# DRAGON VOICE

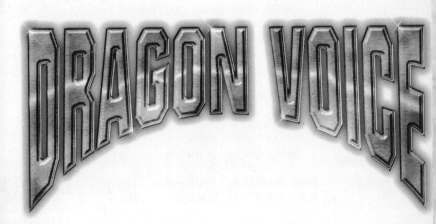

## *Dragon Voice Vol. 2*
## created by Yuriko Nishiyama

Translation - Mike Kiefl
Associate Editor - Troy Lewter
Copy Editors - Alexis Kirsch, Peter Ahlstrom
Retouch and Lettering - Junemoon Studios
Production Artists - James Dashiell
Cover Design - Anna Kernbaum

Editor - Bryce P. Coleman
Digital Imaging Manager - Chris Buford
Pre-Press Manager - Antonio DePietro
Production Managers - Jennifer Miller and Mutsumi Miyazaki
Art Director - Matt Alford
Managing Editor - Jill Freshney
VP of Production - Ron Klamert
President and C.O.O. - John Parker
Publisher and C.E.O. - Stuart Levy

A  Manga

TOKYOPOP Inc.
5900 Wilshire Blvd. Suite 2000
Los Angeles, CA 90036

E-mail: info@TOKYOPOP.com
Come visit us online at www.TOKYOPOP.com

ISBN: 1-59532-120-9

First TOKYOPOP printing: December 2004
10  9  8  7  6  5  4  3  2  1
Printed in the USA

# DRAGON VOICE

## Volume 2
### by
# Yuriko Nishiyama

HAMBURG // LONDON // LOS ANGELES // TOKYO

## The Story So Far in

# DRAGON VOICE

Rin Amami is a good-looking 15-year old kid with a lot of street smarts, but not much in the way of prospects. He's a street dancer, with dreams of becoming a singer and performing his own original music. But with a voice that sounds like a dying bullfrog, he's had to settle for dancing to other people's tunes. That is, until a chance encounter with the newest boyband, THE BEATMEN, forces Rin to follow his ambition. After a series of bizarre circumstances put Rin onstage with THE BEATMEN, the band's manager is convinced that Rin possesses the legendary "Dragon Voice," — filled with "demonic charm and God-like brilliance." Unfortunately, not everyone is so enthusiastic, and it looks like Rin's singing career may be over before it starts. However, Shino, the group's leader, sees something in Rin and convinces him to take another stab at it. With Shino's guidance, Rin improves enough to prompt the manager to make the stunning announcement that Rin Amami is the newest member of THE BEATMEN!

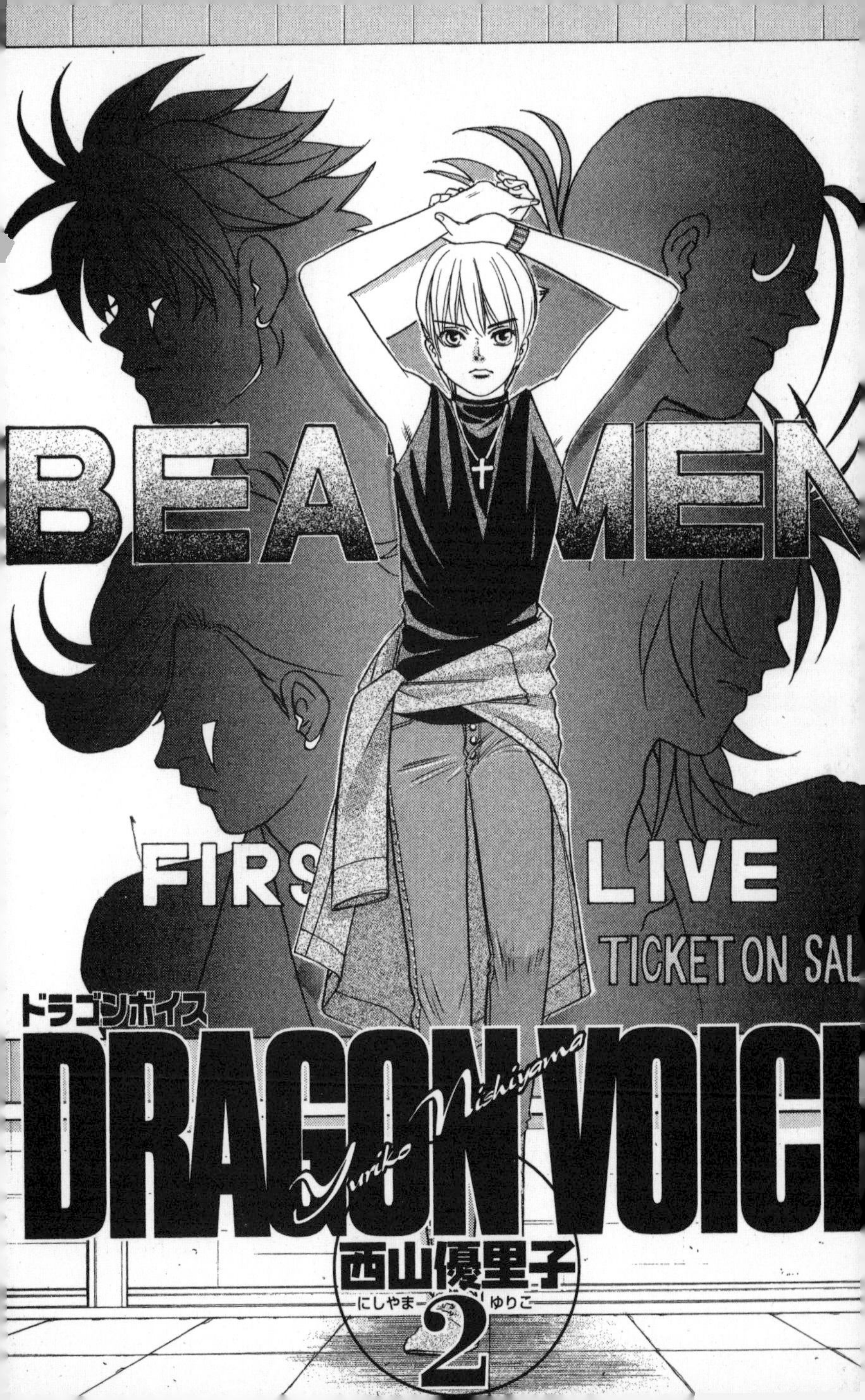
BEA MEN
FIRS LIVE
TICKET ON SAL
ドラゴンボイス
DRAGON VOICE
Yuriko Nishiyama
西山優里子
にしやま ゆりこ
2

KCM-2983

COMPACT
disc
DIGITAL AUDIO

R A G O N  V O I C E

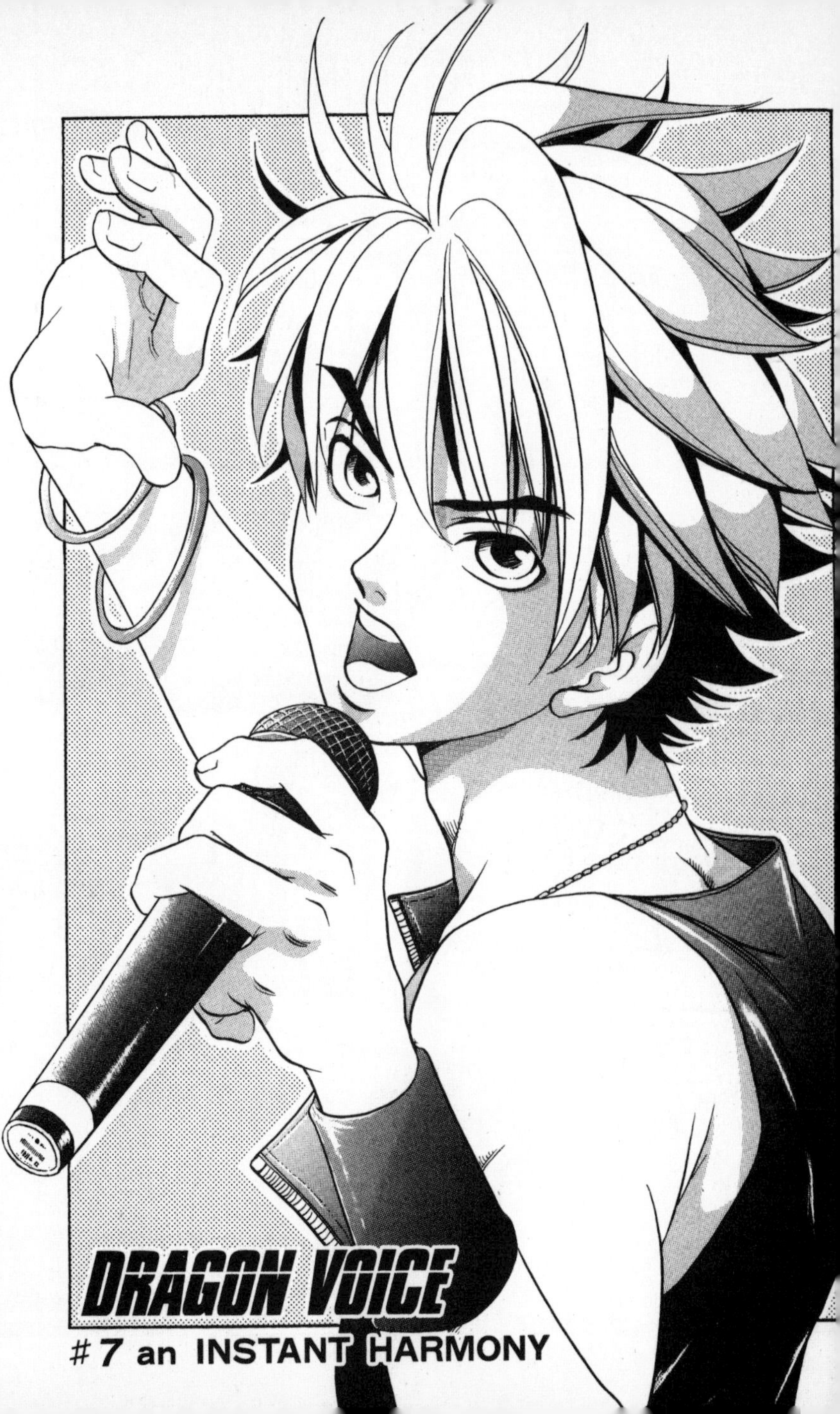

# DRAGON VOICE

## #7 an INSTANT HARMONY

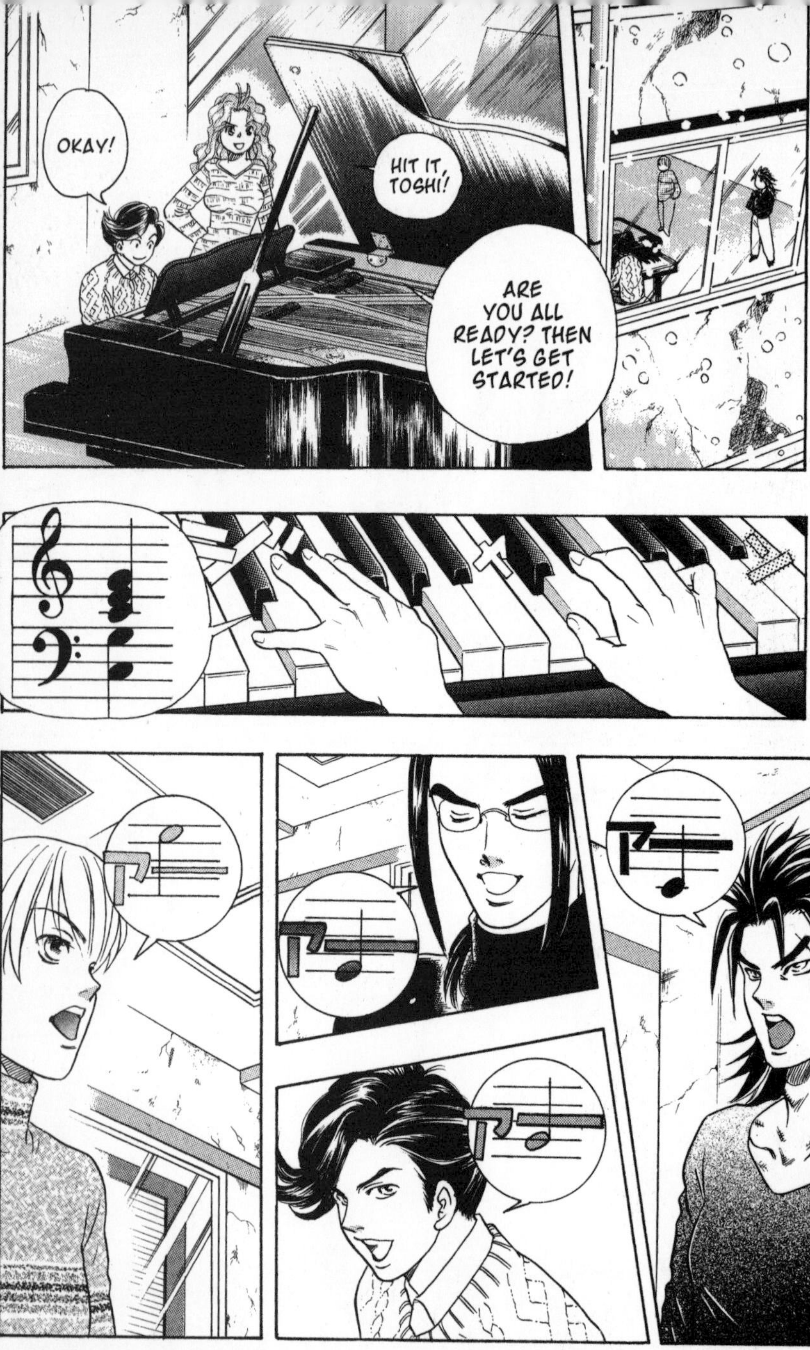
ARE YOU ALL READY? THEN LET'S GET STARTED!
HIT IT, TOSHI!
OKAY!

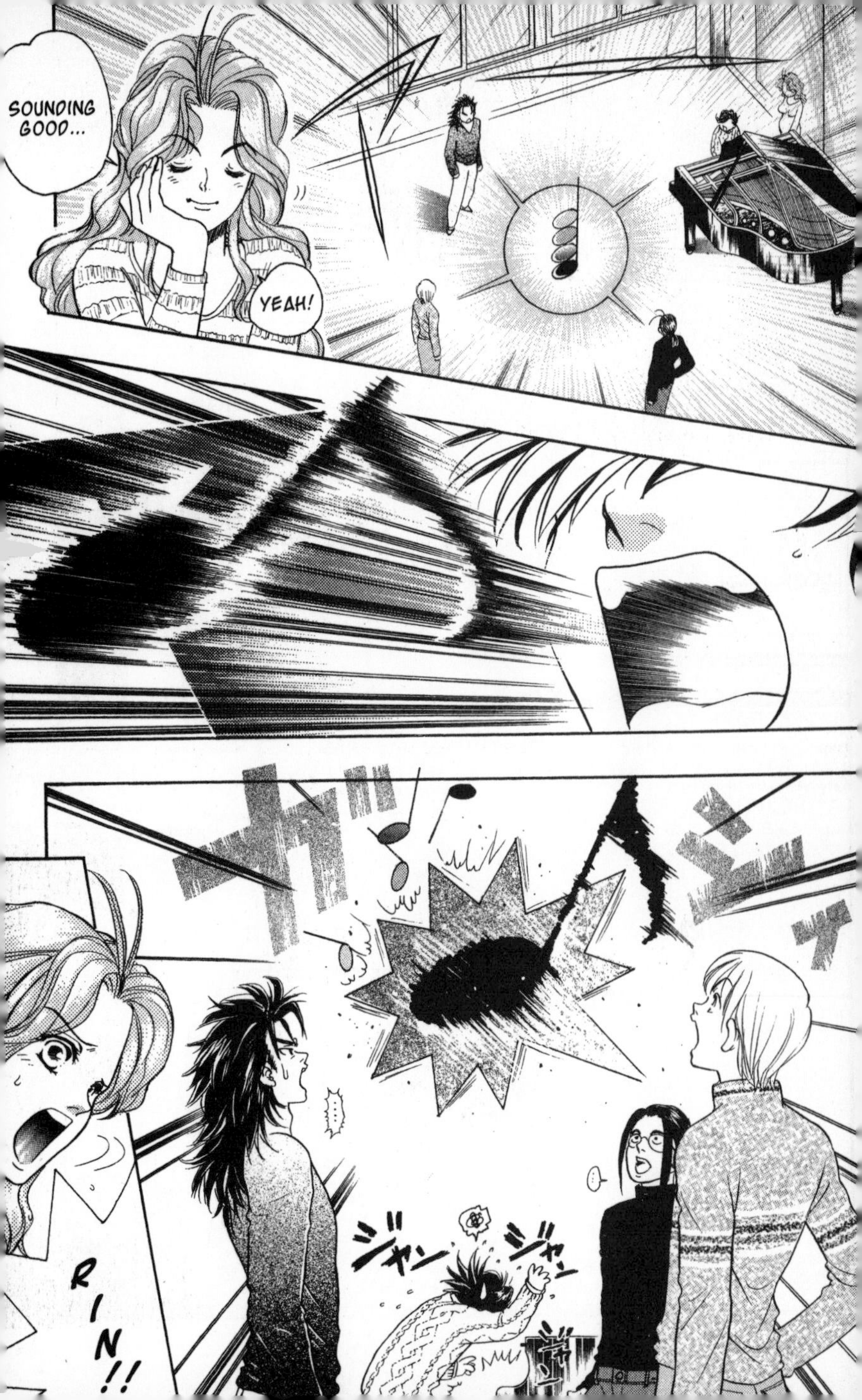
SOUNDING GOOD...
YEAH!
ジャン
ジャン
RIN!!

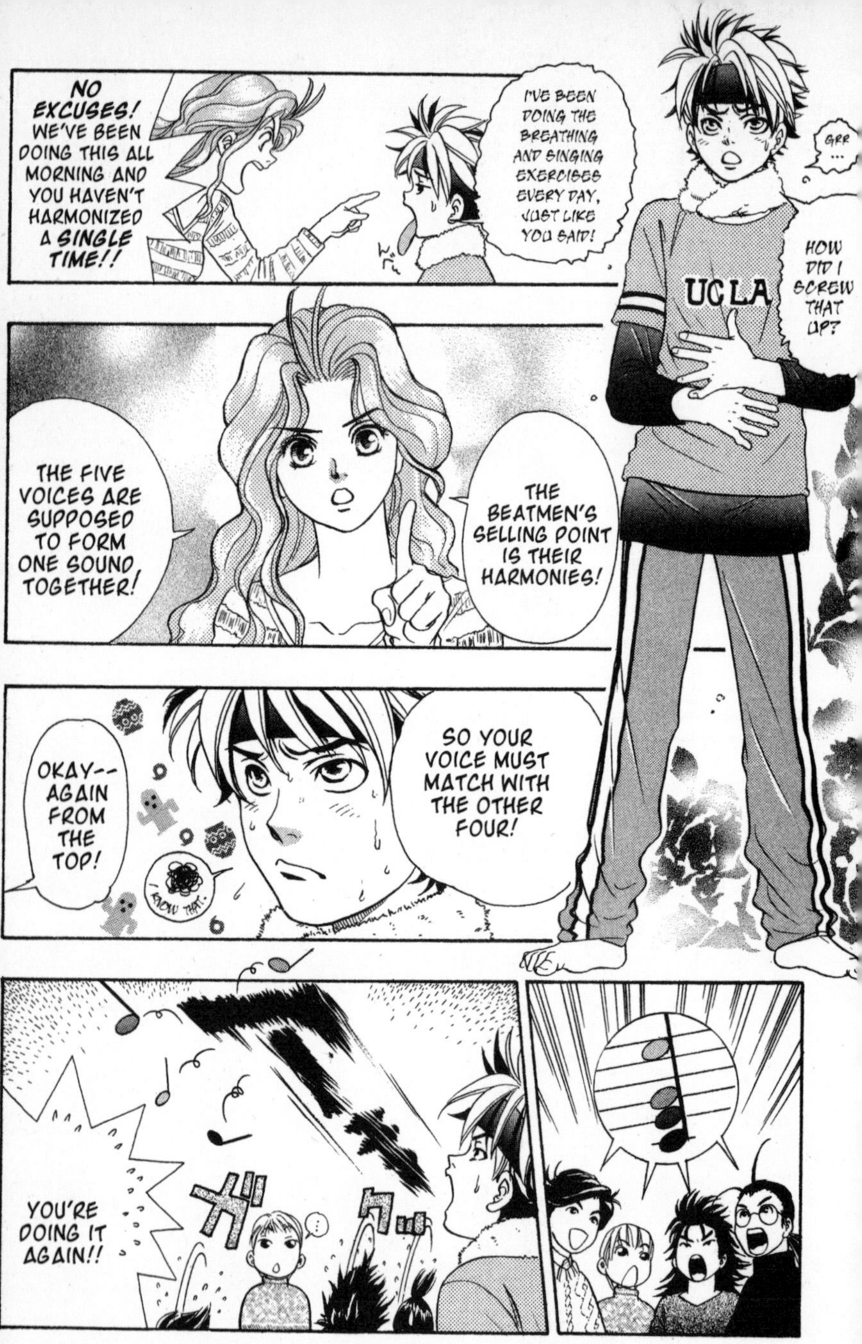
GRR ...
HOW DID I SCREW THAT UP?
I'VE BEEN DOING THE BREATHING AND SINGING EXERCISES EVERY DAY, JUST LIKE YOU SAID!
NO EXCUSES! WE'VE BEEN DOING THIS ALL MORNING AND YOU HAVEN'T HARMONIZED A SINGLE TIME!!
THE BEATMEN'S SELLING POINT IS THEIR HARMONIES!
THE FIVE VOICES ARE SUPPOSED TO FORM ONE SOUND TOGETHER!
SO YOUR VOICE MUST MATCH WITH THE OTHER FOUR!
I KNOW THAT.
OKAY-- AGAIN FROM THE TOP!
...
YOU'RE DOING IT AGAIN!!

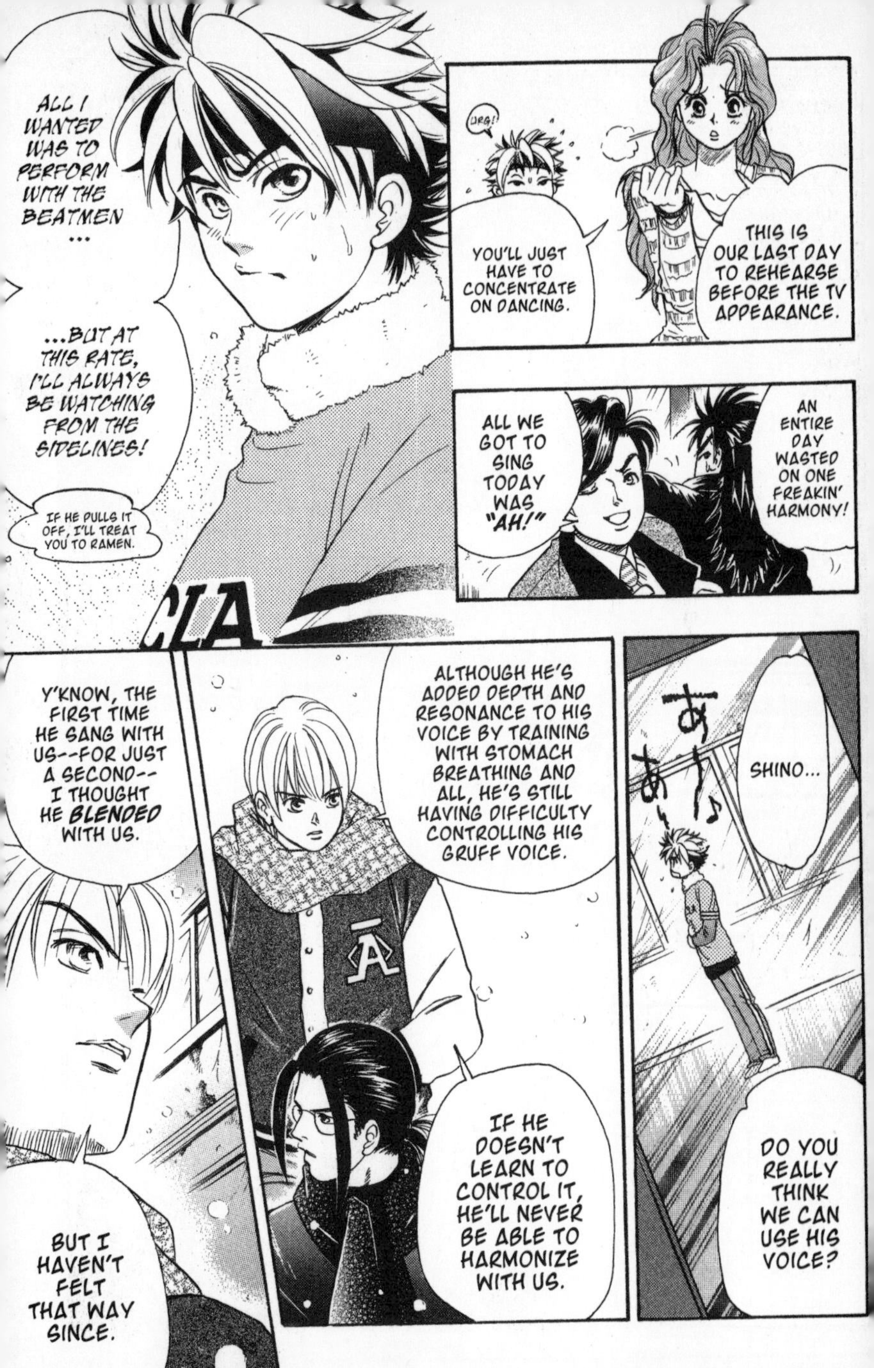
THIS IS OUR LAST DAY TO REHEARSE BEFORE THE TV APPEARANCE.
URG!
YOU'LL JUST HAVE TO CONCENTRATE ON DANCING.
AN ENTIRE DAY WASTED ON ONE FREAKIN' HARMONY!
ALL WE GOT TO SING TODAY WAS "AH!"
ALL I WANTED WAS TO PERFORM WITH THE BEATMEN ...
...BUT AT THIS RATE, I'LL ALWAYS BE WATCHING FROM THE SIDELINES!
IF HE PULLS IT OFF, I'LL TREAT YOU TO RAMEN.
あ～あ～♪
SHINO...
DO YOU REALLY THINK WE CAN USE HIS VOICE?
ALTHOUGH HE'S ADDED DEPTH AND RESONANCE TO HIS VOICE BY TRAINING WITH STOMACH BREATHING AND ALL, HE'S STILL HAVING DIFFICULTY CONTROLLING HIS GRUFF VOICE.
IF HE DOESN'T LEARN TO CONTROL IT, HE'LL NEVER BE ABLE TO HARMONIZE WITH US.
Y'KNOW, THE FIRST TIME HE SANG WITH US--FOR JUST A SECOND--I THOUGHT HE BLENDED WITH US.
BUT I HAVEN'T FELT THAT WAY SINCE.

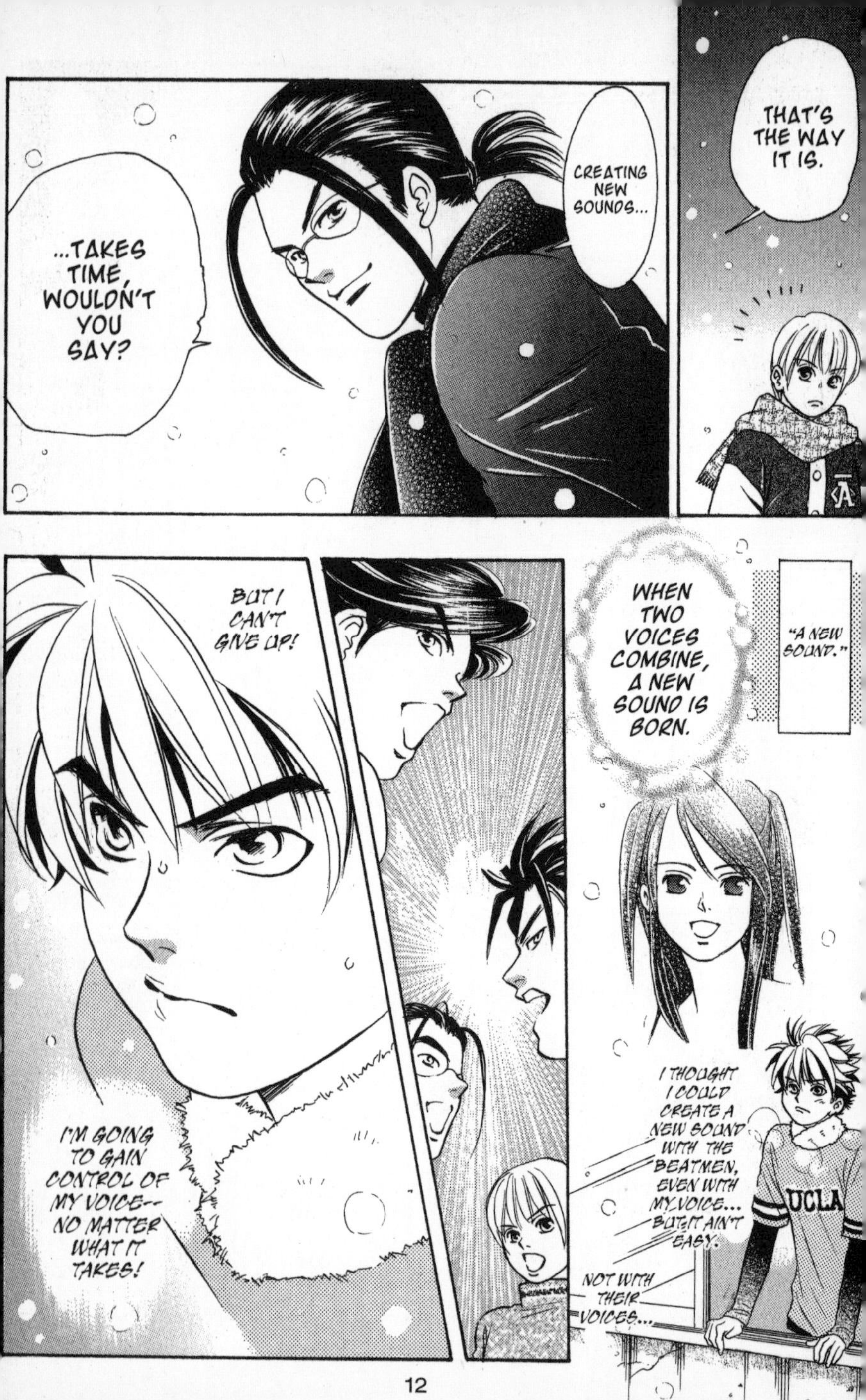
THAT'S THE WAY IT IS.
CREATING NEW SOUNDS...
...TAKES TIME, WOULDN'T YOU SAY?
"A NEW SOUND."
WHEN TWO VOICES COMBINE, A NEW SOUND IS BORN.
I THOUGHT I COULD CREATE A NEW SOUND WITH THE BEATMEN, EVEN WITH MY VOICE... BUT IT AIN'T EASY.
NOT WITH THEIR VOICES...
BUT I CAN'T GIVE UP!
I'M GOING TO GAIN CONTROL OF MY VOICE-- NO MATTER WHAT IT TAKES!

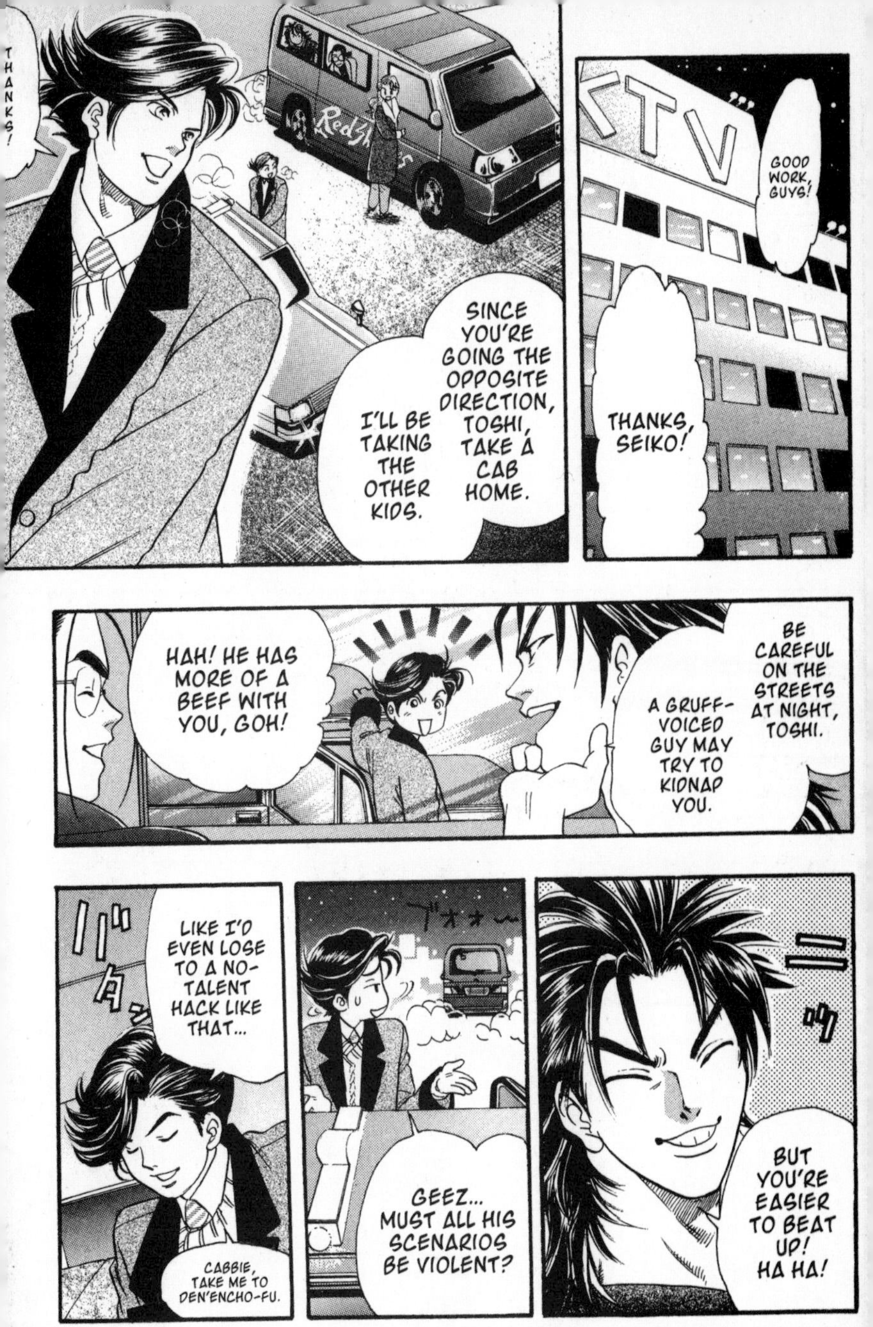
GOOD WORK, GUYS!
THANKS, SEIKO!
SINCE YOU'RE GOING THE OPPOSITE DIRECTION, TOSHI, TAKE A CAB HOME.
I'LL BE TAKING THE OTHER KIDS.
THANKS!
BE CAREFUL ON THE STREETS AT NIGHT, TOSHI.
A GRUFF-VOICED GUY MAY TRY TO KIDNAP YOU.
HAH! HE HAS MORE OF A BEEF WITH YOU, GOH!
BUT YOU'RE EASIER TO BEAT UP! HA HA!
GEEZ... MUST ALL HIS SCENARIOS BE VIOLENT?
LIKE I'D EVEN LOSE TO A NO-TALENT HACK LIKE THAT...
CABBIE, TAKE ME TO DEN'ENCHO-FU.

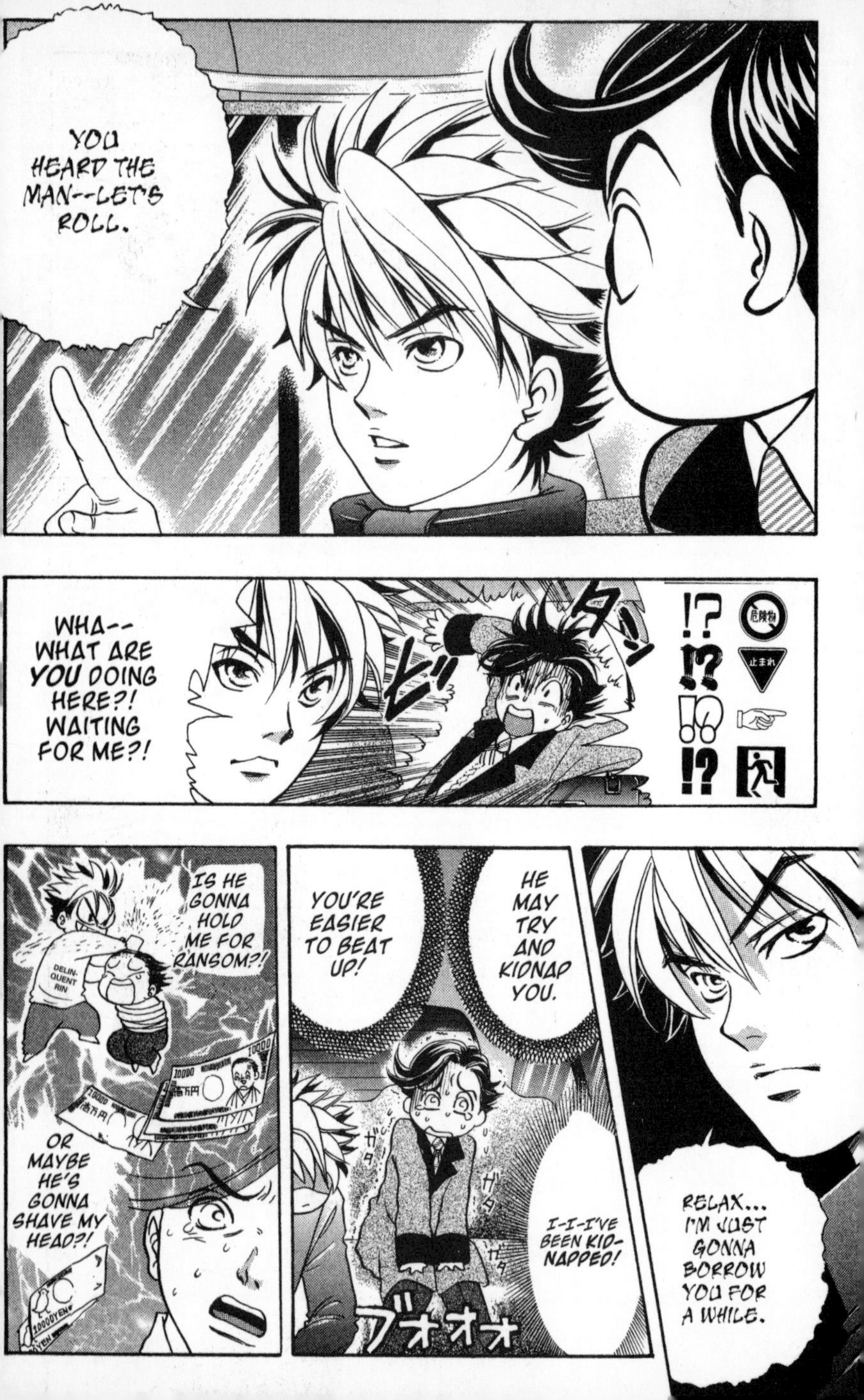
YOU HEARD THE MAN--LET'S ROLL.
WHA-- WHAT ARE YOU DOING HERE?! WAITING FOR ME?!
!? !? !! !?
危険物
止まれ
RELAX... I'M JUST GONNA BORROW YOU FOR A WHILE.
HE MAY TRY AND KIDNAP YOU.
YOU'RE EASIER TO BEAT UP!
I-I-I'VE BEEN KID-NAPPED!
ブオオオ
IS HE GONNA HOLD ME FOR RANSOM?!
DELIN-QUENT RIN
OR MAYBE HE'S GONNA SHAVE MY HEAD?!
10000YEN

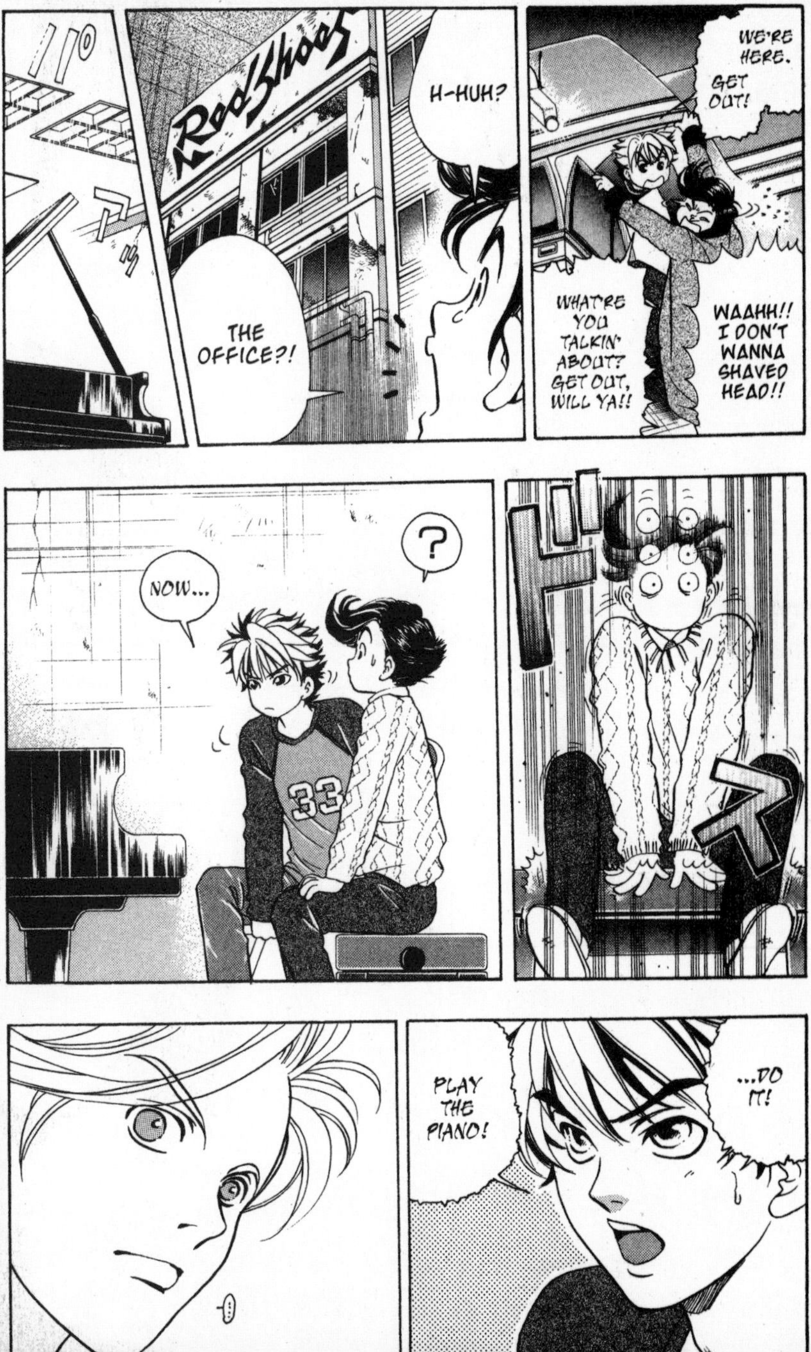
WE'RE HERE.
GET OUT!
WAAHH!! I DON'T WANNA SHAVED HEAD!!
WHAT'RE YOU TALKIN' ABOUT? GET OUT, WILL YA!!
H-HUH?
THE OFFICE?!
?
NOW...
...DO IT!
PLAY THE PIANO!
...

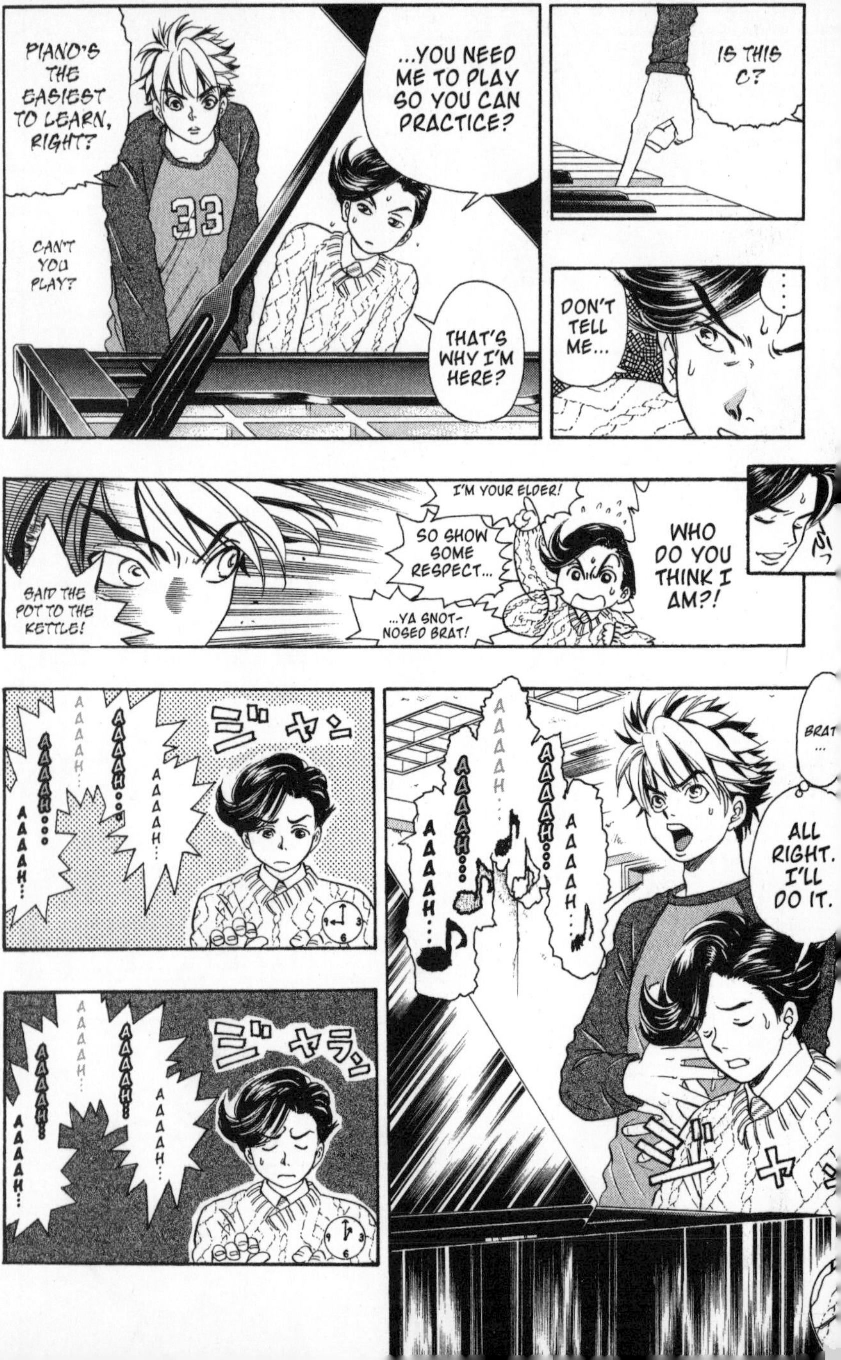
IS THIS C?
...
DON'T TELL ME...
...YOU NEED ME TO PLAY SO YOU CAN PRACTICE?
PIANO'S THE EASIEST TO LEARN, RIGHT?
THAT'S WHY I'M HERE?
CAN'T YOU PLAY?
WHO DO YOU THINK I AM?!
I'M YOUR ELDER!
SO SHOW SOME RESPECT...
...YA SNOT-NOSED BRAT!
SAID THE POT TO THE KETTLE!
BRAT...
ALL RIGHT. I'LL DO IT.
AAAAH... AAAAH... AAAAH... AAAAH...
ジャン
AAAAH... AAAAH... AAAAH... AAAAH...
ジャラン
AAAAH... AAAAH... AAAAH... AAAAH...

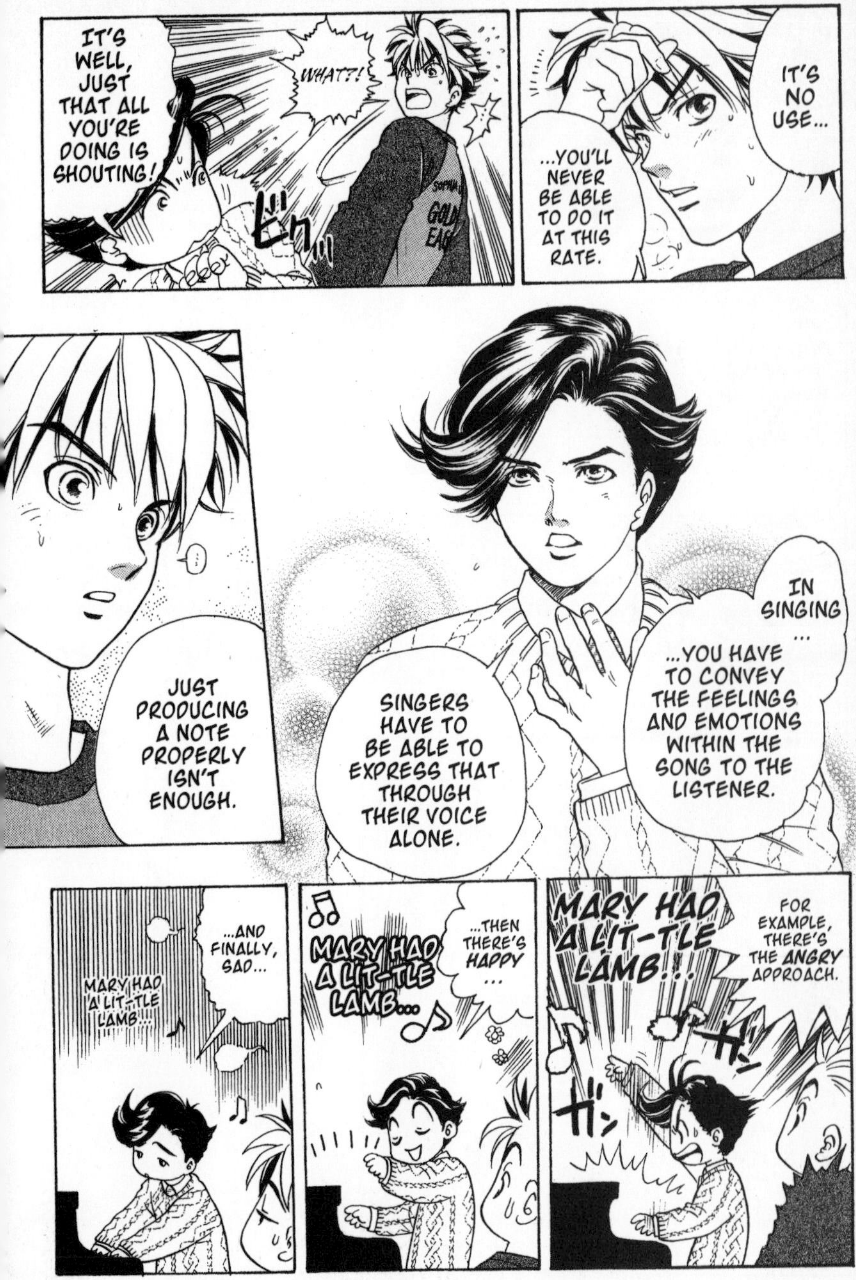
IT'S NO USE...
...YOU'LL NEVER BE ABLE TO DO IT AT THIS RATE.
WHAT?!
IT'S WELL, JUST THAT ALL YOU'RE DOING IS SHOUTING!
IN SINGING...
...YOU HAVE TO CONVEY THE FEELINGS AND EMOTIONS WITHIN THE SONG TO THE LISTENER.
SINGERS HAVE TO BE ABLE TO EXPRESS THAT THROUGH THEIR VOICE ALONE.
...
JUST PRODUCING A NOTE PROPERLY ISN'T ENOUGH.
FOR EXAMPLE, THERE'S THE ANGRY APPROACH.
MARY HAD A LIT-TLE LAMB!!
...THEN THERE'S HAPPY...
MARY HAD A LIT-TLE LAMB...
...AND FINALLY, SAD...
MARY HAD A LIT-TLE LAMB...

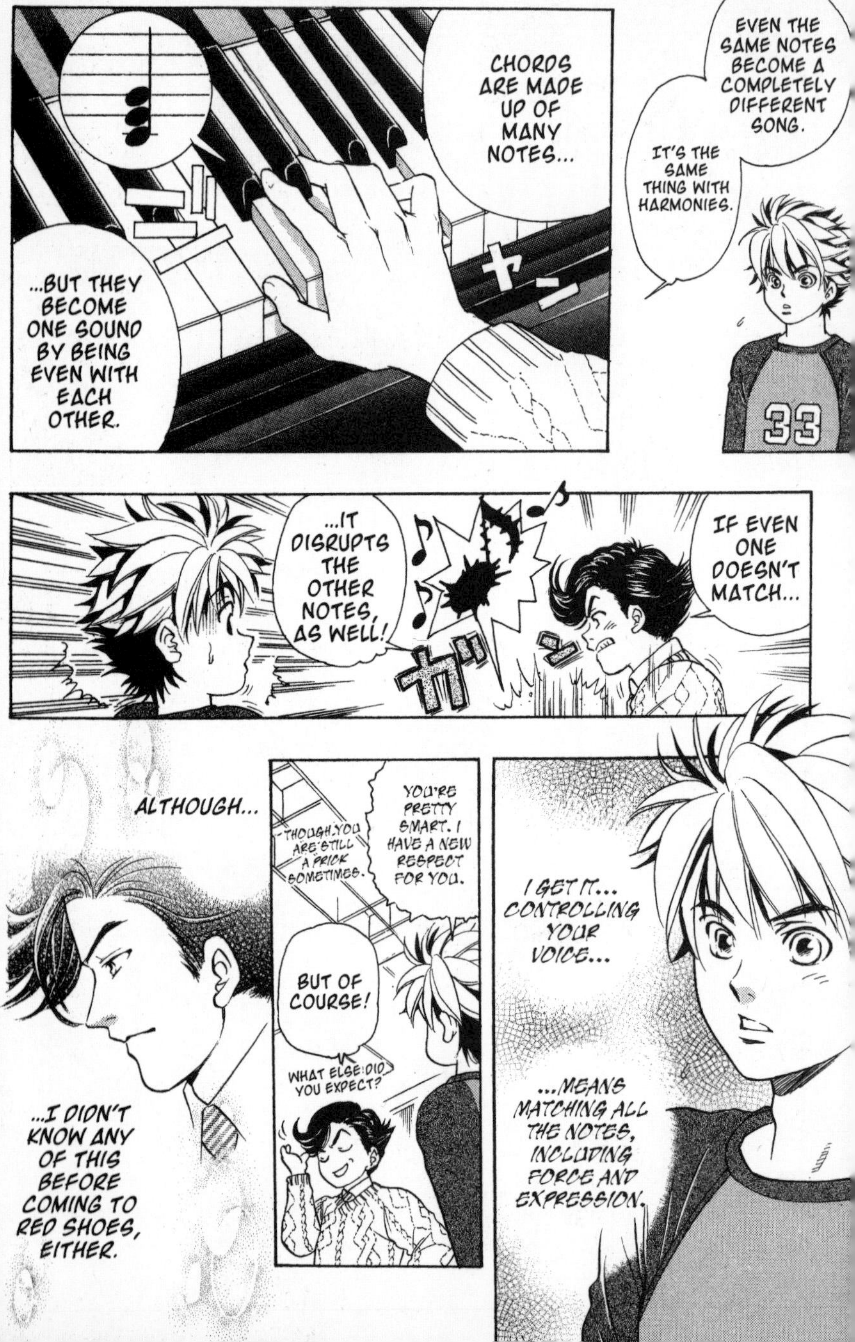
EVEN THE SAME NOTES BECOME A COMPLETELY DIFFERENT SONG.
IT'S THE SAME THING WITH HARMONIES.
CHORDS ARE MADE UP OF MANY NOTES...
ヤー
...BUT THEY BECOME ONE SOUND BY BEING EVEN WITH EACH OTHER.
IF EVEN ONE DOESN'T MATCH...
ガン
...IT DISRUPTS THE OTHER NOTES, AS WELL!
I GET IT... CONTROLLING YOUR VOICE...
...MEANS MATCHING ALL THE NOTES, INCLUDING FORCE AND EXPRESSION.
YOU'RE PRETTY SMART. I HAVE A NEW RESPECT FOR YOU.
THOUGH YOU ARE STILL A PRICK SOMETIMES.
BUT OF COURSE!
WHAT ELSE DID YOU EXPECT?
ALTHOUGH...
...I DIDN'T KNOW ANY OF THIS BEFORE COMING TO RED SHOES, EITHER.

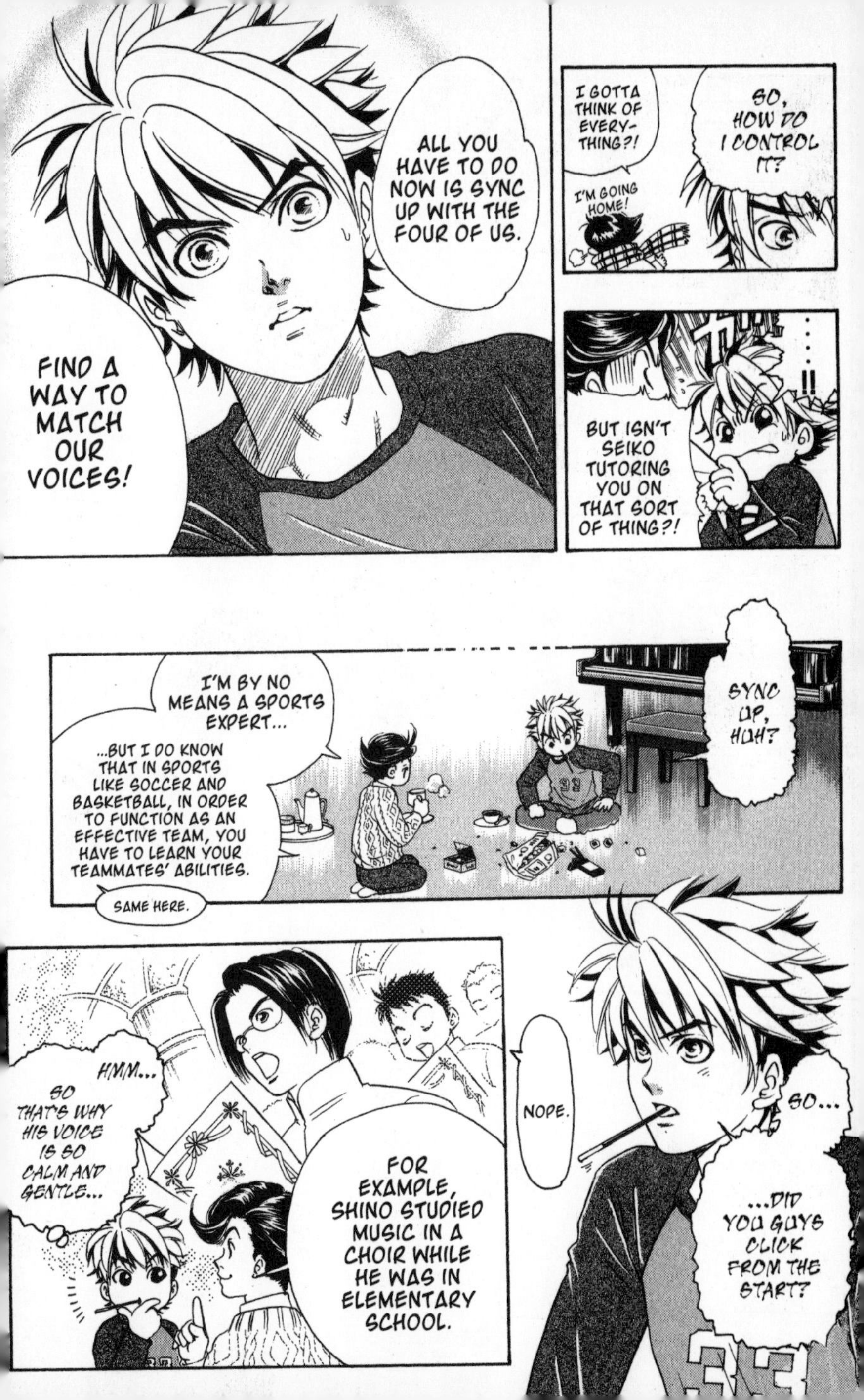
SO, HOW DO I CONTROL IT?
I GOTTA THINK OF EVERY-THING?!
I'M GOING HOME!
BUT ISN'T SEIKO TUTORING YOU ON THAT SORT OF THING?!
ALL YOU HAVE TO DO NOW IS SYNC UP WITH THE FOUR OF US.
FIND A WAY TO MATCH OUR VOICES!
SYNC UP, HUH?
I'M BY NO MEANS A SPORTS EXPERT...
...BUT I DO KNOW THAT IN SPORTS LIKE SOCCER AND BASKETBALL, IN ORDER TO FUNCTION AS AN EFFECTIVE TEAM, YOU HAVE TO LEARN YOUR TEAMMATES' ABILITIES.
SAME HERE.
SO...
...DID YOU GUYS CLICK FROM THE START?
NOPE.
FOR EXAMPLE, SHINO STUDIED MUSIC IN A CHOIR WHILE HE WAS IN ELEMENTARY SCHOOL.
HMM...
SO THAT'S WHY HIS VOICE IS SO CALM AND GENTLE...

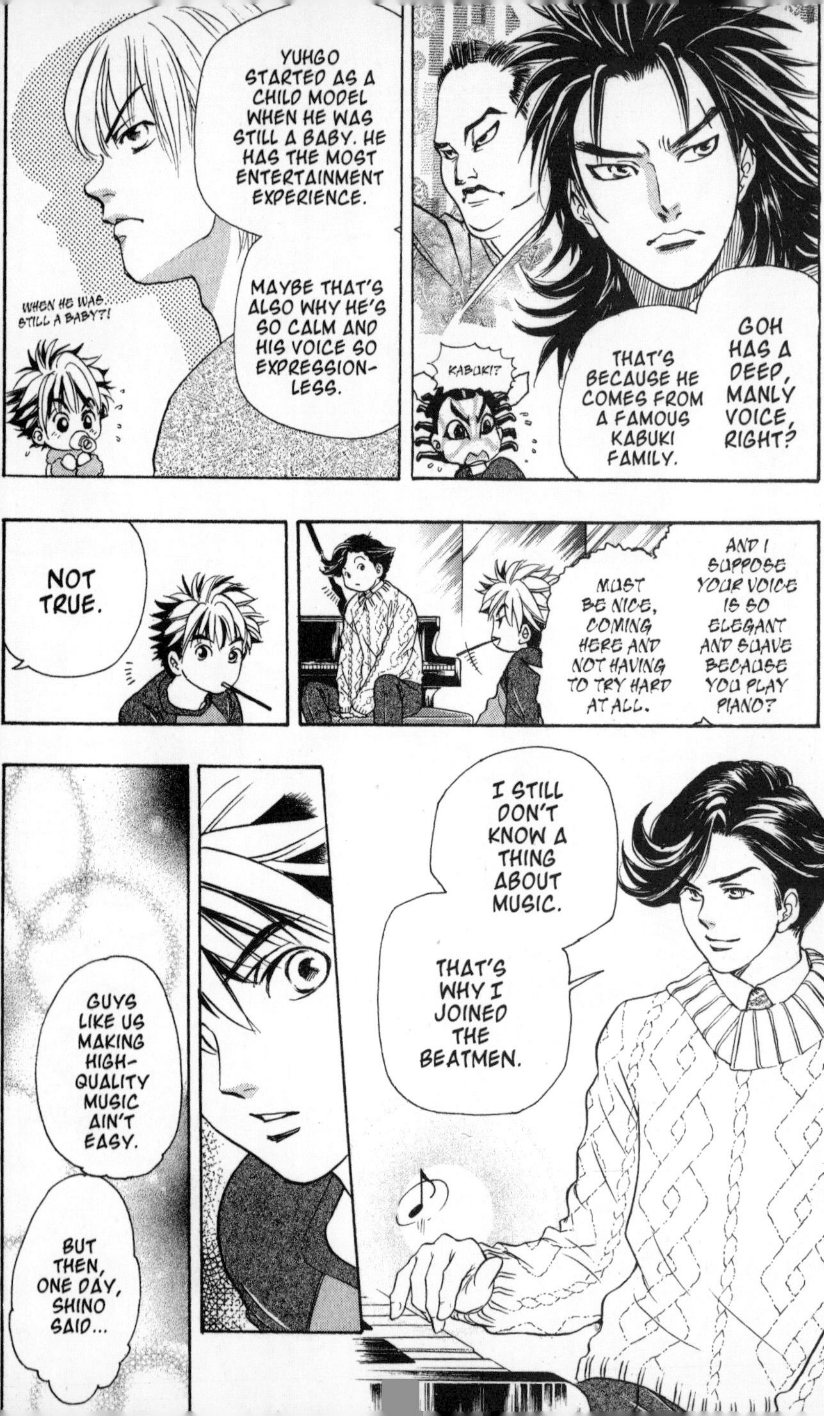
GOH HAS A DEEP, MANLY VOICE, RIGHT?
THAT'S BECAUSE HE COMES FROM A FAMOUS KABUKI FAMILY.
KABUKI!?
YUHGO STARTED AS A CHILD MODEL WHEN HE WAS STILL A BABY. HE HAS THE MOST ENTERTAINMENT EXPERIENCE.
MAYBE THAT'S ALSO WHY HE'S SO CALM AND HIS VOICE SO EXPRESSION-LESS.
WHEN HE WAS STILL A BABY?!
AND I SUPPOSE YOUR VOICE IS SO ELEGANT AND SUAVE BECAUSE YOU PLAY PIANO?
MUST BE NICE, COMING HERE AND NOT HAVING TO TRY HARD AT ALL.
NOT TRUE.
I STILL DON'T KNOW A THING ABOUT MUSIC.
THAT'S WHY I JOINED THE BEATMEN.
GUYS LIKE US MAKING HIGH-QUALITY MUSIC AIN'T EASY.
BUT THEN, ONE DAY, SHINO SAID...

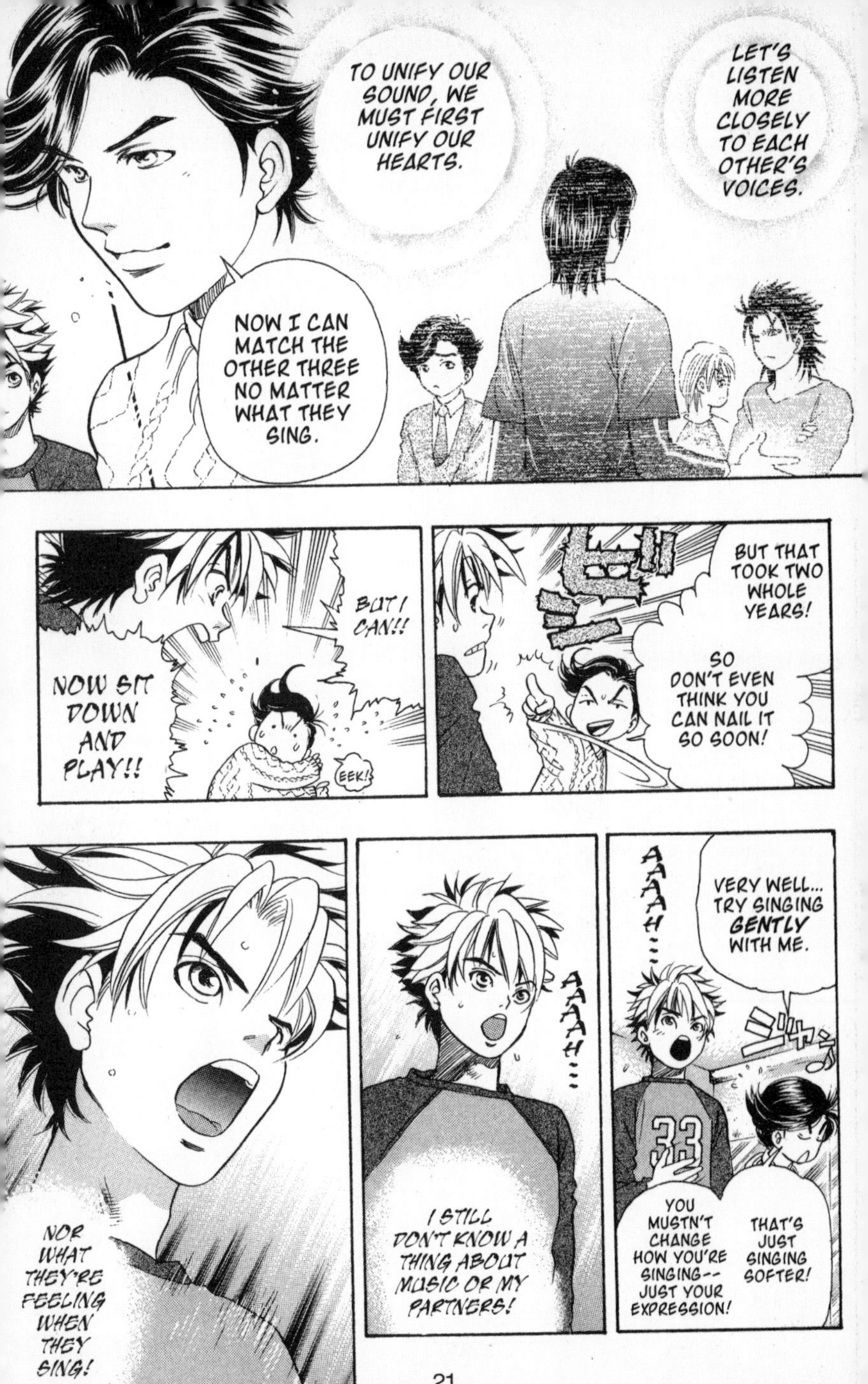
LET'S LISTEN MORE CLOSELY TO EACH OTHER'S VOICES.
TO UNIFY OUR SOUND, WE MUST FIRST UNIFY OUR HEARTS.
NOW I CAN MATCH THE OTHER THREE NO MATTER WHAT THEY SING.
BUT THAT TOOK TWO WHOLE YEARS!
SO DON'T EVEN THINK YOU CAN NAIL IT SO SOON!
BUT I CAN!!
NOW SIT DOWN AND PLAY!!
EEK!
VERY WELL... TRY SINGING **GENTLY** WITH ME.
AAAAH...
THAT'S JUST SINGING SOFTER!
YOU MUSTN'T CHANGE HOW YOU'RE SINGING-- JUST YOUR EXPRESSION!
AAAAH...
I STILL DON'T KNOW A THING ABOUT MUSIC OR MY PARTNERS!
NOR WHAT THEY'RE FEELING WHEN THEY SING!

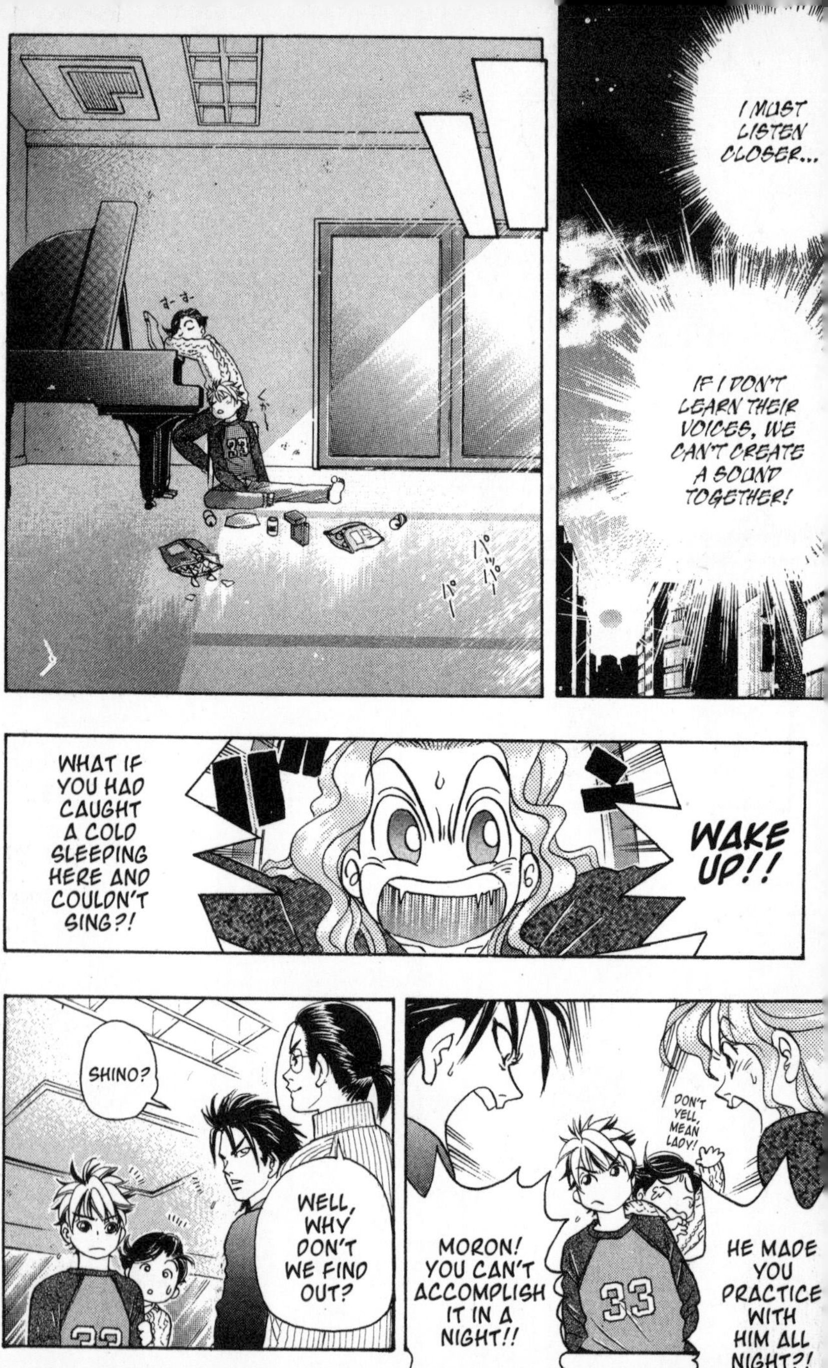
I MUST LISTEN CLOSER...
IF I DON'T LEARN THEIR VOICES, WE CAN'T CREATE A SOUND TOGETHER!
WAKE UP!!
WHAT IF YOU HAD CAUGHT A COLD SLEEPING HERE AND COULDN'T SING?!
HE MADE YOU PRACTICE WITH HIM ALL NIGHT?!
DON'T YELL, MEAN LADY!
MORON! YOU CAN'T ACCOMPLISH IT IN A NIGHT!!
SHINO?
WELL, WHY DON'T WE FIND OUT?

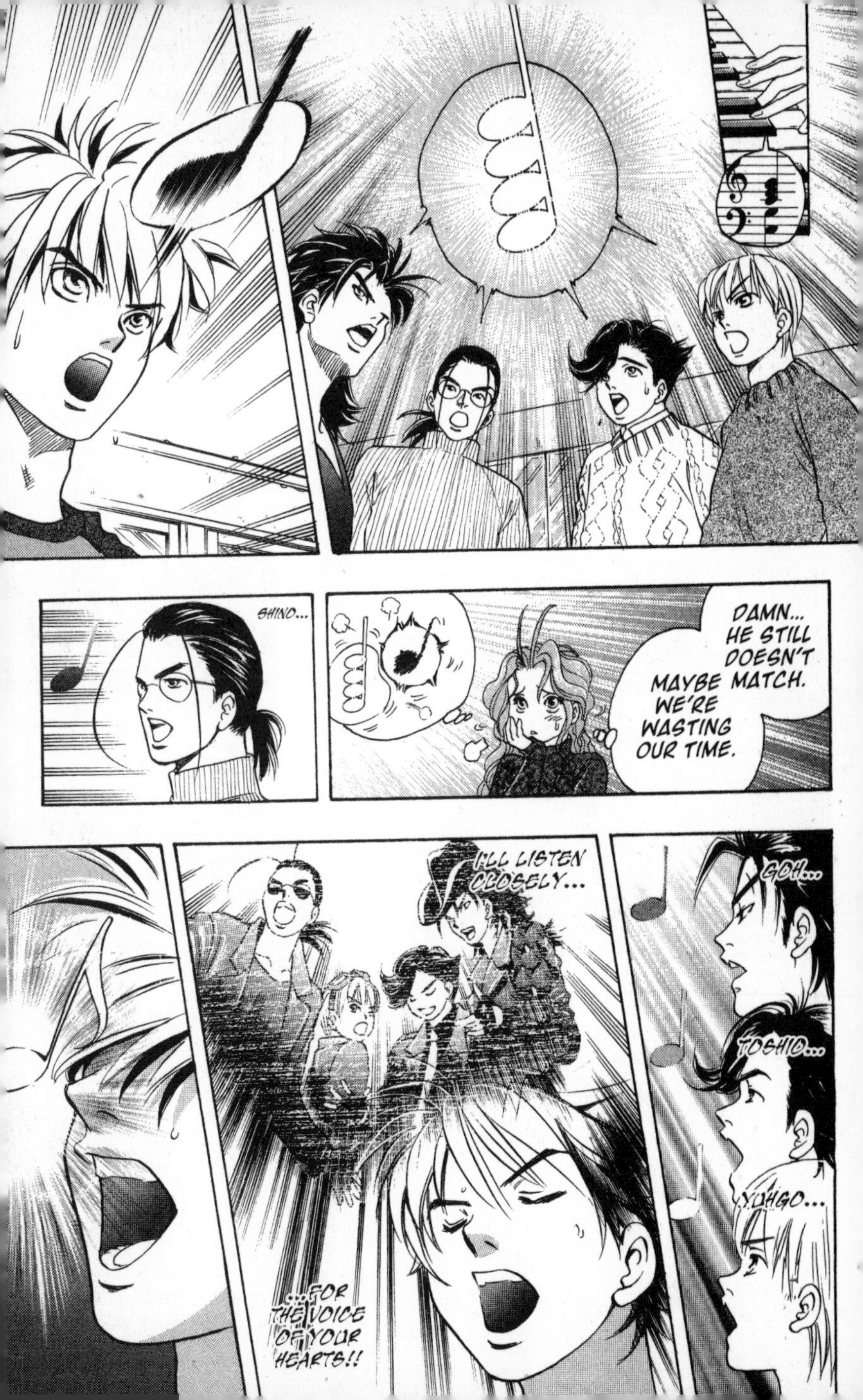
DAMN... HE STILL DOESN'T MATCH. MAYBE WE'RE WASTING OUR TIME.
SHINO...
GOH...
TOSHIO...
YUHGO...
I'LL LISTEN CLOSELY...
...FOR THE VOICE OF YOUR HEARTS!!

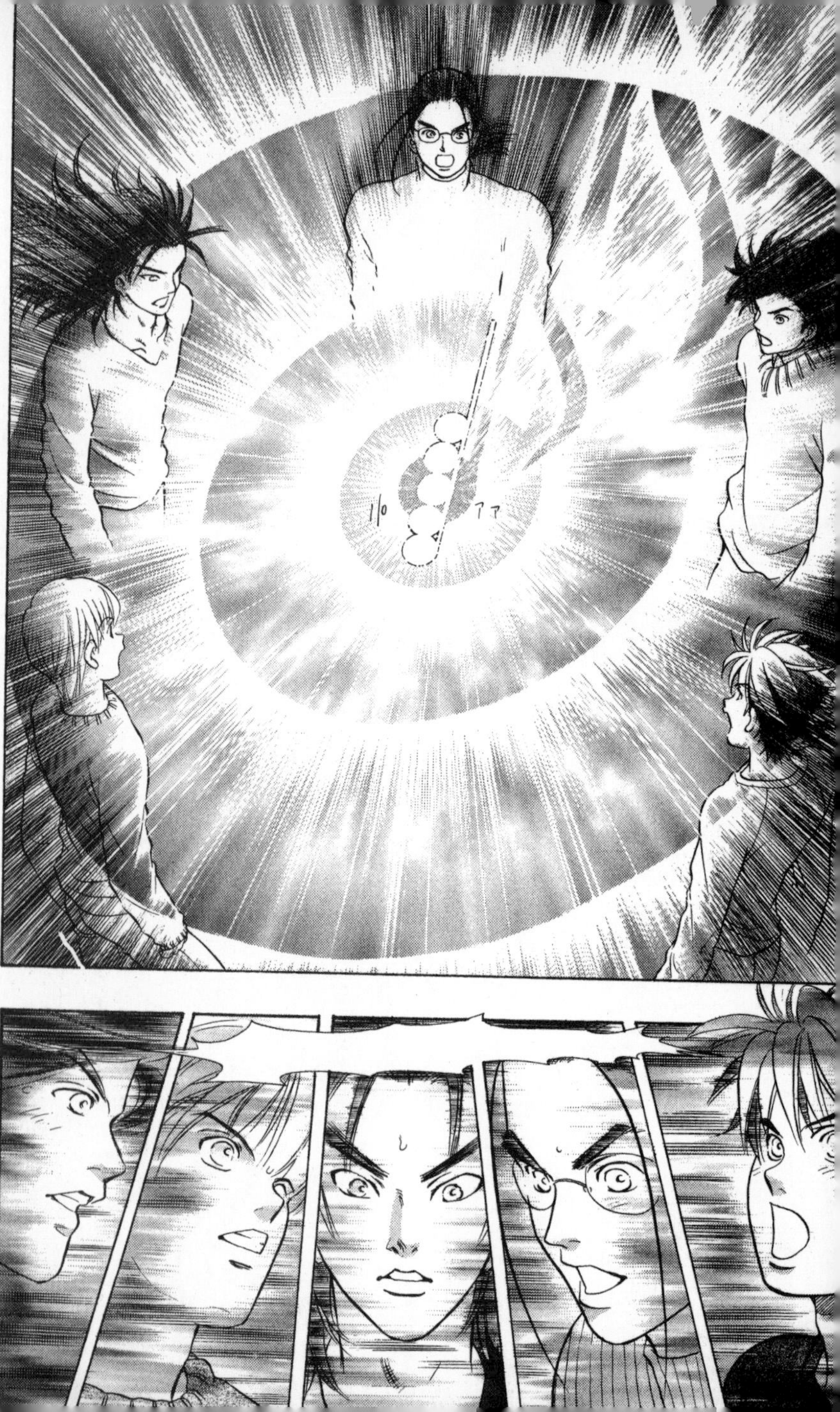
パアア

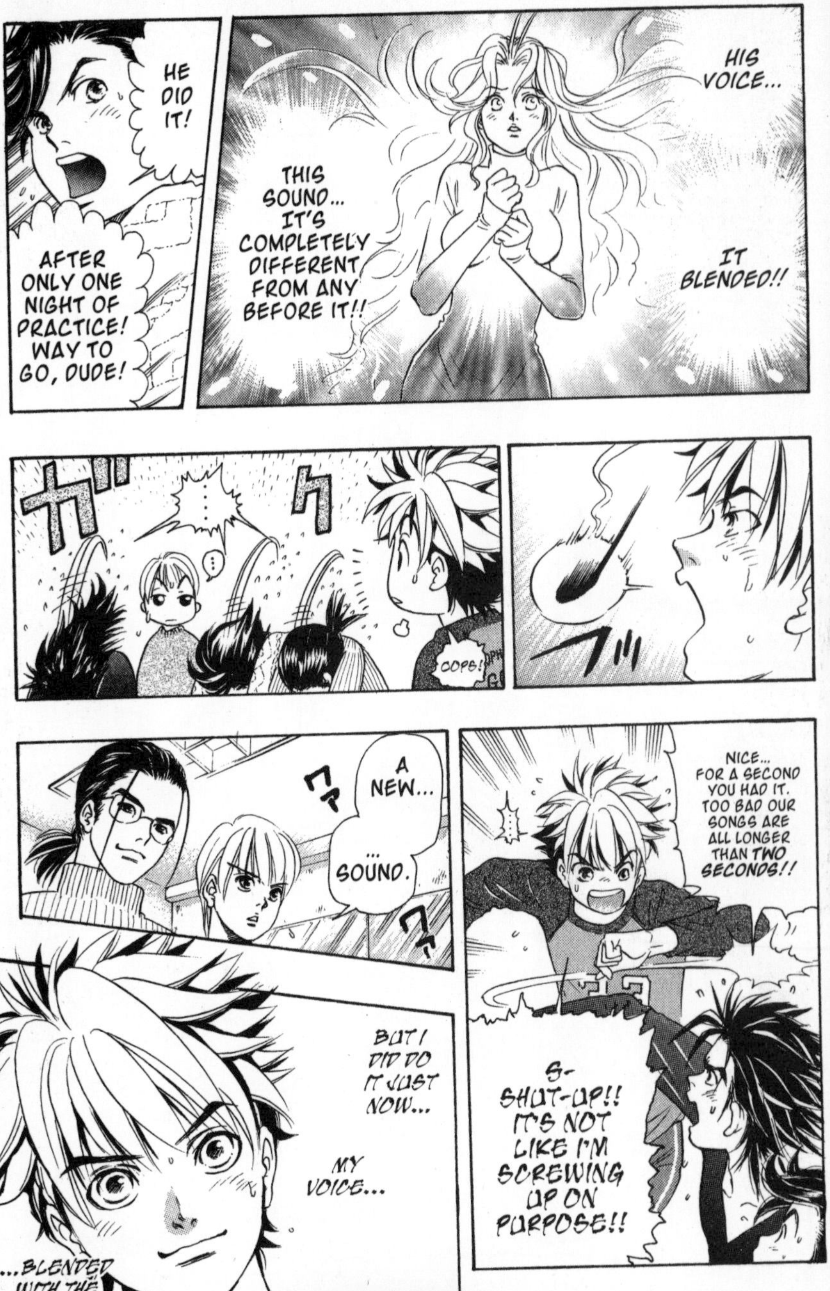
HIS VOICE...
IT BLENDED!!
THIS SOUND... IT'S COMPLETELY DIFFERENT FROM ANY BEFORE IT!!
HE DID IT!
AFTER ONLY ONE NIGHT OF PRACTICE! WAY TO GO, DUDE!
...
...
OOPS!
NICE... FOR A SECOND YOU HAD IT. TOO BAD OUR SONGS ARE ALL LONGER THAN TWO SECONDS!!
!
S-SHUT-UP!! IT'S NOT LIKE I'M SCREWING UP ON PURPOSE!!
A NEW...
...SOUND.
BUT I DID DO IT JUST NOW...
MY VOICE...
...BLENDED WITH THE BEATMEN!

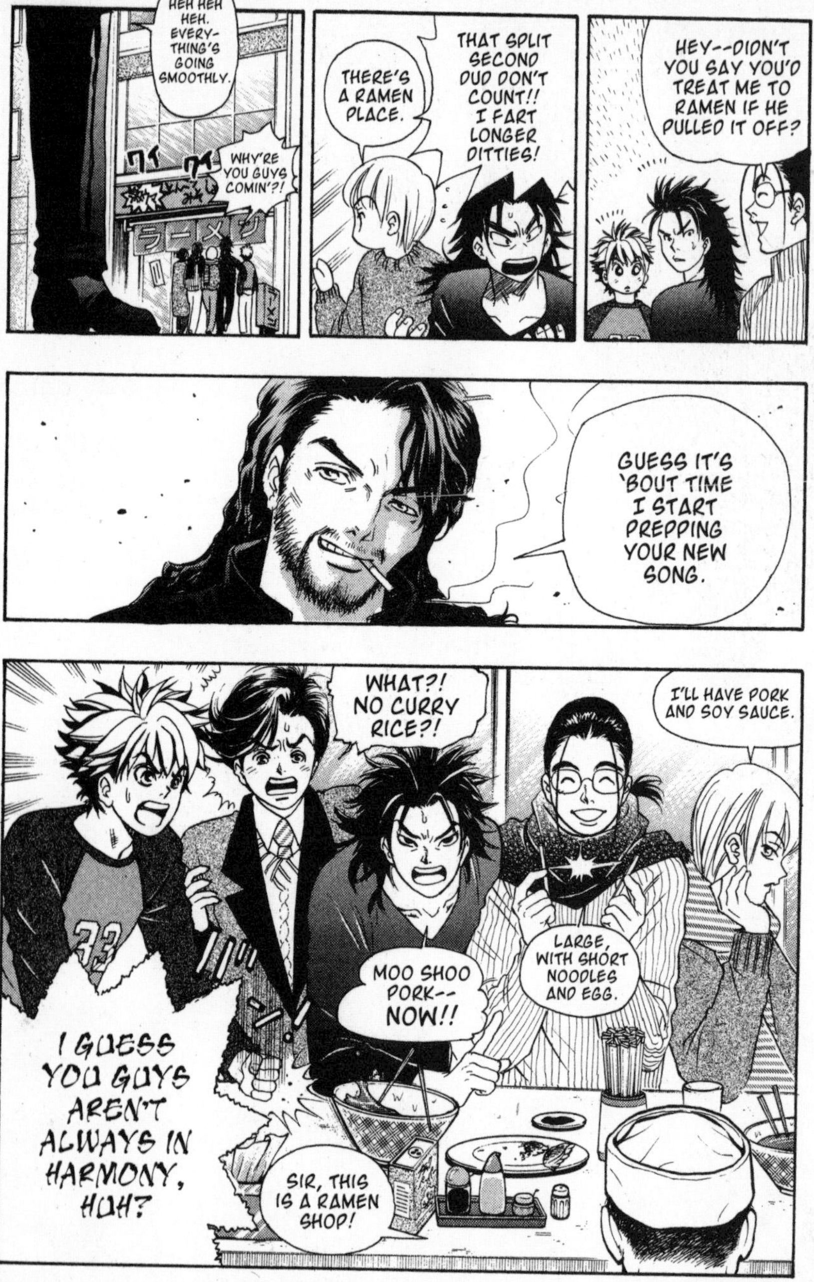
HEY--DIDN'T YOU SAY YOU'D TREAT ME TO RAMEN IF HE PULLED IT OFF?
THAT SPLIT SECOND DUD DON'T COUNT!! I FART LONGER DITTIES!
THERE'S A RAMEN PLACE.
HEH HEH HEH. EVERYTHING'S GOING SMOOTHLY.
WHY'RE YOU GUYS COMIN'?!
GUESS IT'S 'BOUT TIME I START PREPPING YOUR NEW SONG.
I'LL HAVE PORK AND SOY SAUCE.
WHAT?! NO CURRY RICE?!
LARGE, WITH SHORT NOODLES AND EGG.
MOO SHOO PORK--NOW!!
SIR, THIS IS A RAMEN SHOP!
I GUESS YOU GUYS AREN'T ALWAYS IN HARMONY, HUH?

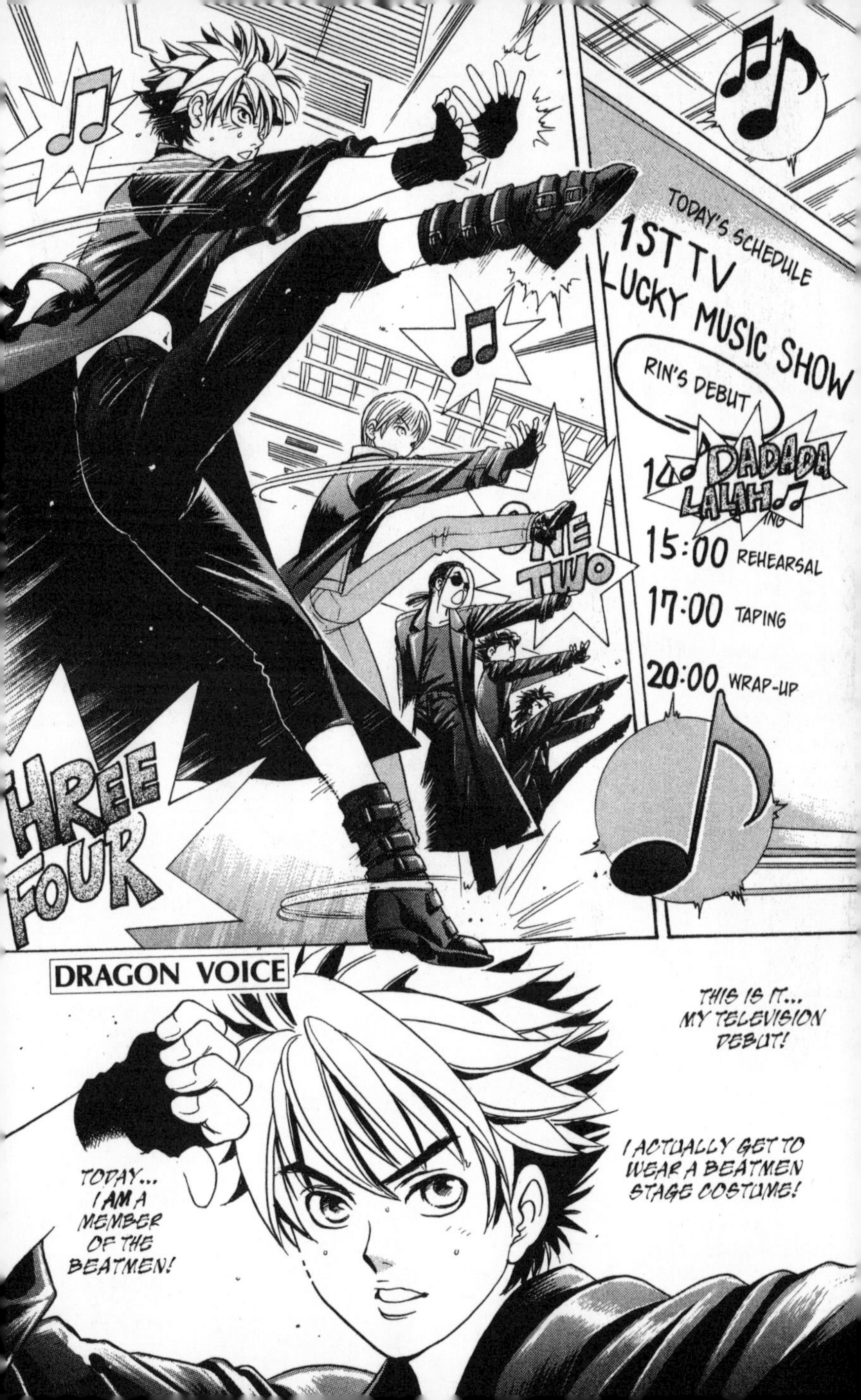

TODAY'S SCHEDULE
1ST TV
LUCKY MUSIC SHOW
RIN'S DEBUT
14
DADADA LALAH
ING
15:00 REHEARSAL
17:00 TAPING
20:00 WRAP-UP
ONE TWO
THREE FOUR
DRAGON VOICE
THIS IS IT... MY TELEVISION DEBUT!
I ACTUALLY GET TO WEAR A BEATMEN STAGE COSTUME!
TODAY... I **AM** A MEMBER OF THE BEATMEN!

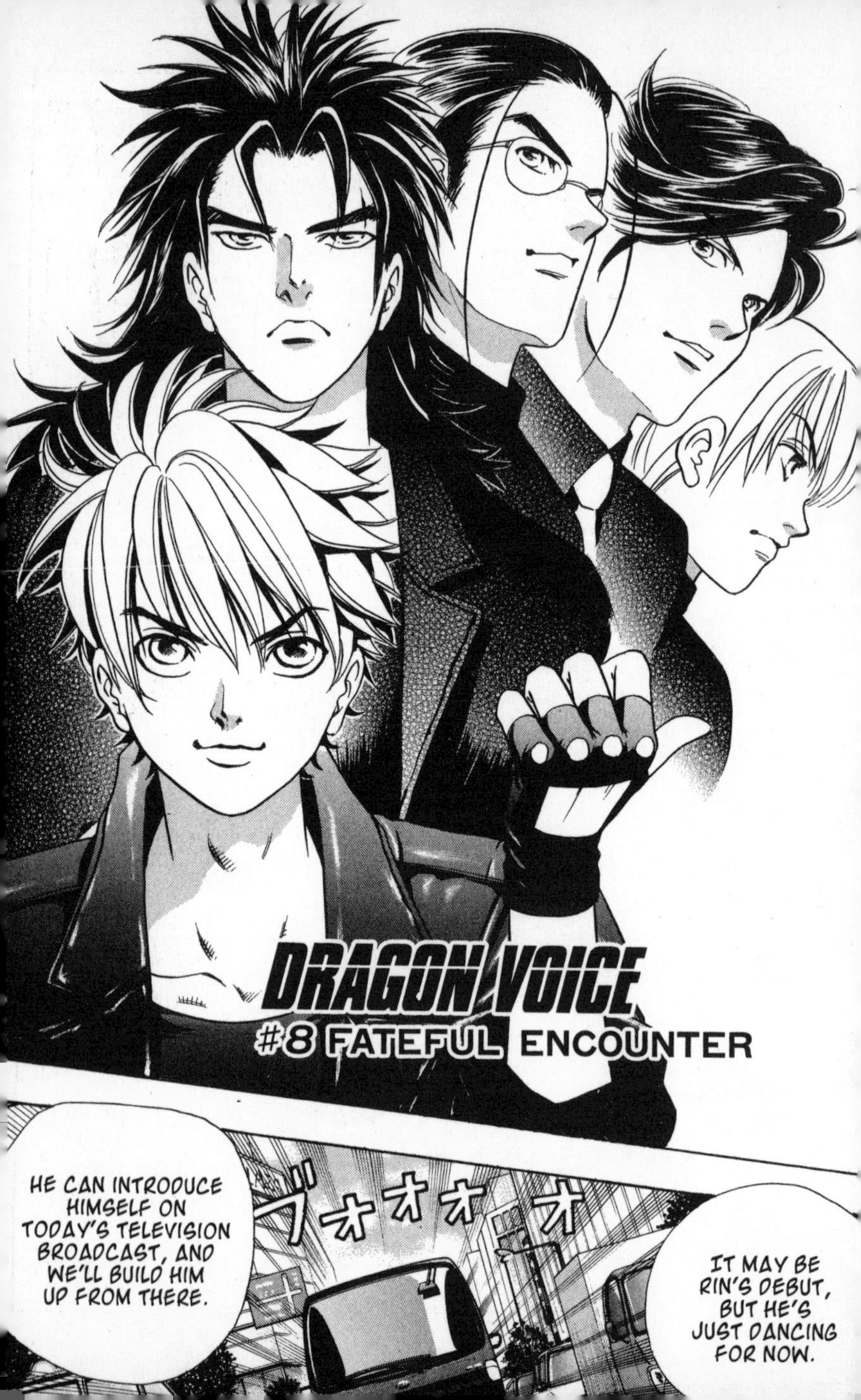
DRAGON VOICE
#8 FATEFUL ENCOUNTER
ヴォオオ・オ
IT MAY BE RIN'S DEBUT, BUT HE'S JUST DANCING FOR NOW.
HE CAN INTRODUCE HIMSELF ON TODAY'S TELEVISION BROADCAST, AND WE'LL BUILD HIM UP FROM THERE.

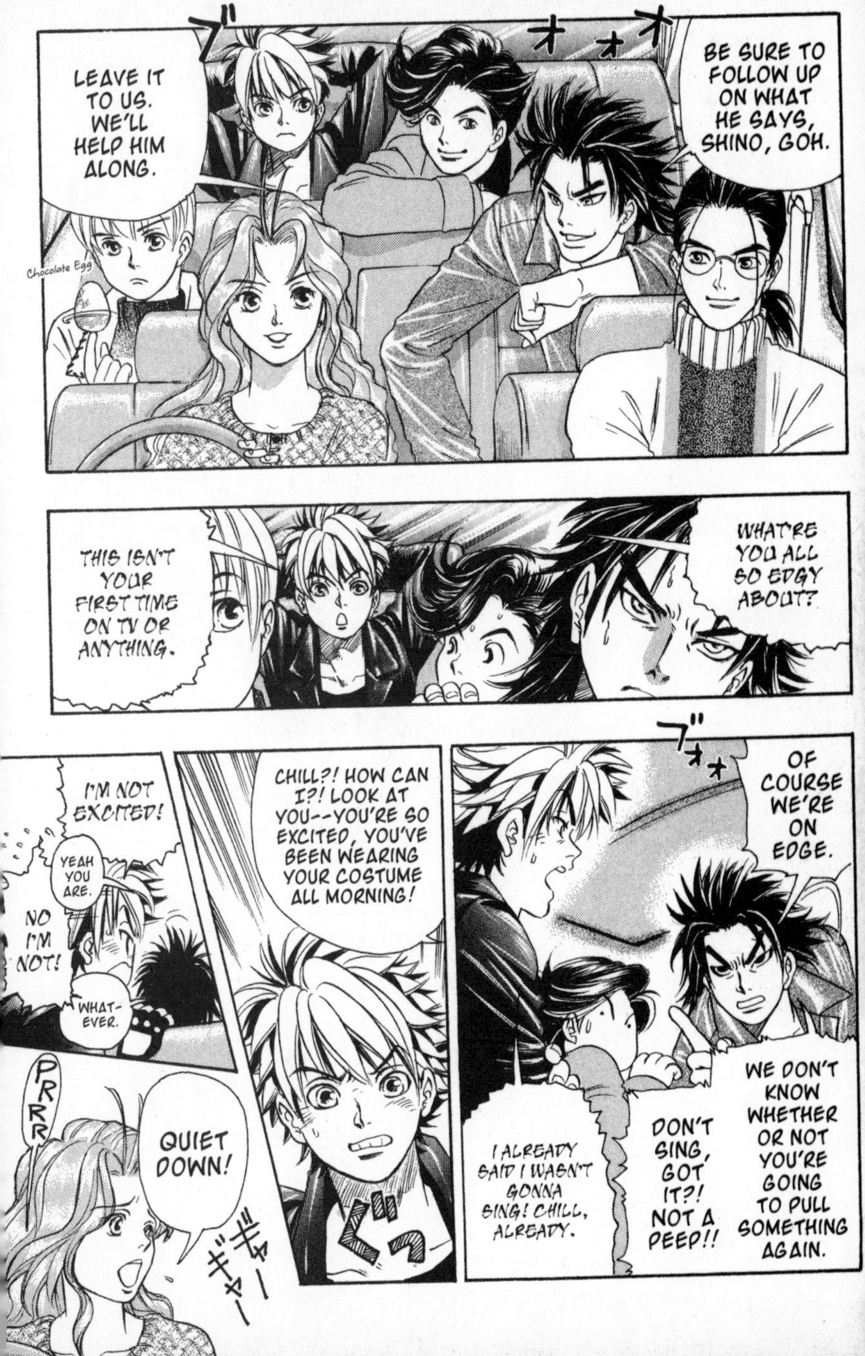
BE SURE TO FOLLOW UP ON WHAT HE SAYS, SHINO, GOH.
LEAVE IT TO US. WE'LL HELP HIM ALONG.
Chocolate Egg
WHAT'RE YOU ALL SO EDGY ABOUT?
THIS ISN'T YOUR FIRST TIME ON TV OR ANYTHING.
OF COURSE WE'RE ON EDGE.
WE DON'T KNOW WHETHER OR NOT YOU'RE GOING TO PULL SOMETHING AGAIN.
DON'T SING, GOT IT?! NOT A PEEP!!
I ALREADY SAID I WASN'T GONNA SING! CHILL, ALREADY.
CHILL?! HOW CAN I?! LOOK AT YOU--YOU'RE SO EXCITED, YOU'VE BEEN WEARING YOUR COSTUME ALL MORNING!
I'M NOT EXCITED!
YEAH YOU ARE.
NO I'M NOT!
WHAT-EVER.
PRRR
QUIET DOWN!

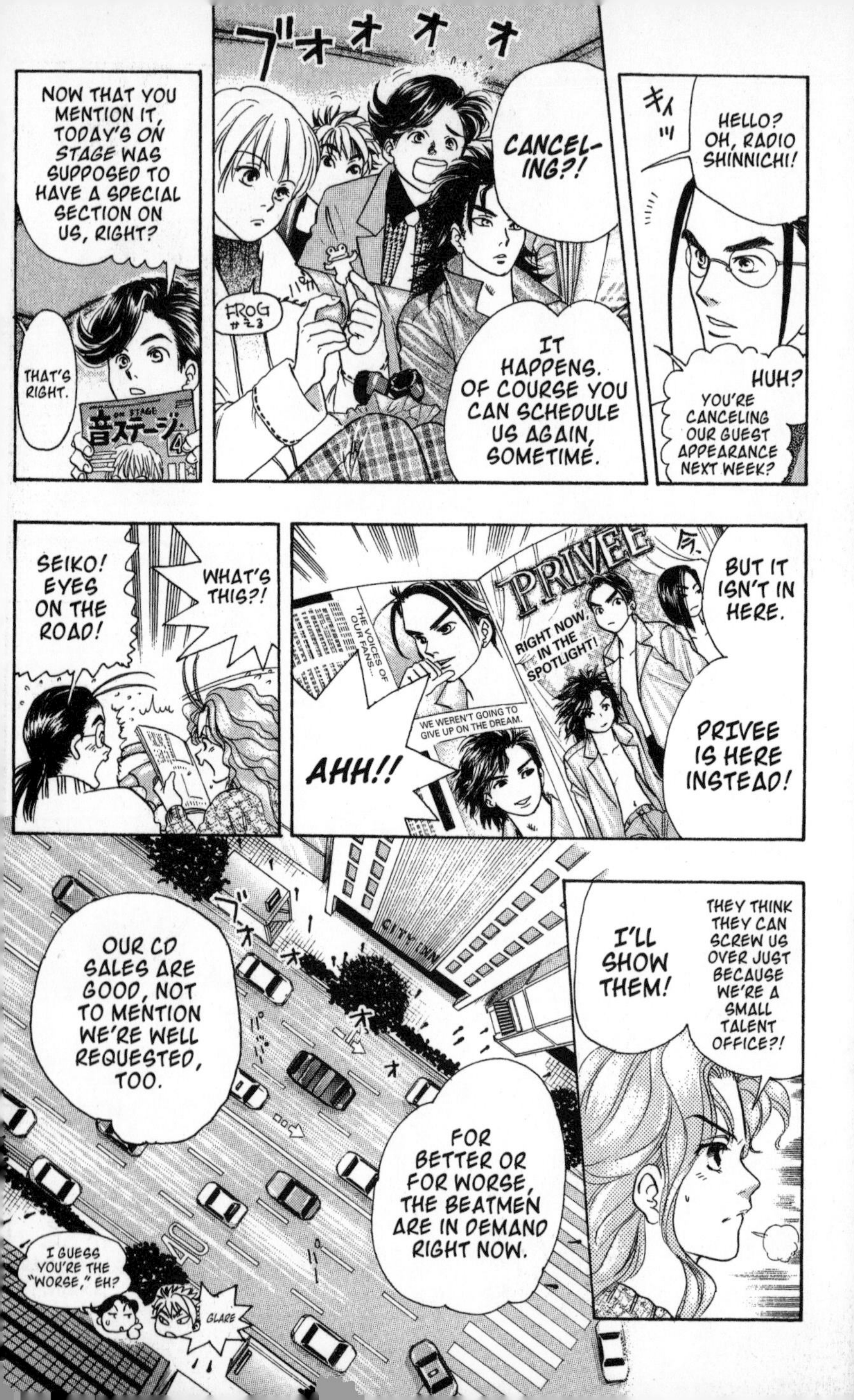
キィッ
HELLO? OH, RADIO SHINNICHI!
HUH? YOU'RE CANCELING OUR GUEST APPEARANCE NEXT WEEK?
ブオオオオオ
CANCEL-ING?!
IT HAPPENS. OF COURSE YOU CAN SCHEDULE US AGAIN, SOMETIME.
FROG かえる
NOW THAT YOU MENTION IT, TODAY'S ON STAGE WAS SUPPOSED TO HAVE A SPECIAL SECTION ON US, RIGHT?
THAT'S RIGHT.
ON STAGE 音ステージ 4
BUT IT ISN'T IN HERE.
PRIVEE IS HERE INSTEAD!
PRIVEE
RIGHT NOW, IN THE SPOTLIGHT!
THE VOICES OF OUR FANS...
WE WEREN'T GOING TO GIVE UP ON THE DREAM.
AHH!!
WHAT'S THIS?!
SEIKO! EYES ON THE ROAD!
THEY THINK THEY CAN SCREW US OVER JUST BECAUSE WE'RE A SMALL TALENT OFFICE?!
I'LL SHOW THEM!
FOR BETTER OR FOR WORSE, THE BEATMEN ARE IN DEMAND RIGHT NOW.
OUR CD SALES ARE GOOD, NOT TO MENTION WE'RE WELL REQUESTED, TOO.
CITY INN
I GUESS YOU'RE THE "WORSE," EH?
GLARE

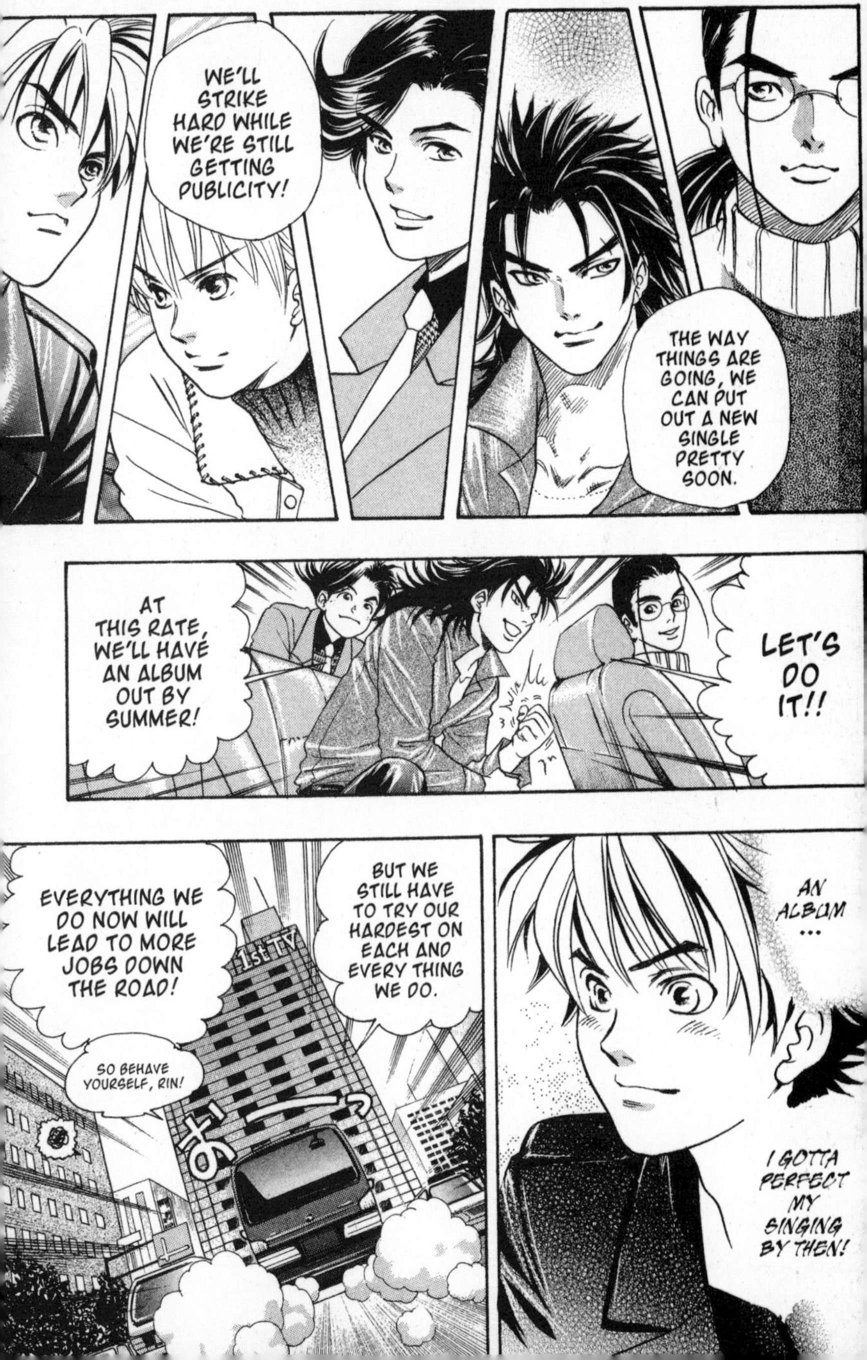
THE WAY THINGS ARE GOING, WE CAN PUT OUT A NEW SINGLE PRETTY SOON.
WE'LL STRIKE HARD WHILE WE'RE STILL GETTING PUBLICITY!
LET'S DO IT!!
AT THIS RATE, WE'LL HAVE AN ALBUM OUT BY SUMMER!
AN ALBUM...
I GOTTA PERFECT MY SINGING BY THEN!
BUT WE STILL HAVE TO TRY OUR HARDEST ON EACH AND EVERY THING WE DO.
EVERYTHING WE DO NOW WILL LEAD TO MORE JOBS DOWN THE ROAD!
1st TV
SO BEHAVE YOURSELF, RIN!
おーーっ

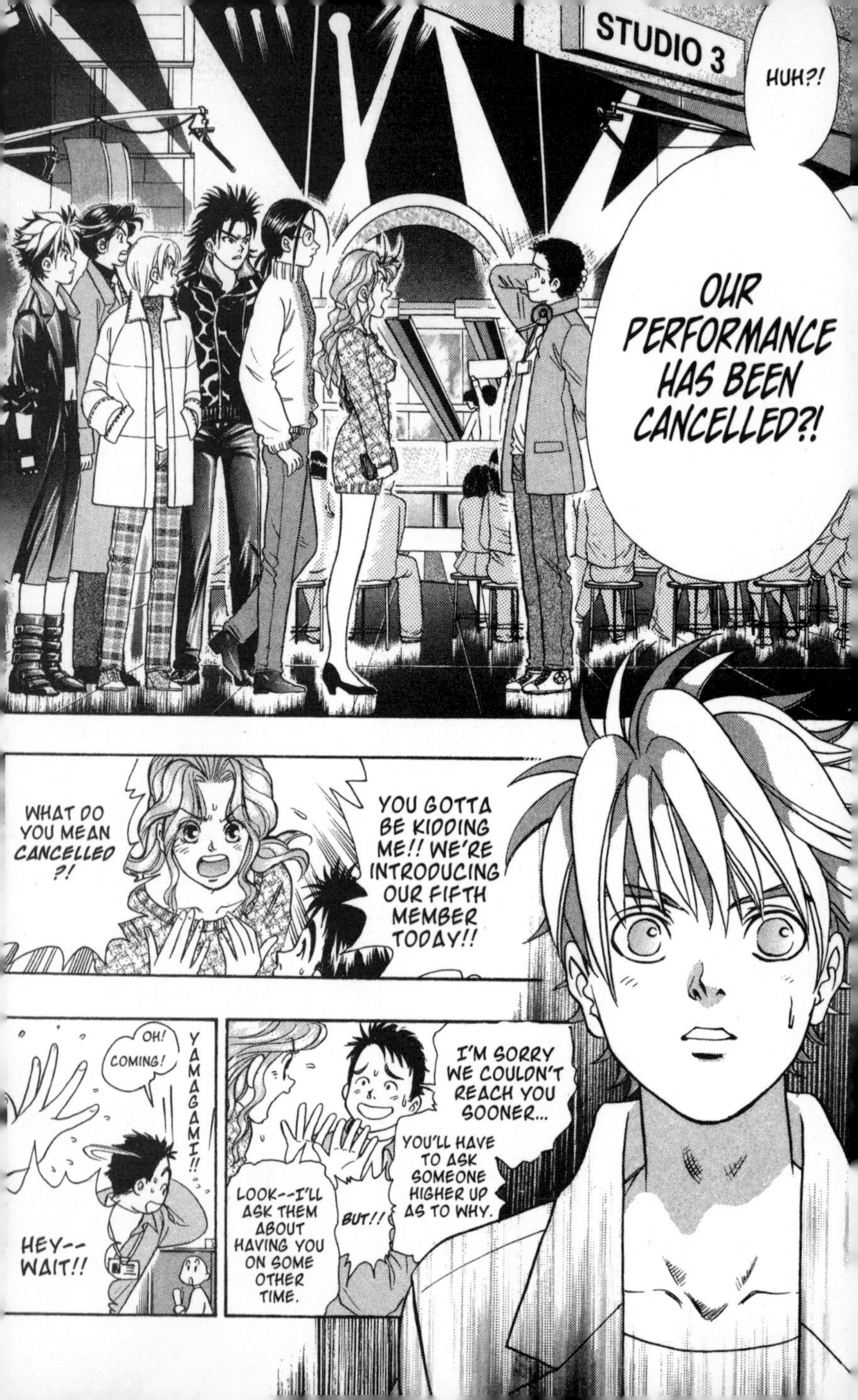
STUDIO 3
HUH?!
OUR PERFORMANCE HAS BEEN CANCELLED?!
YOU GOTTA BE KIDDING ME!! WE'RE INTRODUCING OUR FIFTH MEMBER TODAY!!
WHAT DO YOU MEAN CANCELLED?!
I'M SORRY WE COULDN'T REACH YOU SOONER...
YOU'LL HAVE TO ASK SOMEONE HIGHER UP AS TO WHY.
BUT!!
LOOK--I'LL ASK THEM ABOUT HAVING YOU ON SOME OTHER TIME.
YAMAGAMI!!
OH! COMING!
HEY--WAIT!!

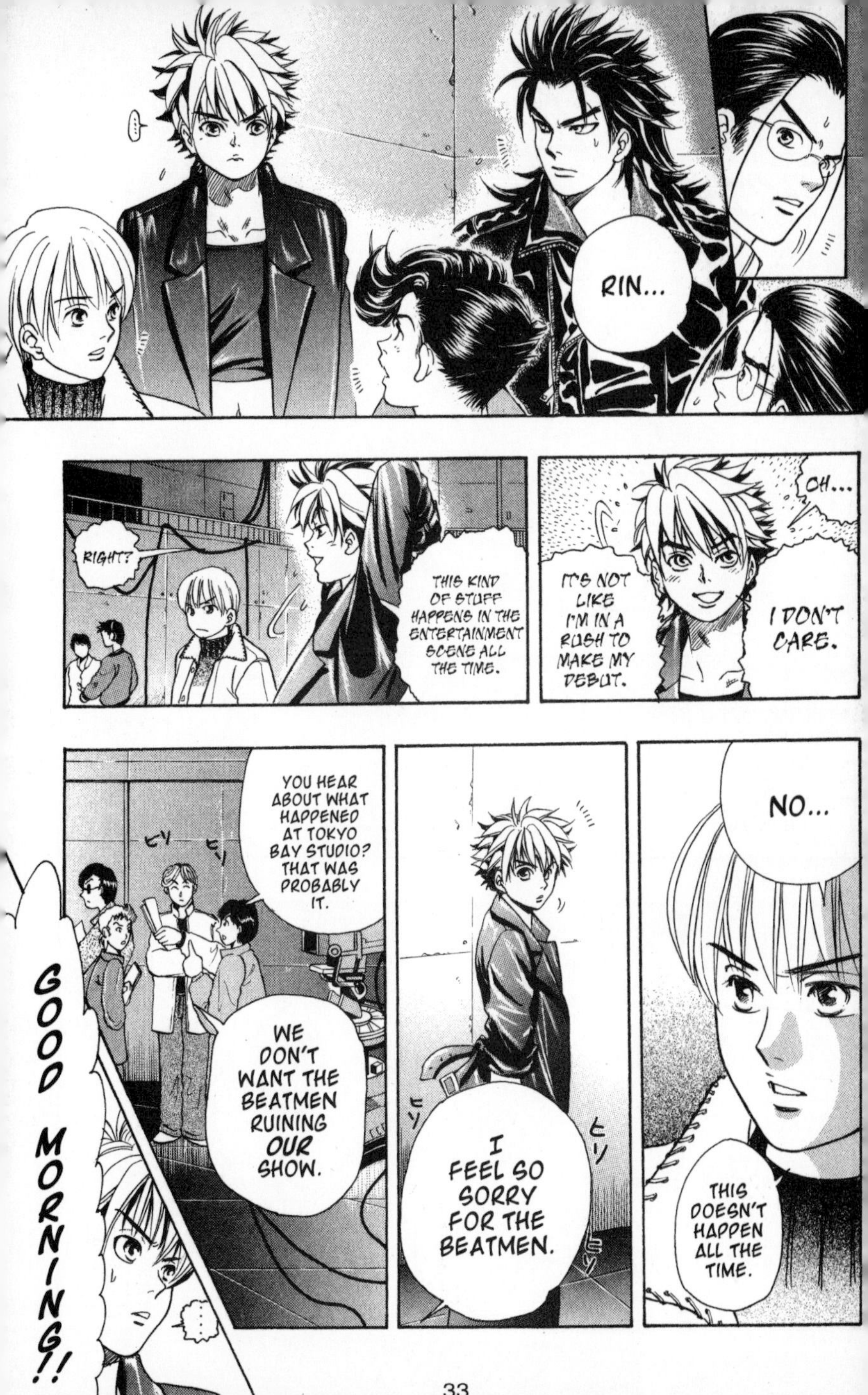
RIN...
...
OH...
I DON'T CARE.
IT'S NOT LIKE I'M IN A RUSH TO MAKE MY DEBUT.
THIS KIND OF STUFF HAPPENS IN THE ENTERTAINMENT SCENE ALL THE TIME.
RIGHT?
NO...
THIS DOESN'T HAPPEN ALL THE TIME.
ヒソ
ヒソ
I FEEL SO SORRY FOR THE BEATMEN.
ヒソ
ヒソ
YOU HEAR ABOUT WHAT HAPPENED AT TOKYO BAY STUDIO? THAT WAS PROBABLY IT.
WE DON'T WANT THE BEATMEN RUINING OUR SHOW.
GOOD MORNING!!
...

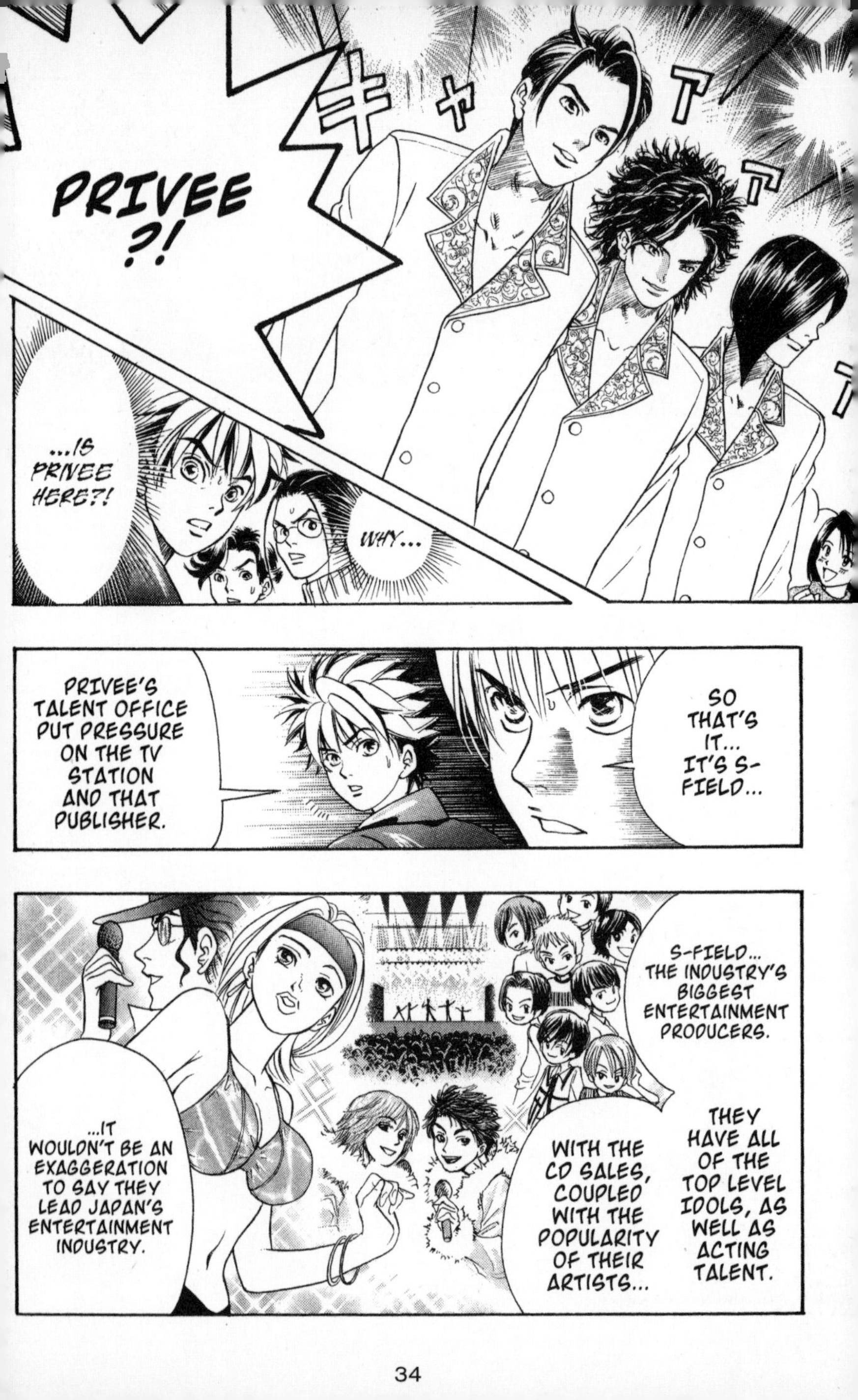
PRIVEE ?!
WHY...
...IS PRIVEE HERE?!
SO THAT'S IT... IT'S S-FIELD...
PRIVEE'S TALENT OFFICE PUT PRESSURE ON THE TV STATION AND THAT PUBLISHER.
S-FIELD... THE INDUSTRY'S BIGGEST ENTERTAINMENT PRODUCERS.
THEY HAVE ALL OF THE TOP LEVEL IDOLS, AS WELL AS ACTING TALENT.
WITH THE CD SALES, COUPLED WITH THE POPULARITY OF THEIR ARTISTS...
...IT WOULDN'T BE AN EXAGGERATION TO SAY THEY LEAD JAPAN'S ENTERTAINMENT INDUSTRY.

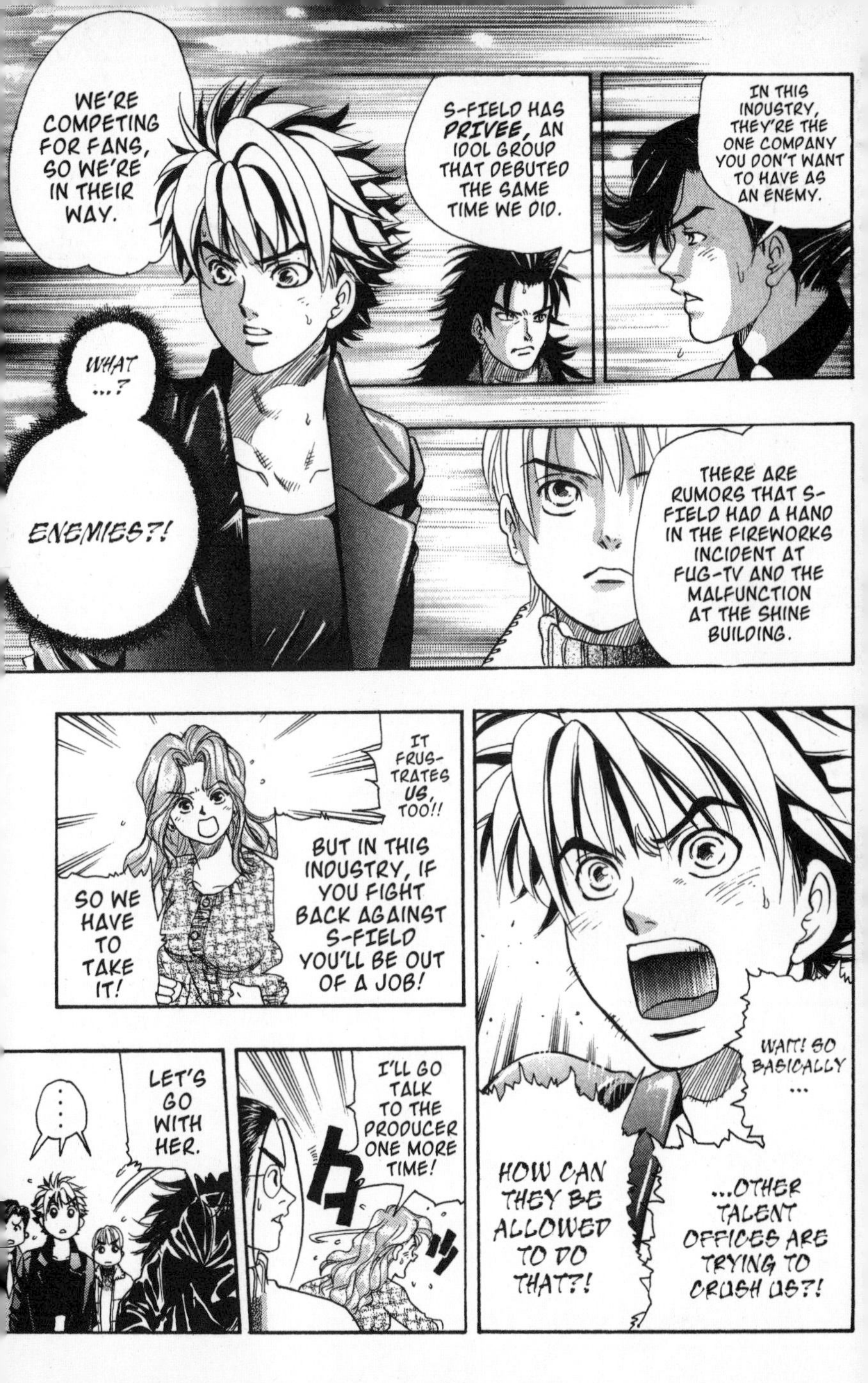

IN THIS INDUSTRY, THEY'RE THE ONE COMPANY YOU DON'T WANT TO HAVE AS AN ENEMY.
S-FIELD HAS PRIVEE, AN IDOL GROUP THAT DEBUTED THE SAME TIME WE DID.
WE'RE COMPETING FOR FANS, SO WE'RE IN THEIR WAY.
WHAT ...?
ENEMIES?!
THERE ARE RUMORS THAT S-FIELD HAD A HAND IN THE FIREWORKS INCIDENT AT FUG-TV AND THE MALFUNCTION AT THE SHINE BUILDING.
WAIT! SO BASICALLY ...
...OTHER TALENT OFFICES ARE TRYING TO CRUSH US?!
HOW CAN THEY BE ALLOWED TO DO THAT?!
IT FRUS-TRATES US, TOO!!
BUT IN THIS INDUSTRY, IF YOU FIGHT BACK AGAINST S-FIELD YOU'LL BE OUT OF A JOB!
SO WE HAVE TO TAKE IT!
I'LL GO TALK TO THE PRODUCER ONE MORE TIME!
LET'S GO WITH HER.
...

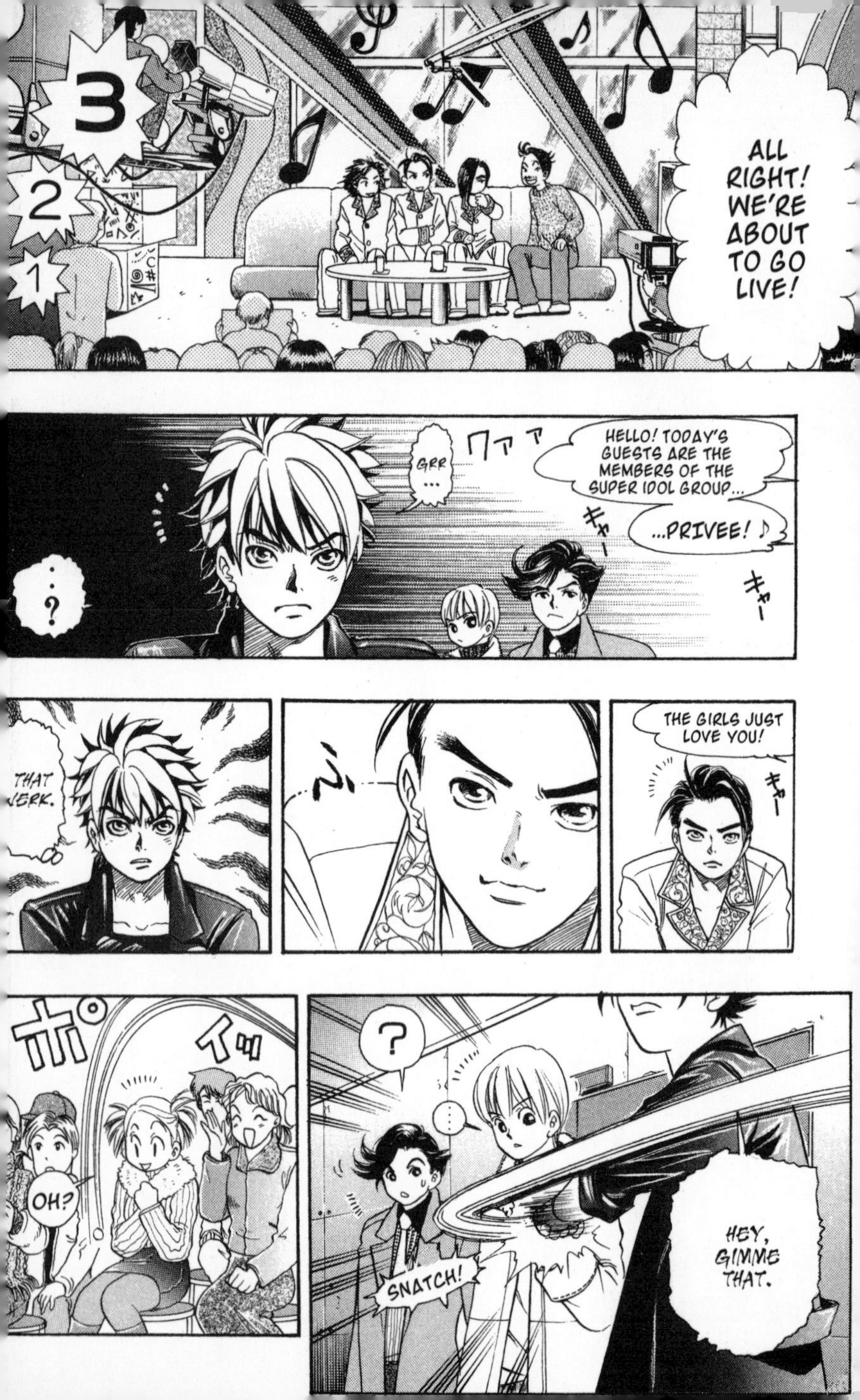
3
2
1
ALL RIGHT! WE'RE ABOUT TO GO LIVE!
HELLO! TODAY'S GUESTS ARE THE MEMBERS OF THE SUPER IDOL GROUP...
...PRIVEE! ♪
キャー
キャー
ワァァ
GRR...
...?
THE GIRLS JUST LOVE YOU!
キャー
ふ
THAT JERK.
?
...
HEY, GIMME THAT.
SNATCH!
ポイッ
OH?

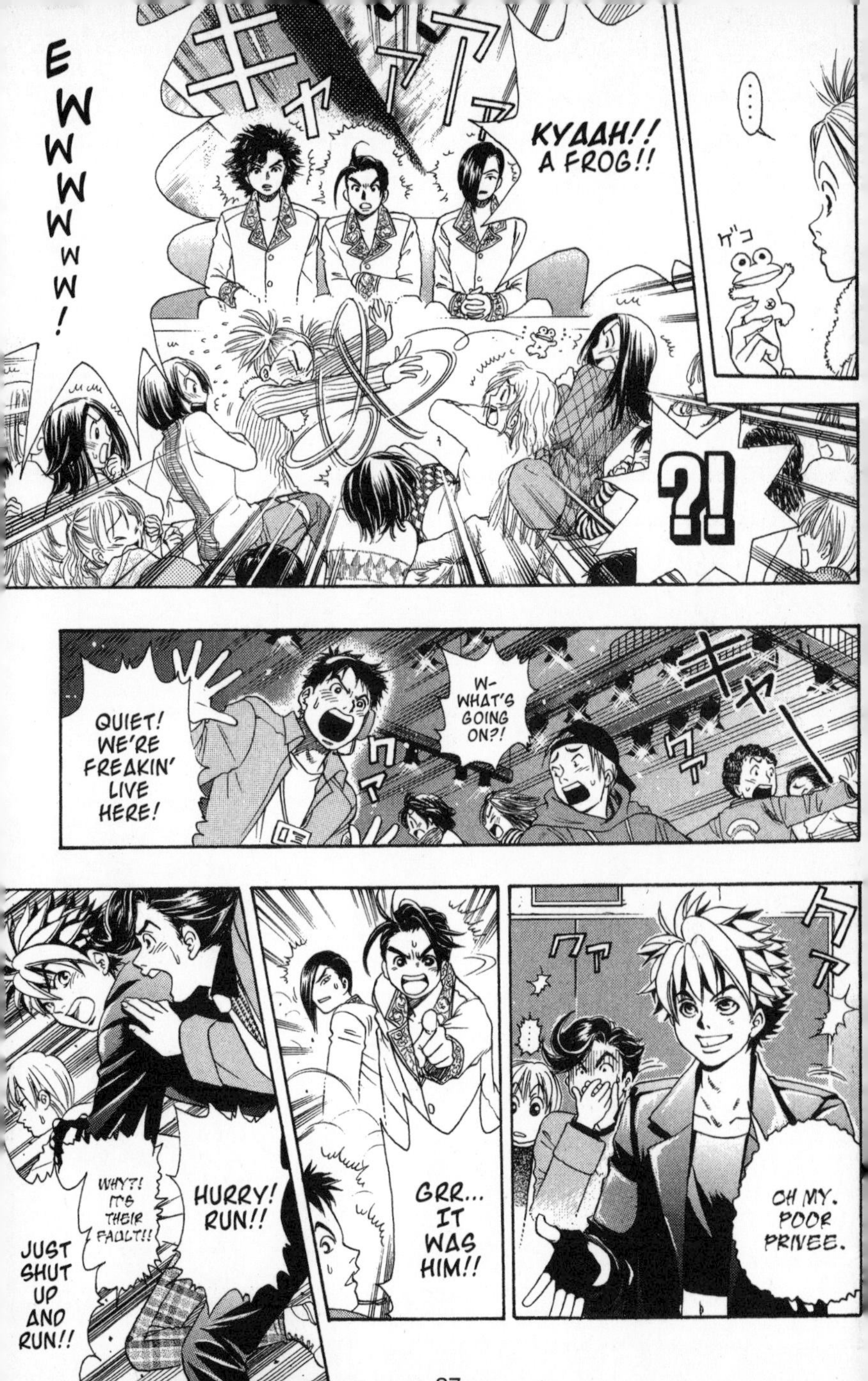
…
ゲコ
KYAAH!! A FROG!!
?!
キャァァ
EWWWWWWWW!
キャー
ワァ
W-WHAT'S GOING ON?!
ワァ
QUIET! WE'RE FREAKIN' LIVE HERE!
ワァ
ワァ
…
OH MY. POOR PRIVEE.
GRR... IT WAS HIM!!
HURRY! RUN!!
WHY?! IT'S THEIR FAULT!!
JUST SHUT UP AND RUN!!

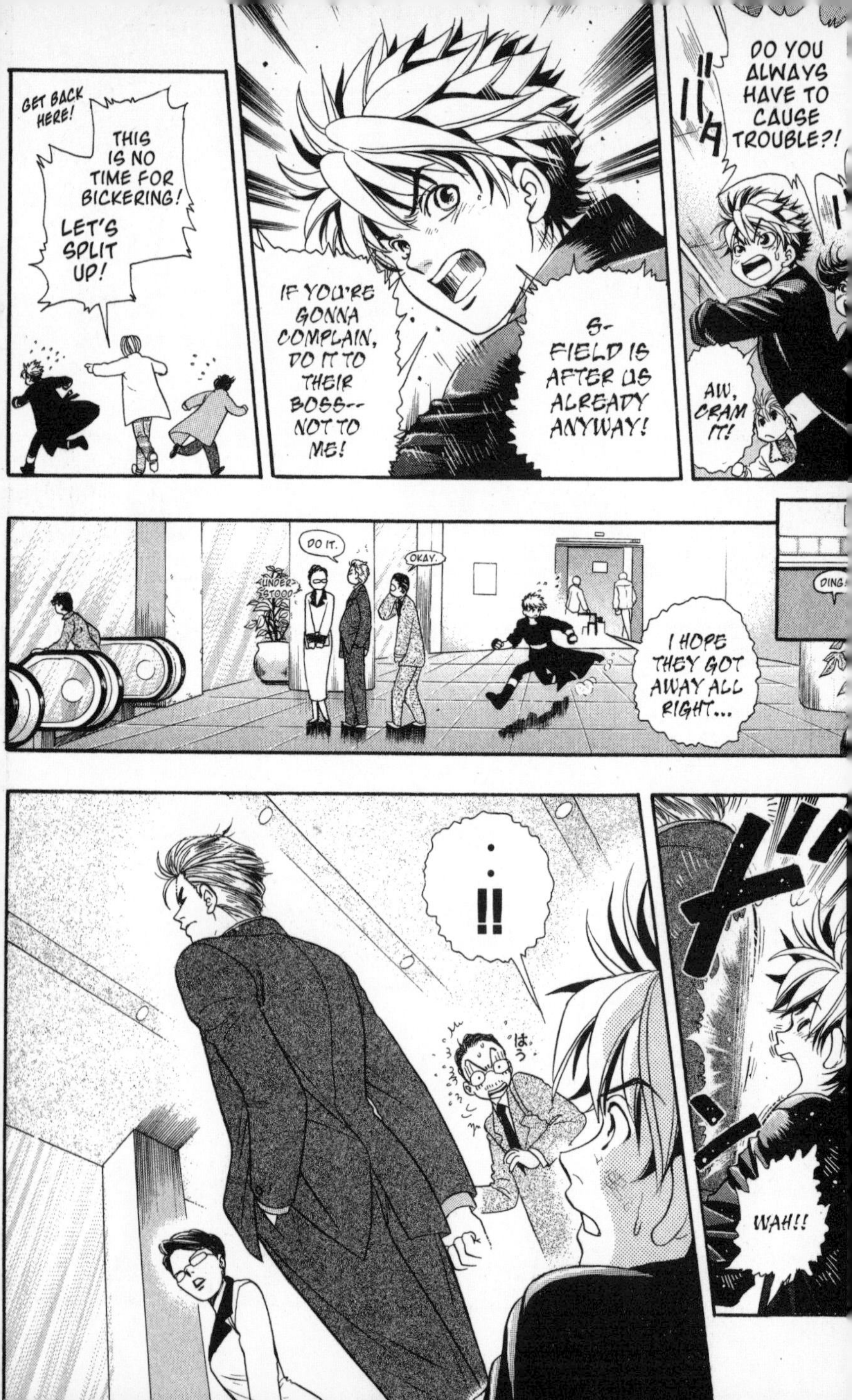
DO YOU ALWAYS HAVE TO CAUSE TROUBLE?!
AW, CRAM IT!
S-FIELD IS AFTER US ALREADY ANYWAY!
IF YOU'RE GONNA COMPLAIN, DO IT TO THEIR BOSS-- NOT TO ME!
THIS IS NO TIME FOR BICKERING! LET'S SPLIT UP!
GET BACK HERE!
DING!
I HOPE THEY GOT AWAY ALL RIGHT...
OKAY.
DO IT.
UNDER-STOOD.
WAH!!
..!!
はう

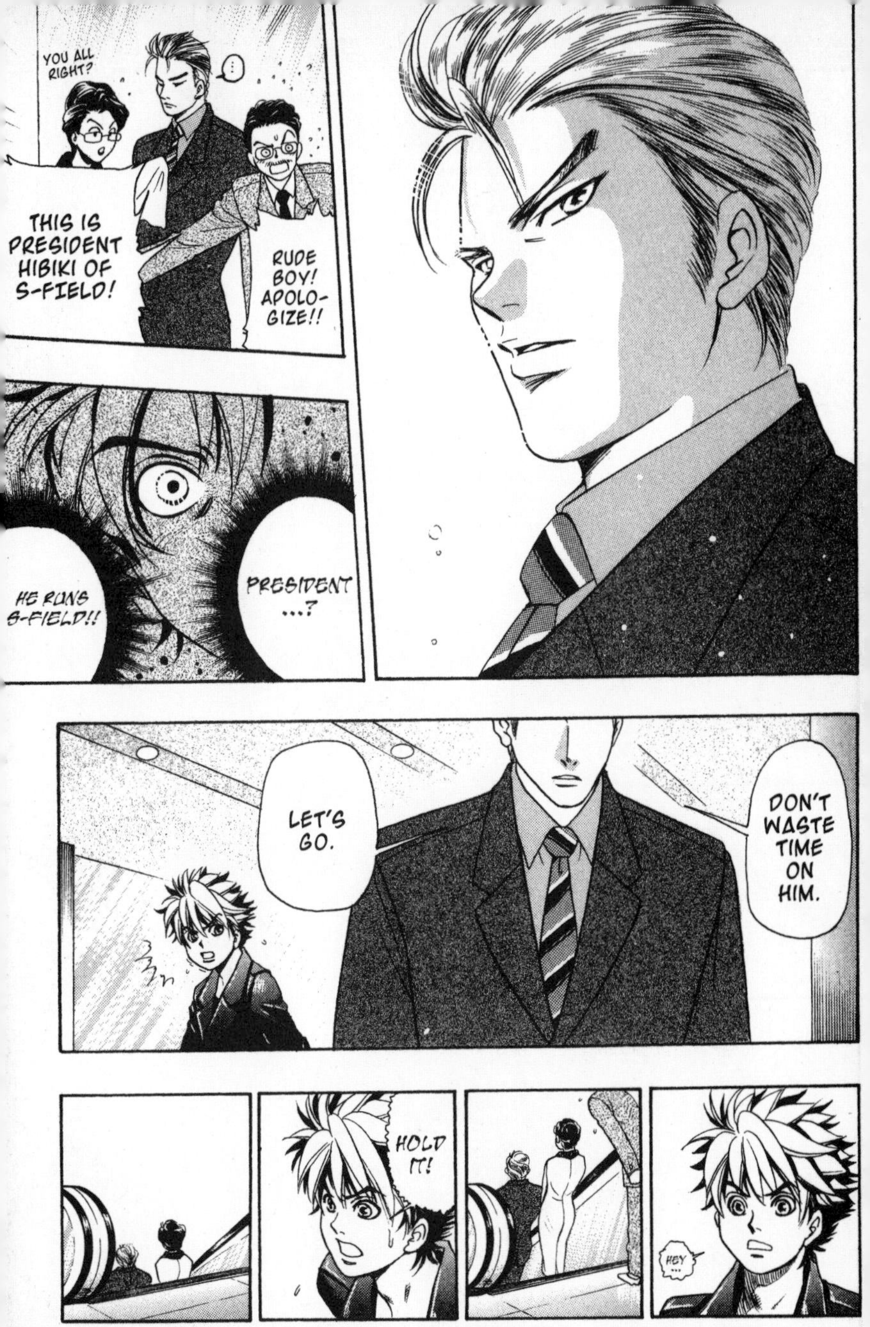

...
YOU ALL RIGHT?
RUDE BOY! APOLOGIZE!!
THIS IS PRESIDENT HIBIKI OF S-FIELD!
PRESIDENT ...?
HE RUNS S-FIELD!!
DON'T WASTE TIME ON HIM.
LET'S GO.
HEY ...
HOLD IT!

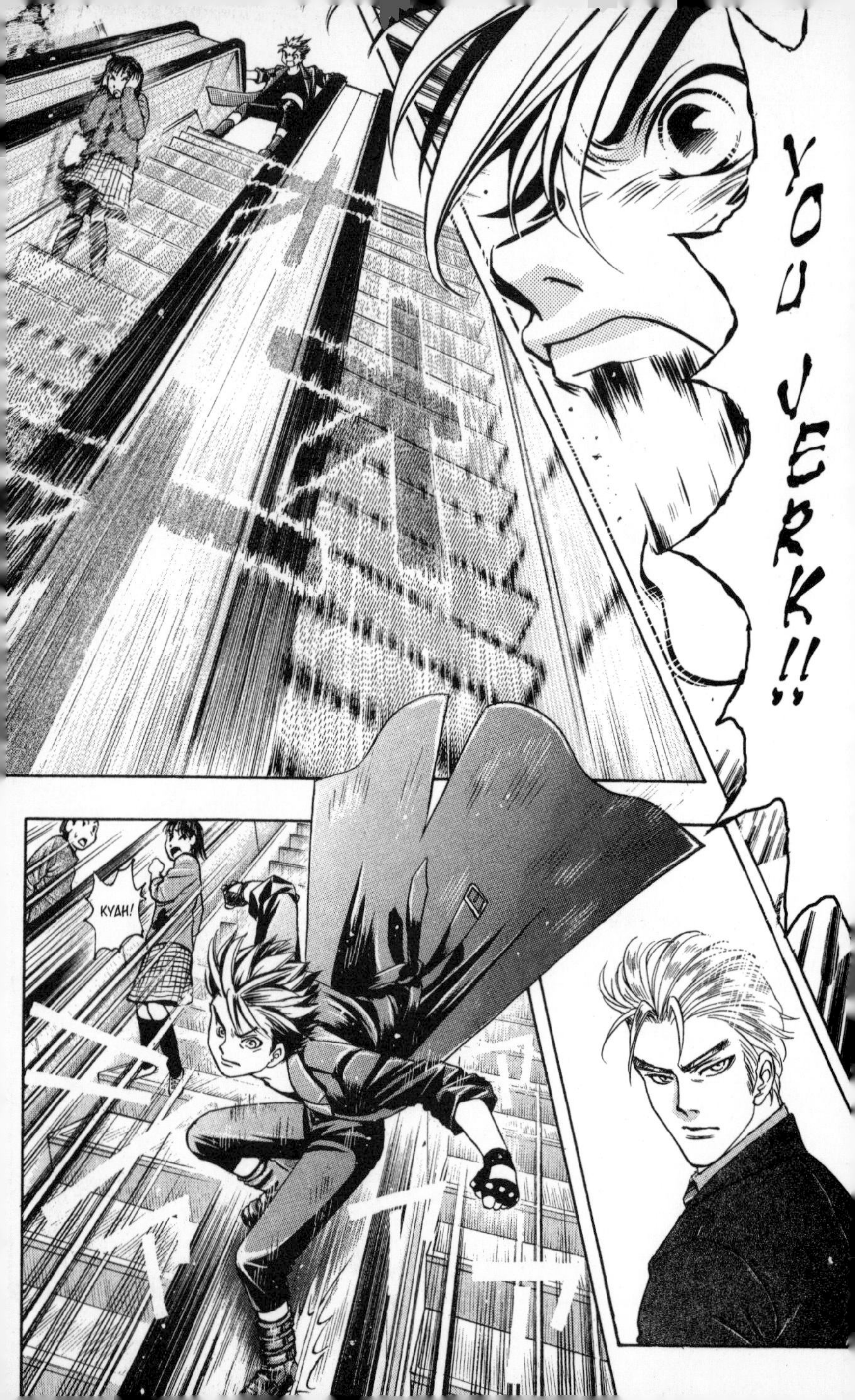
YOU JERK!!
KYAH!

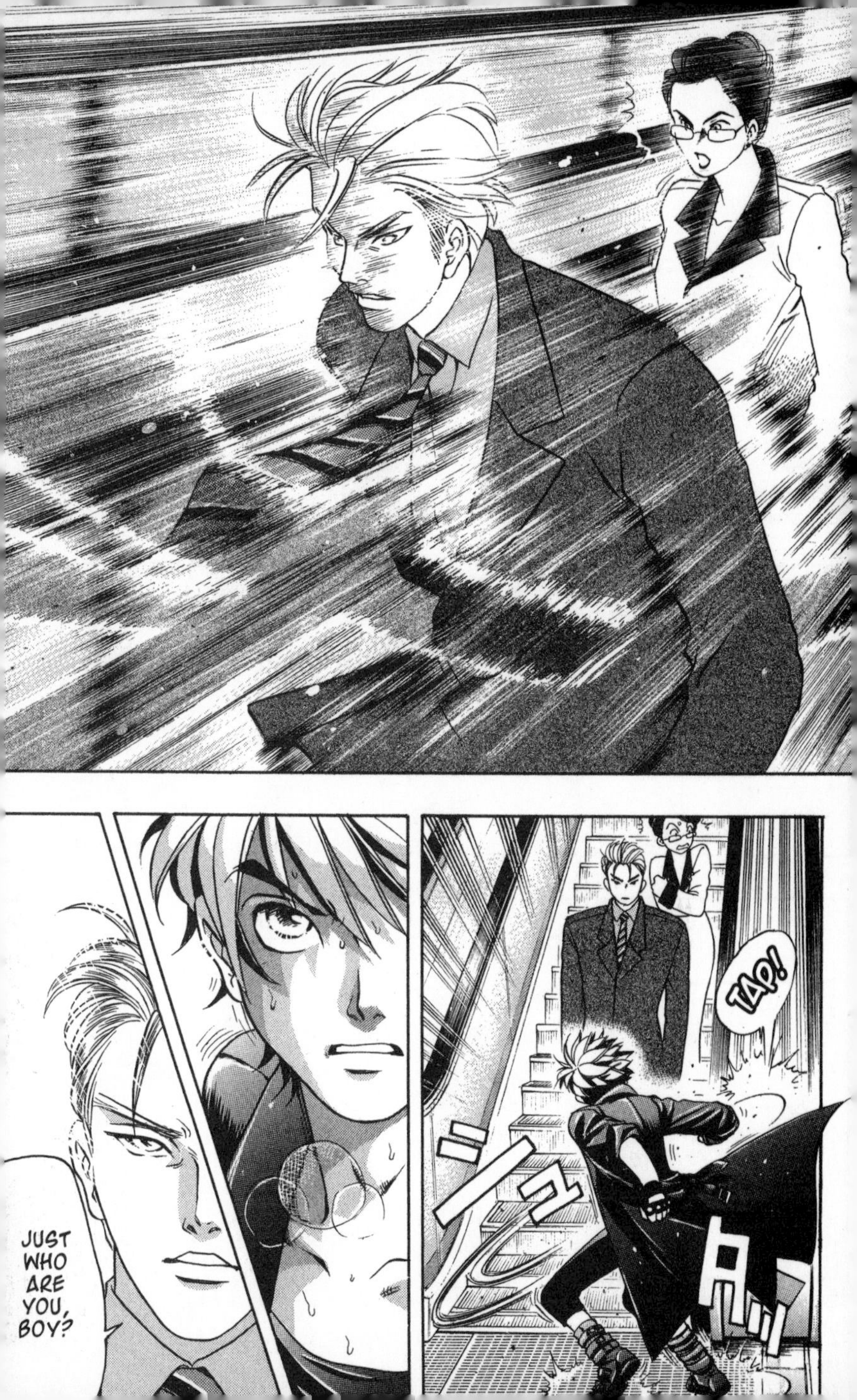
TAP!
JUST WHO ARE YOU, BOY?

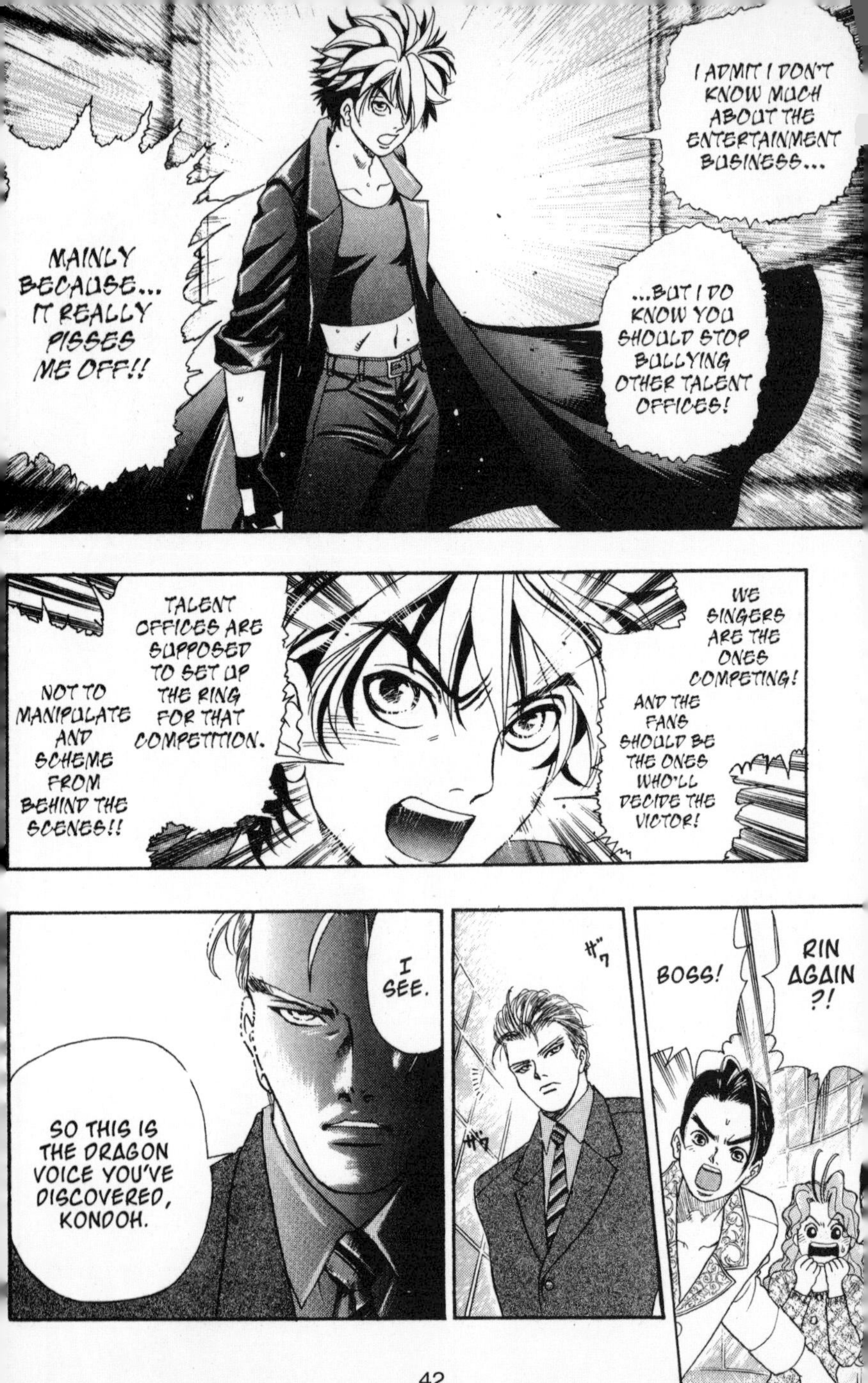
I ADMIT I DON'T KNOW MUCH ABOUT THE ENTERTAINMENT BUSINESS...
...BUT I DO KNOW YOU SHOULD STOP BULLYING OTHER TALENT OFFICES!
MAINLY BECAUSE... IT REALLY PISSES ME OFF!!
WE SINGERS ARE THE ONES COMPETING!
AND THE FANS SHOULD BE THE ONES WHO'LL DECIDE THE VICTOR!
TALENT OFFICES ARE SUPPOSED TO SET UP THE RING FOR THAT COMPETITION.
NOT TO MANIPULATE AND SCHEME FROM BEHIND THE SCENES!!
RIN AGAIN?!
BOSS!
ザッ
ザッ
I SEE.
SO THIS IS THE DRAGON VOICE YOU'VE DISCOVERED, KONDOH.

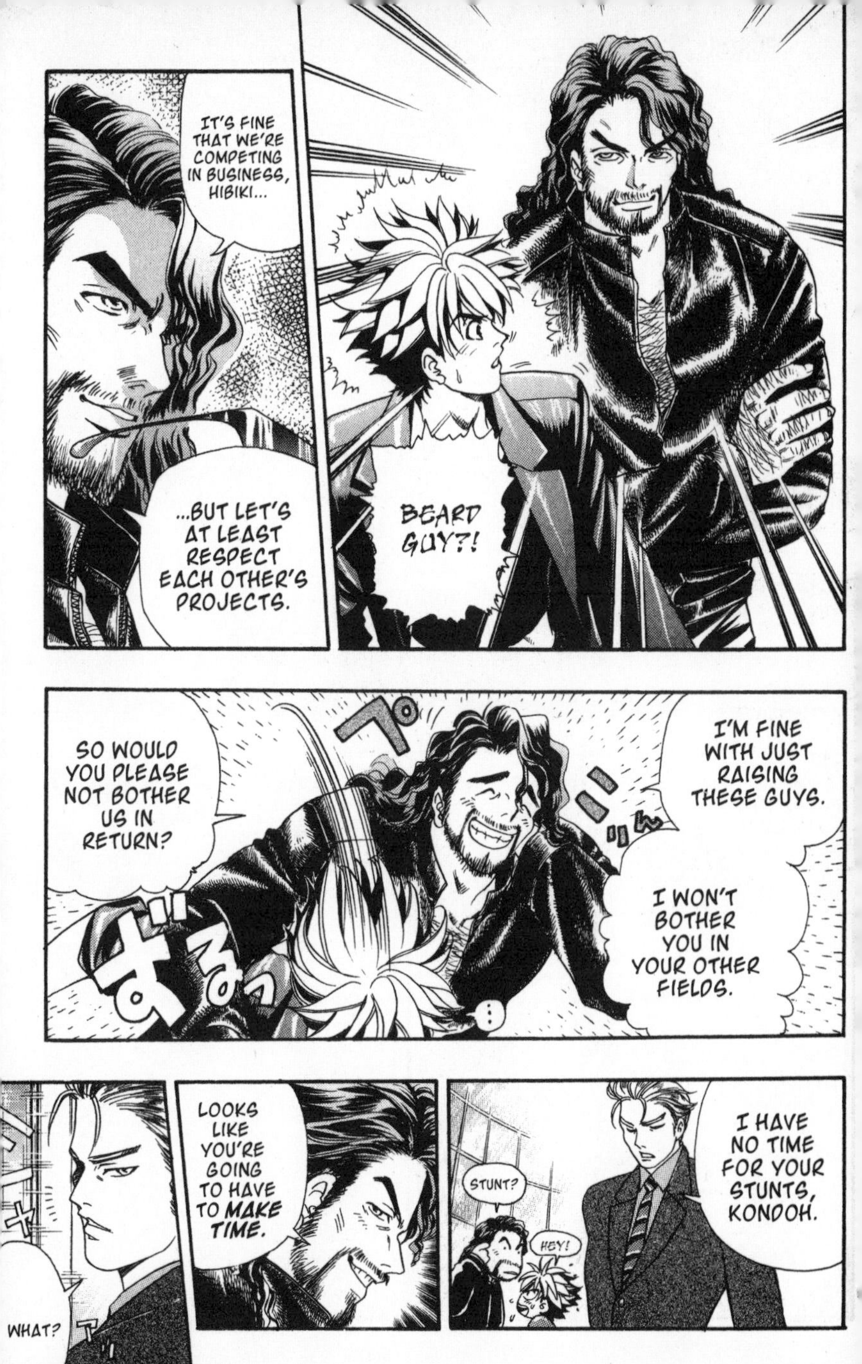
BEARD GUY?!
IT'S FINE THAT WE'RE COMPETING IN BUSINESS, HIBIKI...
...BUT LET'S AT LEAST RESPECT EACH OTHER'S PROJECTS.
I'M FINE WITH JUST RAISING THESE GUYS.
I WON'T BOTHER YOU IN YOUR OTHER FIELDS.
SO WOULD YOU PLEASE NOT BOTHER US IN RETURN?
...
I HAVE NO TIME FOR YOUR STUNTS, KONDOH.
STUNT?
HEY!
LOOKS LIKE YOU'RE GOING TO HAVE TO *MAKE TIME*.
WHAT?

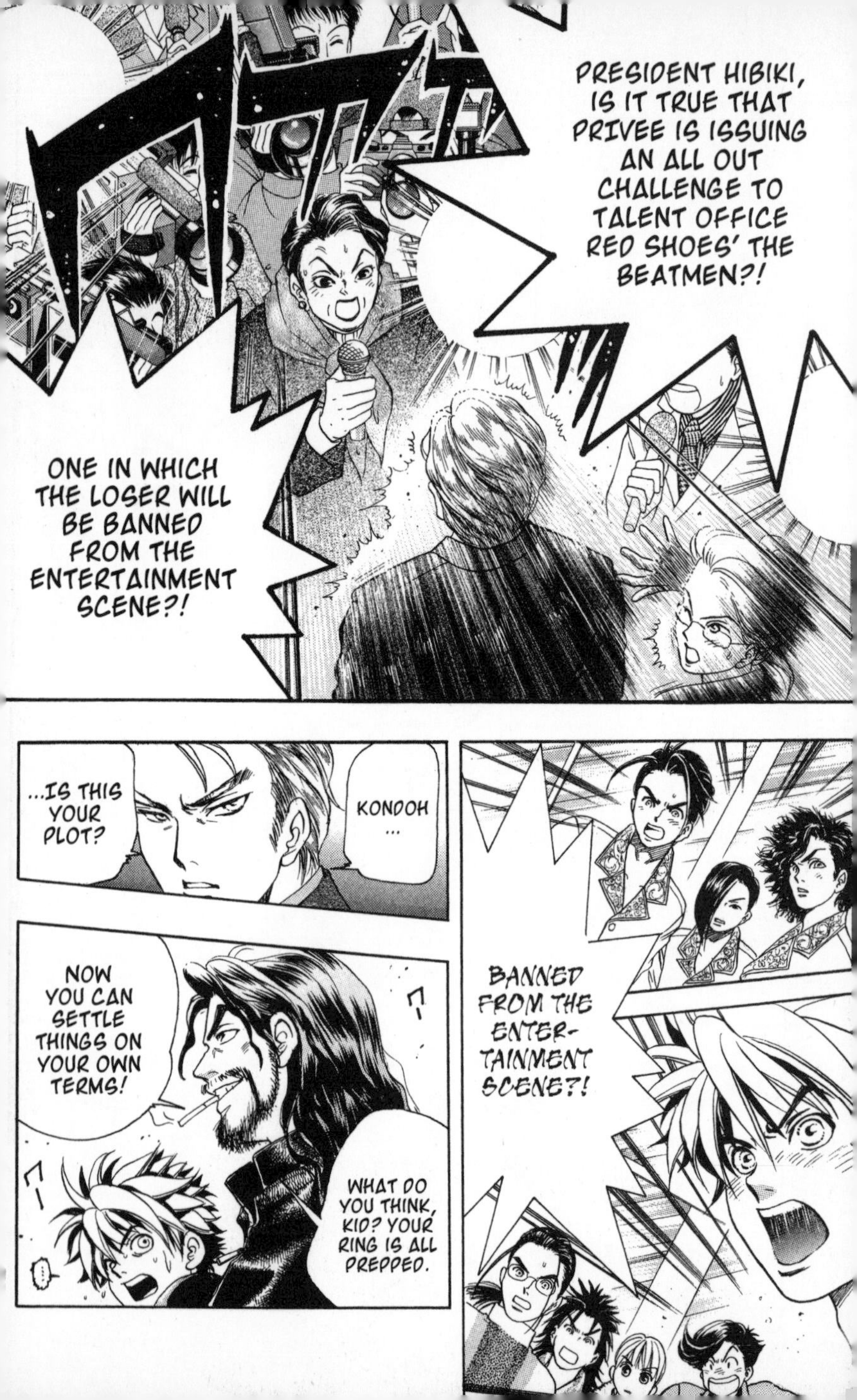
PRESIDENT HIBIKI, IS IT TRUE THAT PRIVEE IS ISSUING AN ALL OUT CHALLENGE TO TALENT OFFICE RED SHOES' THE BEATMEN?!
ONE IN WHICH THE LOSER WILL BE BANNED FROM THE ENTERTAINMENT SCENE?!
BANNED FROM THE ENTER-TAINMENT SCENE?!
KONDOH ...
...IS THIS YOUR PLOT?
!?
NOW YOU CAN SETTLE THINGS ON YOUR OWN TERMS!
WHAT DO YOU THINK, KID? YOUR RING IS ALL PREPPED.
!?
....

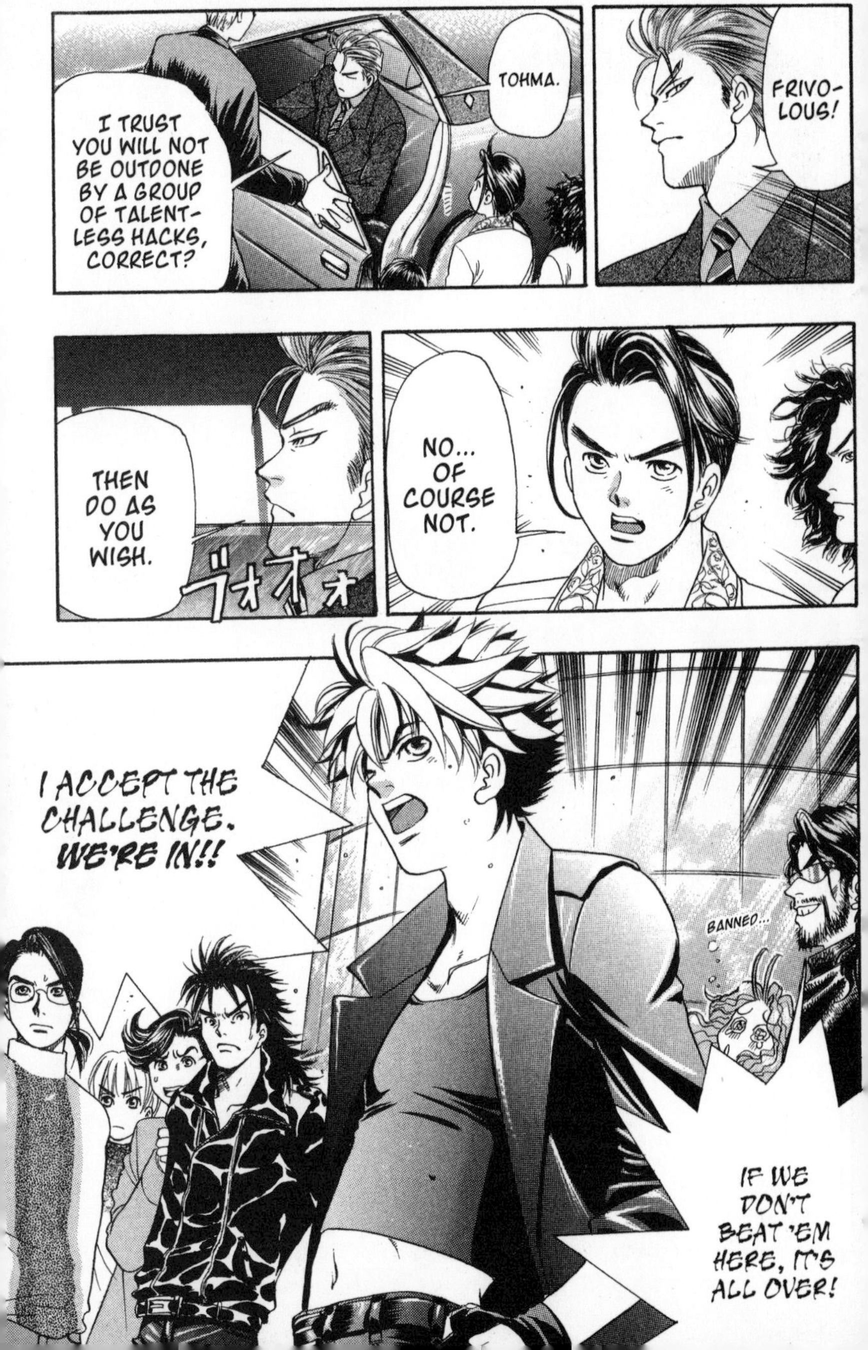
FRIVO-LOUS!
TOHMA.
I TRUST YOU WILL NOT BE OUTDONE BY A GROUP OF TALENT-LESS HACKS, CORRECT?
NO... OF COURSE NOT.
THEN DO AS YOU WISH.
ヴォオォォ
I ACCEPT THE CHALLENGE. WE'RE IN!!
BANNED...
IF WE DON'T BEAT 'EM HERE, IT'S ALL OVER!

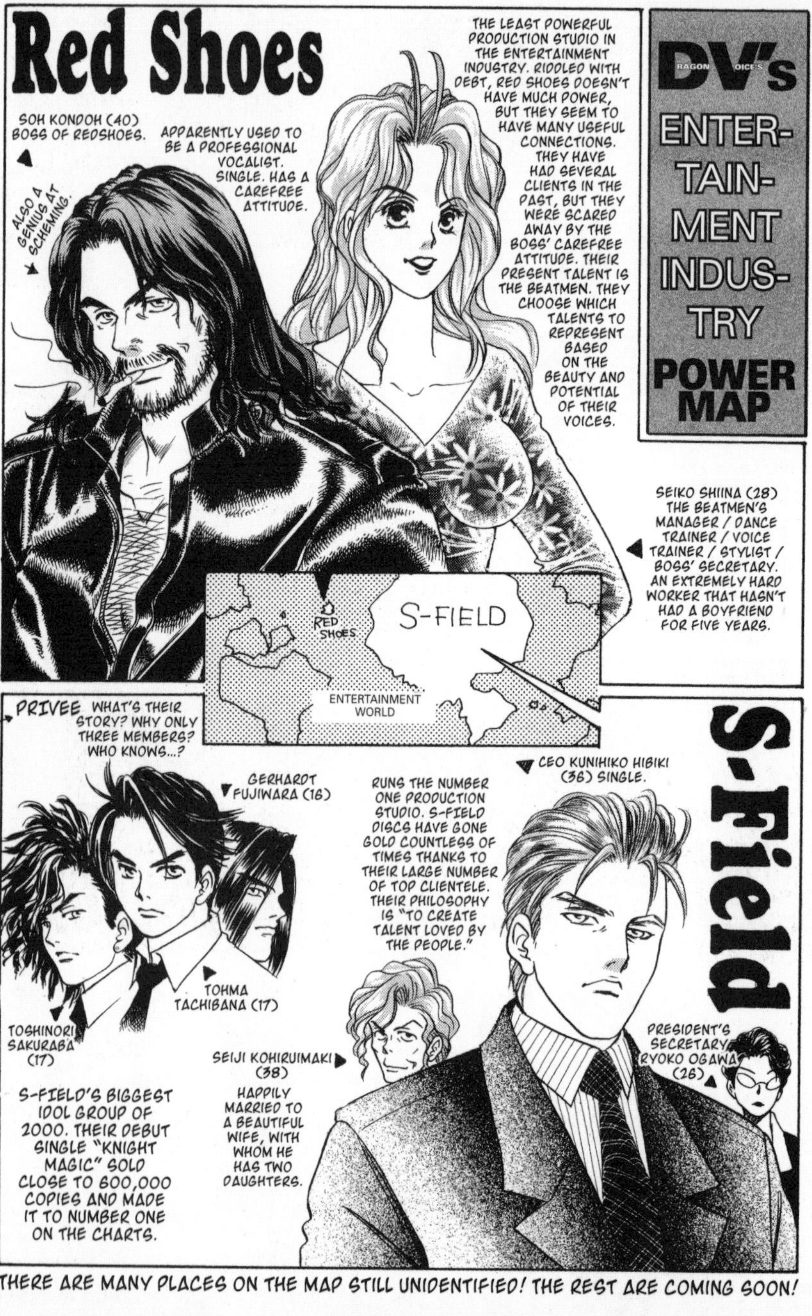
Red Shoes
DV's (DRAGON VOICE'S)
ENTER-TAIN-MENT INDUS-TRY
POWER MAP
THE LEAST POWERFUL PRODUCTION STUDIO IN THE ENTERTAINMENT INDUSTRY. RIDDLED WITH DEBT, RED SHOES DOESN'T HAVE MUCH POWER, BUT THEY SEEM TO HAVE MANY USEFUL CONNECTIONS. THEY HAVE HAD SEVERAL CLIENTS IN THE PAST, BUT THEY WERE SCARED AWAY BY THE BOSS' CAREFREE ATTITUDE. THEIR PRESENT TALENT IS THE BEATMEN. THEY CHOOSE WHICH TALENTS TO REPRESENT BASED ON THE BEAUTY AND POTENTIAL OF THEIR VOICES.
SOH KONDOH (40) BOSS OF REDSHOES.
APPARENTLY USED TO BE A PROFESSIONAL VOCALIST. SINGLE. HAS A CAREFREE ATTITUDE.
ALSO A GENIUS AT SCHEMING.
SEIKO SHIINA (28) THE BEATMEN'S MANAGER / DANCE TRAINER / VOICE TRAINER / STYLIST / BOSS' SECRETARY. AN EXTREMELY HARD WORKER THAT HASN'T HAD A BOYFRIEND FOR FIVE YEARS.
RED SHOES
S-FIELD
ENTERTAINMENT WORLD
S-Field
PRIVEE
WHAT'S THEIR STORY? WHY ONLY THREE MEMBERS? WHO KNOWS...?
PRIVEE MEANS "PRIVATE" IN FRENCH.
GERHARDT FUJIWARA (16)
TOHMA TACHIBANA (17)
TOSHINORI SAKURABA (17)
S-FIELD'S BIGGEST IDOL GROUP OF 2000. THEIR DEBUT SINGLE "KNIGHT MAGIC" SOLD CLOSE TO 600,000 COPIES AND MADE IT TO NUMBER ONE ON THE CHARTS.
CEO KUNIHIKO HIBIKI (36) SINGLE.
RUNS THE NUMBER ONE PRODUCTION STUDIO. S-FIELD DISCS HAVE GONE GOLD COUNTLESS OF TIMES THANKS TO THEIR LARGE NUMBER OF TOP CLIENTELE. THEIR PHILOSOPHY IS "TO CREATE TALENT LOVED BY THE PEOPLE."
SEIJI KOHIRUIMAKI (38)
HAPPILY MARRIED TO A BEAUTIFUL WIFE, WITH WHOM HE HAS TWO DAUGHTERS.
PRESIDENT'S SECRETARY RYOKO OGAWA (26)

THERE ARE MANY PLACES ON THE MAP STILL UNIDENTIFIED! THE REST ARE COMING SOON!

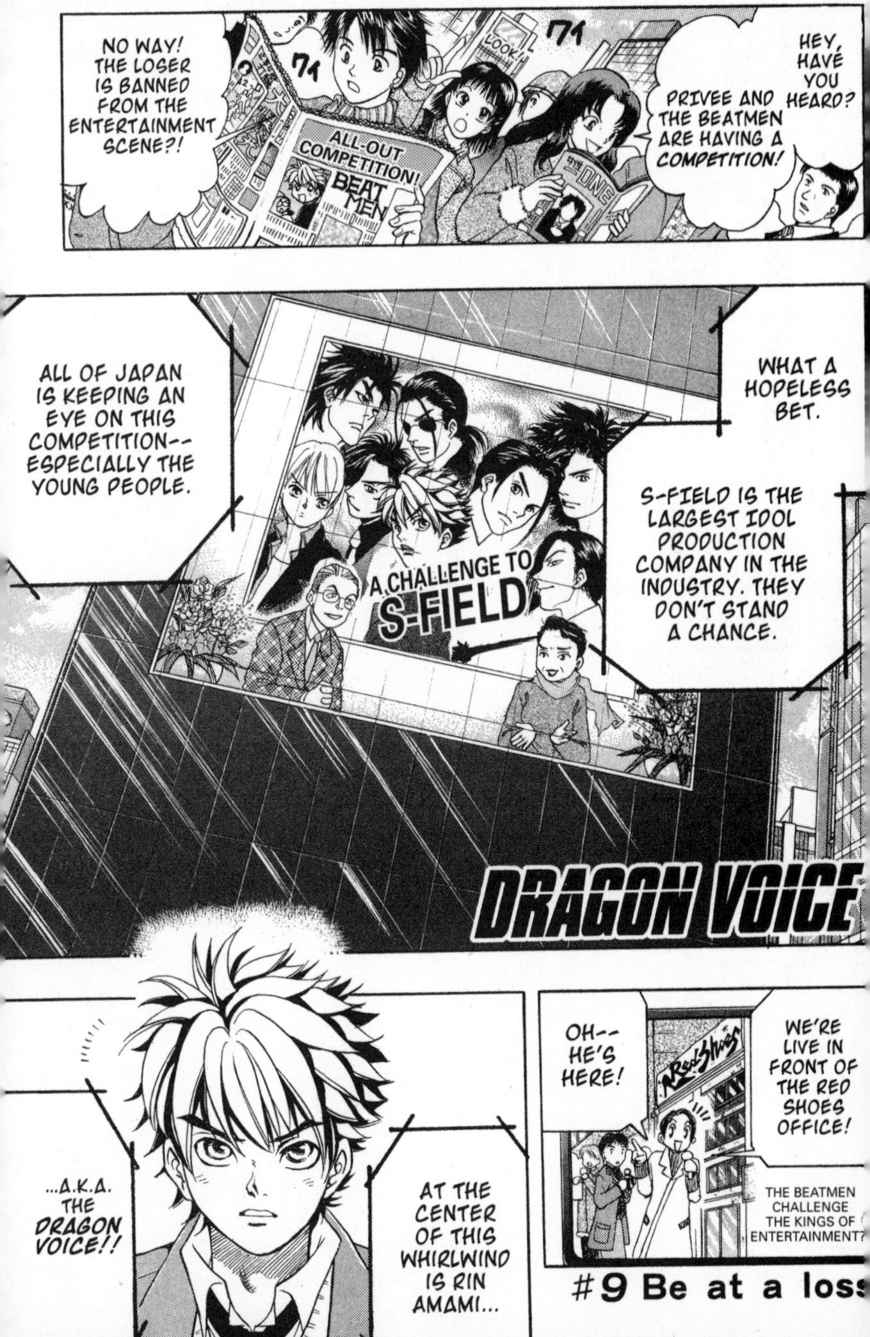
HEY, HAVE YOU HEARD?
PRIVEE AND THE BEATMEN ARE HAVING A COMPETITION!
LOOK!
ONE
NO WAY! THE LOSER IS BANNED FROM THE ENTERTAINMENT SCENE?!
ALL-OUT COMPETITION!
BEAT MEN
WHAT A HOPELESS BET.
S-FIELD IS THE LARGEST IDOL PRODUCTION COMPANY IN THE INDUSTRY. THEY DON'T STAND A CHANCE.
A CHALLENGE TO S-FIELD
ALL OF JAPAN IS KEEPING AN EYE ON THIS COMPETITION--ESPECIALLY THE YOUNG PEOPLE.
DRAGON VOICE
WE'RE LIVE IN FRONT OF THE RED SHOES OFFICE!
Red Shoes
OH--HE'S HERE!
THE BEATMEN CHALLENGE THE KINGS OF ENTERTAINMENT?
#9 Be at a loss
AT THE CENTER OF THIS WHIRLWIND IS RIN AMAMI...
...A.K.A. THE DRAGON VOICE!!

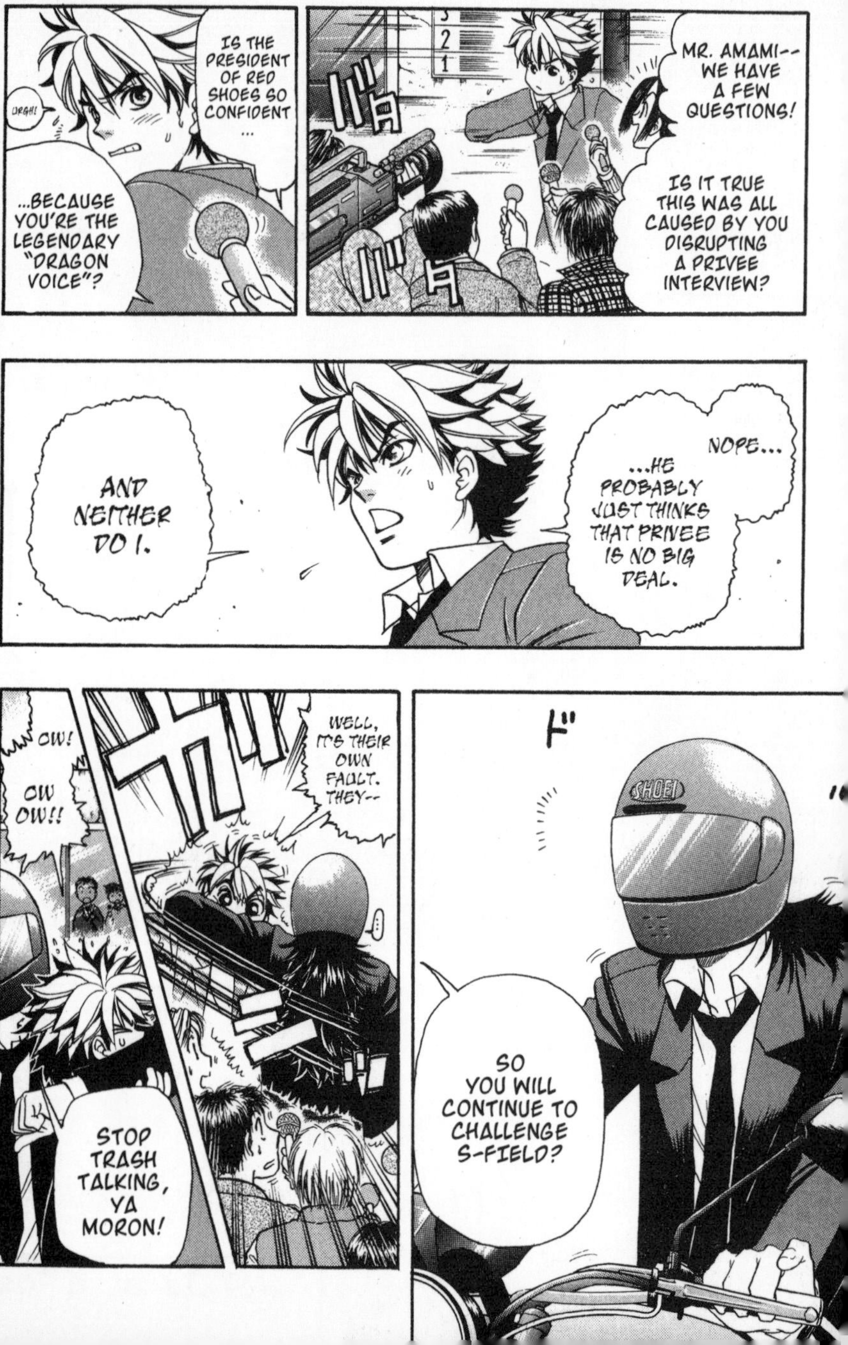
MR. AMAMI-- WE HAVE A FEW QUESTIONS!
IS IT TRUE THIS WAS ALL CAUSED BY YOU DISRUPTING A PRIVEE INTERVIEW?
IS THE PRESIDENT OF RED SHOES SO CONFIDENT ...
URGH!
...BECAUSE YOU'RE THE LEGENDARY "DRAGON VOICE"?
NOPE...
...HE PROBABLY JUST THINKS THAT PRIVEE IS NO BIG DEAL.
AND NEITHER DO I.
ド
SHOEI
SO YOU WILL CONTINUE TO CHALLENGE S-FIELD?
WELL, IT'S THEIR OWN FAULT. THEY--
OW!
OW OW!!
STOP TRASH TALKING, YA MORON!

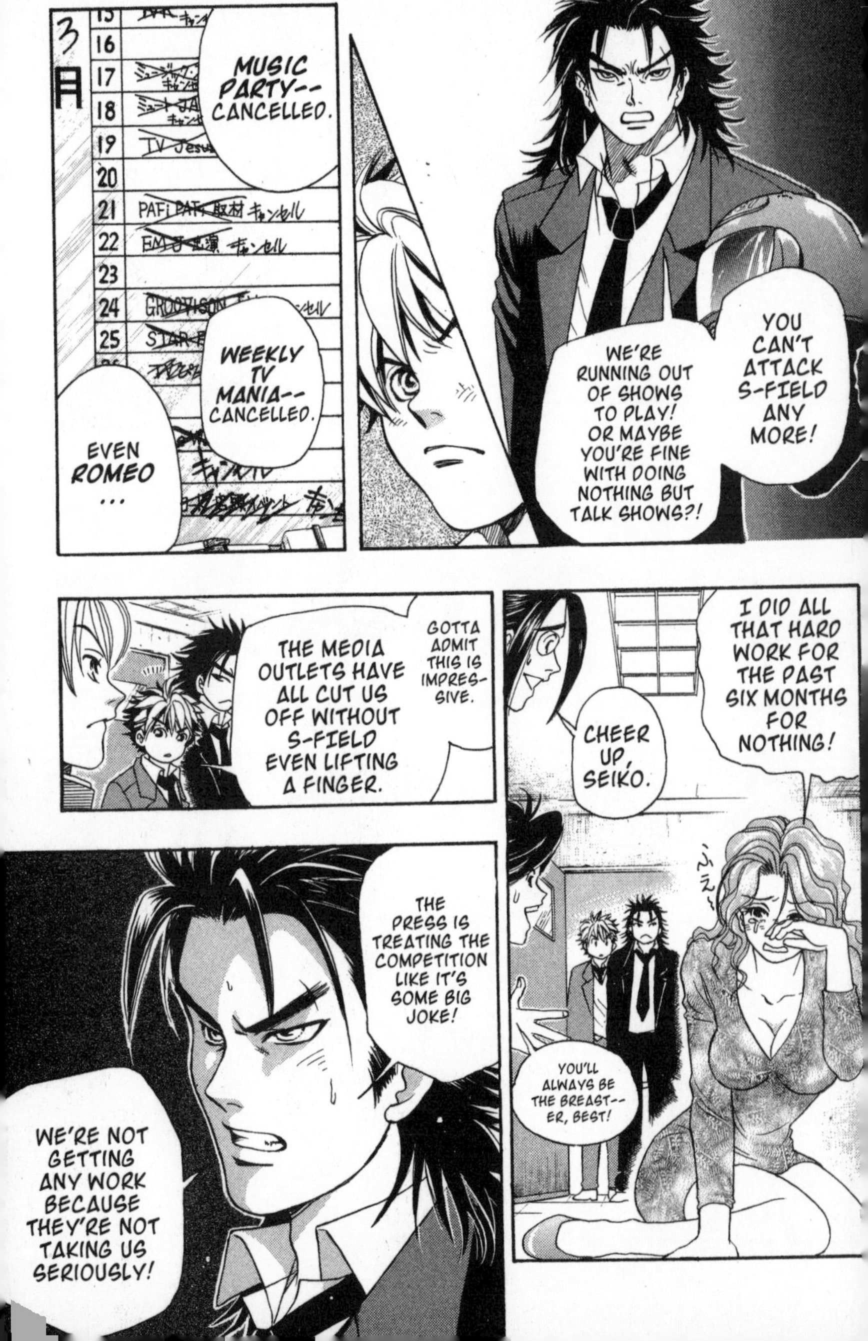
YOU CAN'T ATTACK S-FIELD ANY MORE!
WE'RE RUNNING OUT OF SHOWS TO PLAY! OR MAYBE YOU'RE FINE WITH DOING NOTHING BUT TALK SHOWS?!
MUSIC PARTY--CANCELLED.
WEEKLY TV MANIA--CANCELLED.
EVEN ROMEO...
I DID ALL THAT HARD WORK FOR THE PAST SIX MONTHS FOR NOTHING!
CHEER UP, SEIKO.
ふぇ～
YOU'LL ALWAYS BE THE BREASTER--ER, BEST!
GOTTA ADMIT THIS IS IMPRESSIVE.
THE MEDIA OUTLETS HAVE ALL CUT US OFF WITHOUT S-FIELD EVEN LIFTING A FINGER.
THE PRESS IS TREATING THE COMPETITION LIKE IT'S SOME BIG JOKE!
WE'RE NOT GETTING ANY WORK BECAUSE THEY'RE NOT TAKING US SERIOUSLY!

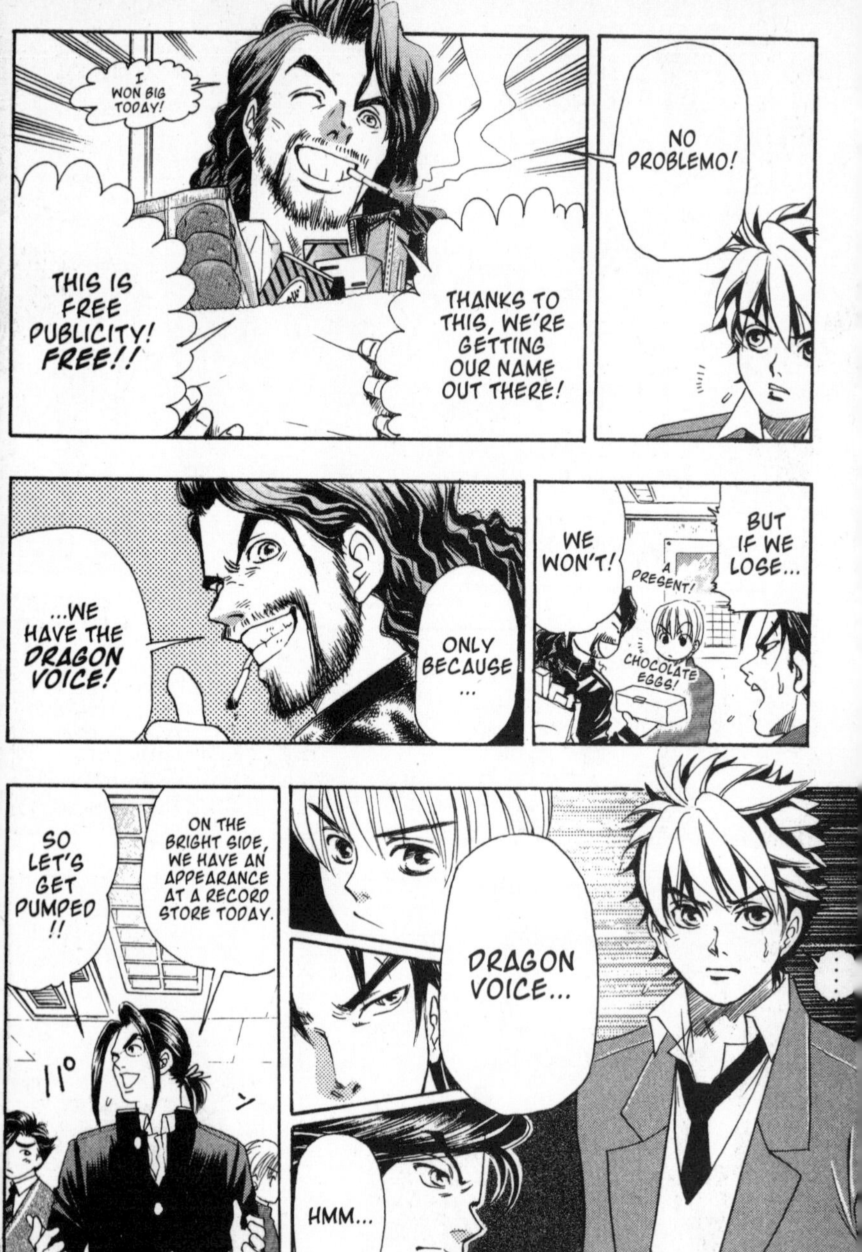
NO PROBLEMO!
I WON BIG TODAY!
THANKS TO THIS, WE'RE GETTING OUR NAME OUT THERE!
THIS IS FREE PUBLICITY! FREE!!
BUT IF WE LOSE...
WE WON'T!
A PRESENT!
CHOCOLATE EGGS!
ONLY BECAUSE ...
...WE HAVE THE DRAGON VOICE!
...
DRAGON VOICE...
HMM...
ON THE BRIGHT SIDE, WE HAVE AN APPEARANCE AT A RECORD STORE TODAY.
SO LET'S GET PUMPED!!

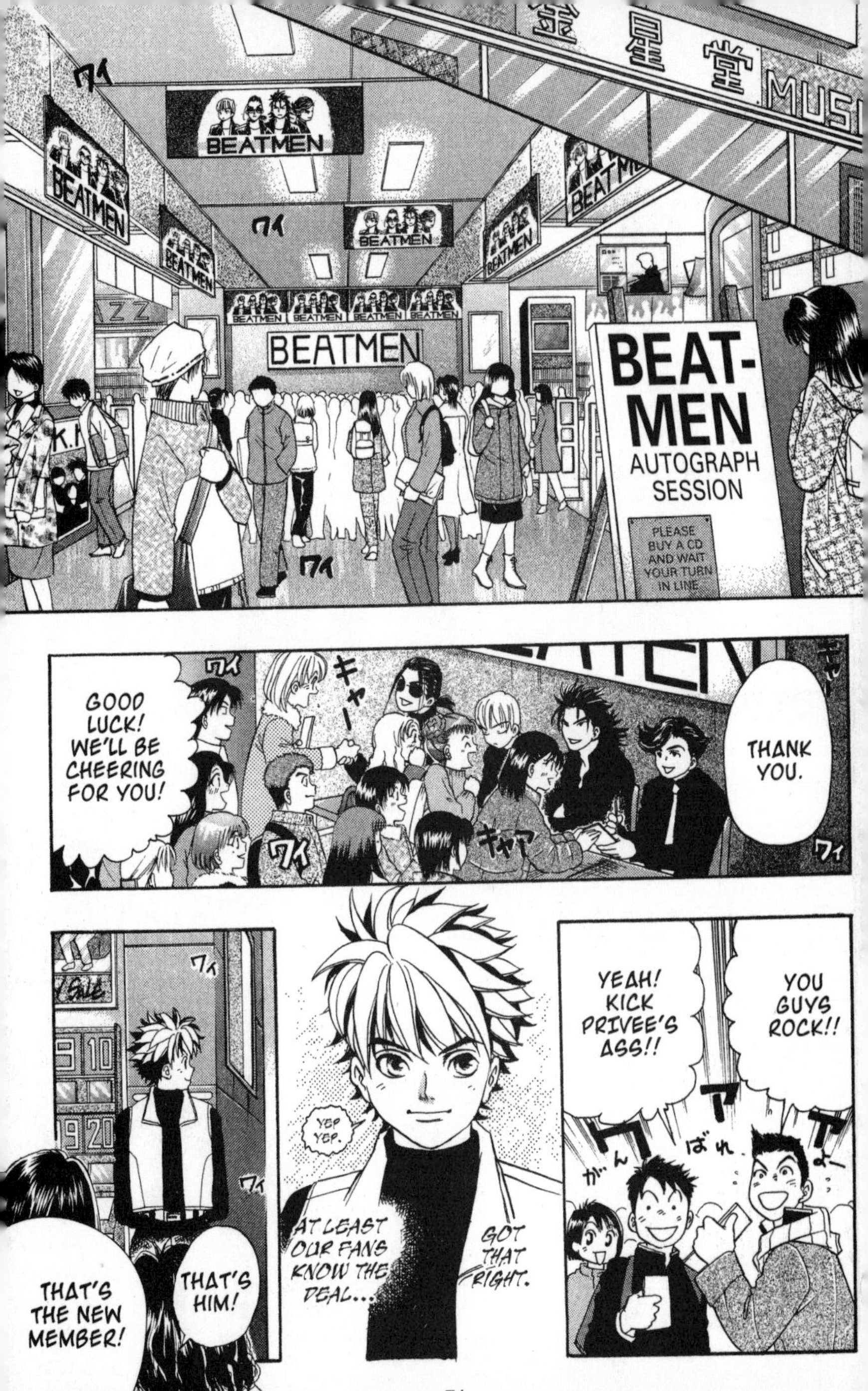

金星堂
BEATMEN
BEAT-MEN AUTOGRAPH SESSION
PLEASE BUY A CD AND WAIT YOUR TURN IN LINE
THANK YOU.
GOOD LUCK! WE'LL BE CHEERING FOR YOU!
YOU GUYS ROCK!!
YEAH! KICK PRIVEE'S ASS!!
YEP YEP.
GOT THAT RIGHT.
AT LEAST OUR FANS KNOW THE DEAL...
THAT'S HIM!
THAT'S THE NEW MEMBER!

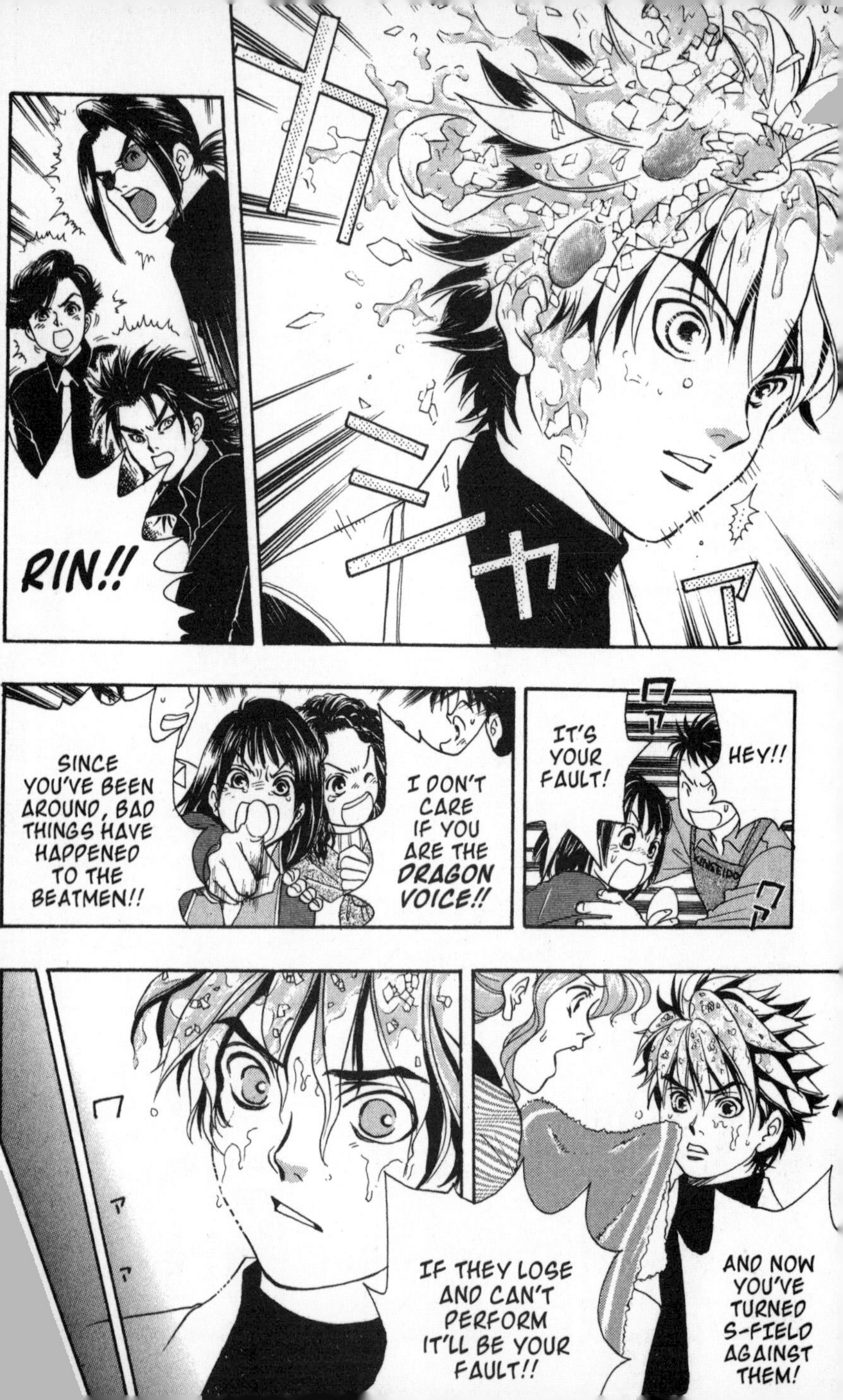
RIN!!
HEY!!
IT'S YOUR FAULT!
I DON'T CARE IF YOU ARE THE DRAGON VOICE!!
SINCE YOU'VE BEEN AROUND, BAD THINGS HAVE HAPPENED TO THE BEATMEN!!
AND NOW YOU'VE TURNED S-FIELD AGAINST THEM!
IF THEY LOSE AND CAN'T PERFORM IT'LL BE YOUR FAULT!!

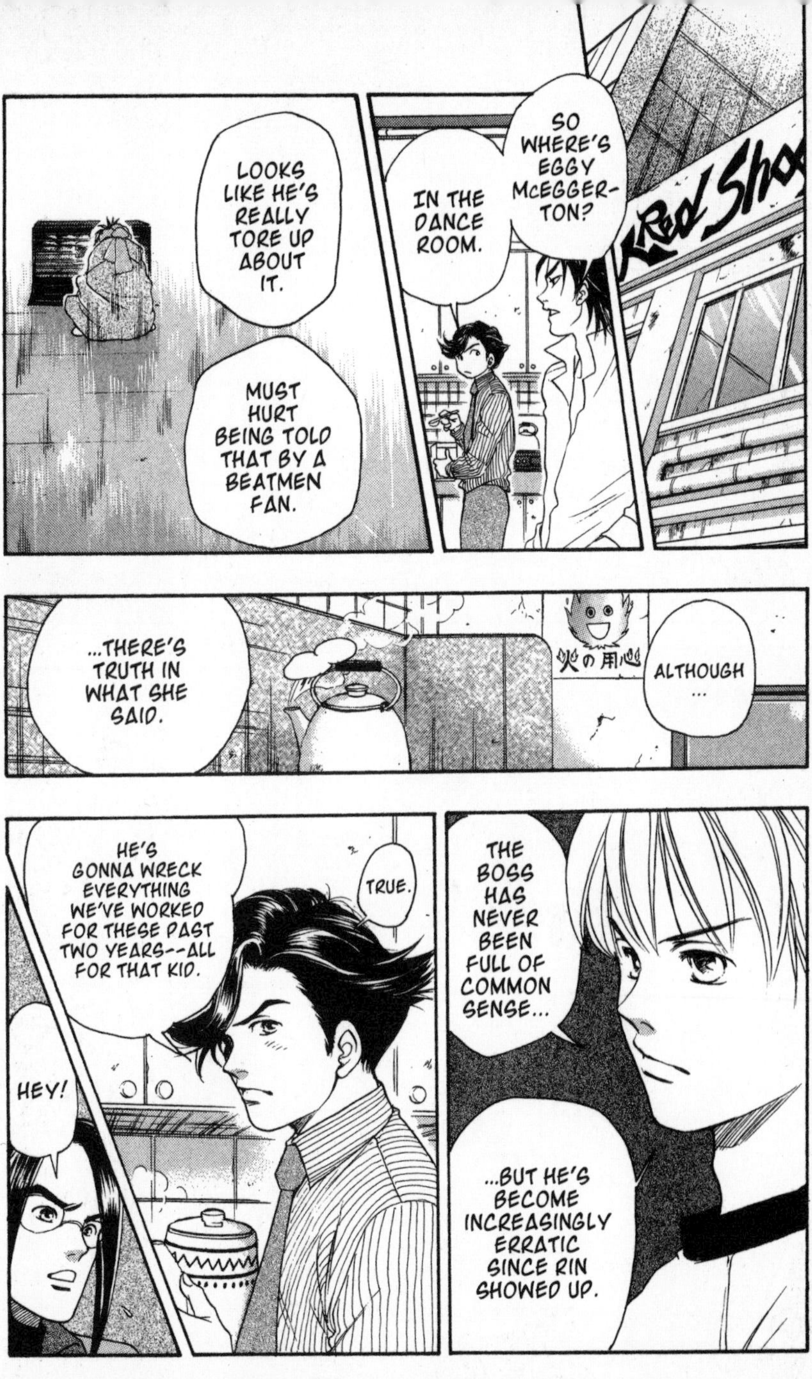
SO WHERE'S EGGY McEGGERTON?
IN THE DANCE ROOM.
LOOKS LIKE HE'S REALLY TORE UP ABOUT IT.
MUST HURT BEING TOLD THAT BY A BEATMEN FAN.
ALTHOUGH...
火の用心
...THERE'S TRUTH IN WHAT SHE SAID.
THE BOSS HAS NEVER BEEN FULL OF COMMON SENSE...
...BUT HE'S BECOME INCREASINGLY ERRATIC SINCE RIN SHOWED UP.
TRUE.
HE'S GONNA WRECK EVERYTHING WE'VE WORKED FOR THESE PAST TWO YEARS--ALL FOR THAT KID.
HEY!

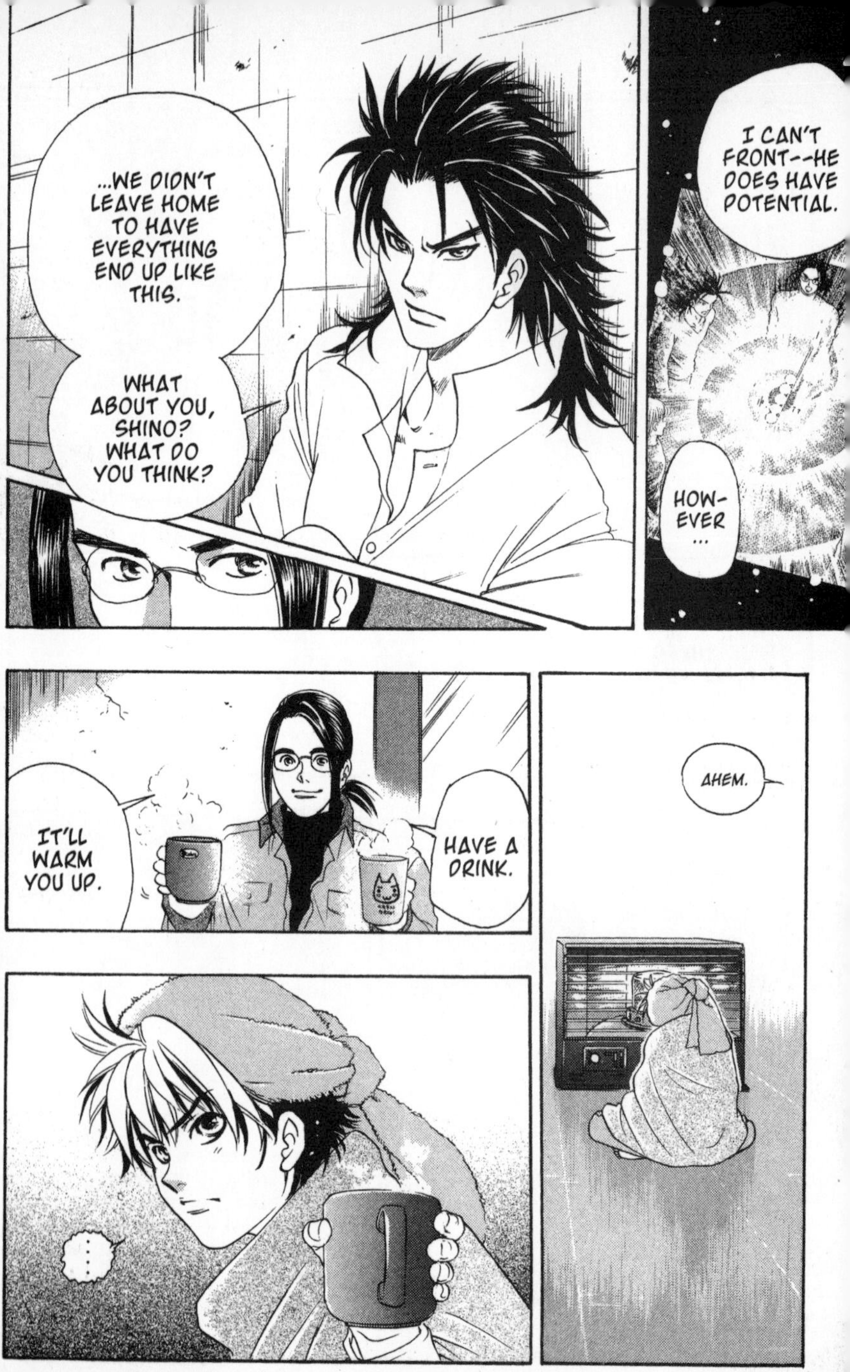
I CAN'T FRONT--HE DOES HAVE POTENTIAL.
HOW-EVER ...
...WE DIDN'T LEAVE HOME TO HAVE EVERYTHING END UP LIKE THIS.
WHAT ABOUT YOU, SHINO? WHAT DO YOU THINK?
AHEM.
HAVE A DRINK.
IT'LL WARM YOU UP.
...

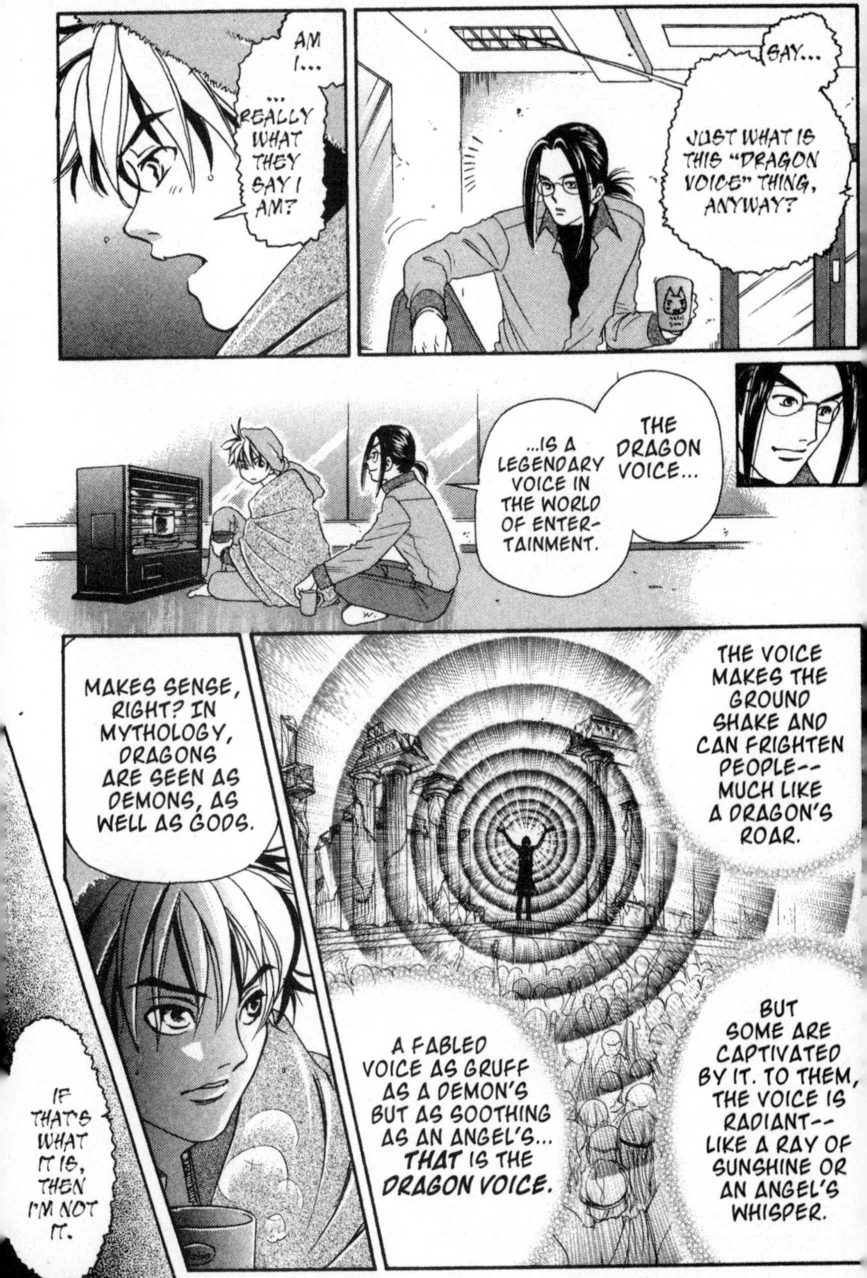
SAY...
JUST WHAT IS THIS "DRAGON VOICE" THING, ANYWAY?
AM I...
...REALLY WHAT THEY SAY I AM?
THE DRAGON VOICE...
...IS A LEGENDARY VOICE IN THE WORLD OF ENTERTAINMENT.
THE VOICE MAKES THE GROUND SHAKE AND CAN FRIGHTEN PEOPLE--MUCH LIKE A DRAGON'S ROAR.
BUT SOME ARE CAPTIVATED BY IT. TO THEM, THE VOICE IS RADIANT--LIKE A RAY OF SUNSHINE OR AN ANGEL'S WHISPER.
A FABLED VOICE AS GRUFF AS A DEMON'S BUT AS SOOTHING AS AN ANGEL'S... THAT IS THE DRAGON VOICE.
MAKES SENSE, RIGHT? IN MYTHOLOGY, DRAGONS ARE SEEN AS DEMONS, AS WELL AS GODS.
IF THAT'S WHAT IT IS, THEN I'M NOT IT.

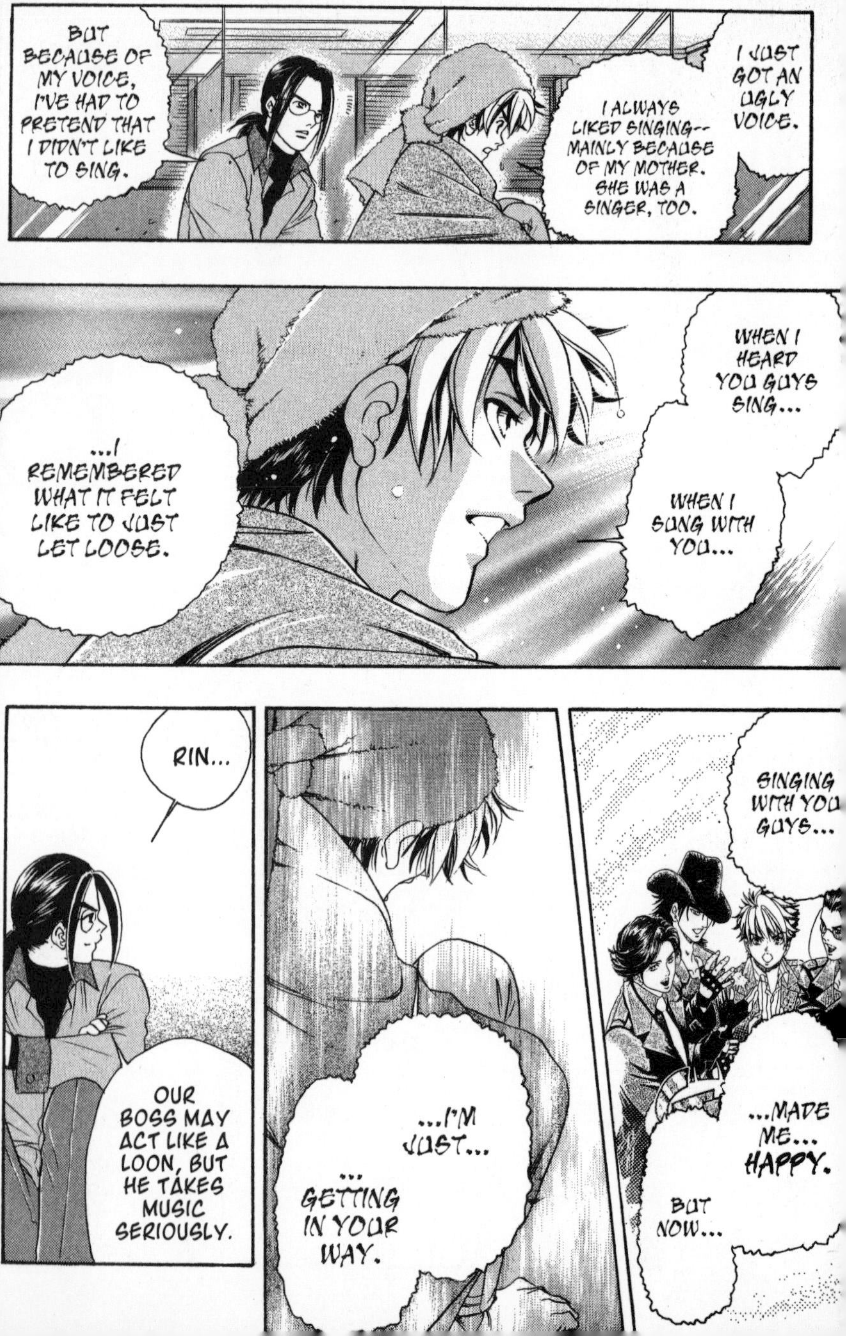
I JUST GOT AN UGLY VOICE.
I ALWAYS LIKED SINGING-- MAINLY BECAUSE OF MY MOTHER. SHE WAS A SINGER, TOO.
BUT BECAUSE OF MY VOICE, I'VE HAD TO PRETEND THAT I DIDN'T LIKE TO SING.
WHEN I HEARD YOU GUYS SING...
WHEN I SUNG WITH YOU...
...I REMEMBERED WHAT IT FELT LIKE TO JUST LET LOOSE.
SINGING WITH YOU GUYS...
...MADE ME... HAPPY.
BUT NOW...
...I'M JUST...
...GETTING IN YOUR WAY.
RIN...
OUR BOSS MAY ACT LIKE A LOON, BUT HE TAKES MUSIC SERIOUSLY.

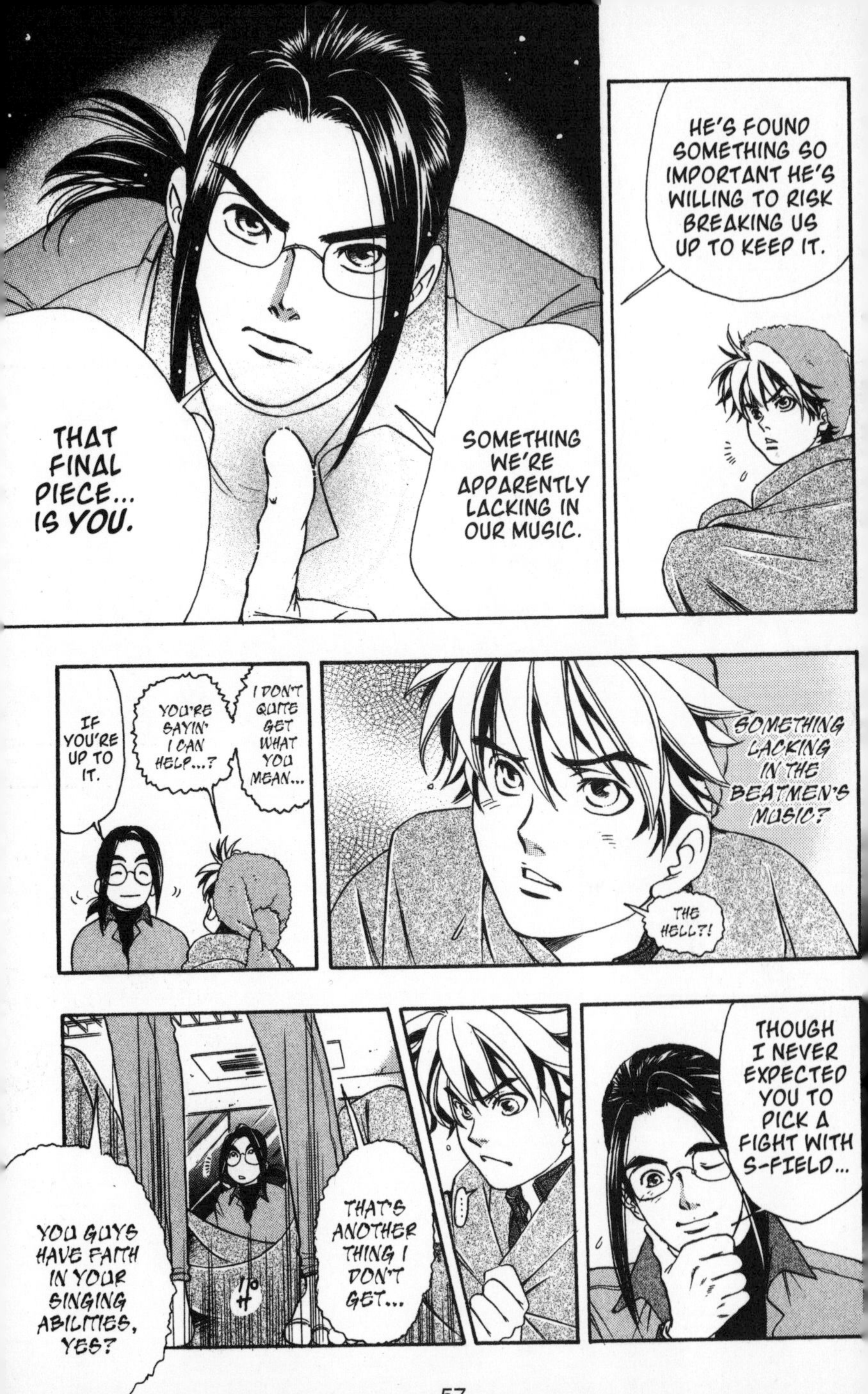
HE'S FOUND SOMETHING SO IMPORTANT HE'S WILLING TO RISK BREAKING US UP TO KEEP IT.
SOMETHING WE'RE APPARENTLY LACKING IN OUR MUSIC.
THAT FINAL PIECE... IS *YOU.*
SOMETHING LACKING IN THE BEATMEN'S MUSIC?
THE HELL?!
I DON'T QUITE GET WHAT YOU MEAN...
YOU'RE SAYIN' I CAN HELP...?
IF YOU'RE UP TO IT.
THOUGH I NEVER EXPECTED YOU TO PICK A FIGHT WITH S-FIELD...
...
THAT'S ANOTHER THING I DON'T GET...
YOU GUYS HAVE FAITH IN YOUR SINGING ABILITIES, YES?

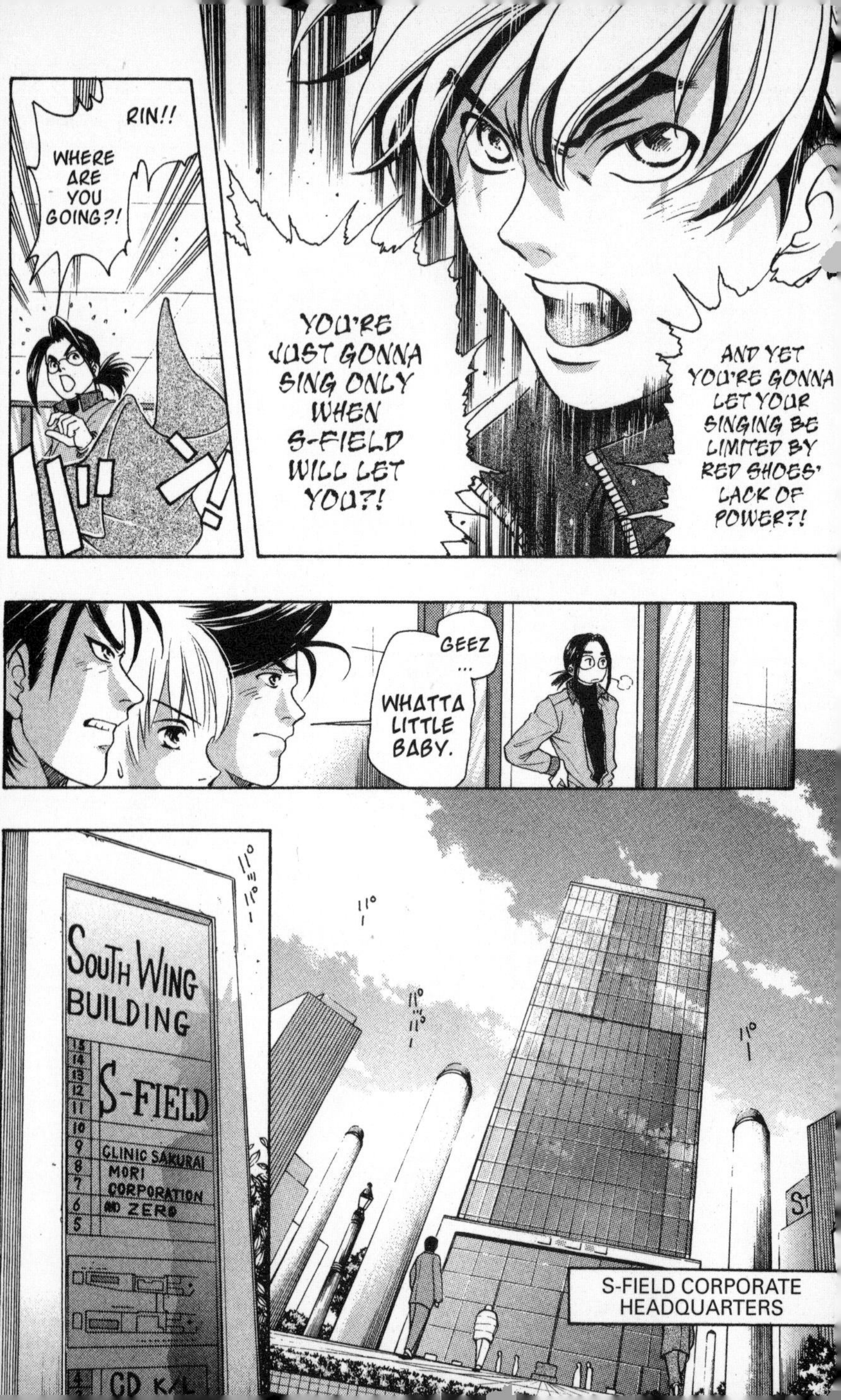
AND YET YOU'RE GONNA LET YOUR SINGING BE LIMITED BY RED SHOES' LACK OF POWER?!
YOU'RE JUST GONNA SING ONLY WHEN S-FIELD WILL LET YOU?!
RIN!!
WHERE ARE YOU GOING?!
GEEZ ... WHATTA LITTLE BABY.
SOUTH WING BUILDING
S-FIELD
CLINIC SAKURAI
MORI CORPORATION
ZERO
S-FIELD CORPORATE HEADQUARTERS

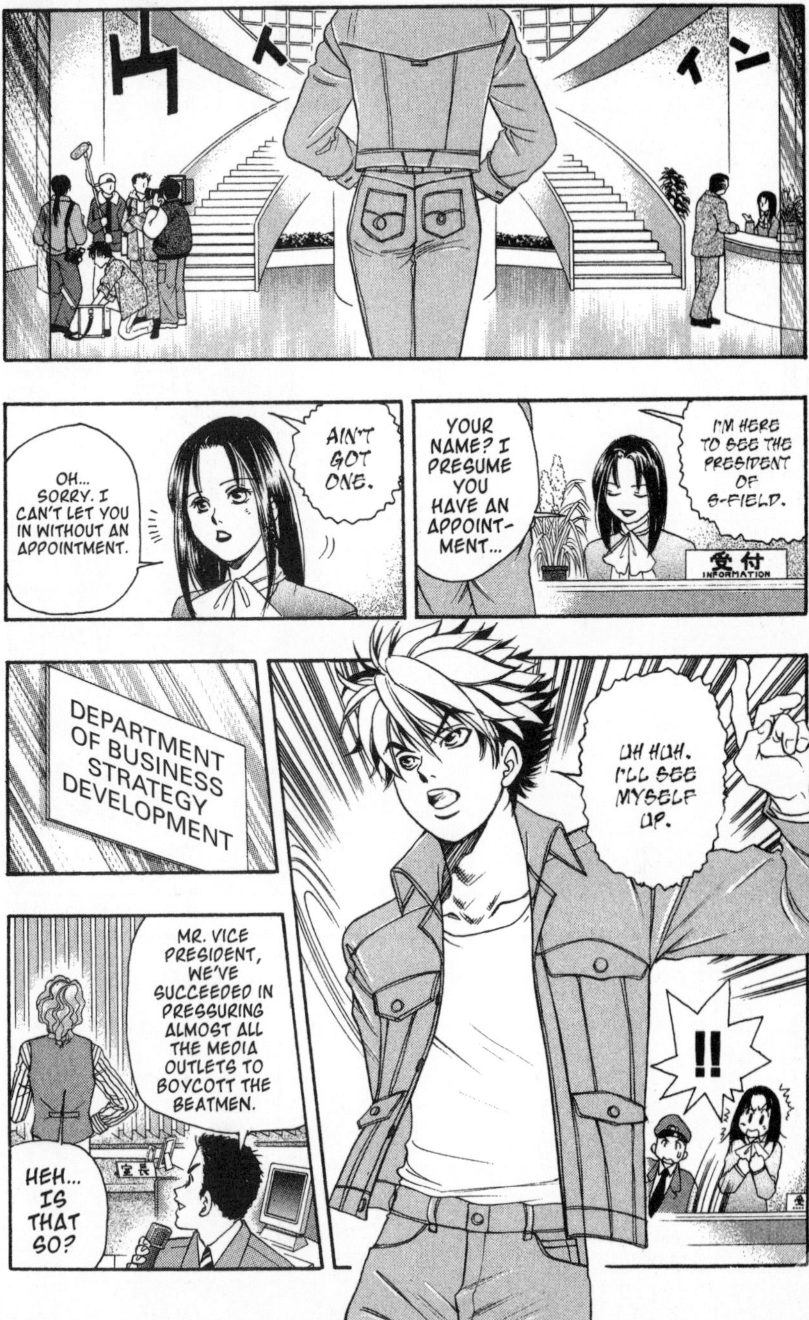
I'M HERE TO SEE THE PRESIDENT OF S-FIELD.
YOUR NAME? I PRESUME YOU HAVE AN APPOINTMENT...
受付 INFORMATION
AIN'T GOT ONE.
OH... SORRY. I CAN'T LET YOU IN WITHOUT AN APPOINTMENT.
UH HUH. I'LL SEE MYSELF UP.
!!
DEPARTMENT OF BUSINESS STRATEGY DEVELOPMENT
MR. VICE PRESIDENT, WE'VE SUCCEEDED IN PRESSURING ALMOST ALL THE MEDIA OUTLETS TO BOYCOTT THE BEATMEN.
室長
HEH... IS THAT SO?

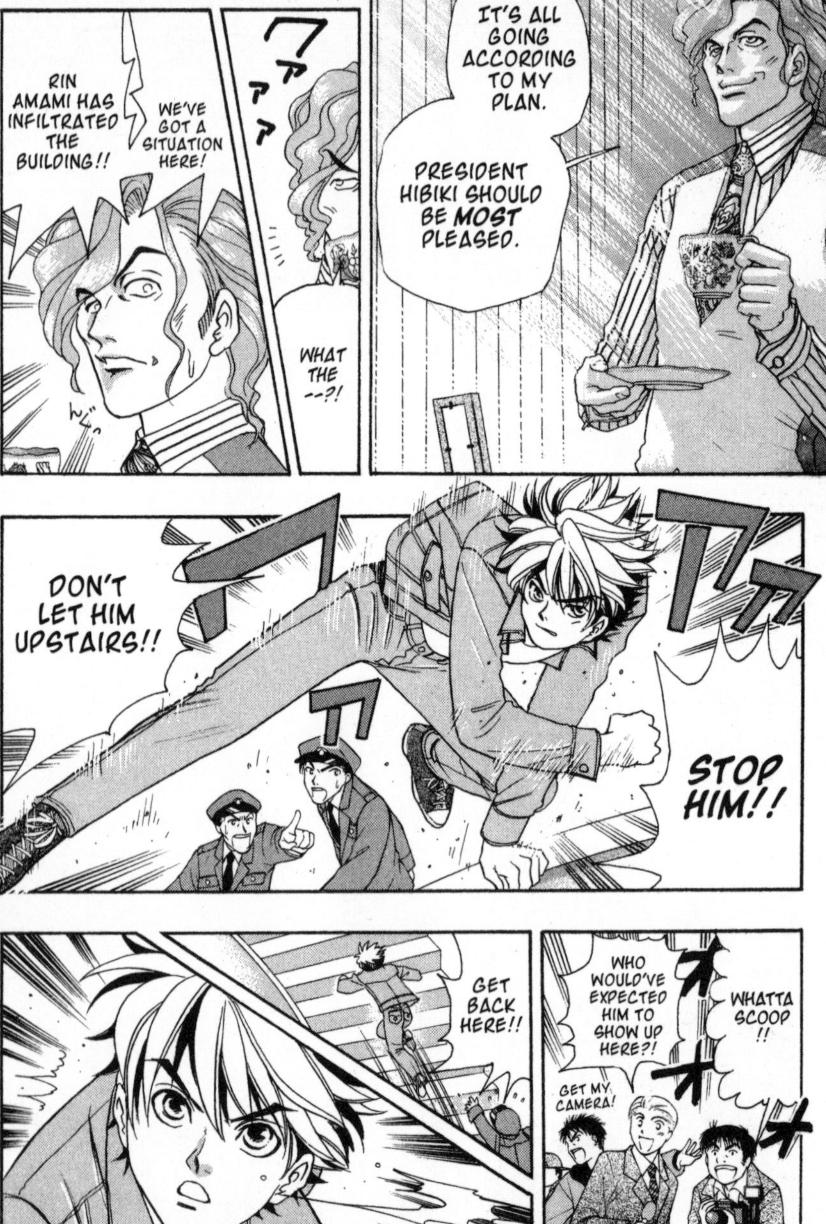
IT'S ALL GOING ACCORDING TO MY PLAN.
PRESIDENT HIBIKI SHOULD BE **MOST** PLEASED.
WHAT THE --?!
WE'VE GOT A SITUATION HERE!
RIN AMAMI HAS INFILTRATED THE BUILDING!!
STOP HIM!!
DON'T LET HIM UPSTAIRS!!
WHATTA SCOOP!!
WHO WOULD'VE EXPECTED HIM TO SHOW UP HERE?!
GET MY CAMERA!
GET BACK HERE!!

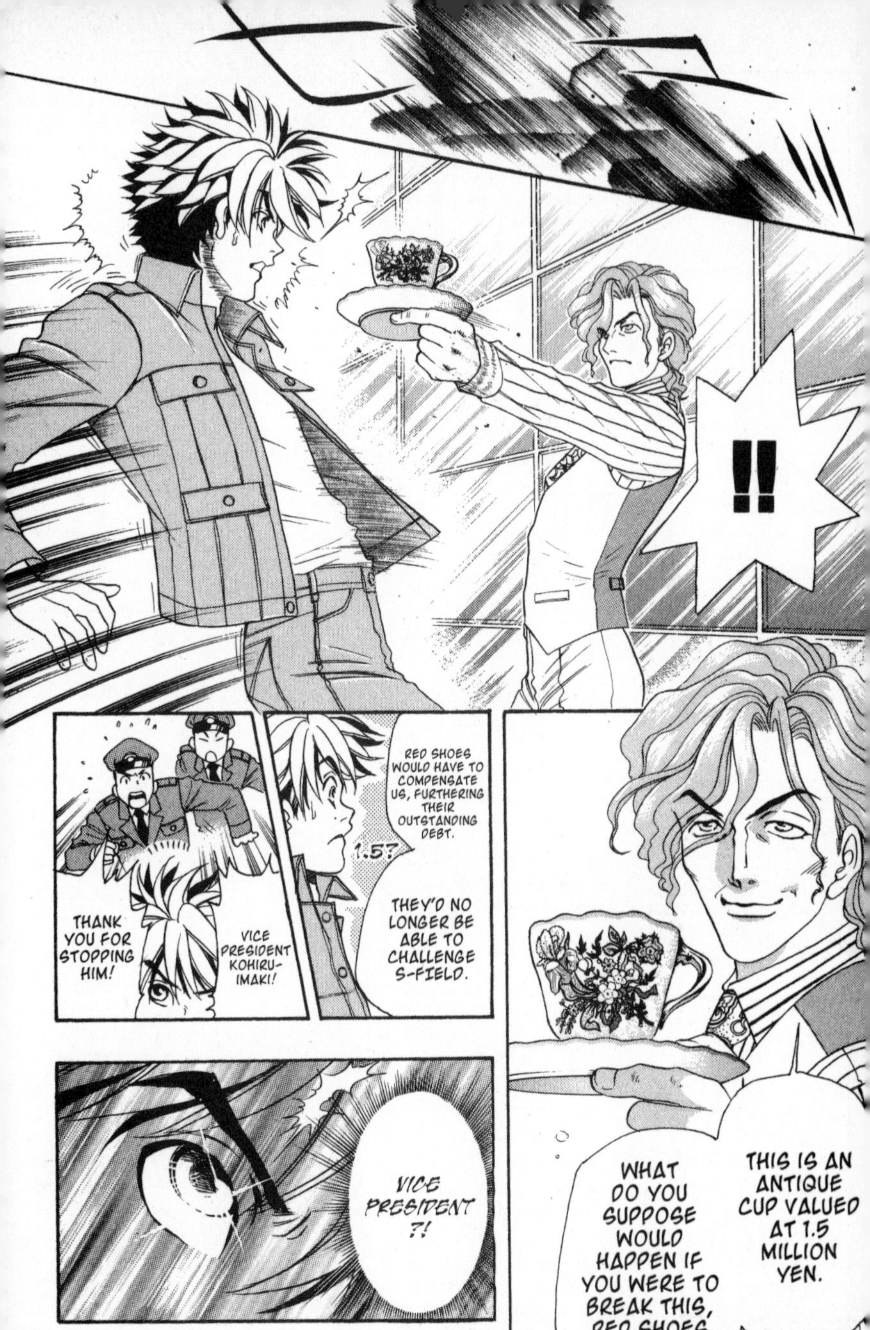
!!
THIS IS AN ANTIQUE CUP VALUED AT 1.5 MILLION YEN.
WHAT DO YOU SUPPOSE WOULD HAPPEN IF YOU WERE TO BREAK THIS, RED SHOES BOY?
1.5?
RED SHOES WOULD HAVE TO COMPENSATE US, FURTHERING THEIR OUTSTANDING DEBT.
THEY'D NO LONGER BE ABLE TO CHALLENGE S-FIELD.
VICE PRESIDENT KOHIRU-IMAKI!
THANK YOU FOR STOPPING HIM!
VICE PRESIDENT ?!

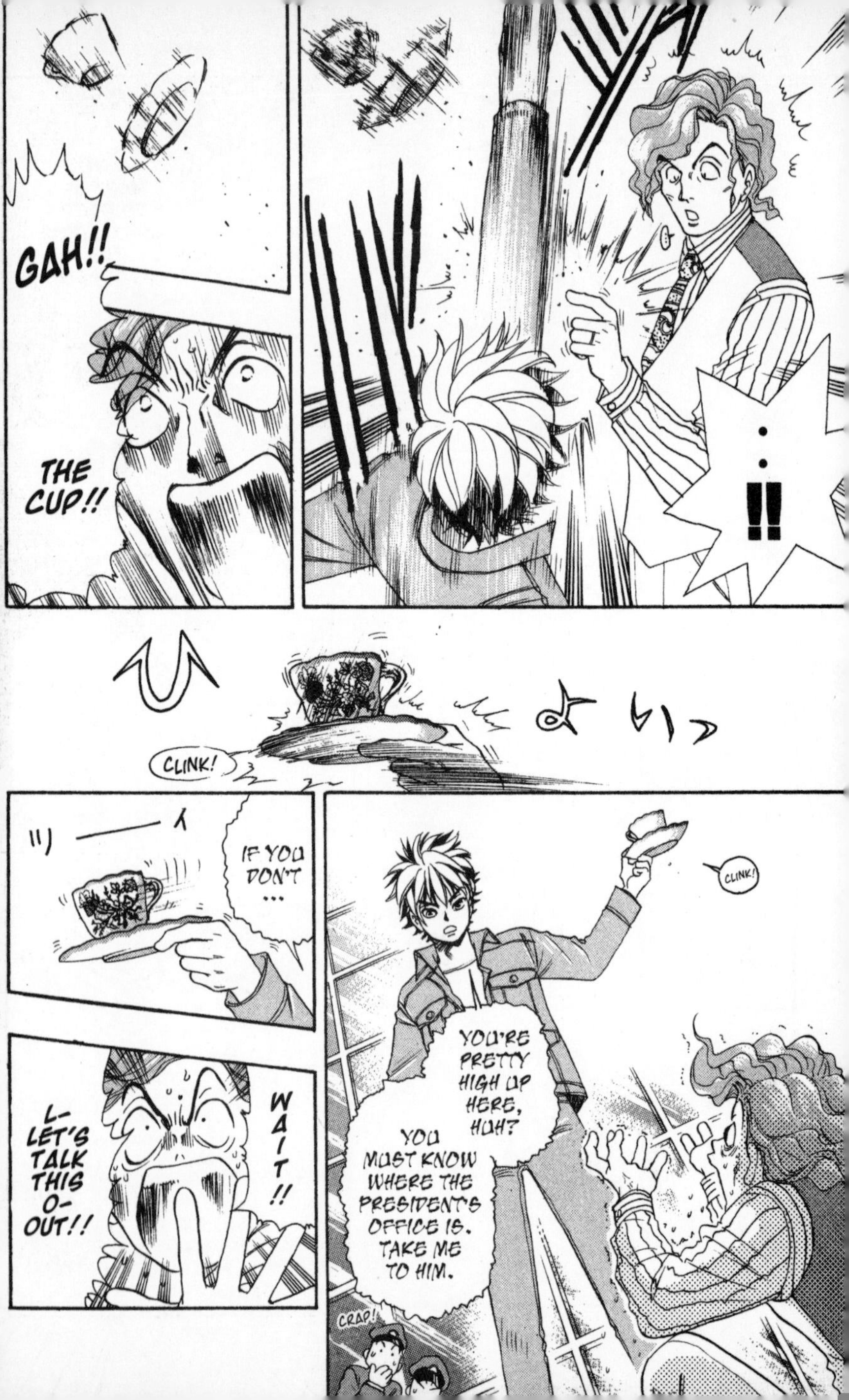
..!!
GAH!!
THE CUP!!
CLINK!
CLINK!
YOU'RE PRETTY HIGH UP HERE, HUH?
YOU MUST KNOW WHERE THE PRESIDENT'S OFFICE IS. TAKE ME TO HIM.
CRAP!
IF YOU DON'T...
WAIT!!
L-LET'S TALK THIS O-OUT!!

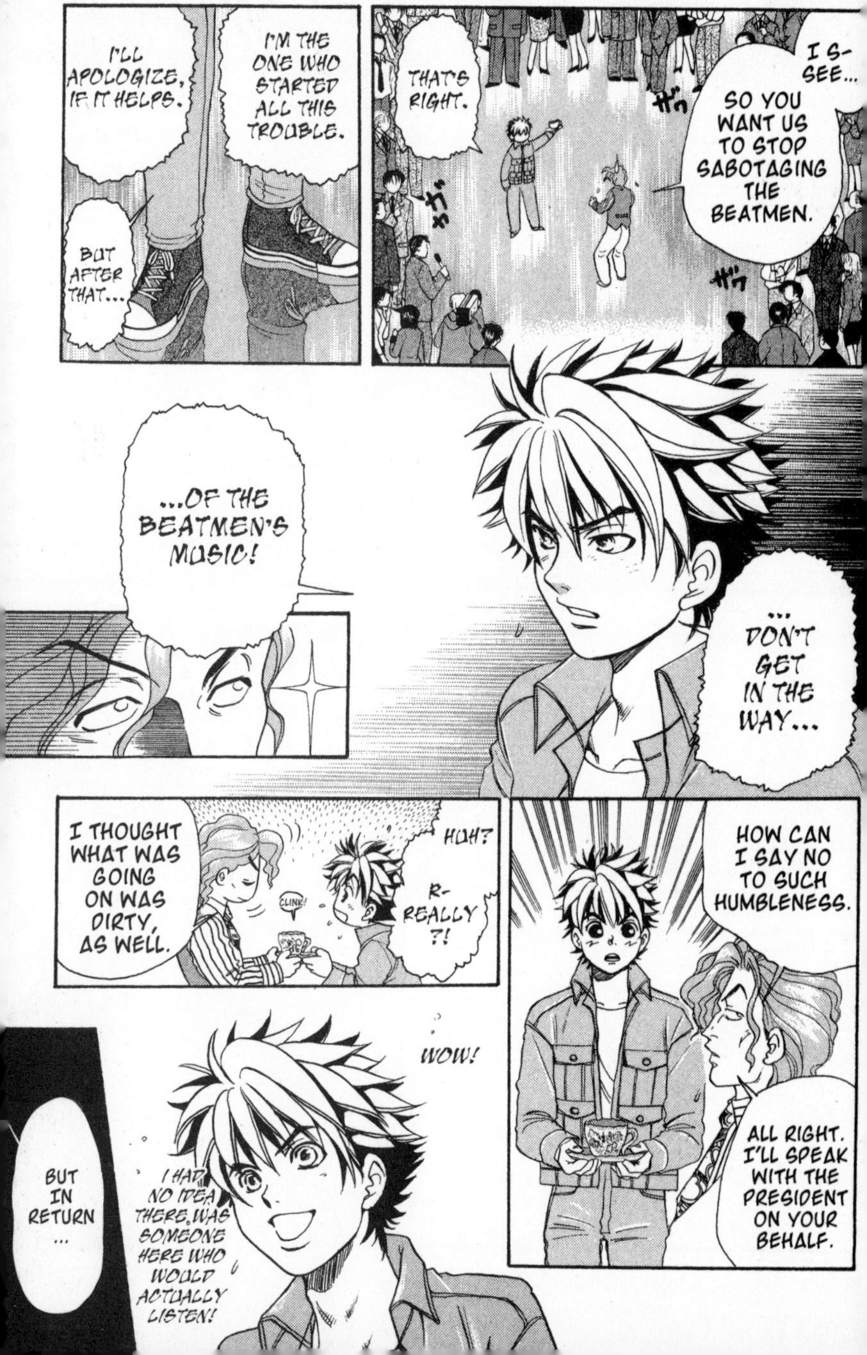
I S-SEE...
SO YOU WANT US TO STOP SABOTAGING THE BEATMEN.
THAT'S RIGHT.
I'M THE ONE WHO STARTED ALL THIS TROUBLE.
I'LL APOLOGIZE, IF IT HELPS.
BUT AFTER THAT...
... DON'T GET IN THE WAY...
...OF THE BEATMEN'S MUSIC!
HOW CAN I SAY NO TO SUCH HUMBLENESS.
ALL RIGHT. I'LL SPEAK WITH THE PRESIDENT ON YOUR BEHALF.
HUH?
R-REALLY ?!
CLINK!
I THOUGHT WHAT WAS GOING ON WAS DIRTY, AS WELL.
WOW!
I HAD NO IDEA THERE WAS SOMEONE HERE WHO WOULD ACTUALLY LISTEN!
BUT IN RETURN ...

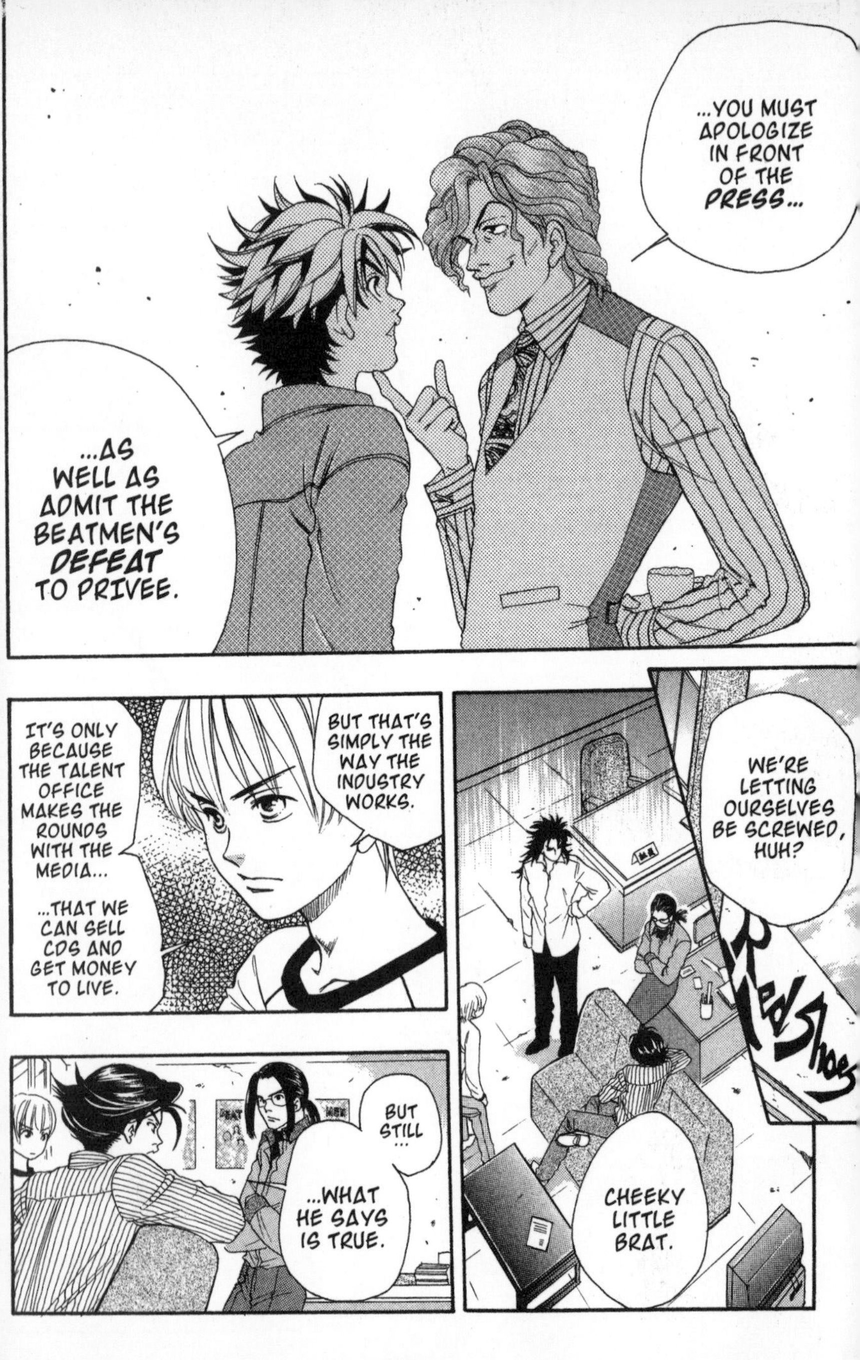
...YOU MUST APOLOGIZE IN FRONT OF THE PRESS...
...AS WELL AS ADMIT THE BEATMEN'S DEFEAT TO PRIVEE.
WE'RE LETTING OURSELVES BE SCREWED, HUH?
Red Shoes
CHEEKY LITTLE BRAT.
BUT THAT'S SIMPLY THE WAY THE INDUSTRY WORKS.
IT'S ONLY BECAUSE THE TALENT OFFICE MAKES THE ROUNDS WITH THE MEDIA...
...THAT WE CAN SELL CDS AND GET MONEY TO LIVE.
BUT STILL...
...WHAT HE SAYS IS TRUE.

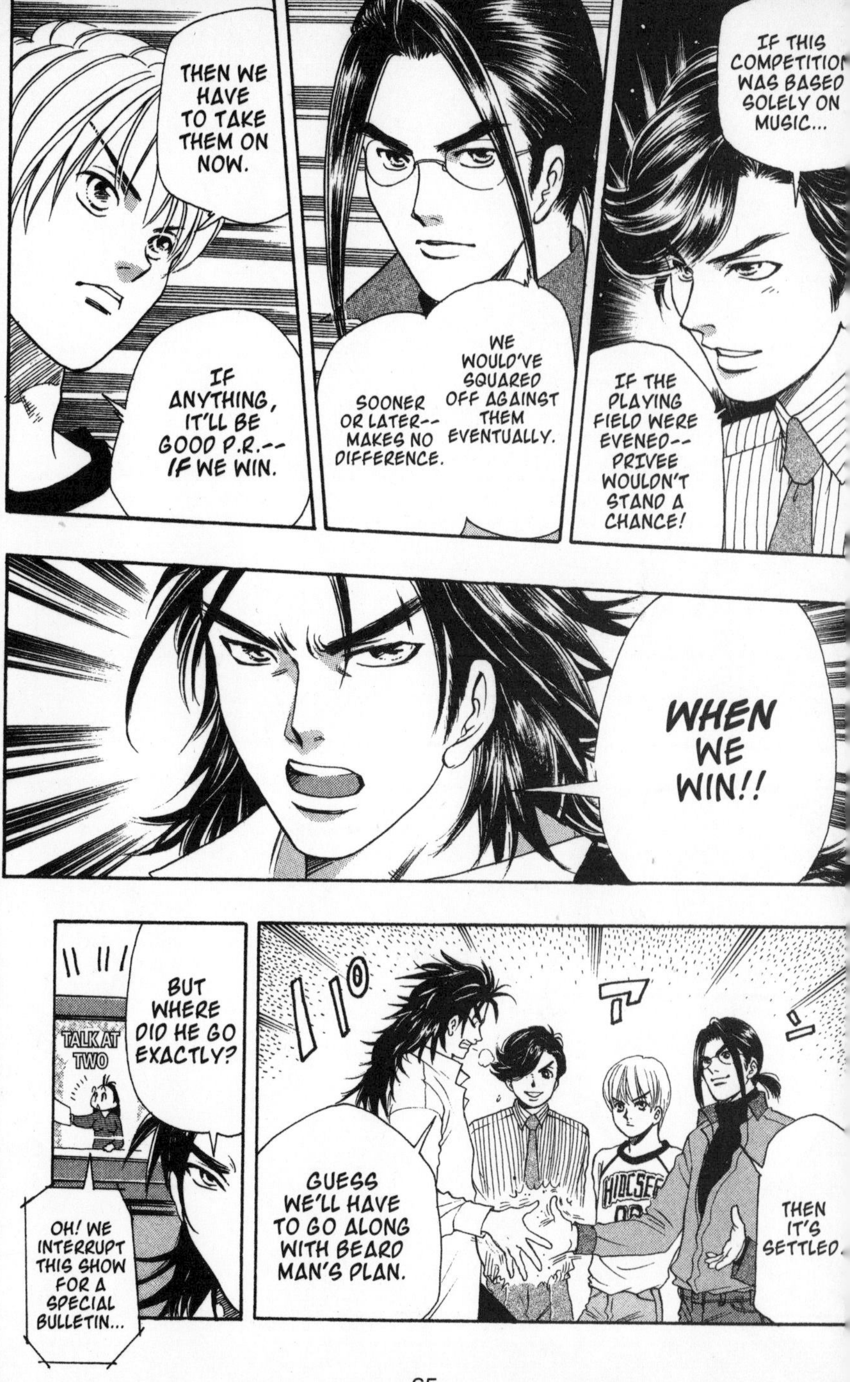
IF THIS COMPETITION WAS BASED SOLELY ON MUSIC...
IF THE PLAYING FIELD WERE EVENED-- PRIVEE WOULDN'T STAND A CHANCE!
WE WOULD'VE SQUARED OFF AGAINST THEM EVENTUALLY.
SOONER OR LATER-- MAKES NO DIFFERENCE.
THEN WE HAVE TO TAKE THEM ON NOW.
IF ANYTHING, IT'LL BE GOOD P.R.-- *IF* WE WIN.
WHEN WE WIN!!
THEN IT'S SETTLED.
GUESS WE'LL HAVE TO GO ALONG WITH BEARD MAN'S PLAN.
BUT WHERE DID HE GO EXACTLY?
TALK AT TWO
OH! WE INTERRUPT THIS SHOW FOR A SPECIAL BULLETIN...

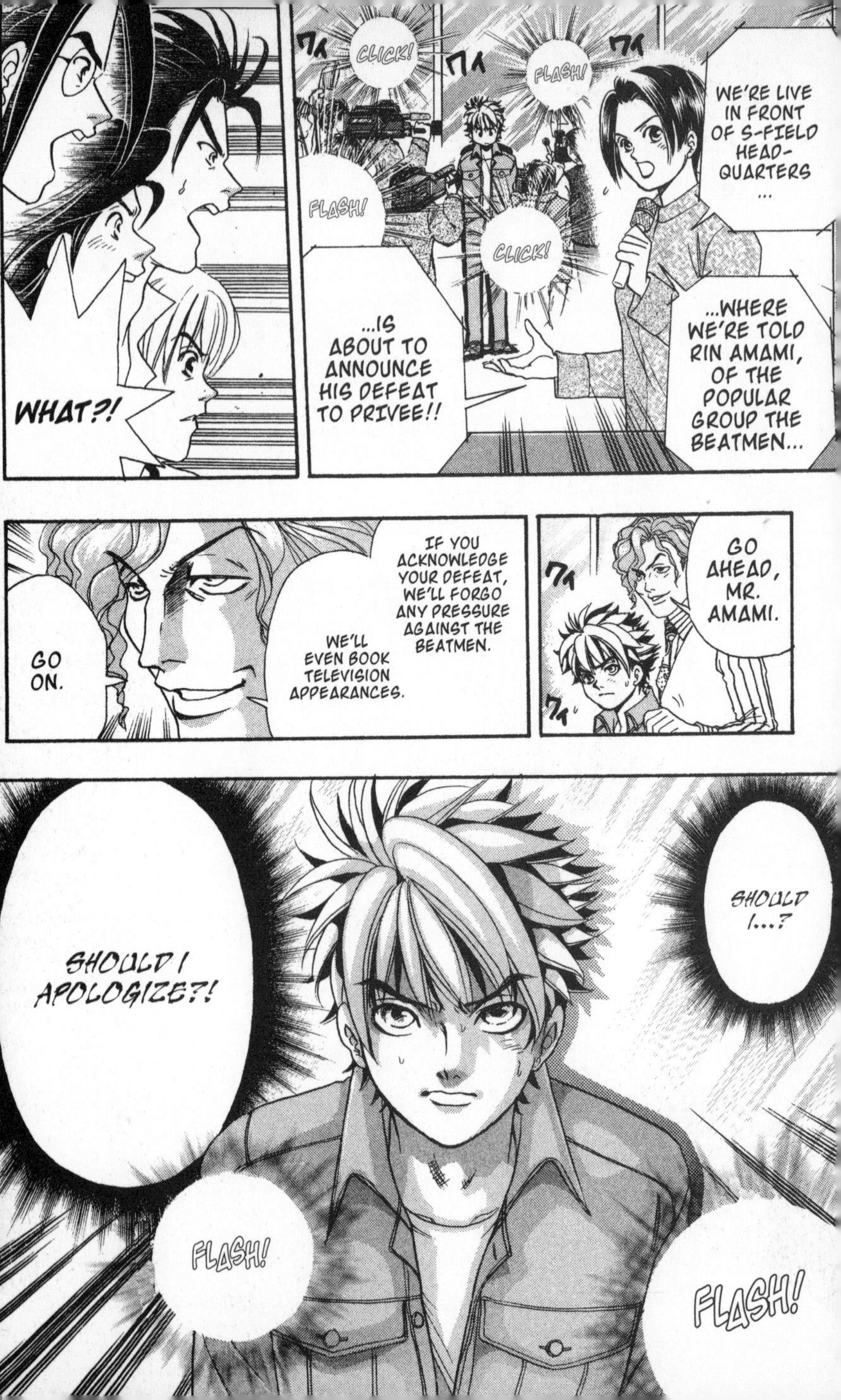
ワイ
CLICK!
ワイ
FLASH!
ワイ
WE'RE LIVE IN FRONT OF S-FIELD HEAD-QUARTERS ...
...WHERE WE'RE TOLD RIN AMAMI, OF THE POPULAR GROUP THE BEATMEN...
FLASH!
CLICK!
...IS ABOUT TO ANNOUNCE HIS DEFEAT TO PRIVEE!!
WHAT?!
ワイ
GO AHEAD, MR. AMAMI.
ワイ
IF YOU ACKNOWLEDGE YOUR DEFEAT, WE'LL FORGO ANY PRESSURE AGAINST THE BEATMEN.
WE'LL EVEN BOOK TELEVISION APPEARANCES.
GO ON.
SHOULD I...?
SHOULD I APOLOGIZE?!
FLASH!
FLASH!

# DRAGON VOICE

## #10 We're BEATMEN

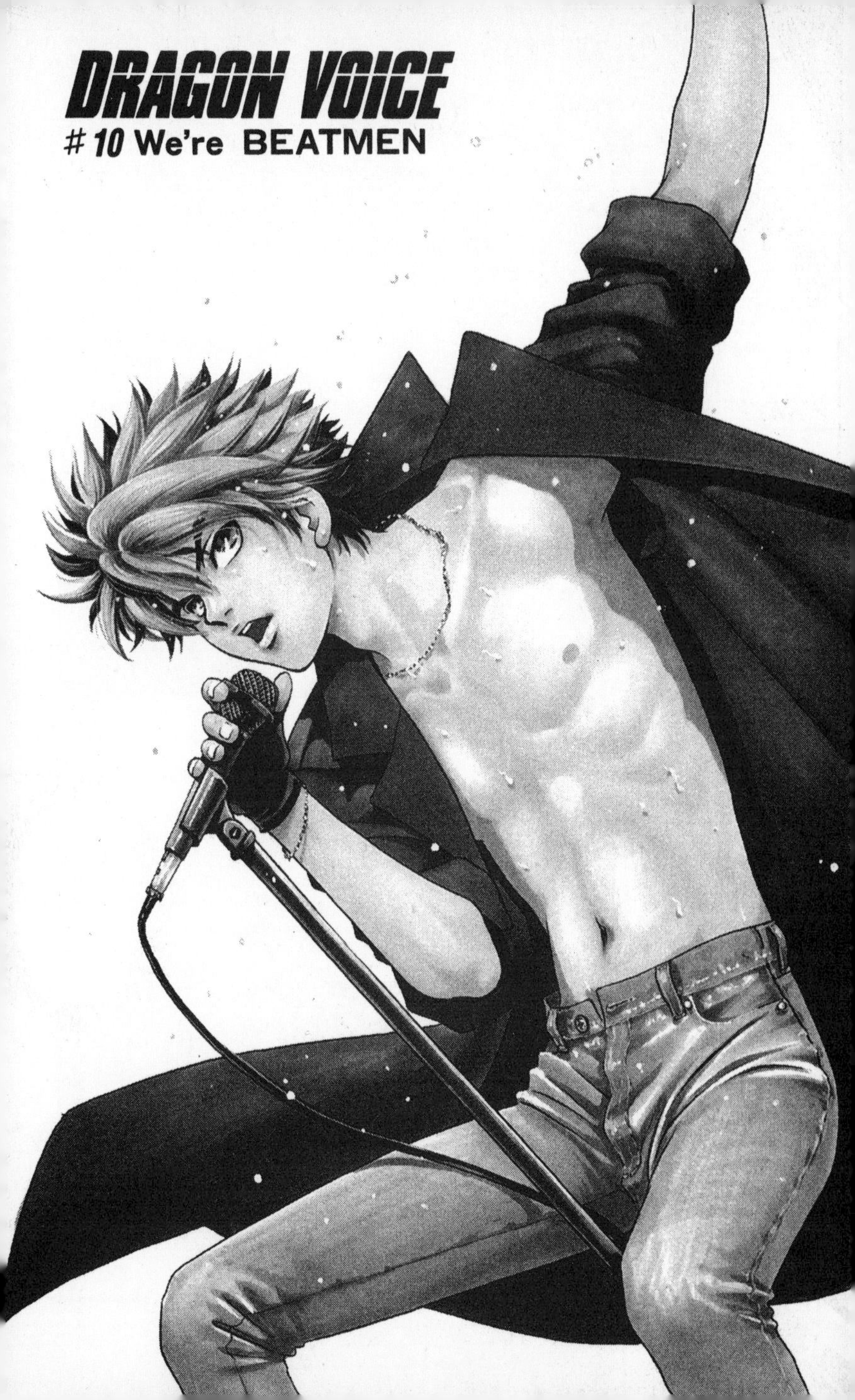

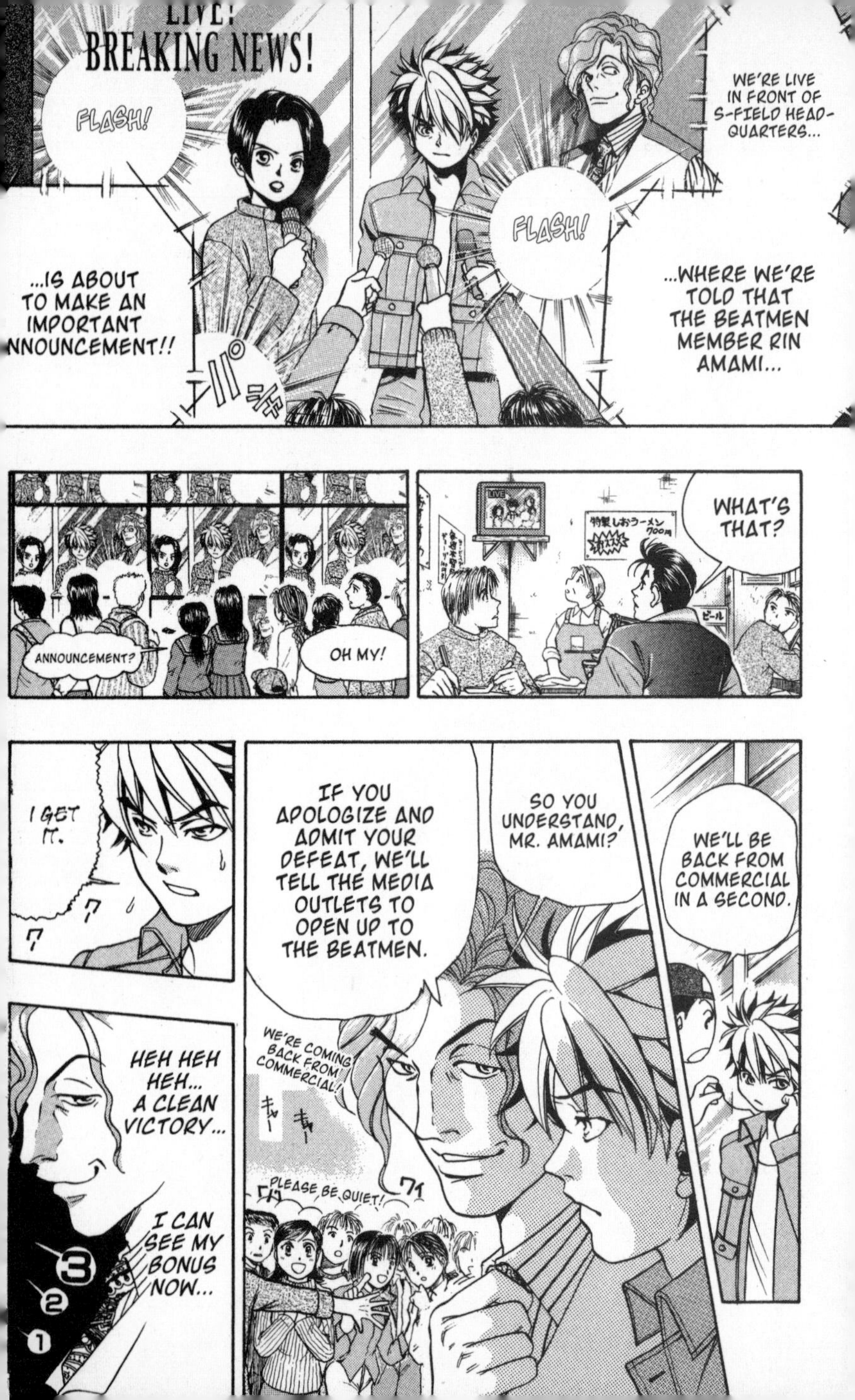
WE'RE LIVE IN FRONT OF S-FIELD HEAD-QUARTERS...
FLASH!
...WHERE WE'RE TOLD THAT THE BEATMEN MEMBER RIN AMAMI...
LIVE! BREAKING NEWS!
FLASH!
...IS ABOUT TO MAKE AN IMPORTANT NNOUNCEMENT!!
WHAT'S THAT?
LIVE
特製しおラーメン 700円
ビール
OH MY!
ANNOUNCEMENT?
WE'LL BE BACK FROM COMMERCIAL IN A SECOND.
SO YOU UNDERSTAND, MR. AMAMI?
IF YOU APOLOGIZE AND ADMIT YOUR DEFEAT, WE'LL TELL THE MEDIA OUTLETS TO OPEN UP TO THE BEATMEN.
WE'RE COMING BACK FROM COMMERCIAL!
キャー
キャー
PLEASE BE QUIET!
ワイ
I GET IT.
HEH HEH HEH... A CLEAN VICTORY...
I CAN SEE MY BONUS NOW...
3
2
1

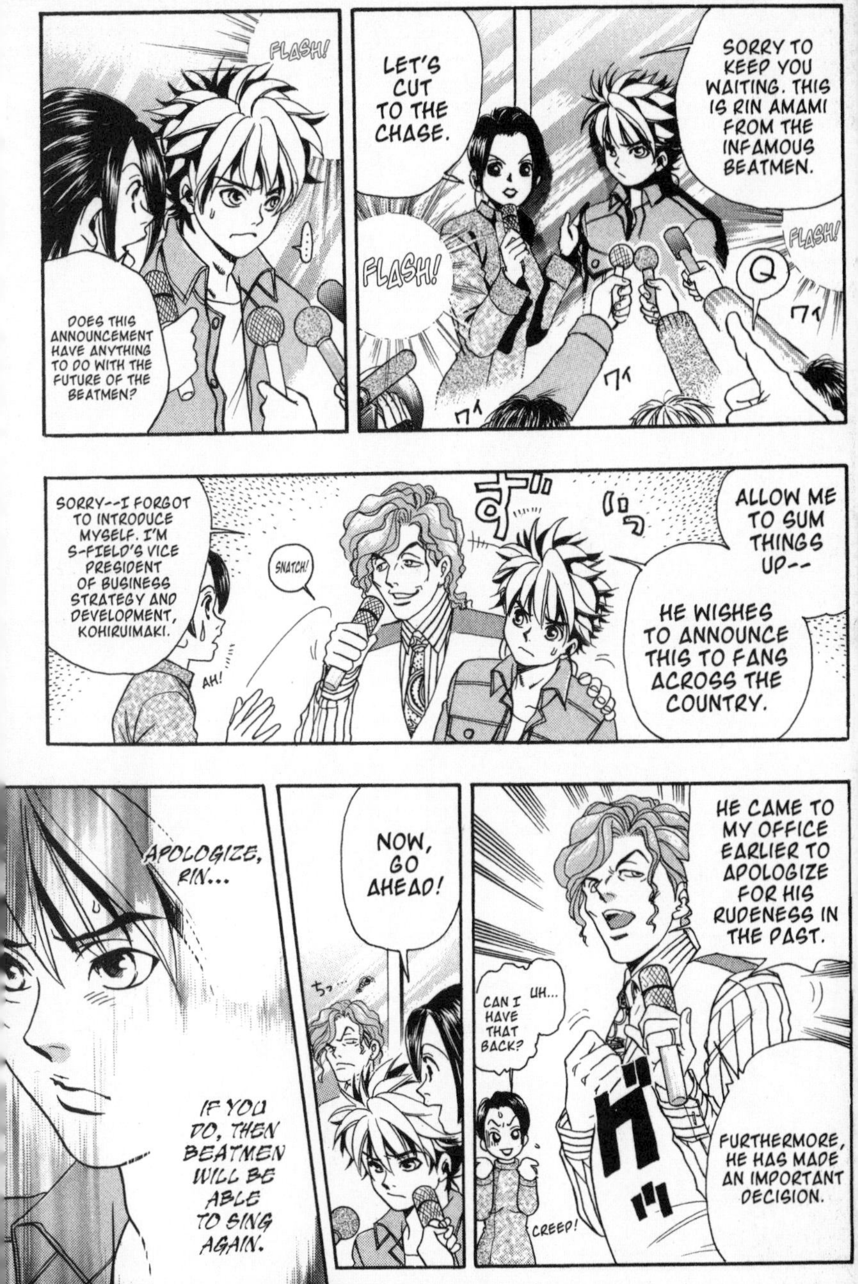
SORRY TO KEEP YOU WAITING. THIS IS RIN AMAMI FROM THE INFAMOUS BEATMEN.
FLASH!
Q
ワイ
LET'S CUT TO THE CHASE.
FLASH!
ワイ
ワイ
FLASH!
...
DOES THIS ANNOUNCEMENT HAVE ANYTHING TO DO WITH THE FUTURE OF THE BEATMEN?
ALLOW ME TO SUM THINGS UP--
HE WISHES TO ANNOUNCE THIS TO FANS ACROSS THE COUNTRY.
SNATCH!
SORRY--I FORGOT TO INTRODUCE MYSELF. I'M S-FIELD'S VICE PRESIDENT OF BUSINESS STRATEGY AND DEVELOPMENT, KOHIRUIMAKI.
AH!
HE CAME TO MY OFFICE EARLIER TO APOLOGIZE FOR HIS RUDENESS IN THE PAST.
UH...
CAN I HAVE THAT BACK?
FURTHERMORE, HE HAS MADE AN IMPORTANT DECISION.
CREEP!
NOW, GO AHEAD!
APOLOGIZE, RIN...
IF YOU DO, THEN BEATMEN WILL BE ABLE TO SING AGAIN.

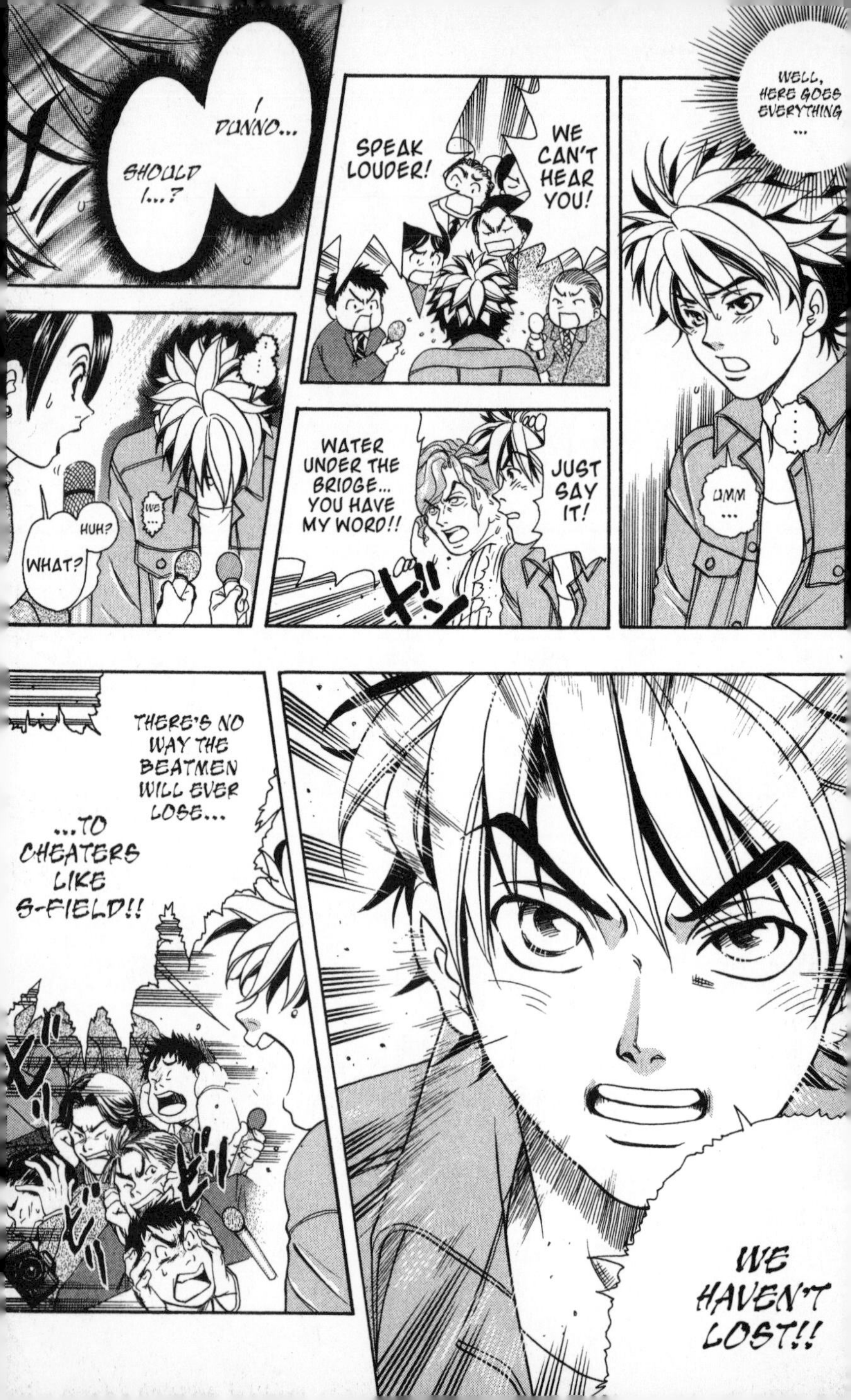
WELL, HERE GOES EVERYTHING ...
UMM ...
WE CAN'T HEAR YOU!
SPEAK LOUDER!
JUST SAY IT!
WATER UNDER THE BRIDGE... YOU HAVE MY WORD!!
I DUNNO...
SHOULD I...?
WE ...
HUH?
WHAT?
WE HAVEN'T LOST!!
THERE'S NO WAY THE BEATMEN WILL EVER LOSE...
...TO CHEATERS LIKE S-FIELD!!

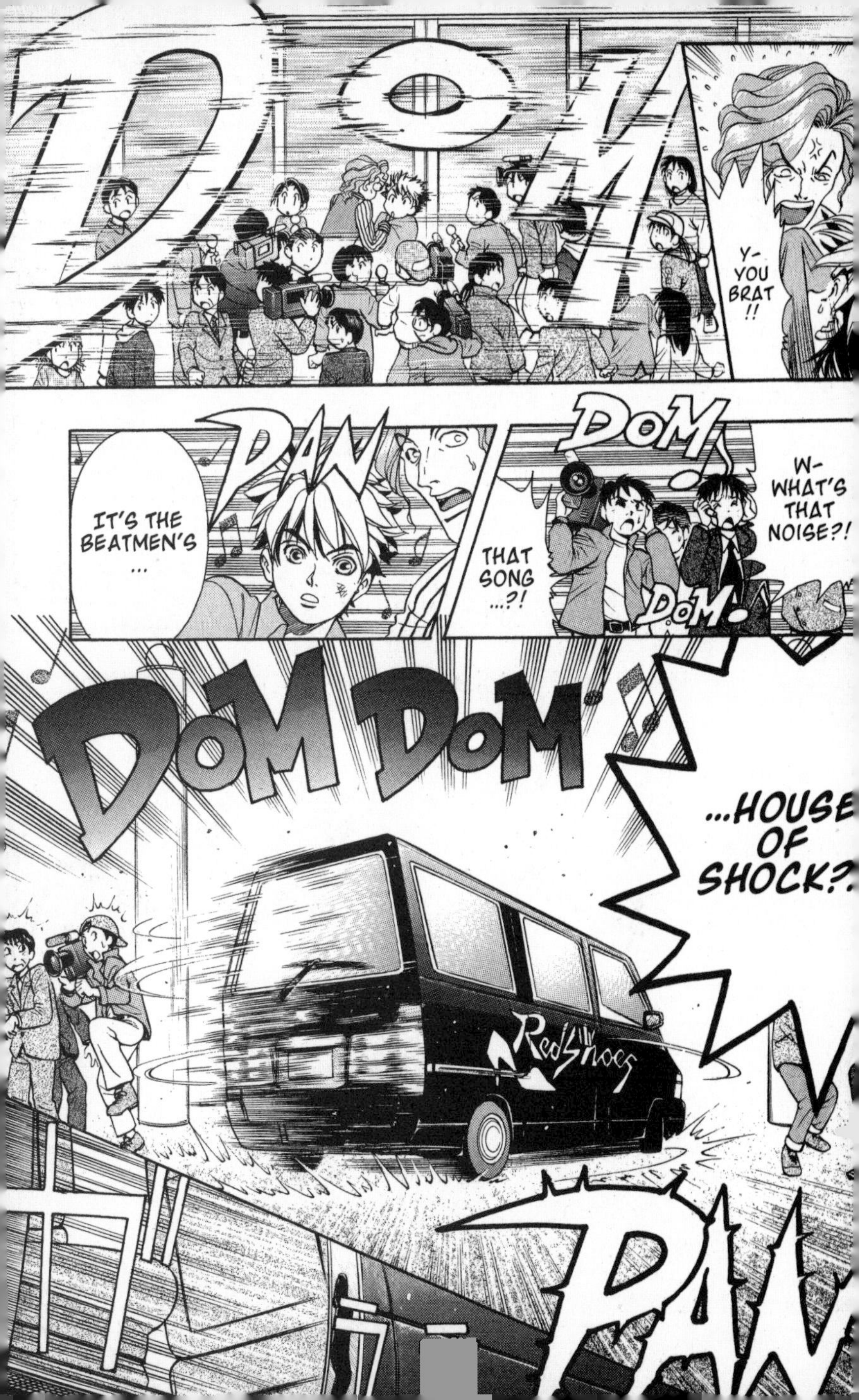
DOM
Y- YOU BRAT!!
DOM
W- WHAT'S THAT NOISE?!
THAT SONG ...?!
DOM!
DAN
IT'S THE BEATMEN'S ...
DOM DOM
...HOUSE OF SHOCK?!
RedShoes

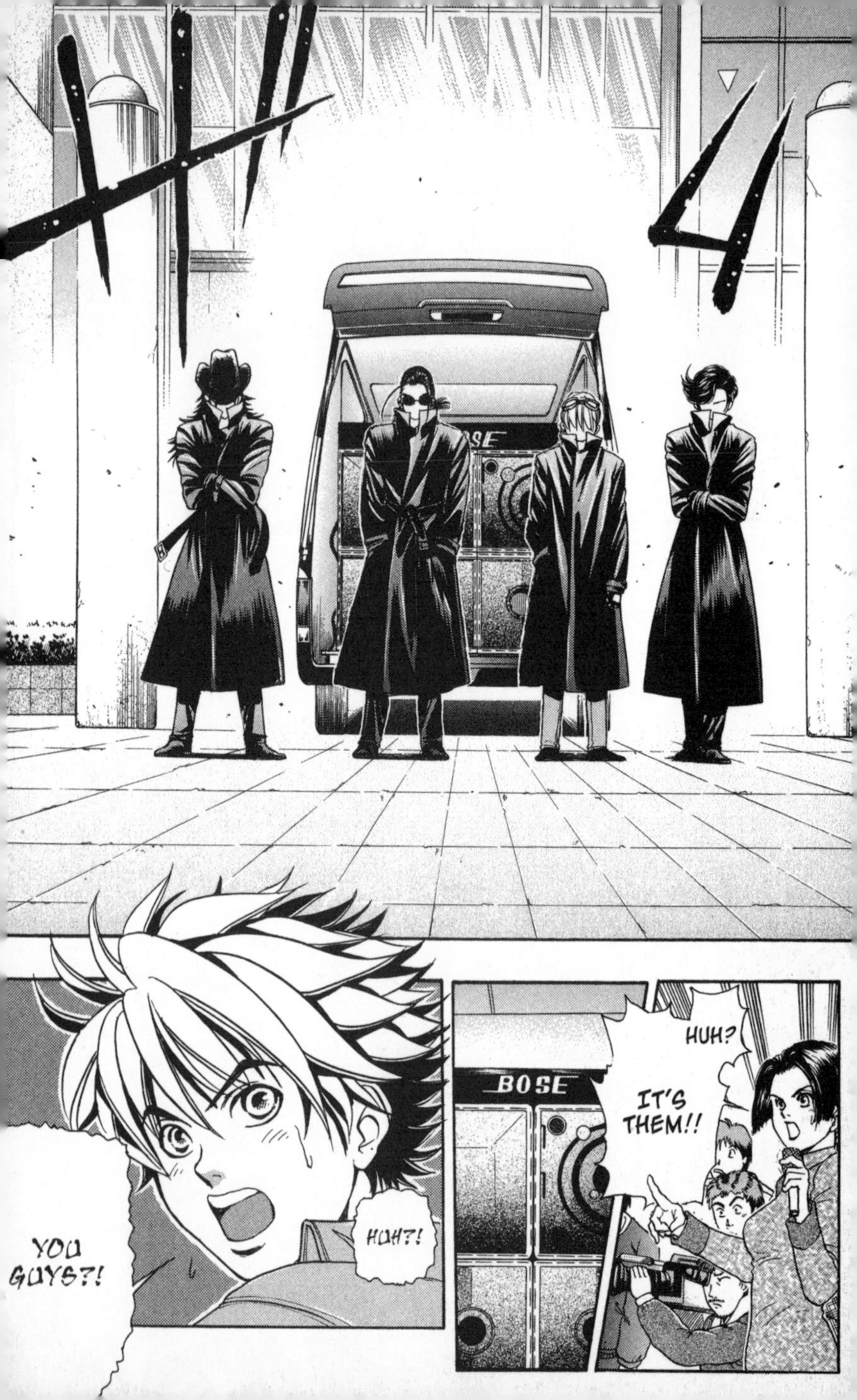
BOSE
HUH?
IT'S THEM!!
BOSE
HUH?!
YOU GUYS?!

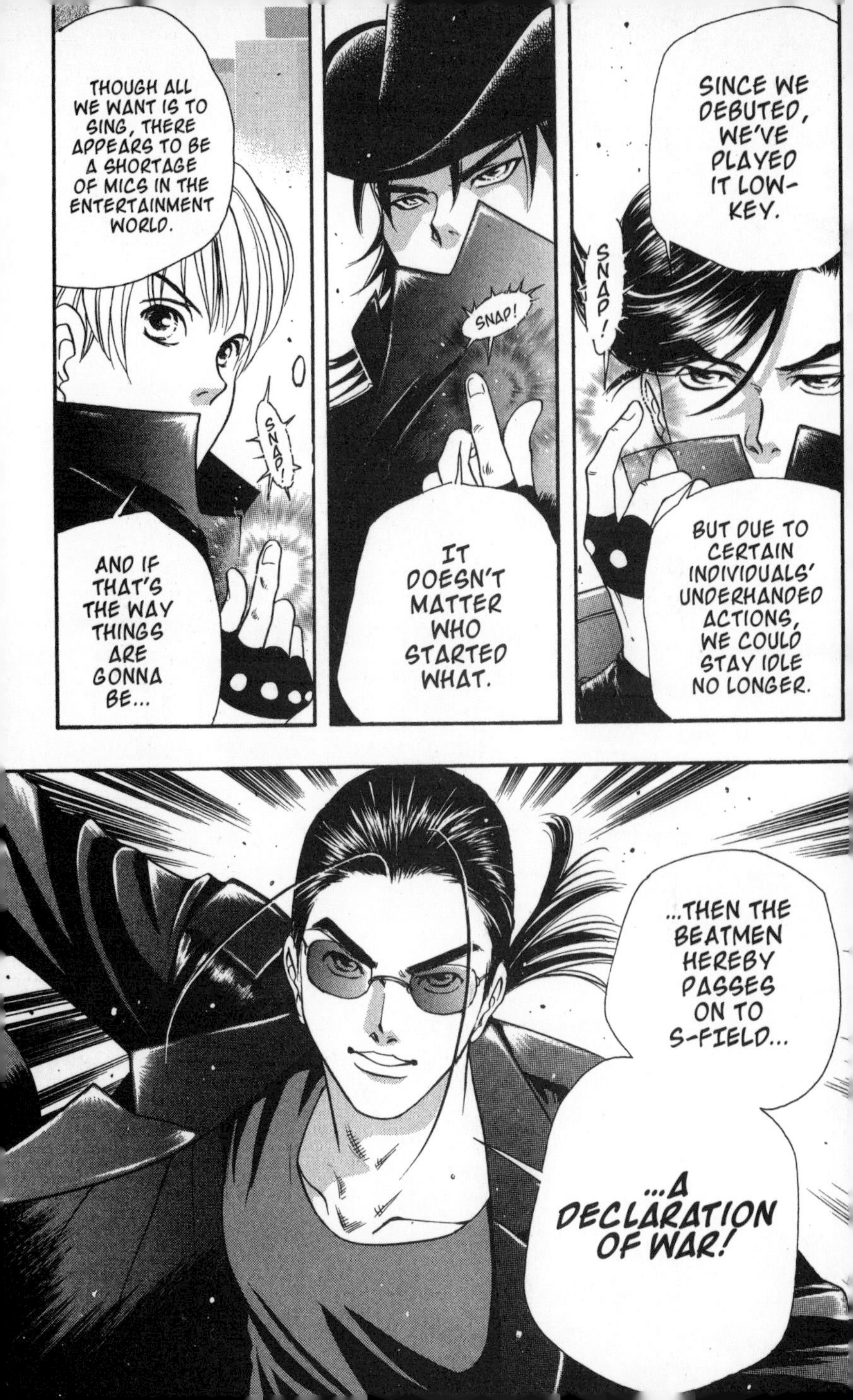
SINCE WE DEBUTED, WE'VE PLAYED IT LOW-KEY.
SNAP!
BUT DUE TO CERTAIN INDIVIDUALS' UNDERHANDED ACTIONS, WE COULD STAY IDLE NO LONGER.
SNAP!
IT DOESN'T MATTER WHO STARTED WHAT.
THOUGH ALL WE WANT IS TO SING, THERE APPEARS TO BE A SHORTAGE OF MICS IN THE ENTERTAINMENT WORLD.
SNAP!
AND IF THAT'S THE WAY THINGS ARE GONNA BE...
...THEN THE BEATMEN HEREBY PASSES ON TO S-FIELD...
...A DECLARATION OF WAR!

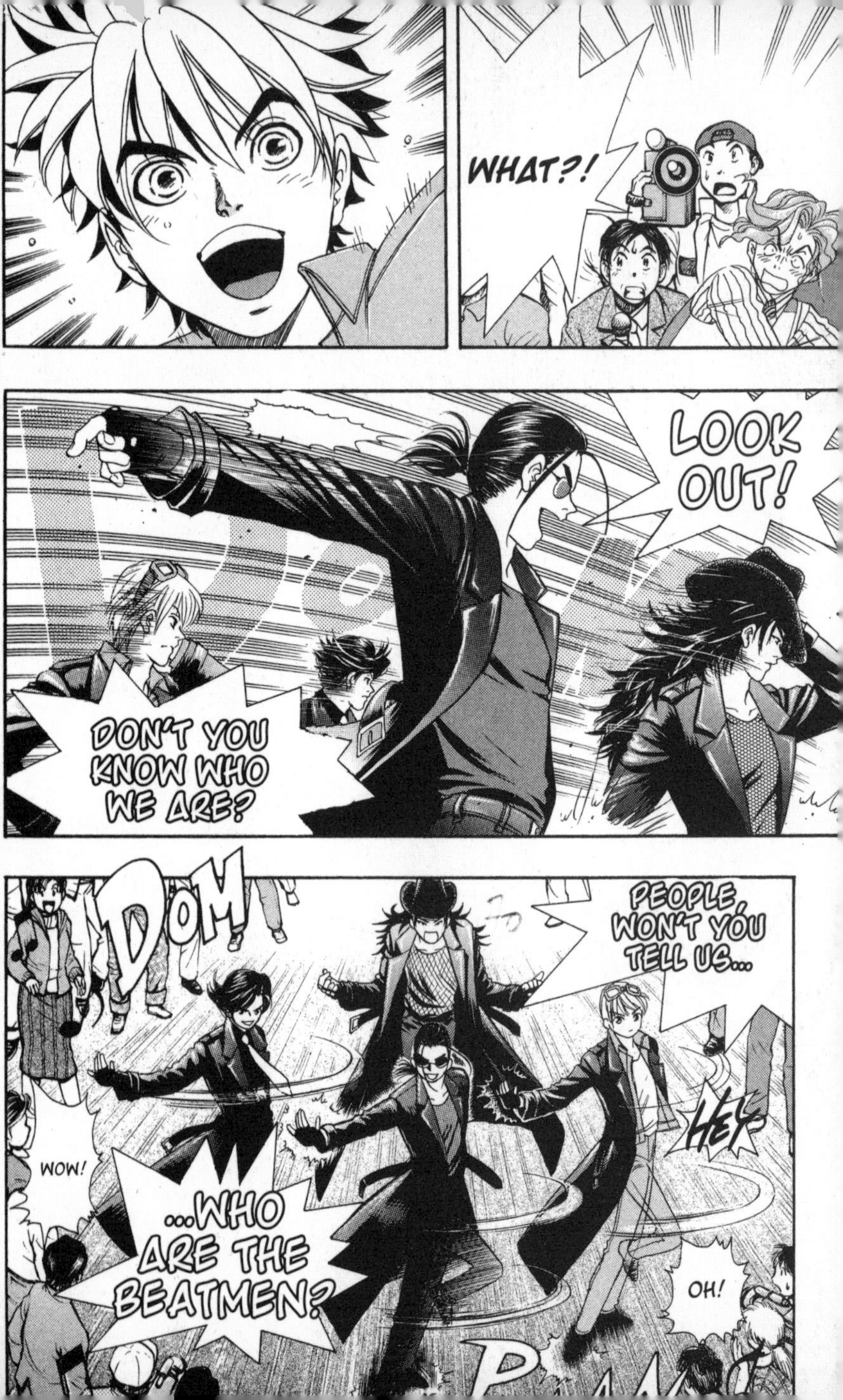
WHAT?!
LOOK OUT!
DON'T YOU KNOW WHO WE ARE?
PEOPLE, WON'T YOU TELL US...
DOM
HEY
OH!
...WHO ARE THE BEATMEN?
WOW!

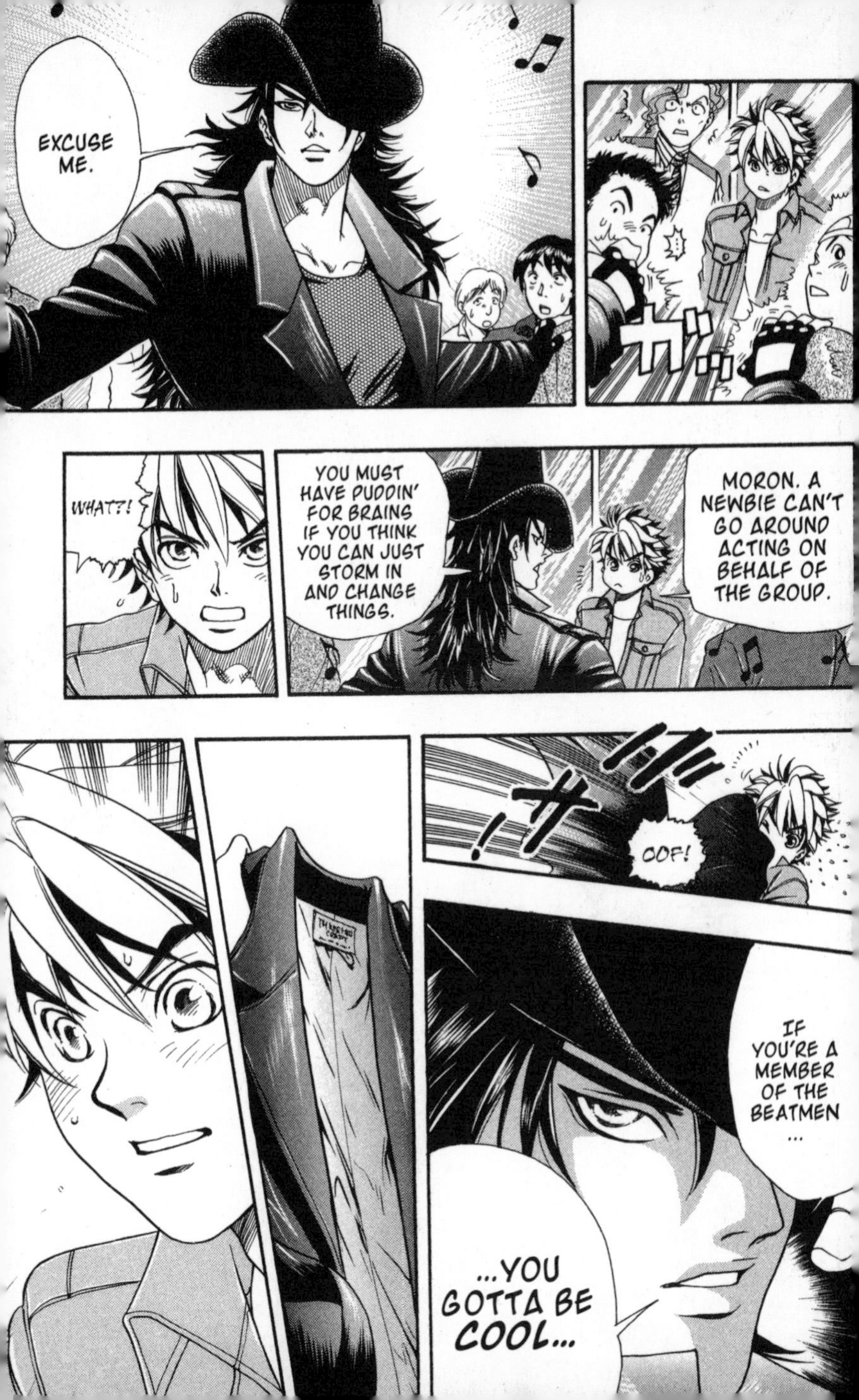
EXCUSE ME.
MORON. A NEWBIE CAN'T GO AROUND ACTING ON BEHALF OF THE GROUP.
YOU MUST HAVE PUDDIN' FOR BRAINS IF YOU THINK YOU CAN JUST STORM IN AND CHANGE THINGS.
WHAT?!
OOF!
IF YOU'RE A MEMBER OF THE BEATMEN ...
...YOU GOTTA BE COOL...

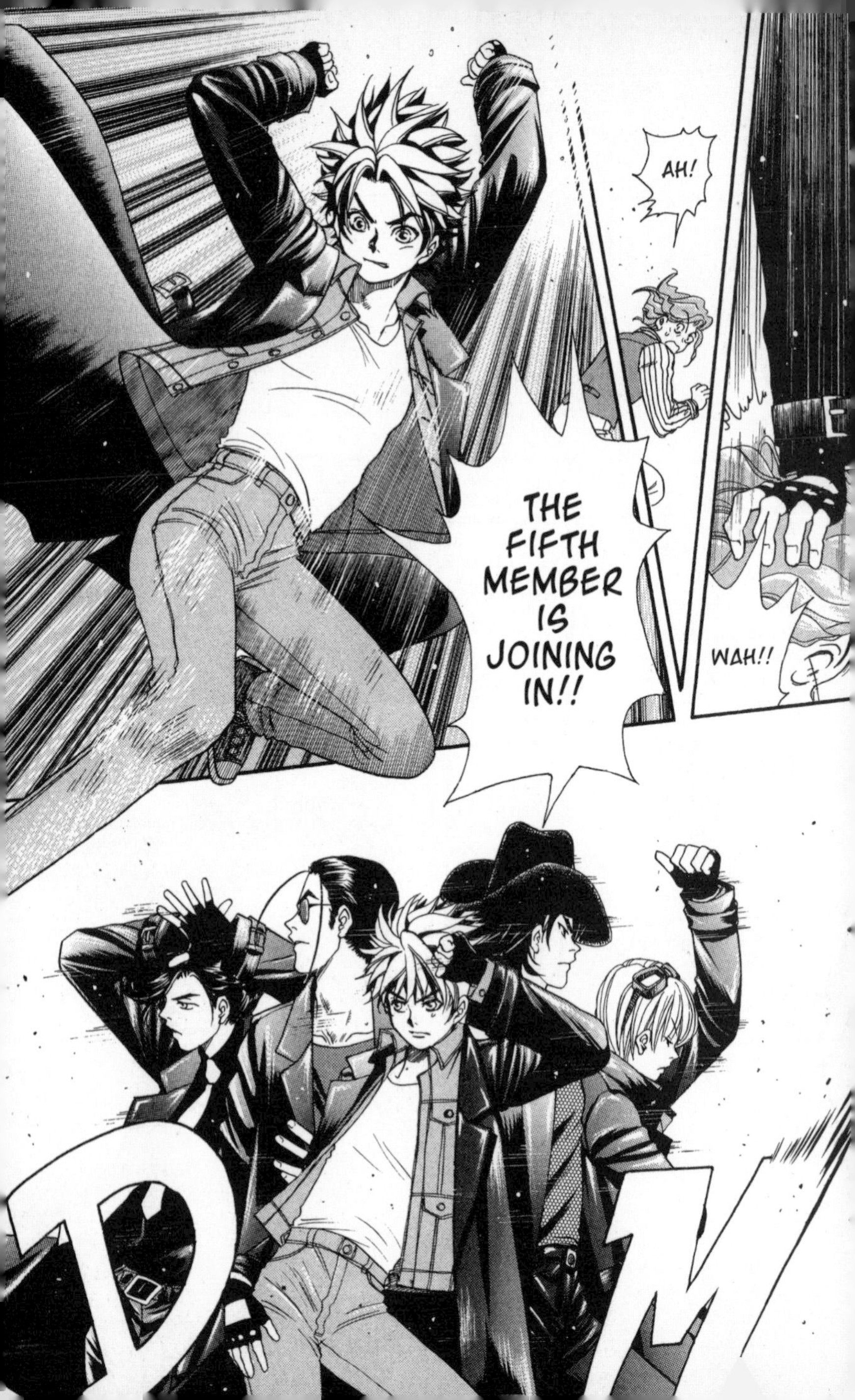
WAH!!
AH!
THE FIFTH MEMBER IS JOINING IN!!

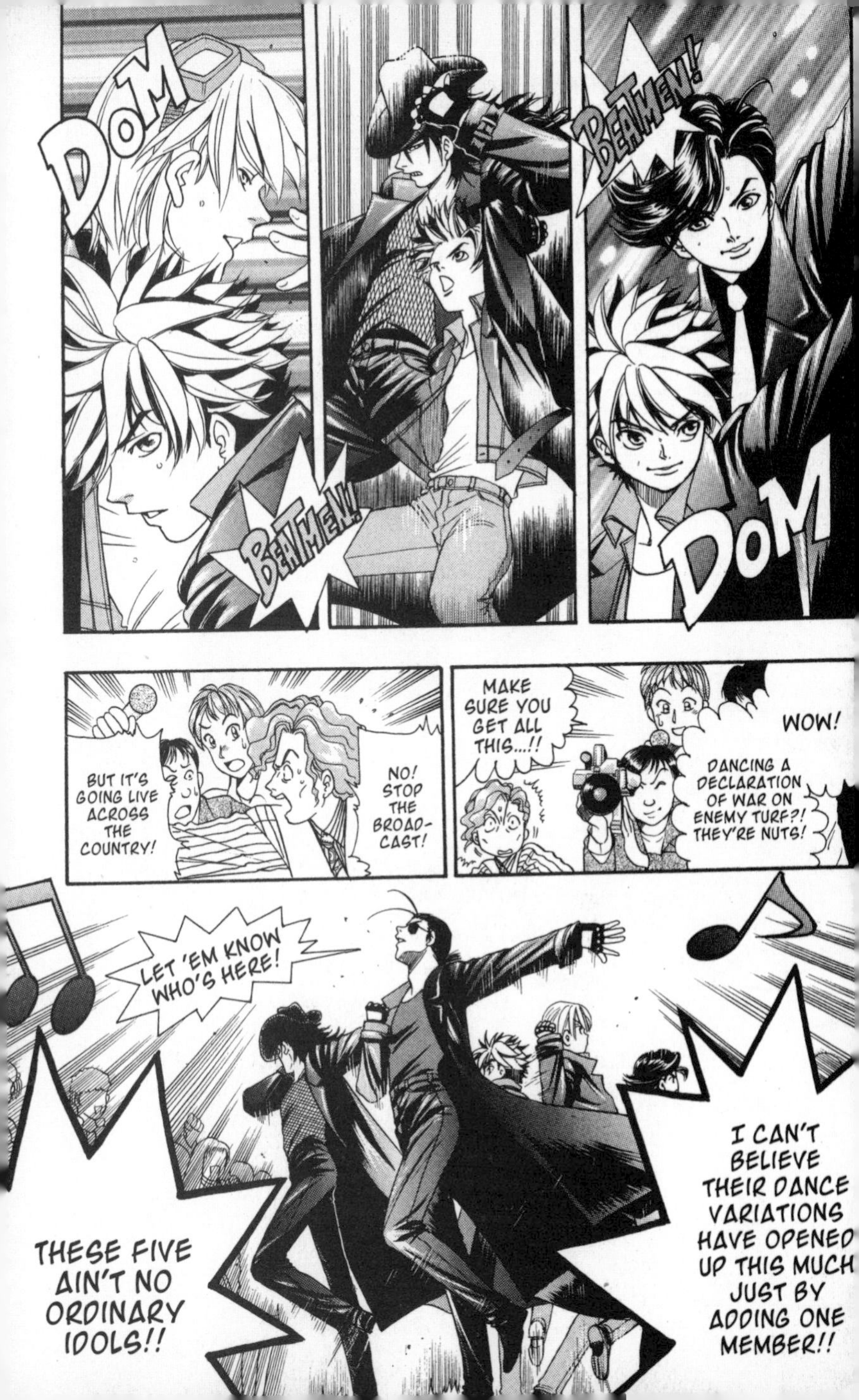
BEATMEN!
DOM
BEATMEN!
DOM
WOW!
DANCING A DECLARATION OF WAR ON ENEMY TURF?! THEY'RE NUTS!
MAKE SURE YOU GET ALL THIS...!!
NO! STOP THE BROAD-CAST!
BUT IT'S GOING LIVE ACROSS THE COUNTRY!
LET 'EM KNOW WHO'S HERE!
I CAN'T BELIEVE THEIR DANCE VARIATIONS HAVE OPENED UP THIS MUCH JUST BY ADDING ONE MEMBER!!
THESE FIVE AIN'T NO ORDINARY IDOLS!!

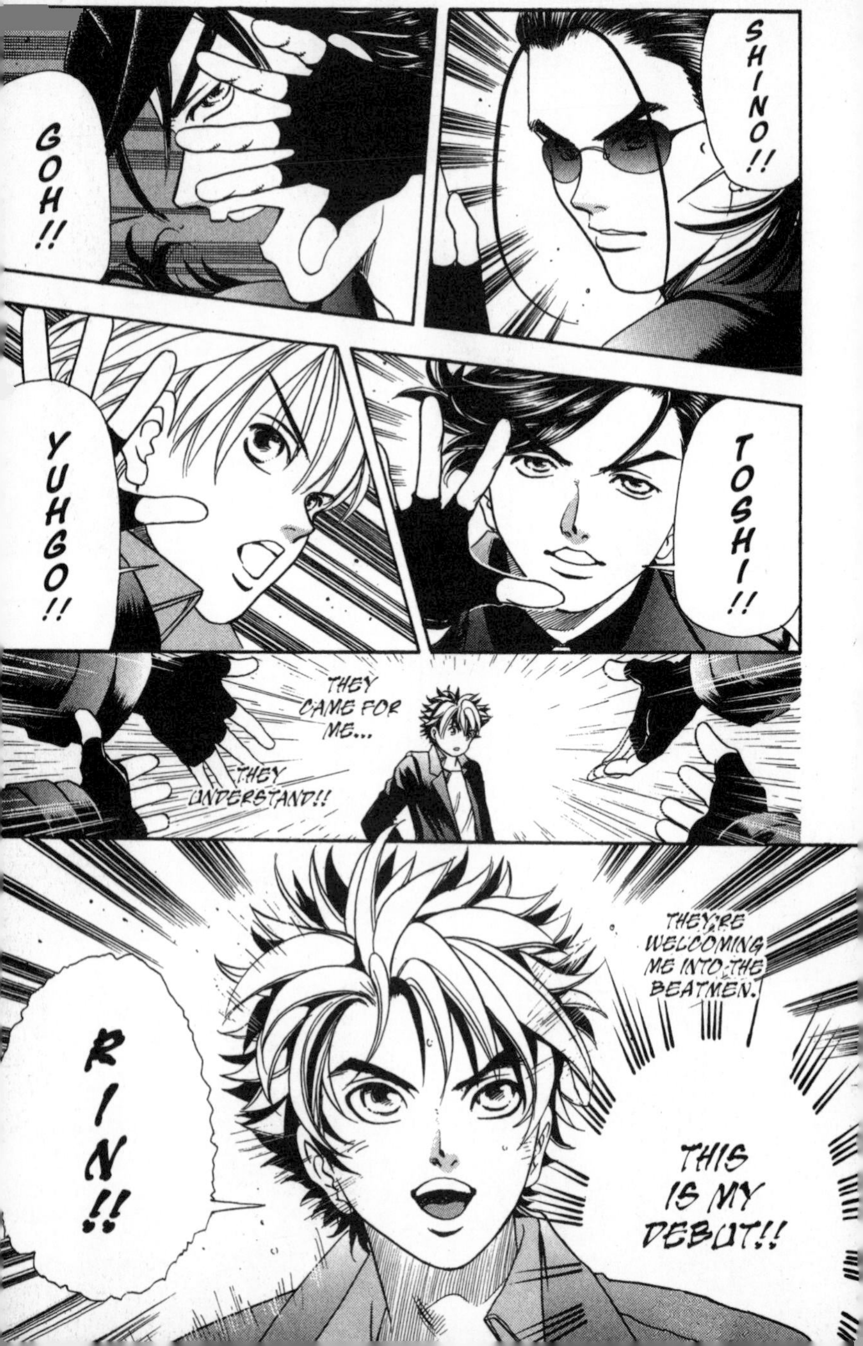
SHINO!!
GOH!!
TOSHI!!
YUHGO!!
THEY CAME FOR ME...
THEY UNDERSTAND!!
THEY'RE WELCOMING ME INTO THE BEATMEN.
THIS IS MY DEBUT!!
RIN!!

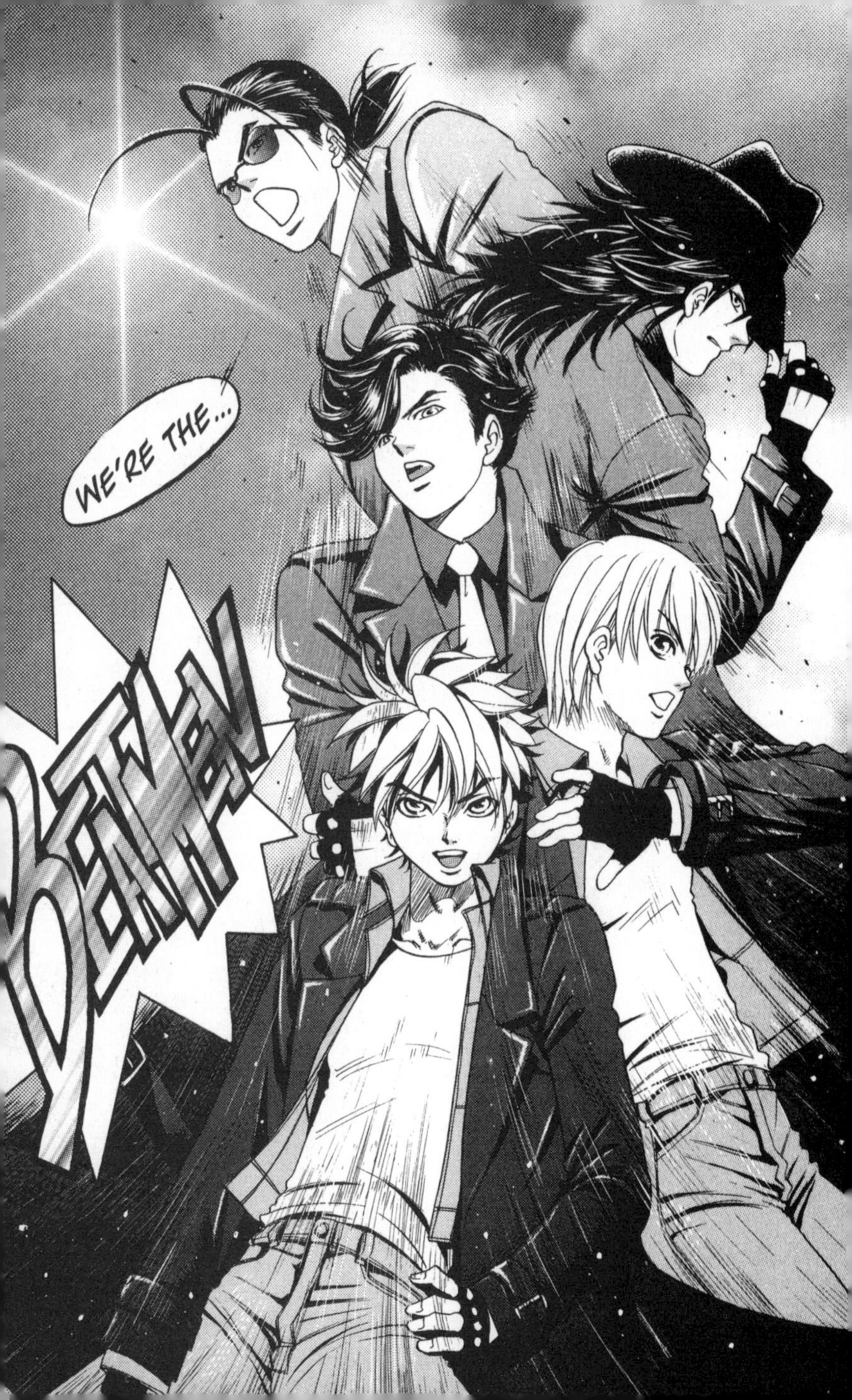
WE'RE THE...

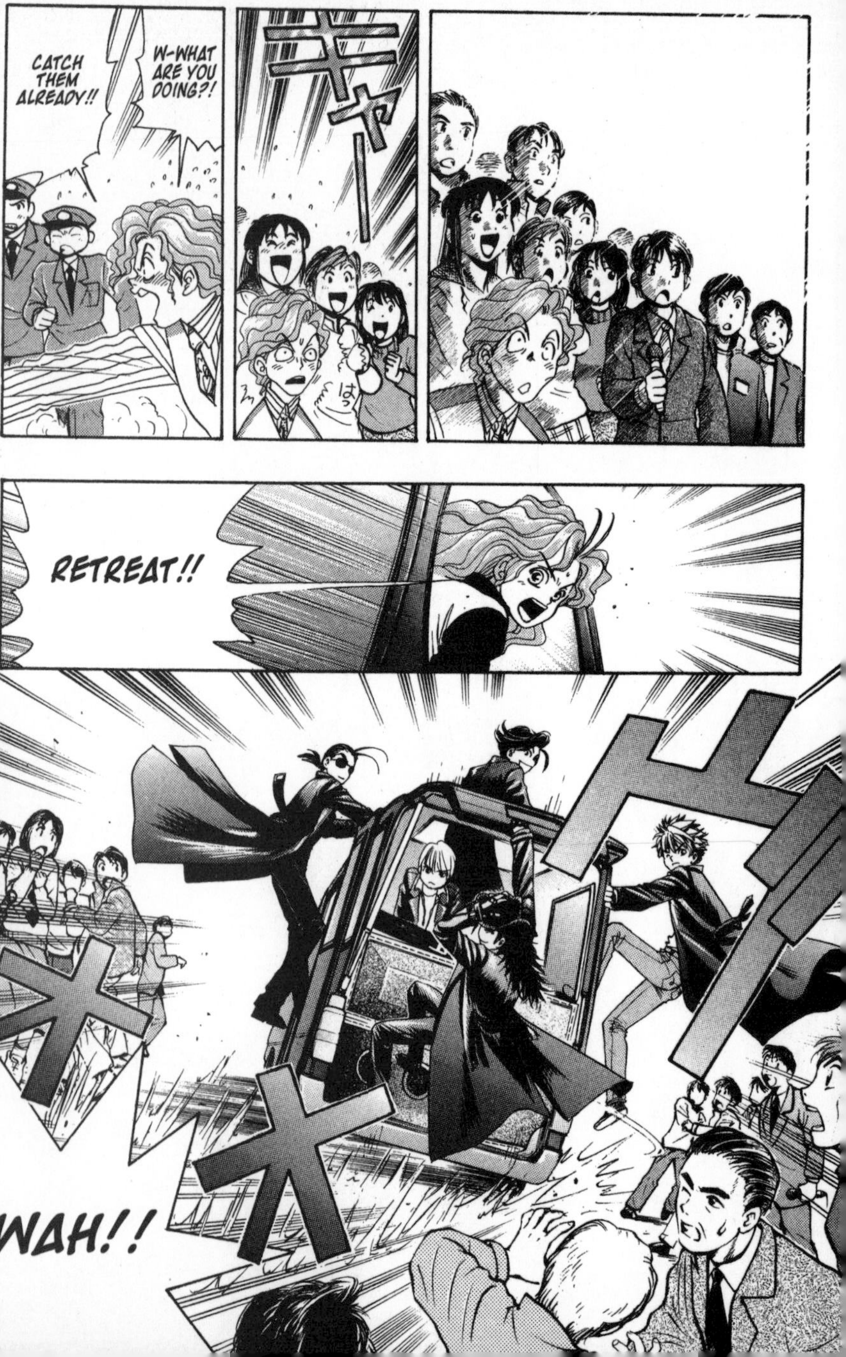
キャー
W-WHAT ARE YOU DOING?!
CATCH THEM ALREADY!!
RETREAT!!
WAH!!

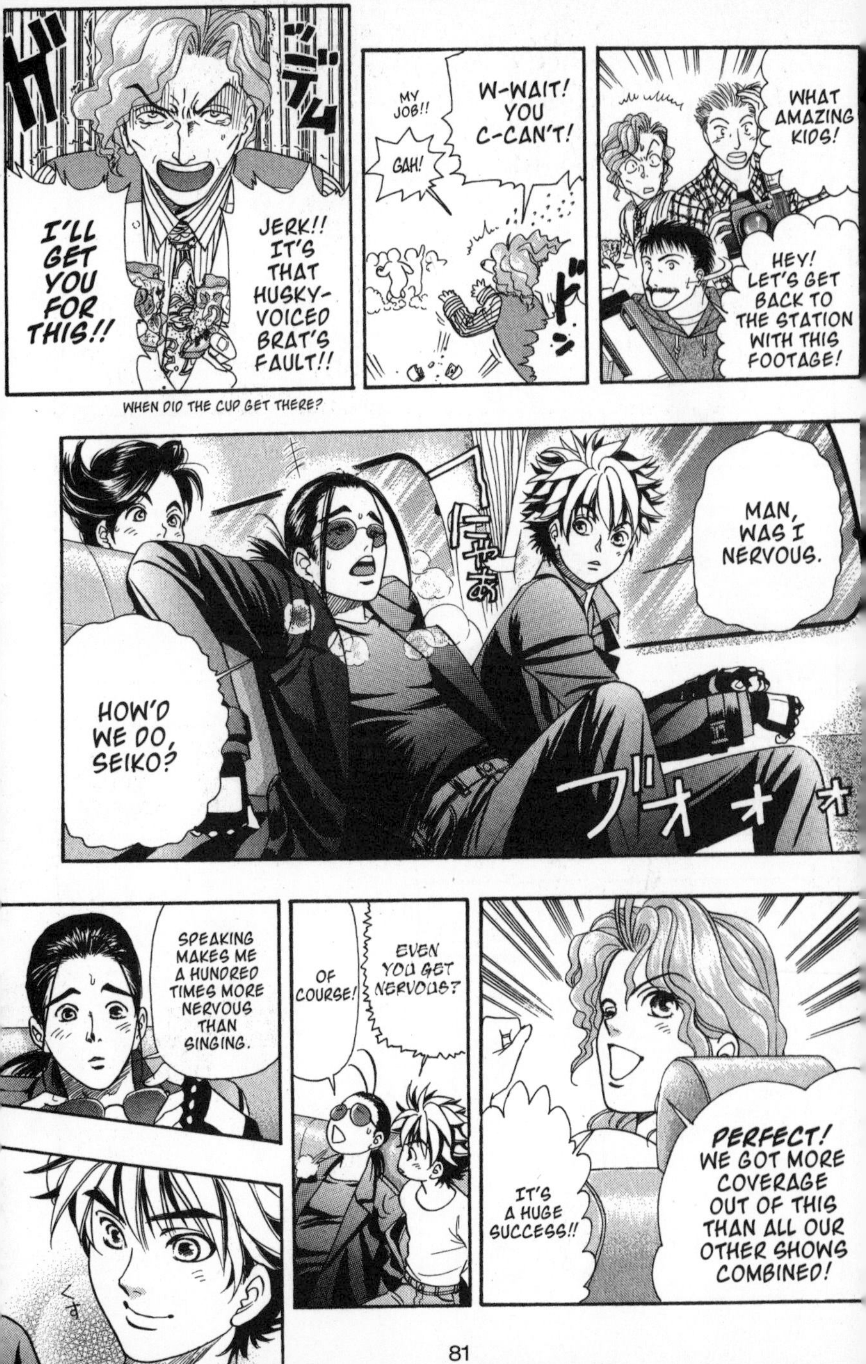
WHAT AMAZING KIDS!
HEY! LET'S GET BACK TO THE STATION WITH THIS FOOTAGE!
W-WAIT! YOU C-CAN'T!
MY JOB!!
GAH!
JERK!! IT'S THAT HUSKY-VOICED BRAT'S FAULT!!
I'LL GET YOU FOR THIS!!
WHEN DID THE CUP GET THERE?
MAN, WAS I NERVOUS.
HOW'D WE DO, SEIKO?
PERFECT! WE GOT MORE COVERAGE OUT OF THIS THAN ALL OUR OTHER SHOWS COMBINED!
IT'S A HUGE SUCCESS!!
EVEN YOU GET NERVOUS?
OF COURSE!
SPEAKING MAKES ME A HUNDRED TIMES MORE NERVOUS THAN SINGING.

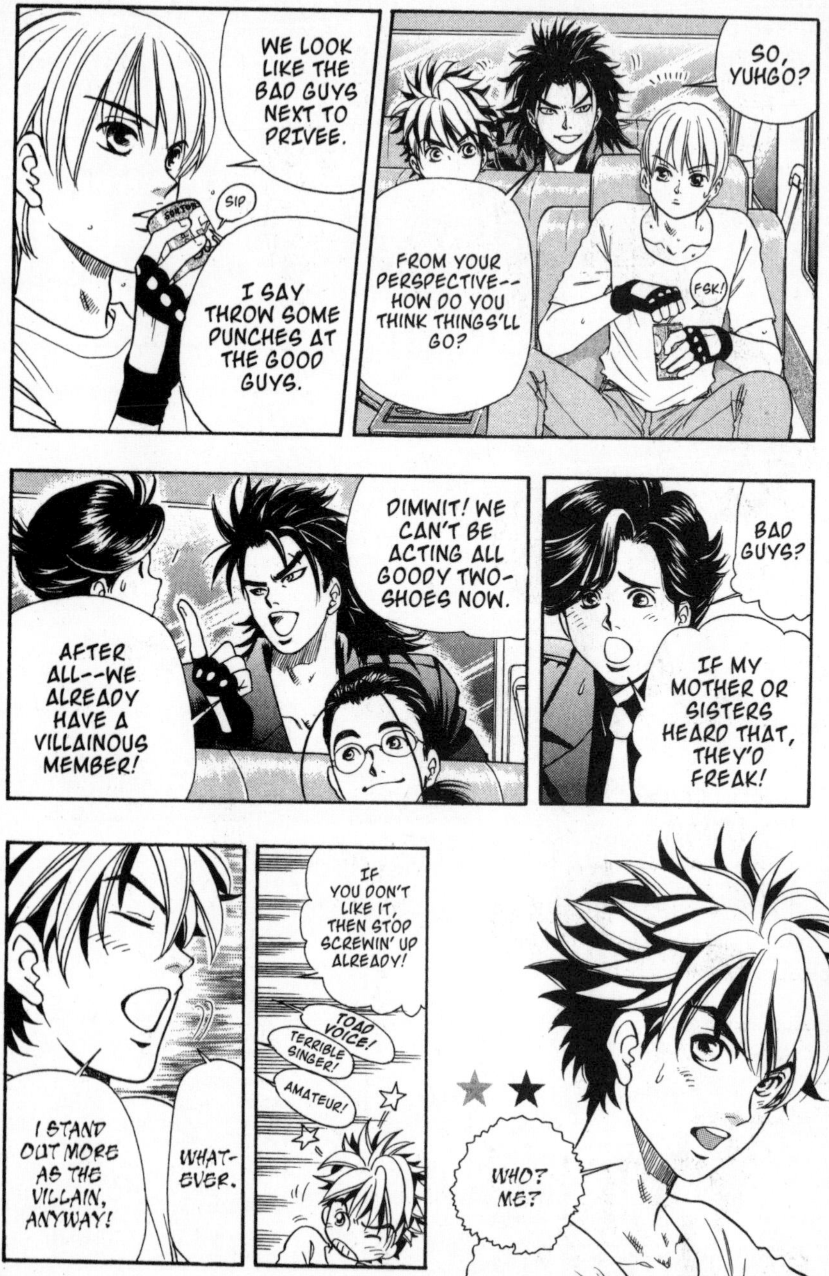
SO, YUHGO?
FROM YOUR PERSPECTIVE--HOW DO YOU THINK THINGS'LL GO?
FSK!
WE LOOK LIKE THE BAD GUYS NEXT TO PRIVEE.
SIP
I SAY THROW SOME PUNCHES AT THE GOOD GUYS.
BAD GUYS?
IF MY MOTHER OR SISTERS HEARD THAT, THEY'D FREAK!
DIMWIT! WE CAN'T BE ACTING ALL GOODY TWO-SHOES NOW.
AFTER ALL--WE ALREADY HAVE A VILLAINOUS MEMBER!
WHO? ME?
IF YOU DON'T LIKE IT, THEN STOP SCREWIN' UP ALREADY!
TOAD VOICE!
TERRIBLE SINGER!
AMATEUR!
WHAT-EVER.
I STAND OUT MORE AS THE VILLAIN, ANYWAY!

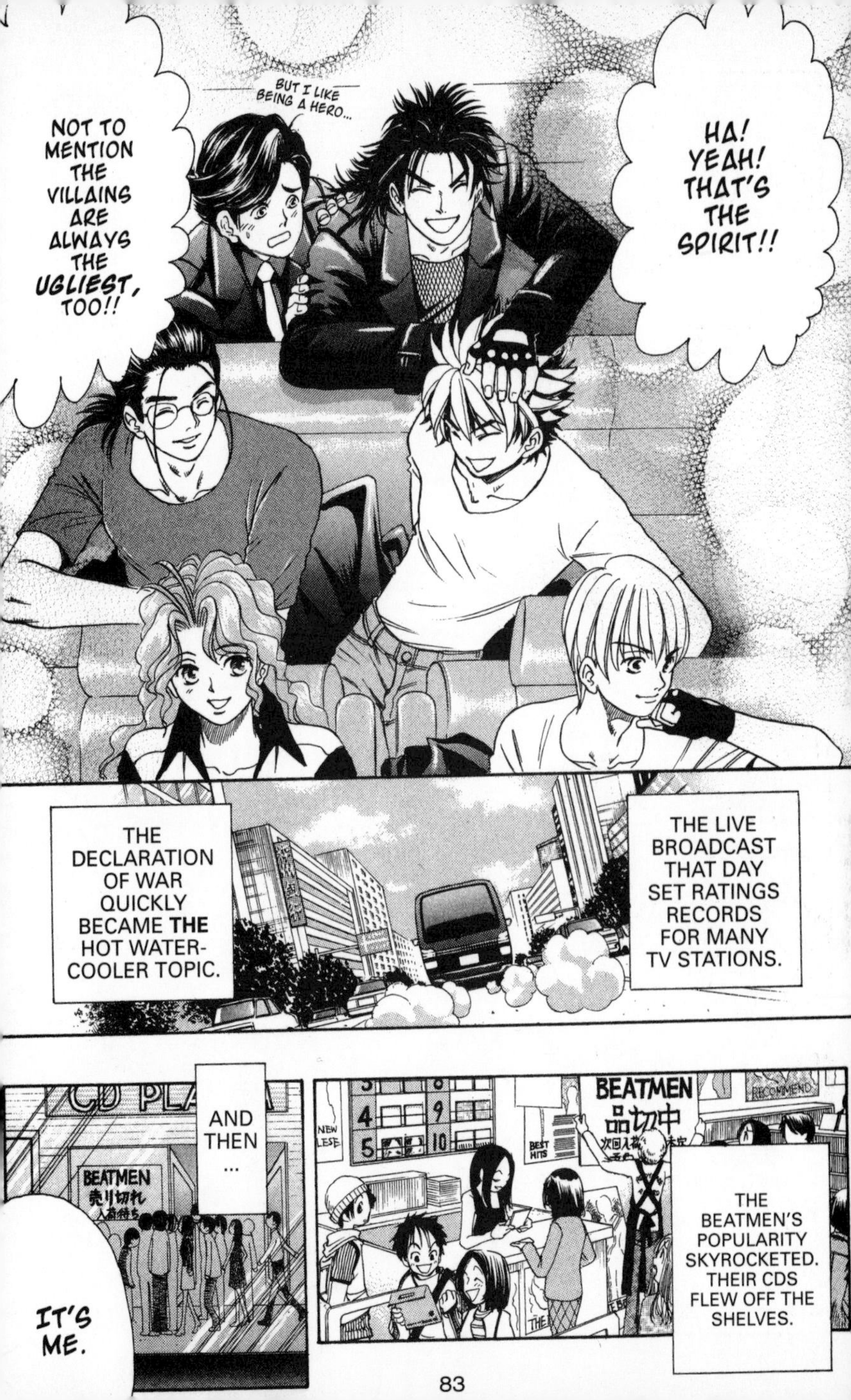
HA! YEAH! THAT'S THE SPIRIT!!
BUT I LIKE BEING A HERO...
NOT TO MENTION THE VILLAINS ARE ALWAYS THE *UGLIEST*, TOO!!
THE LIVE BROADCAST THAT DAY SET RATINGS RECORDS FOR MANY TV STATIONS.
THE DECLARATION OF WAR QUICKLY BECAME **THE** HOT WATER-COOLER TOPIC.
BEATMEN
品切中
BEST HITS
THE BEATMEN'S POPULARITY SKYROCKETED. THEIR CDS FLEW OFF THE SHELVES.
AND THEN ...
BEATMEN
売り切れ
入荷待ち
IT'S ME.

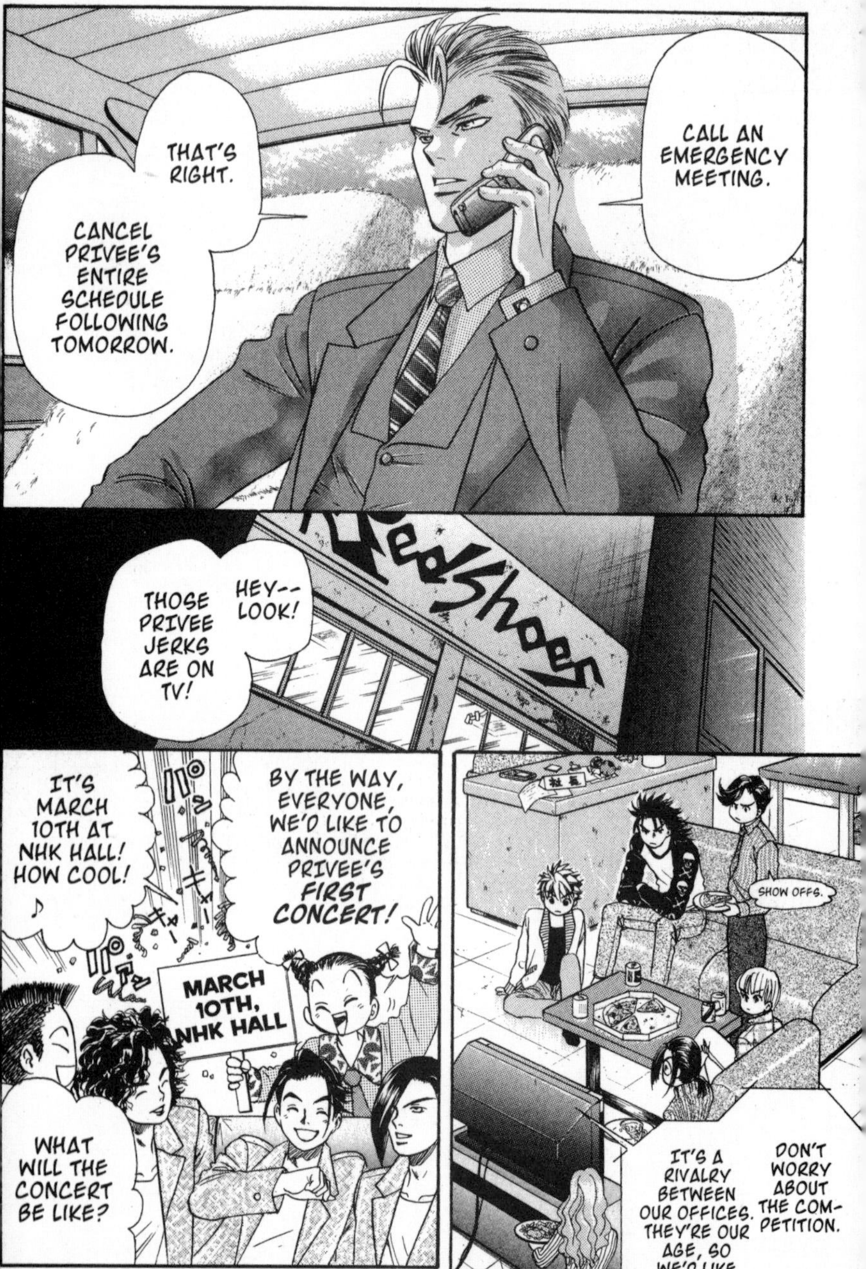
CALL AN EMERGENCY MEETING.
THAT'S RIGHT.
CANCEL PRIVEE'S ENTIRE SCHEDULE FOLLOWING TOMORROW.
RedShoes
HEY--LOOK!
THOSE PRIVEE JERKS ARE ON TV!
SHOW OFFS.
DON'T WORRY ABOUT THE COMPETITION.
IT'S A RIVALRY BETWEEN OUR OFFICES. THEY'RE OUR AGE, SO WE'D LIKE TO GET TO KNOW THEM.
BY THE WAY, EVERYONE, WE'D LIKE TO ANNOUNCE PRIVEE'S FIRST CONCERT!
MARCH 10TH, NHK HALL
IT'S MARCH 10TH AT NHK HALL! HOW COOL! ♪
WHAT WILL THE CONCERT BE LIKE?

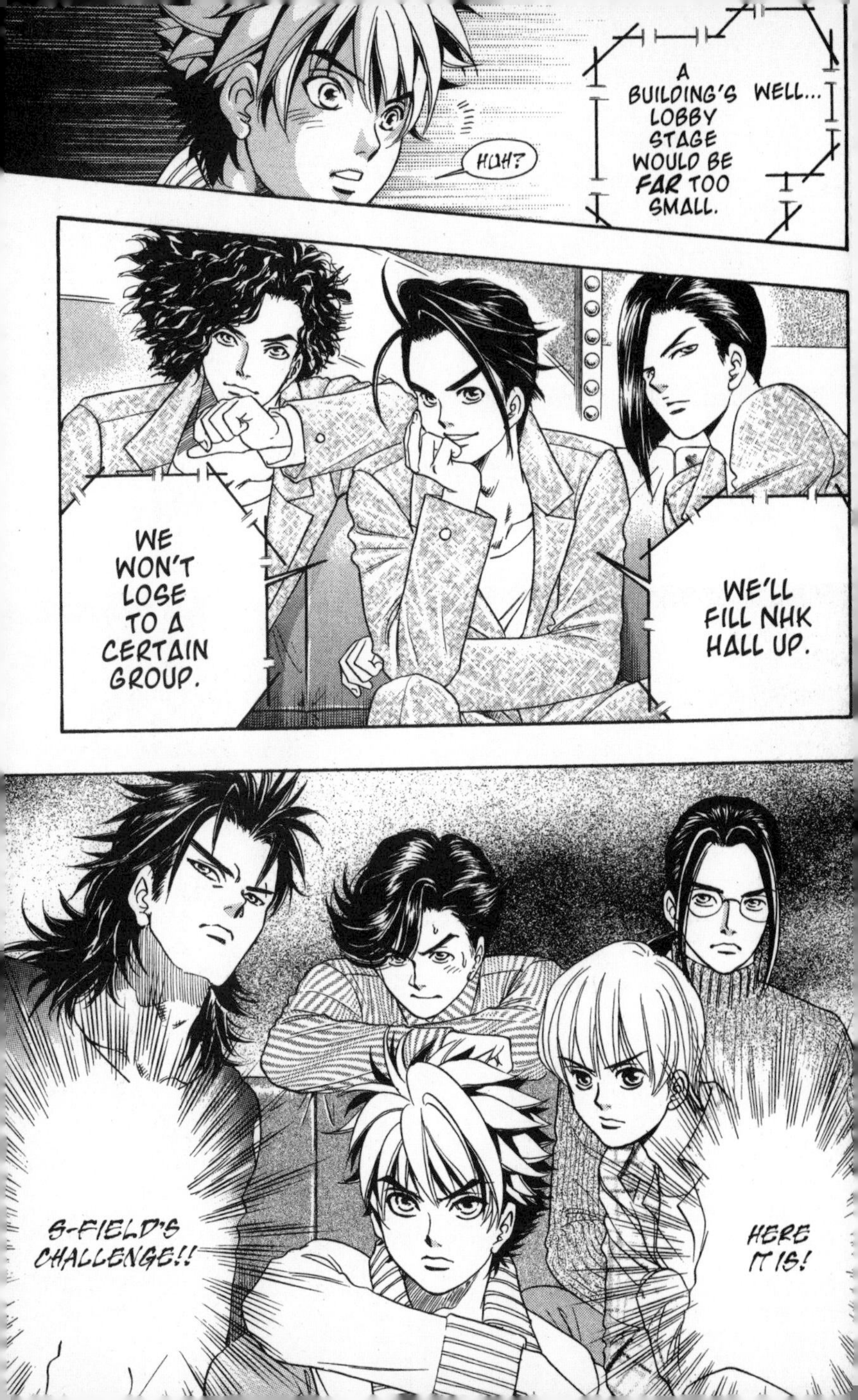
WELL...
A BUILDING'S LOBBY STAGE WOULD BE FAR TOO SMALL.
HUH?
WE'LL FILL NHK HALL UP.
WE WON'T LOSE TO A CERTAIN GROUP.
HERE IT IS!
S-FIELD'S CHALLENGE!!

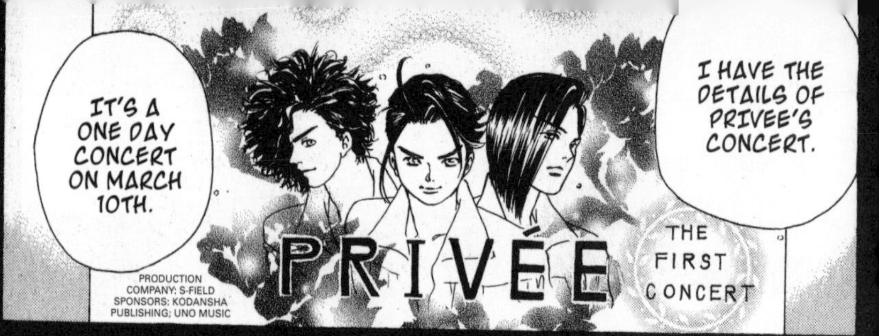
I HAVE THE DETAILS OF PRIVEE'S CONCERT.
IT'S A ONE DAY CONCERT ON MARCH 10TH.
PRIVÉE
THE FIRST CONCERT
PRODUCTION COMPANY: S-FIELD
SPONSORS: KODANSHA PUBLISHING; UNO MUSIC

# DRAGON VOICE #11 treachery

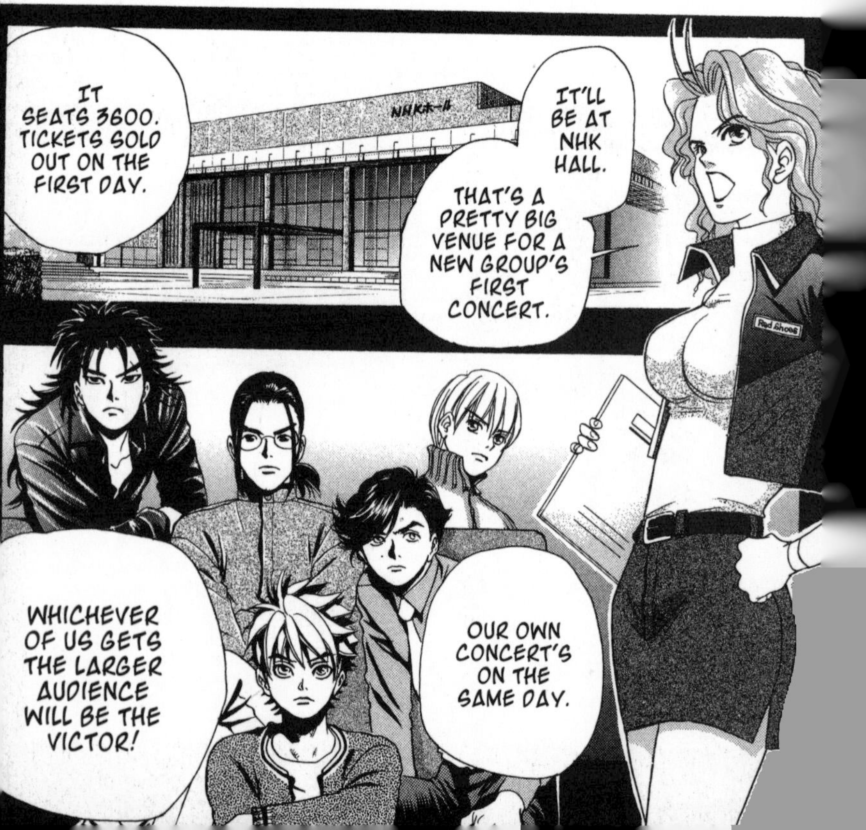
IT'LL BE AT NHK HALL.
THAT'S A PRETTY BIG VENUE FOR A NEW GROUP'S FIRST CONCERT.
NHKホール
IT SEATS 3600. TICKETS SOLD OUT ON THE FIRST DAY.
Red Shoes
OUR OWN CONCERT'S ON THE SAME DAY.
WHICHEVER OF US GETS THE LARGER AUDIENCE WILL BE THE VICTOR!

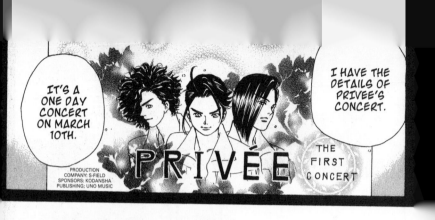

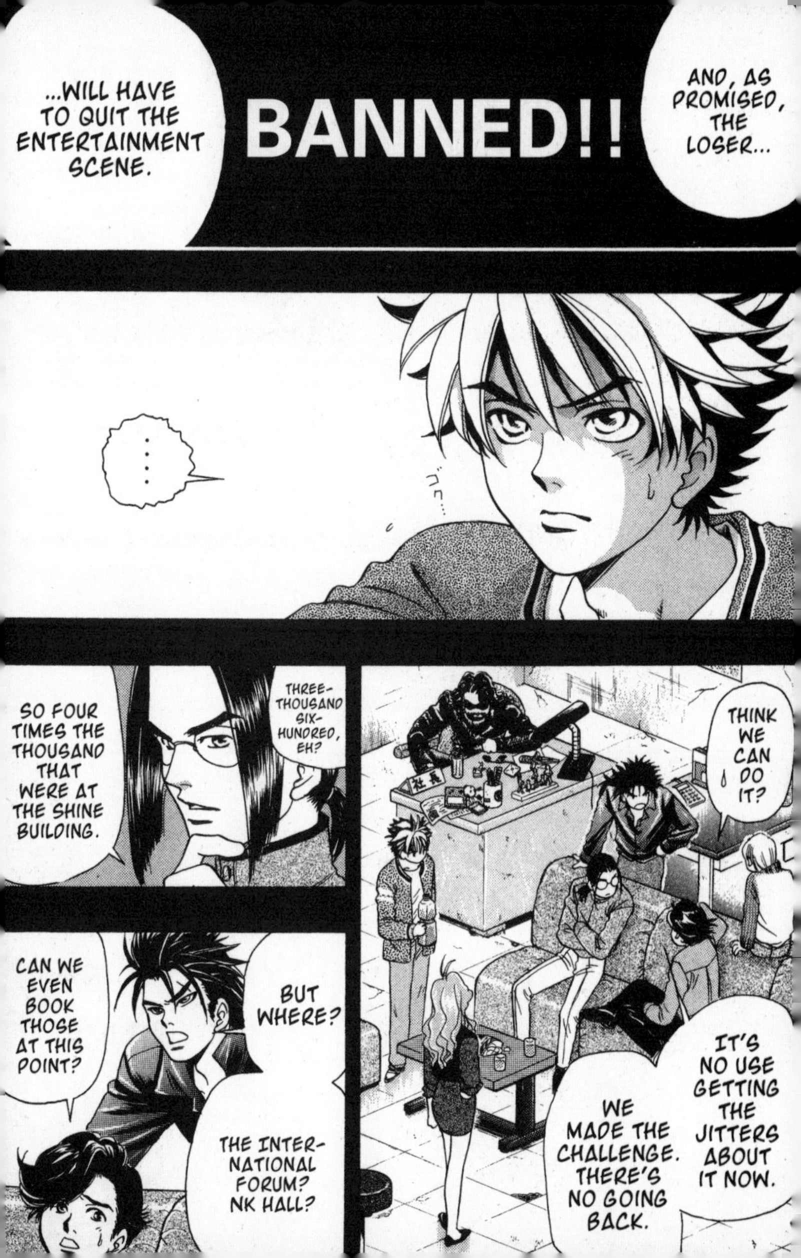
AND, AS PROMISED, THE LOSER...
BANNED!!
...WILL HAVE TO QUIT THE ENTERTAINMENT SCENE.
.....
ゴク…
THINK WE CAN DO IT?
IT'S NO USE GETTING THE JITTERS ABOUT IT NOW.
WE MADE THE CHALLENGE. THERE'S NO GOING BACK.
THREE-THOUSAND SIX-HUNDRED, EH?
SO FOUR TIMES THE THOUSAND THAT WERE AT THE SHINE BUILDING.
BUT WHERE?
THE INTERNATIONAL FORUM? NK HALL?
CAN WE EVEN BOOK THOSE AT THIS POINT?

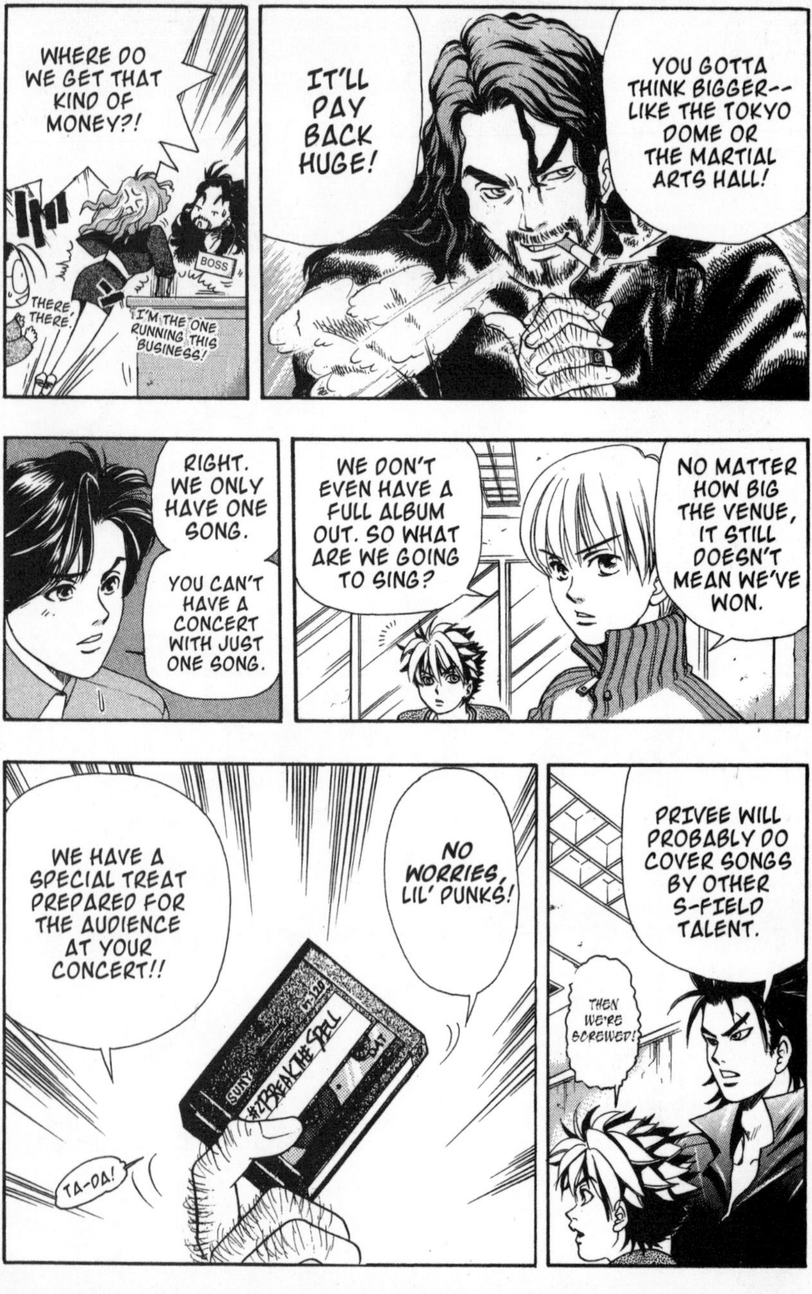
YOU GOTTA THINK BIGGER--LIKE THE TOKYO DOME OR THE MARTIAL ARTS HALL!
IT'LL PAY BACK HUGE!
WHERE DO WE GET THAT KIND OF MONEY?!
BOSS
THERE, THERE.
I'M THE ONE RUNNING THIS BUSINESS!
NO MATTER HOW BIG THE VENUE, IT STILL DOESN'T MEAN WE'VE WON.
WE DON'T EVEN HAVE A FULL ALBUM OUT. SO WHAT ARE WE GOING TO SING?
RIGHT. WE ONLY HAVE ONE SONG.
YOU CAN'T HAVE A CONCERT WITH JUST ONE SONG.
PRIVEE WILL PROBABLY DO COVER SONGS BY OTHER S-FIELD TALENT.
THEN WE'RE SCREWED!
NO WORRIES, LIL' PUNKS!
WE HAVE A SPECIAL TREAT PREPARED FOR THE AUDIENCE AT YOUR CONCERT!!
#2 BREAK THE SPELL
TA-DA!

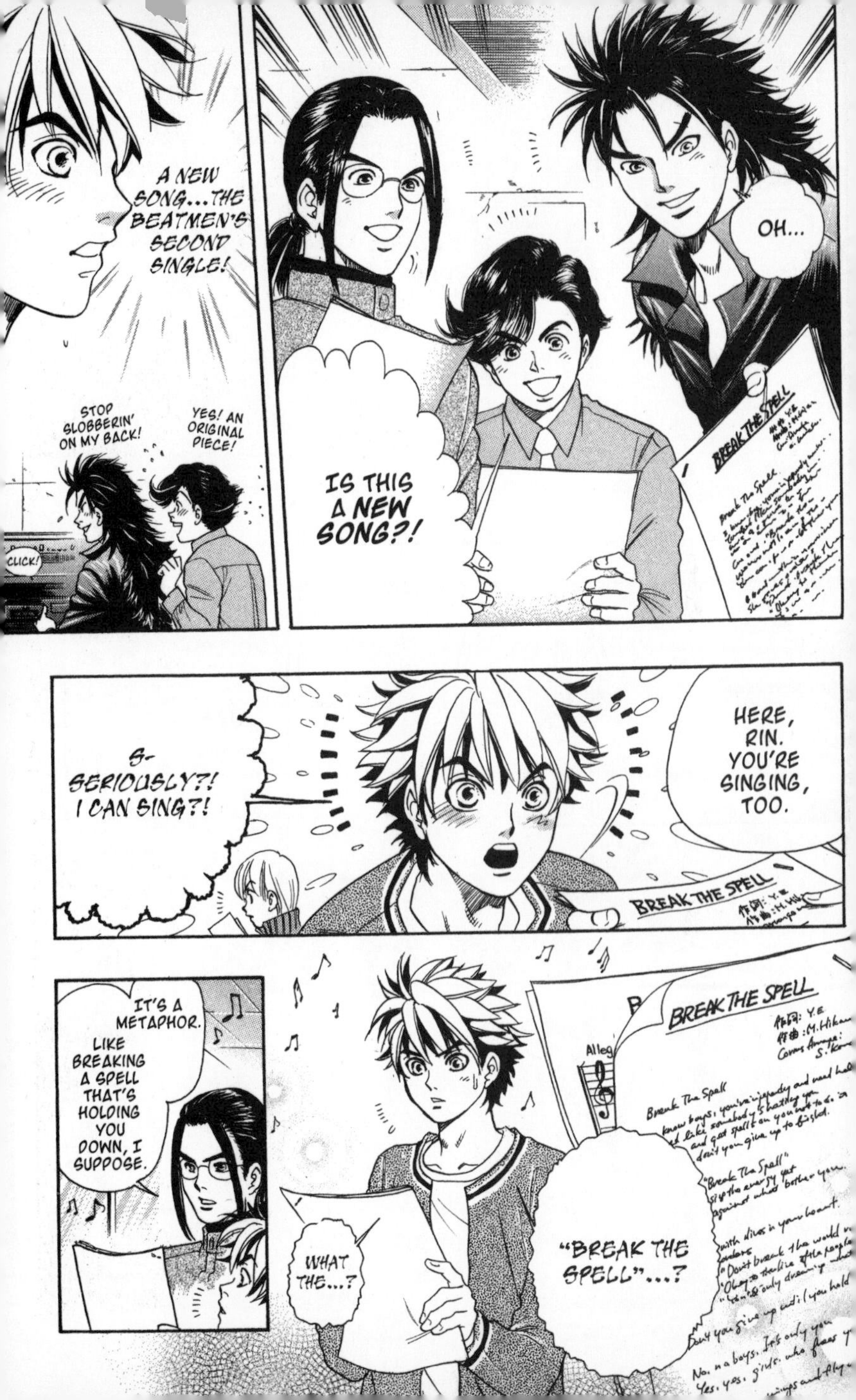

OH...
IS THIS A NEW SONG?!
BREAK THE SPELL
A NEW SONG...THE BEATMEN'S SECOND SINGLE!
YES! AN ORIGINAL PIECE!
STOP SLOBBERIN' ON MY BACK!
CLICK!
HERE, RIN. YOU'RE SINGING, TOO.
BREAK THE SPELL
S-SERIOUSLY?! I CAN SING?!
BREAK THE SPELL
"BREAK THE SPELL"...?
WHAT THE...?
IT'S A METAPHOR. LIKE BREAKING A SPELL THAT'S HOLDING YOU DOWN, I SUPPOSE.

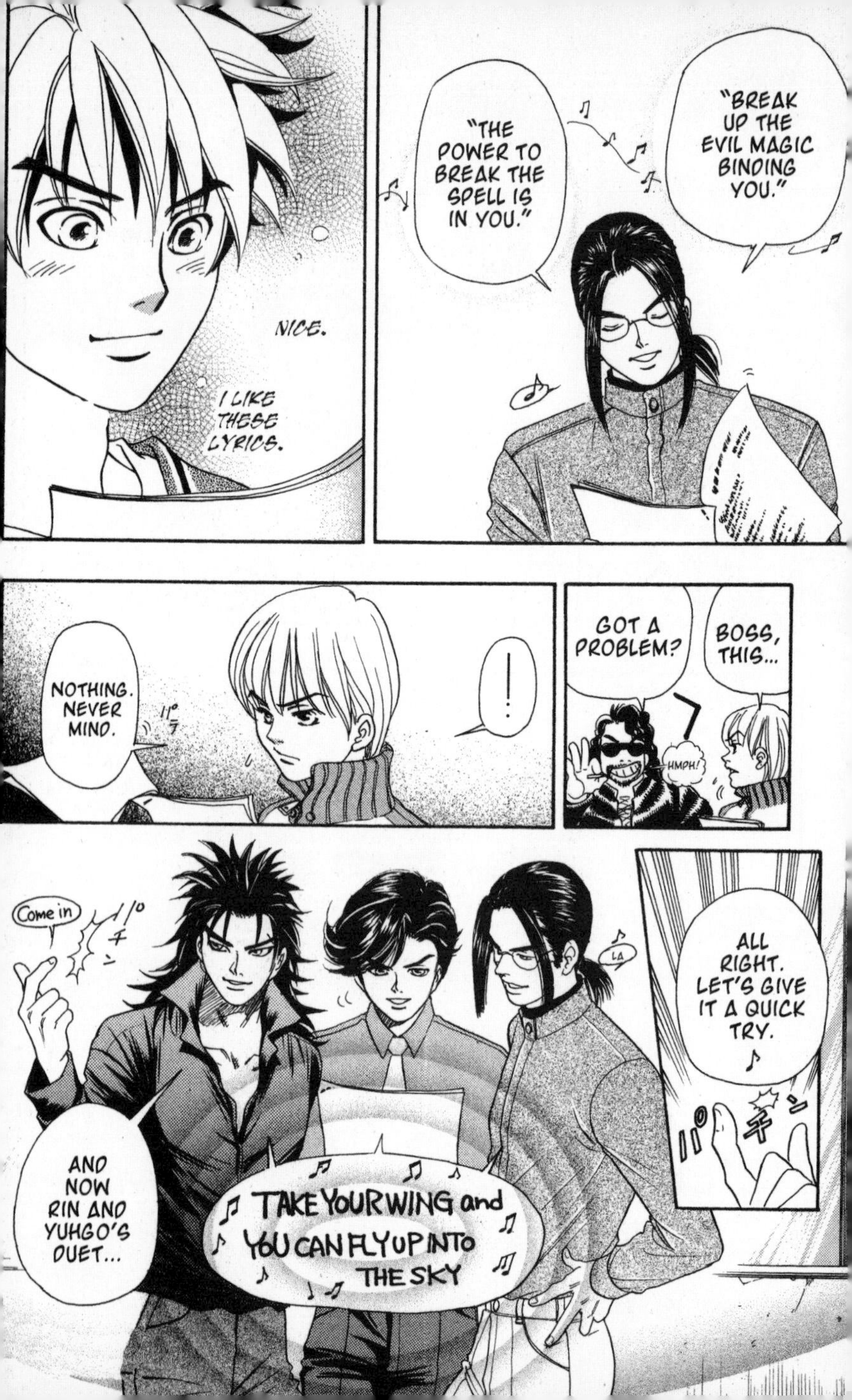
"BREAK UP THE EVIL MAGIC BINDING YOU."
"THE POWER TO BREAK THE SPELL IS IN YOU."
NICE.
I LIKE THESE LYRICS.
BOSS, THIS...
GOT A PROBLEM?
HMPH!
!
NOTHING. NEVER MIND.
ALL RIGHT. LET'S GIVE IT A QUICK TRY.
LA
Come in
AND NOW RIN AND YUHGO'S DUET...
TAKE YOUR WING and YOU CAN FLY UP INTO THE SKY

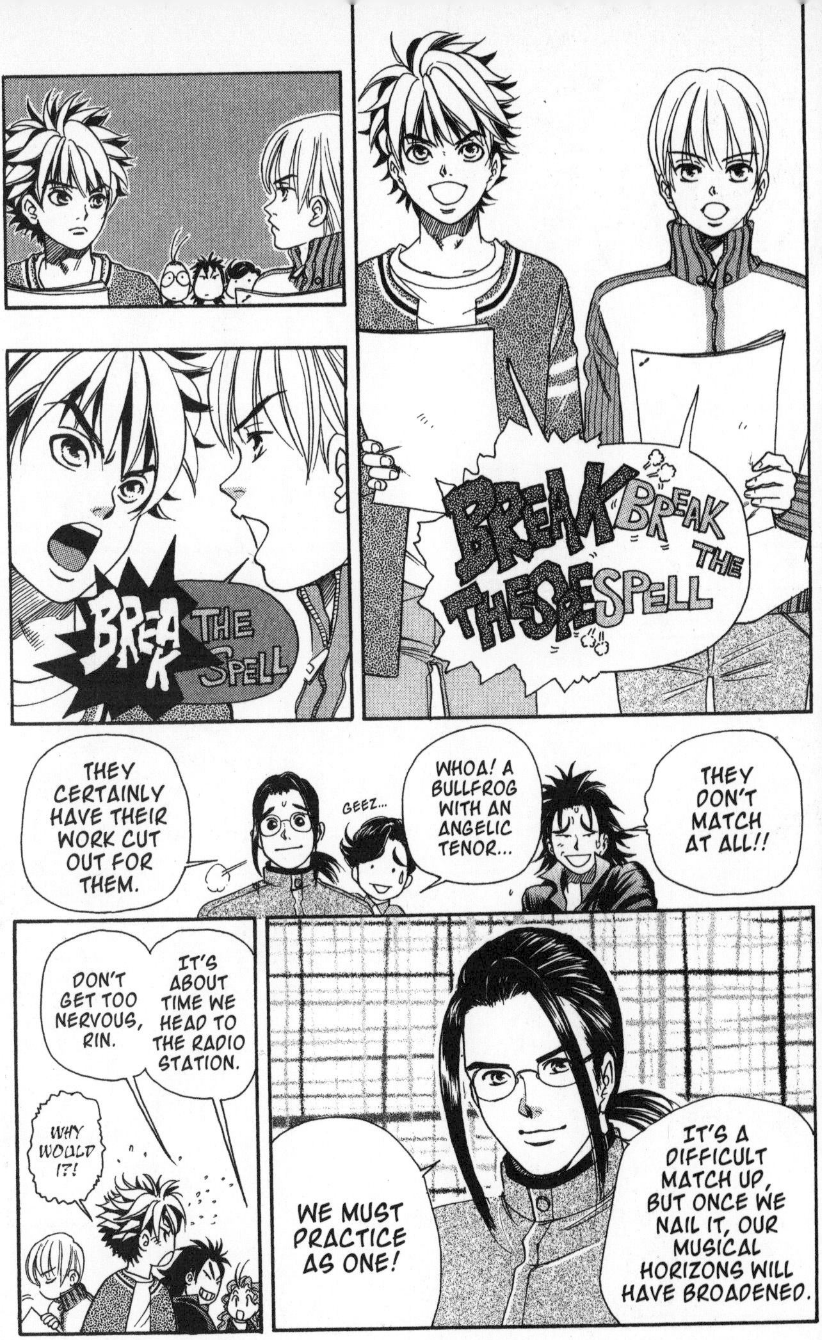
BREAK BREAK THE
THE SPE SPELL
BREAK THE SPELL
THEY DON'T MATCH AT ALL!!
WHOA! A BULLFROG WITH AN ANGELIC TENOR...
GEEZ...
THEY CERTAINLY HAVE THEIR WORK CUT OUT FOR THEM.
IT'S A DIFFICULT MATCH UP, BUT ONCE WE NAIL IT, OUR MUSICAL HORIZONS WILL HAVE BROADENED.
WE MUST PRACTICE AS ONE!
IT'S ABOUT TIME WE HEAD TO THE RADIO STATION.
DON'T GET TOO NERVOUS, RIN.
WHY WOULD I?!

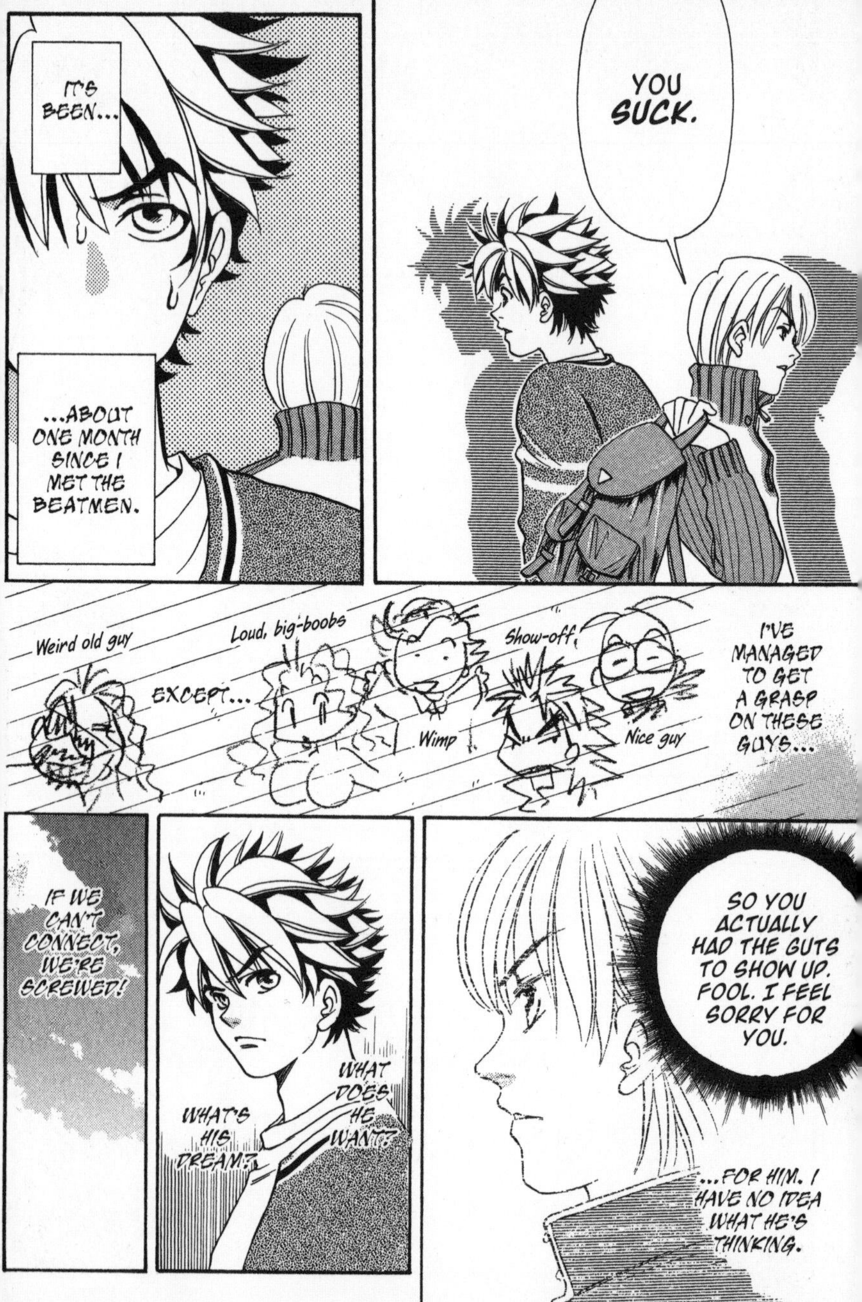
YOU SUCK.
IT'S BEEN...
...ABOUT ONE MONTH SINCE I MET THE BEATMEN.
I'VE MANAGED TO GET A GRASP ON THESE GUYS...
Nice guy
Show-off
Wimp
Loud, big-boobs
EXCEPT...
Weird old guy
SO YOU ACTUALLY HAD THE GUTS TO SHOW UP. FOOL. I FEEL SORRY FOR YOU.
...FOR HIM. I HAVE NO IDEA WHAT HE'S THINKING.
WHAT DOES HE WANT?
WHAT'S HIS DREAM?
IF WE CAN'T CONNECT, WE'RE SCREWED!

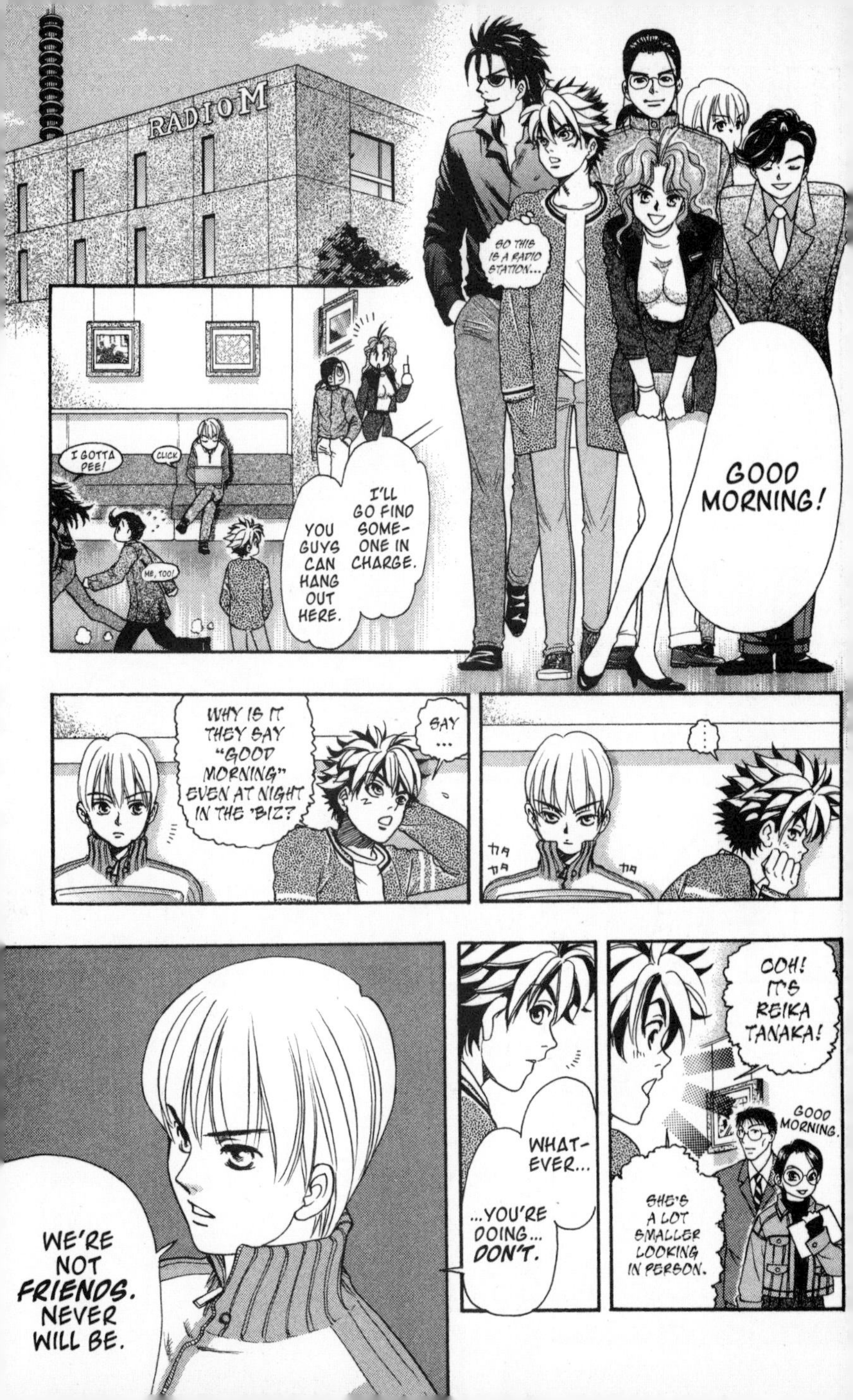
GOOD MORNING!
SO THIS IS A RADIO STATION...
RADIO M
I'LL GO FIND SOME-ONE IN CHARGE.
YOU GUYS CAN HANG OUT HERE.
CLICK
I GOTTA PEE!
ME, TOO!
...
カタ
カタ カタ
SAY ...
WHY IS IT THEY SAY "GOOD MORNING" EVEN AT NIGHT IN THE 'BIZ?
OOH! IT'S REIKA TANAKA!
GOOD MORNING.
SHE'S A LOT SMALLER LOOKING IN PERSON.
WHAT-EVER...
...YOU'RE DOING... DON'T.
WE'RE NOT FRIENDS. NEVER WILL BE.

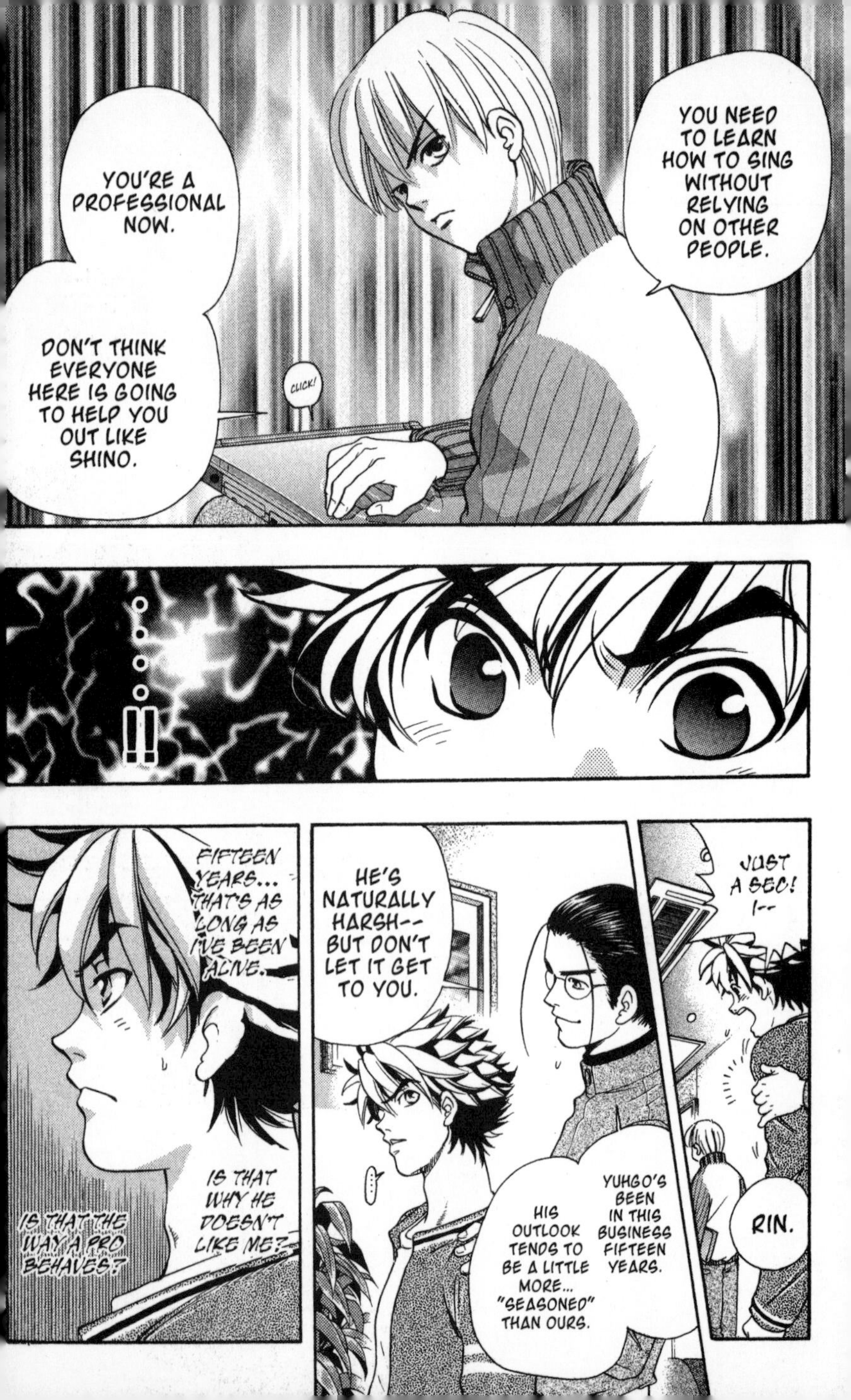
YOU NEED TO LEARN HOW TO SING WITHOUT RELYING ON OTHER PEOPLE.
YOU'RE A PROFESSIONAL NOW.
CLICK!
DON'T THINK EVERYONE HERE IS GOING TO HELP YOU OUT LIKE SHINO.
......!!
JUST A SEC! I--
RIN.
HE'S NATURALLY HARSH-- BUT DON'T LET IT GET TO YOU.
YUHGO'S BEEN IN THIS BUSINESS FIFTEEN YEARS.
HIS OUTLOOK TENDS TO BE A LITTLE MORE... "SEASONED" THAN OURS.
...
FIFTEEN YEARS... THAT'S AS LONG AS I'VE BEEN ALIVE.
IS THAT WHY HE DOESN'T LIKE ME?
IS THAT THE WAY A PRO BEHAVES?

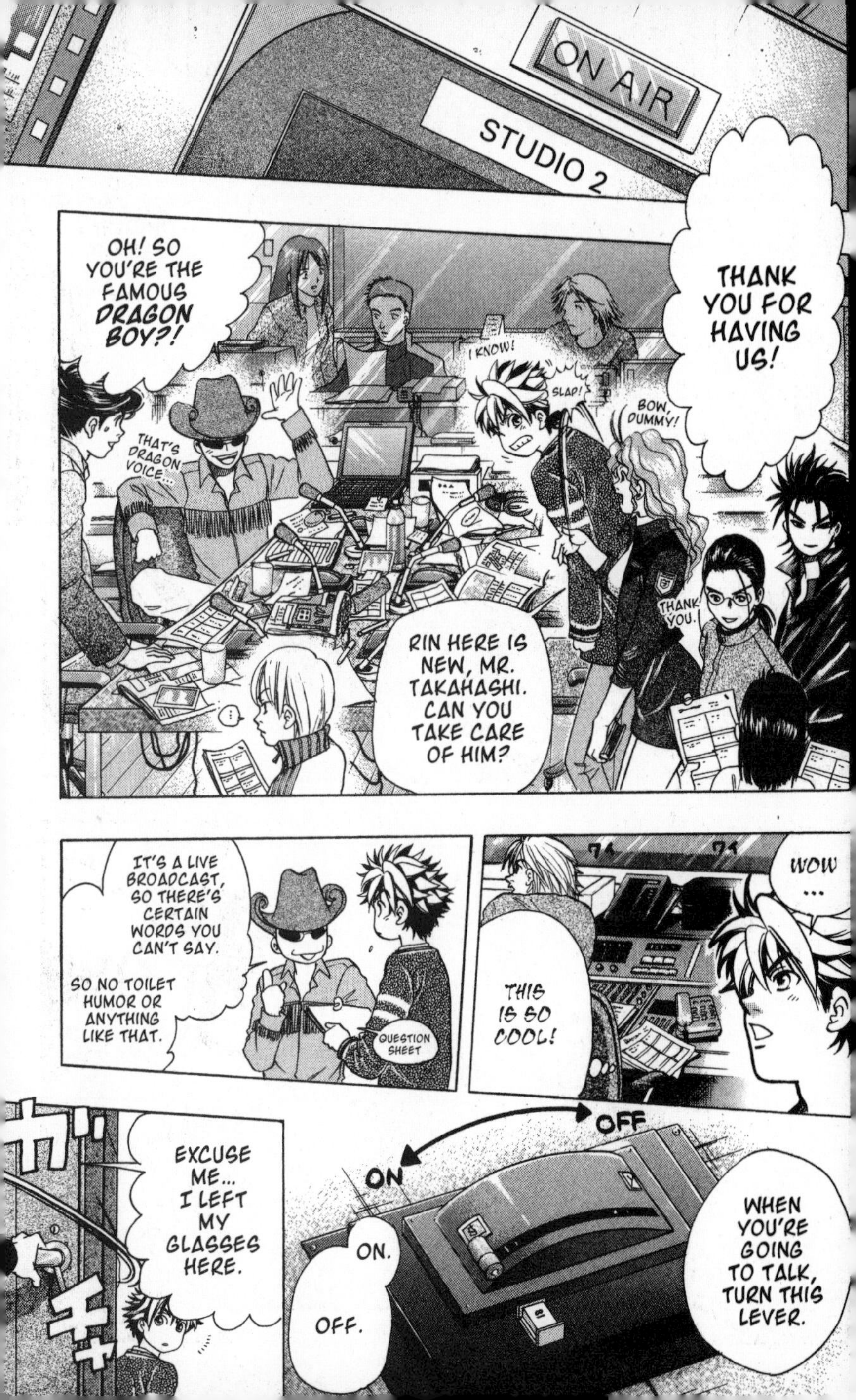
ON AIR
STUDIO 2
THANK YOU FOR HAVING US!
BOW, DUMMY!
SLAP!
I KNOW!
THANK YOU.
OH! SO YOU'RE THE FAMOUS DRAGON BOY?!
THAT'S DRAGON VOICE...
RIN HERE IS NEW, MR. TAKAHASHI. CAN YOU TAKE CARE OF HIM?
WOW...
THIS IS SO COOL!
IT'S A LIVE BROADCAST, SO THERE'S CERTAIN WORDS YOU CAN'T SAY.
SO NO TOILET HUMOR OR ANYTHING LIKE THAT.
QUESTION SHEET
WHEN YOU'RE GOING TO TALK, TURN THIS LEVER.
OFF
ON
ON.
OFF.
EXCUSE ME... I LEFT MY GLASSES HERE.

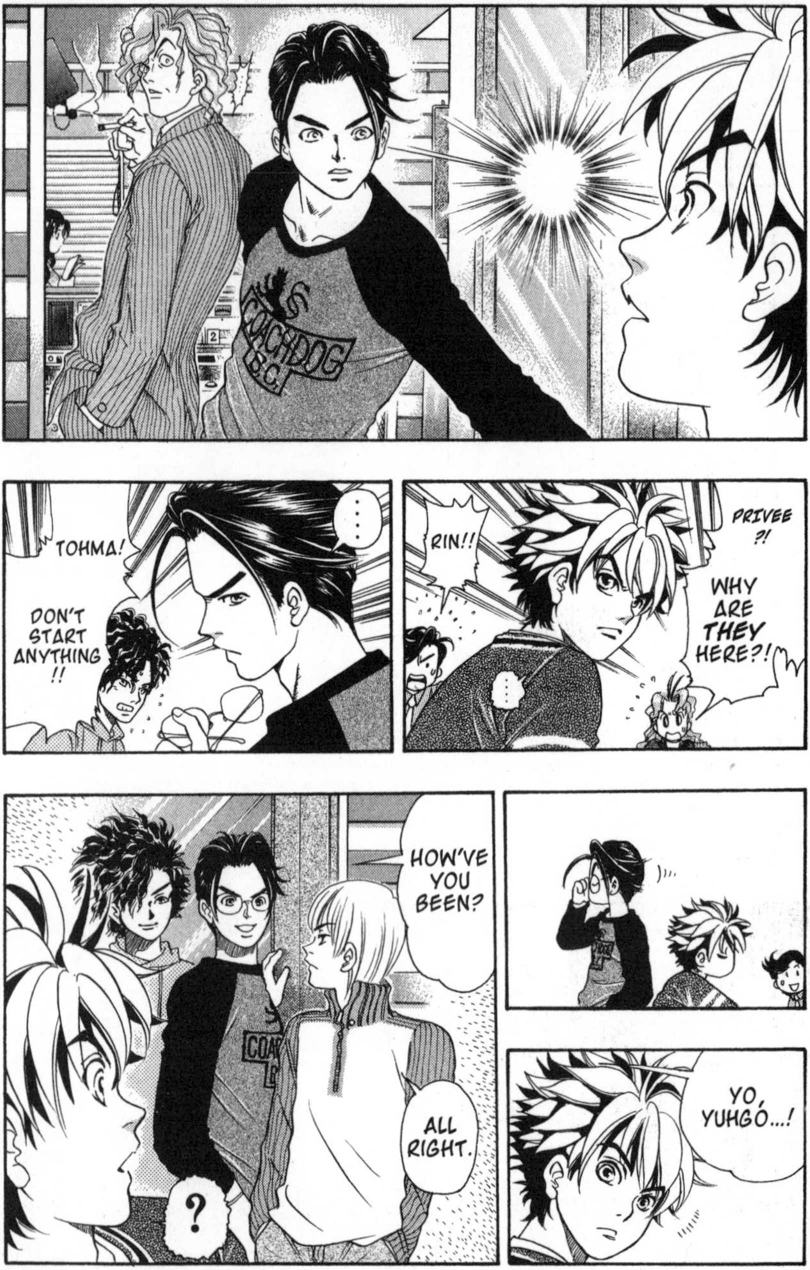
PRIVEE ?!
RIN!!
WHY ARE THEY HERE?!
. . .
TOHMA!
DON'T START ANYTHING !!
YO, YUHGO...!
HOW'VE YOU BEEN?
ALL RIGHT.
?

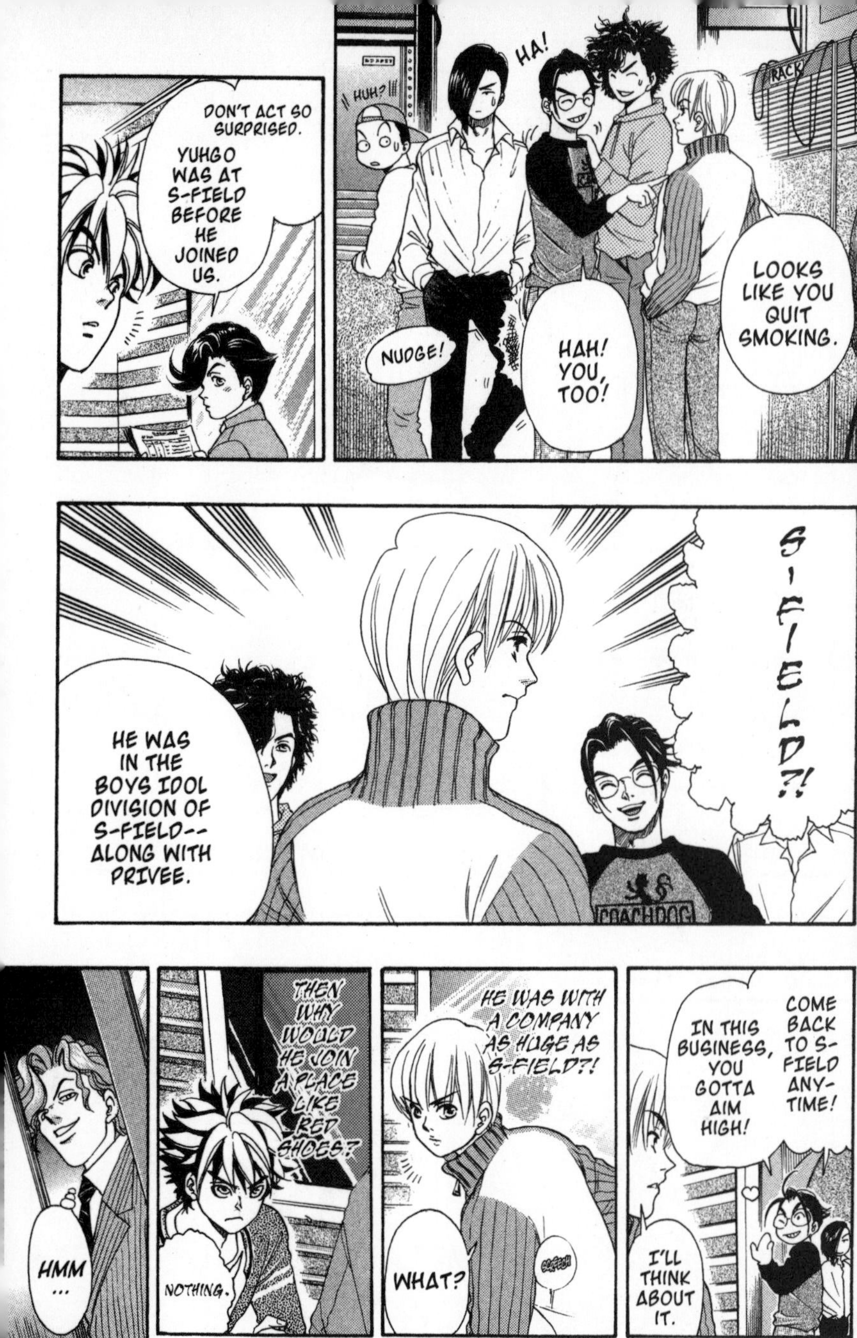
RACK
LOOKS LIKE YOU QUIT SMOKING.
HA!
HAH! YOU, TOO!
HUH?
NUDGE!
DON'T ACT SO SURPRISED.
YUHGO WAS AT S-FIELD BEFORE HE JOINED US.
S-FIELD?!
HE WAS IN THE BOYS IDOL DIVISION OF S-FIELD--ALONG WITH PRIVEE.
COACHDOG
COME BACK TO S-FIELD ANYTIME!
IN THIS BUSINESS, YOU GOTTA AIM HIGH!
I'LL THINK ABOUT IT.
HE WAS WITH A COMPANY AS HUGE AS S-FIELD?!
SCRATCH
WHAT?
THEN WHY WOULD HE JOIN A PLACE LIKE RED SHOES?
NOTHING.
HMM ...

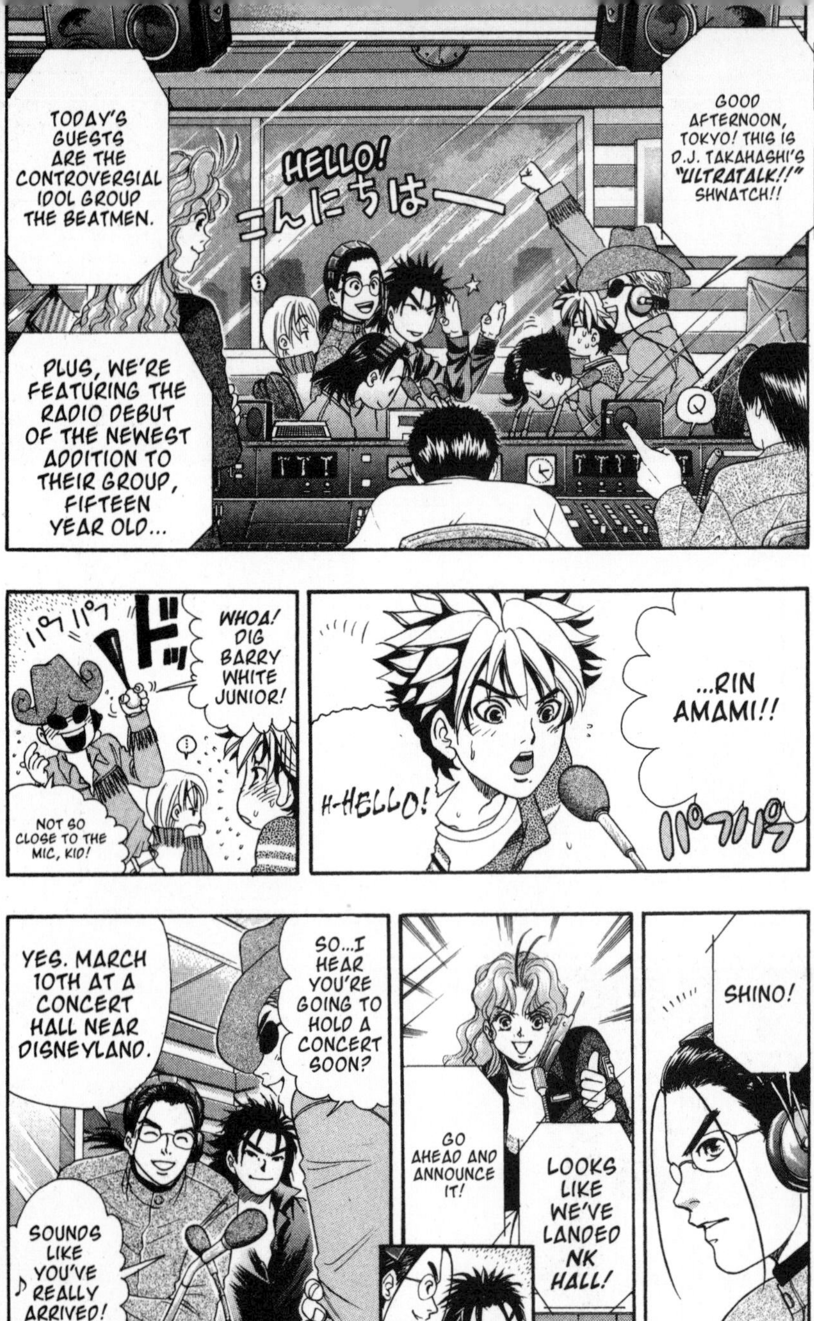
GOOD AFTERNOON, TOKYO! THIS IS D.J. TAKAHASHI'S "ULTRATALK!!" SHWATCH!!
HELLO!
こんにちはー
TODAY'S GUESTS ARE THE CONTROVERSIAL IDOL GROUP THE BEATMEN.
Q
PLUS, WE'RE FEATURING THE RADIO DEBUT OF THE NEWEST ADDITION TO THEIR GROUP, FIFTEEN YEAR OLD...
...RIN AMAMI!!
パフパ
H-HELLO!
WHOA! DIG BARRY WHITE JUNIOR!
ドッ
パフパフ
NOT SO CLOSE TO THE MIC, KID!
SHINO!
LOOKS LIKE WE'VE LANDED NK HALL!
GO AHEAD AND ANNOUNCE IT!
SO...I HEAR YOU'RE GOING TO HOLD A CONCERT SOON?
YES. MARCH 10TH AT A CONCERT HALL NEAR DISNEYLAND.
SOUNDS LIKE YOU'VE REALLY ARRIVED! ♪

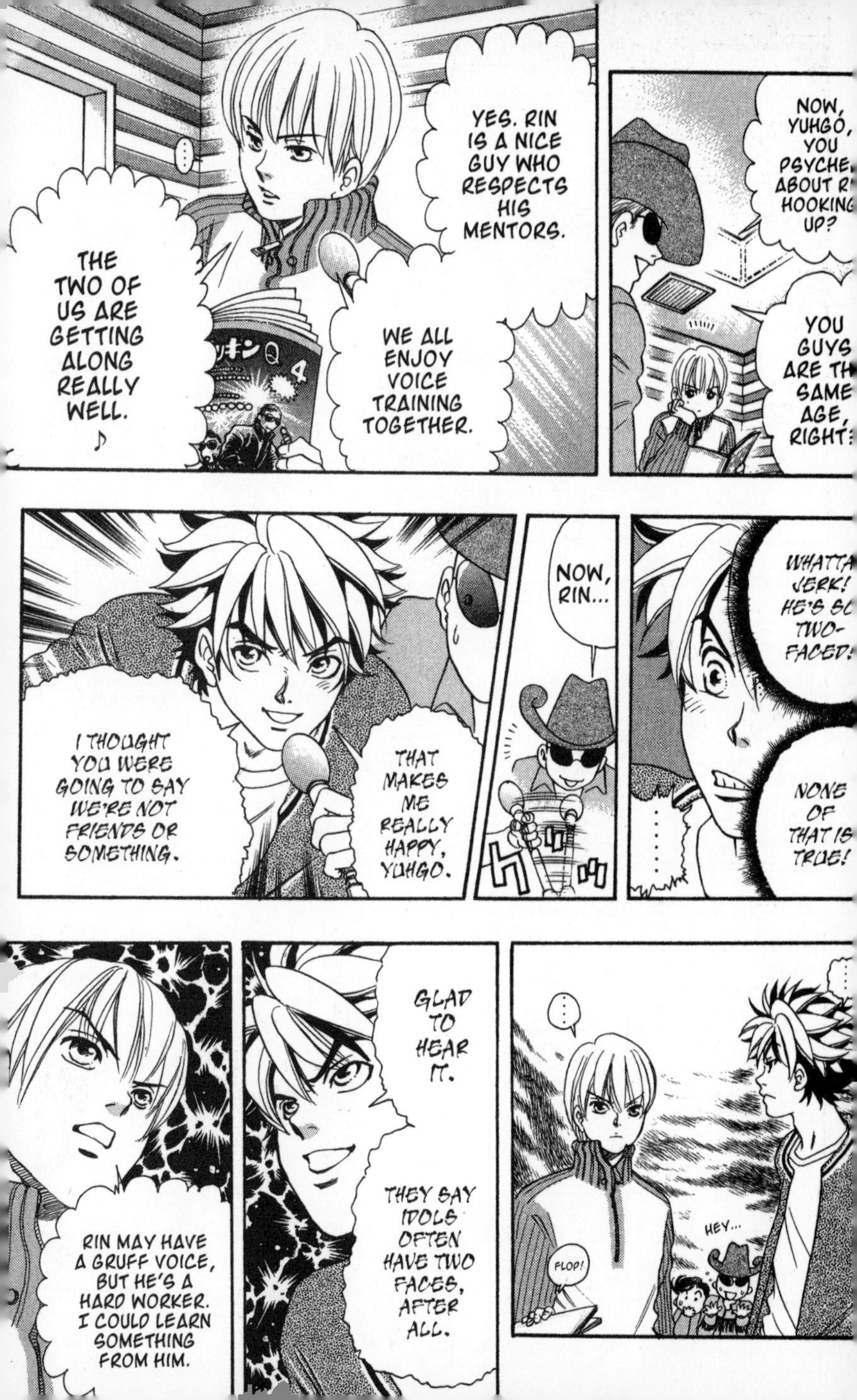
NOW, YUHGO, YOU PSYCHE ABOUT R HOOKING UP?
YOU GUYS ARE TH SAME AGE, RIGHT?
YES. RIN IS A NICE GUY WHO RESPECTS HIS MENTORS.
...
WE ALL ENJOY VOICE TRAINING TOGETHER.
THE TWO OF US ARE GETTING ALONG REALLY WELL. ♪
WHATTA JERK! HE'S SO TWO-FACED!
NONE OF THAT IS TRUE!
......
NOW, RIN...
THAT MAKES ME REALLY HAPPY, YUHGO.
I THOUGHT YOU WERE GOING TO SAY WE'RE NOT FRIENDS OR SOMETHING.
...
...
HEY...
FLOP!
GLAD TO HEAR IT.
THEY SAY IDOLS OFTEN HAVE TWO FACES, AFTER ALL.
RIN MAY HAVE A GRUFF VOICE, BUT HE'S A HARD WORKER. I COULD LEARN SOMETHING FROM HIM.

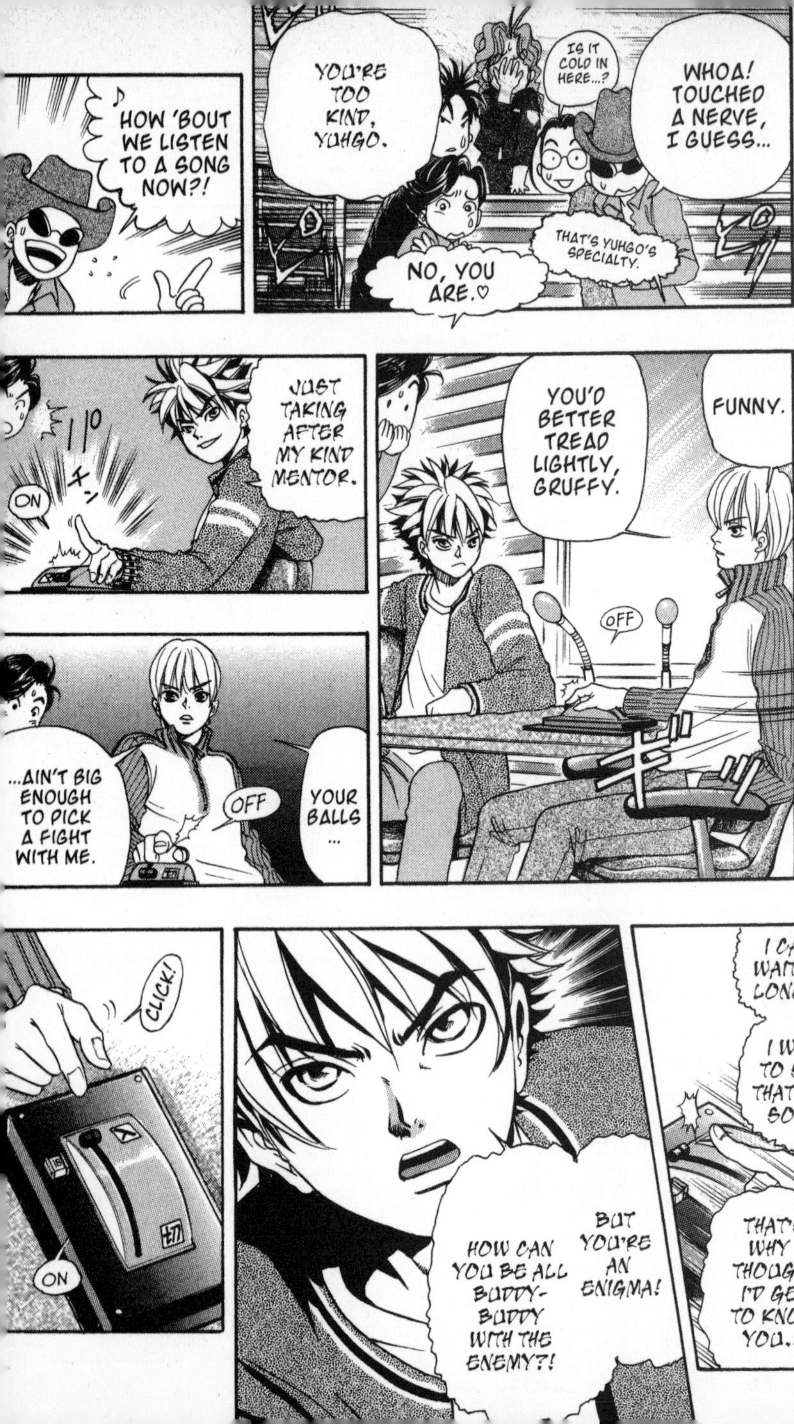
WHOA! TOUCHED A NERVE, I GUESS...
IS IT COLD IN HERE...?
YOU'RE TOO KIND, YUHGO.
THAT'S YUHGO'S SPECIALTY.
NO, YOU ARE.♡
♪ HOW 'BOUT WE LISTEN TO A SONG NOW?!
FUNNY.
YOU'D BETTER TREAD LIGHTLY, GRUFFY.
OFF
JUST TAKING AFTER MY KIND MENTOR.
ON
YOUR BALLS ...
...AIN'T BIG ENOUGH TO PICK A FIGHT WITH ME.
OFF
I CAN'T WAIT ANY LONGER.
I WANT TO SING THAT NEW SONG!
THAT'S WHY I THOUGHT I'D GET TO KNOW YOU...
BUT YOU'RE AN ENIGMA!
HOW CAN YOU BE ALL BUDDY-BUDDY WITH THE ENEMY?!
CLICK!
ON

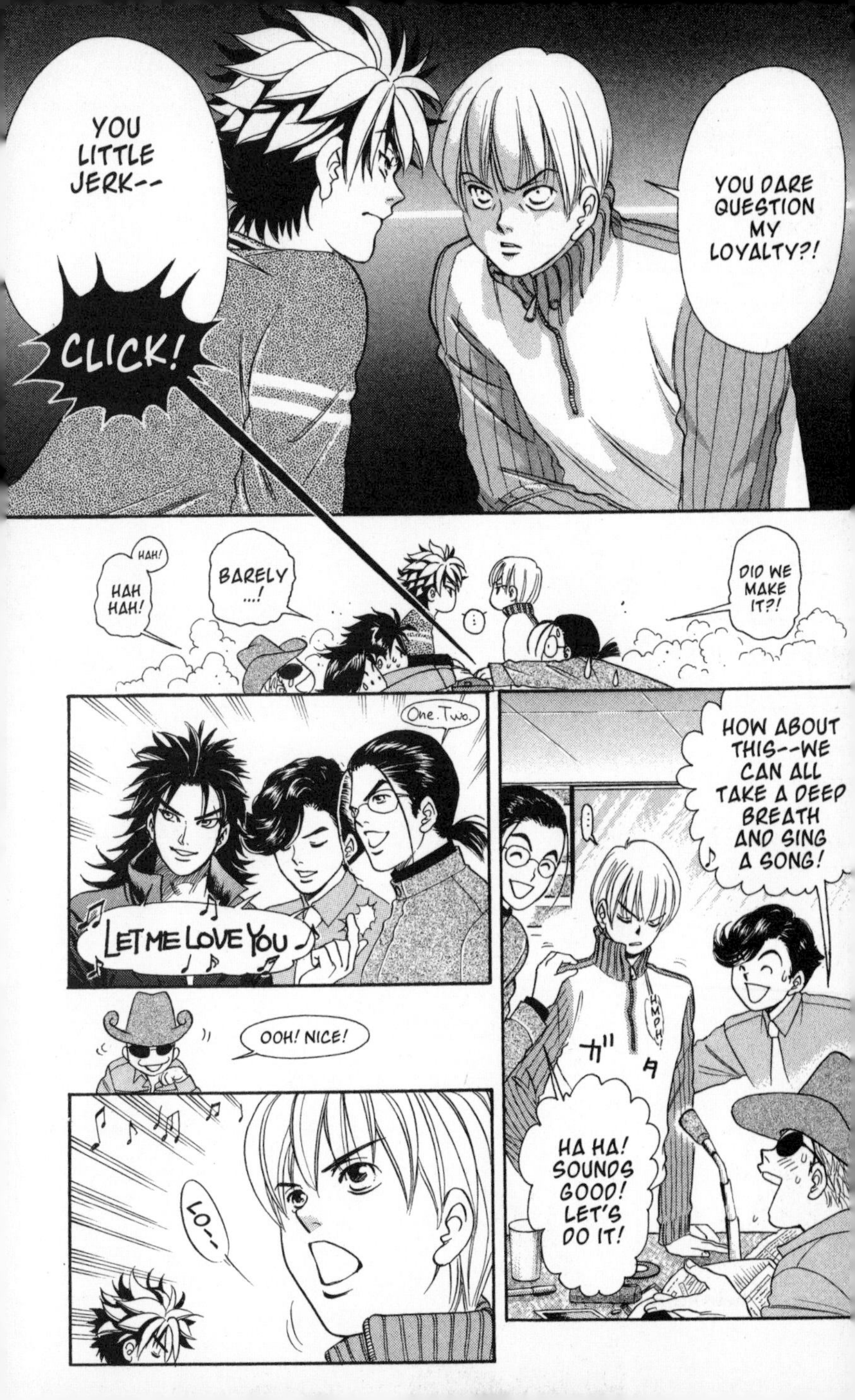
YOU DARE QUESTION MY LOYALTY?!
YOU LITTLE JERK--
CLICK!
DID WE MAKE IT?!
...
BARELY ...!
HAH!
HAH HAH!
HOW ABOUT THIS--WE CAN ALL TAKE A DEEP BREATH AND SING A SONG!
...
HMPH!
ガタ
HA HA! SOUNDS GOOD! LET'S DO IT!
One. Two.
LET ME LOVE YOU
OOH! NICE!
LO--

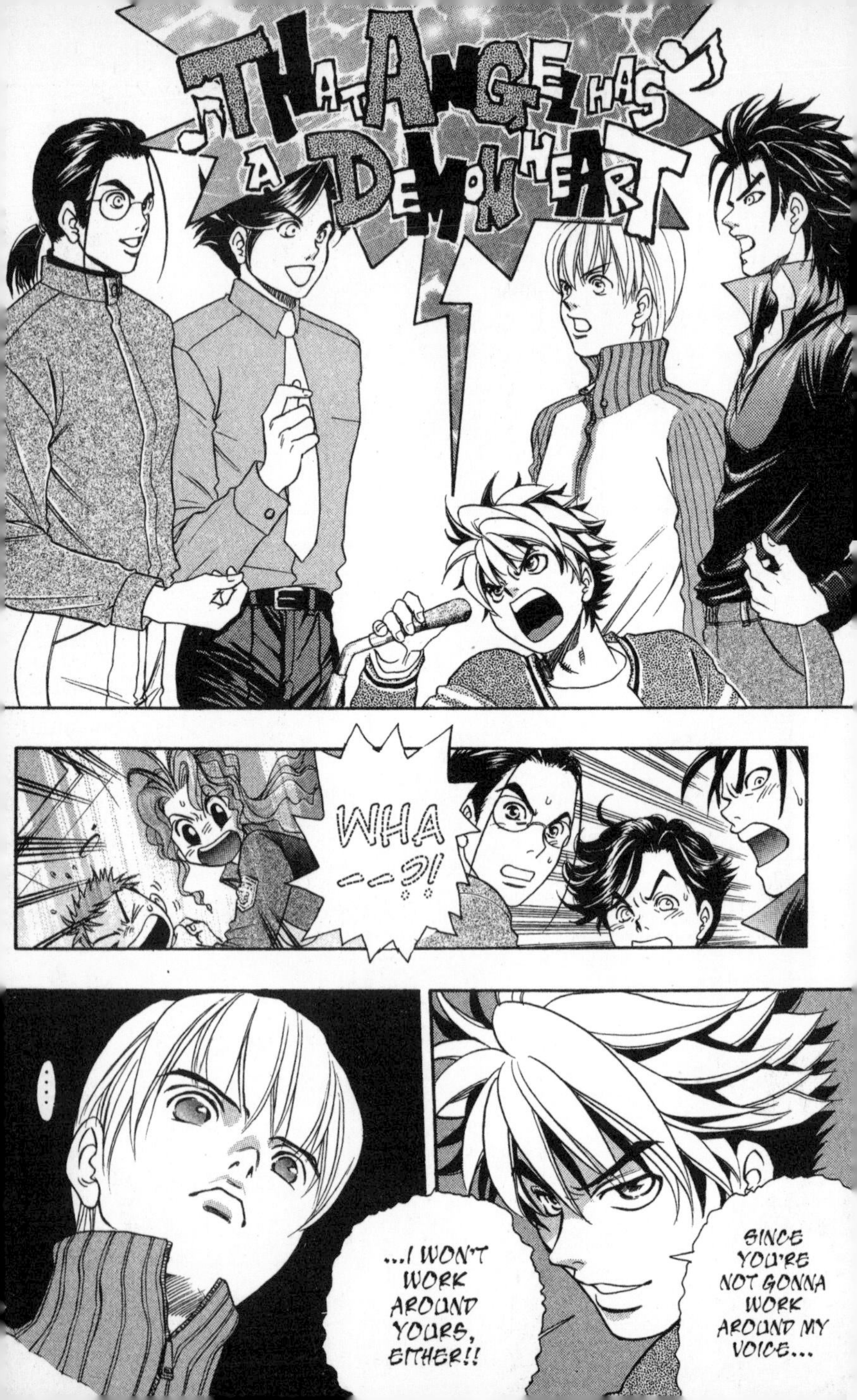

THAT ANGEL HAS A DEMON HEART
WHA---?!
SINCE YOU'RE NOT GONNA WORK AROUND MY VOICE...
...I WON'T WORK AROUND YOURS, EITHER!!
...

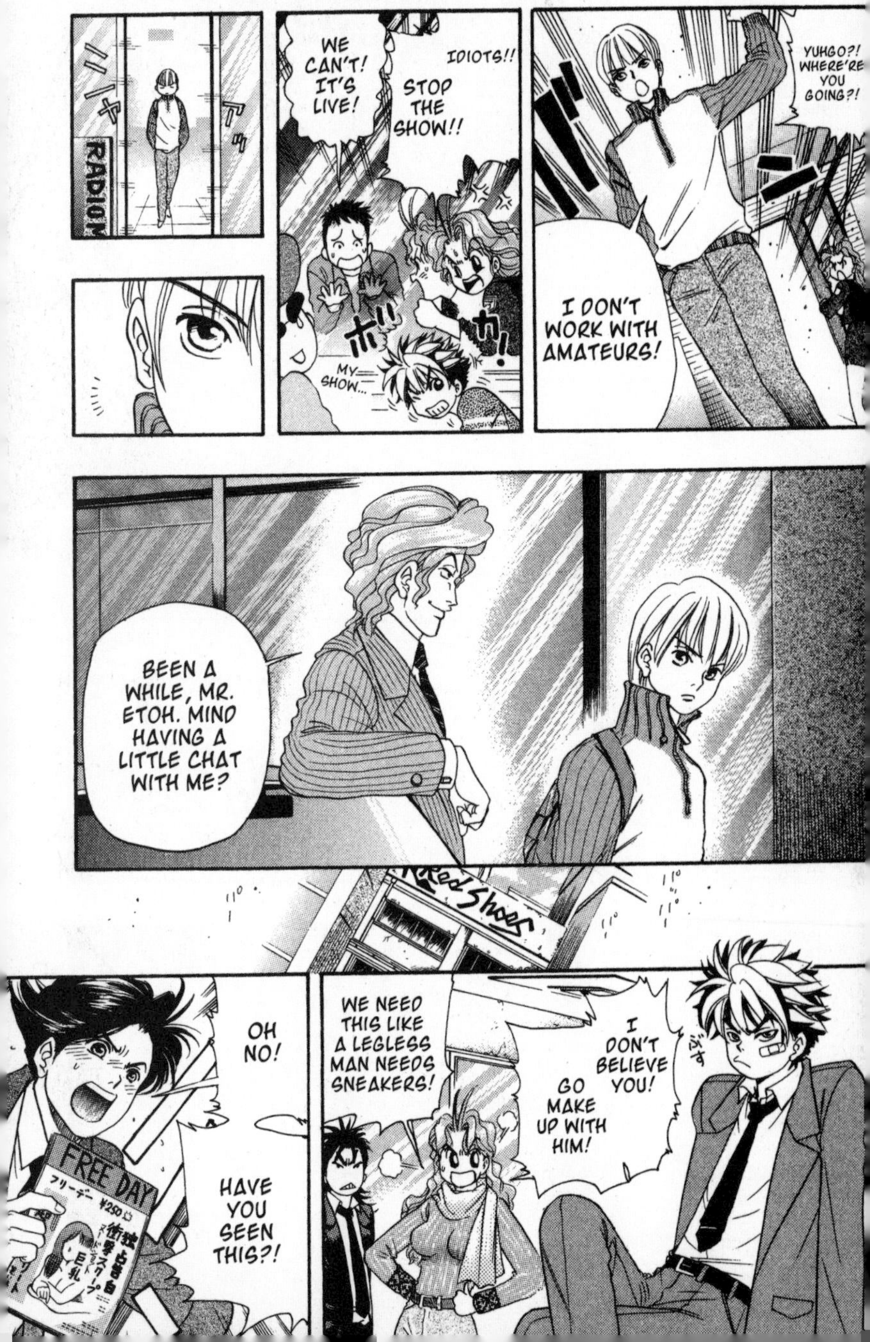
YUHGO?! WHERE'RE YOU GOING?!
I DON'T WORK WITH AMATEURS!
IDIOTS!!
STOP THE SHOW!!
WE CAN'T! IT'S LIVE!
MY SHOW...
RADIO M
BEEN A WHILE, MR. ETOH. MIND HAVING A LITTLE CHAT WITH ME?
Red Shoes
I DON'T BELIEVE YOU!
GO MAKE UP WITH HIM!
WE NEED THIS LIKE A LEGLESS MAN NEEDS SNEAKERS!
OH NO!
HAVE YOU SEEN THIS?!
FREE DAY
フリーデー ¥250

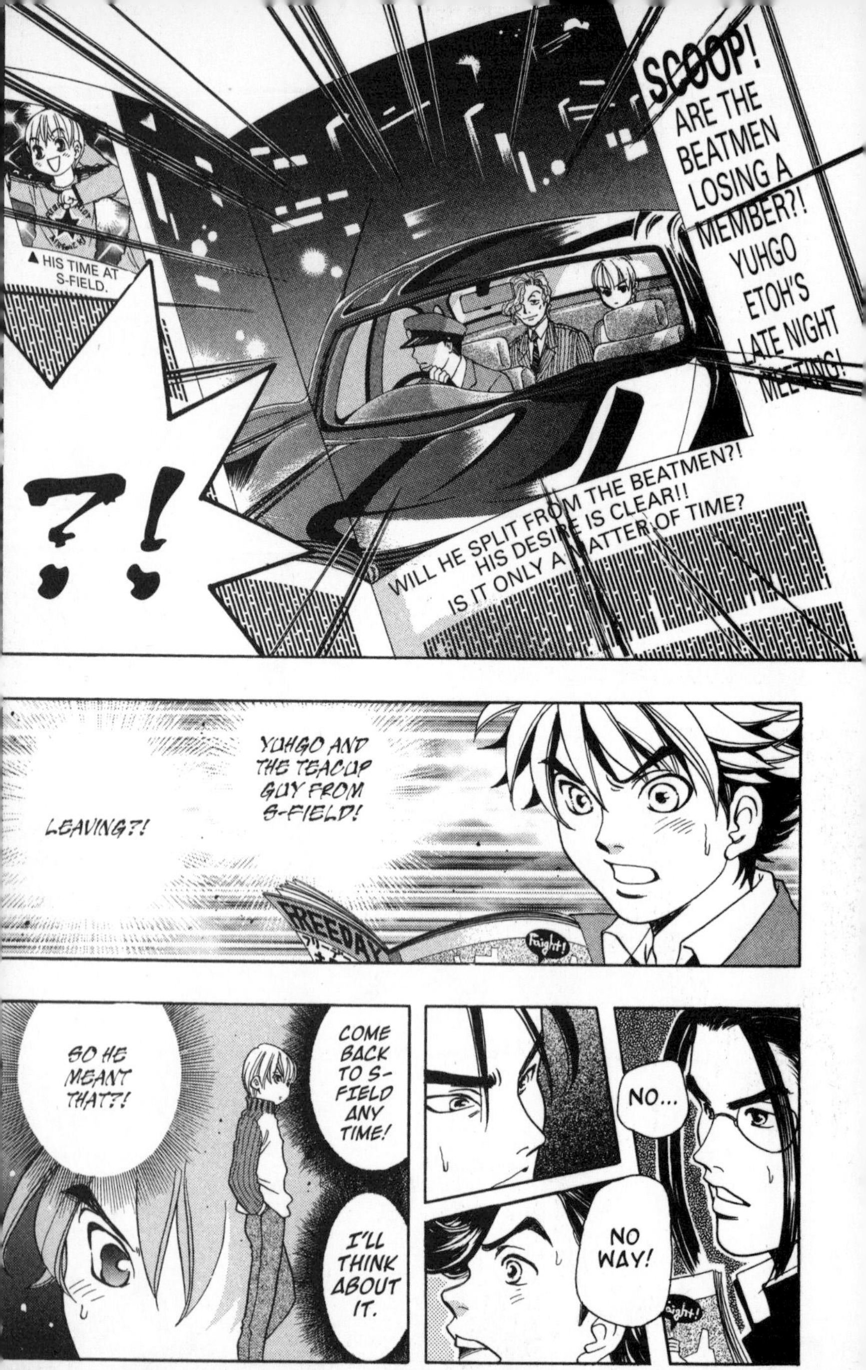
SCOOP!
ARE THE BEATMEN LOSING A MEMBER?! YUHGO ETOH'S LATE NIGHT MEETING!
WILL HE SPLIT FROM THE BEATMEN?! HIS DESIRE IS CLEAR!! IS IT ONLY A MATTER OF TIME?
▲ HIS TIME AT S-FIELD.
?!
YUHGO AND THE TEACUP GUY FROM S-FIELD!
LEAVING?!
FREEDAY
Faight!
NO...
NO WAY!
Faight!
COME BACK TO S-FIELD ANY TIME!
I'LL THINK ABOUT IT.
SO HE MEANT THAT?!

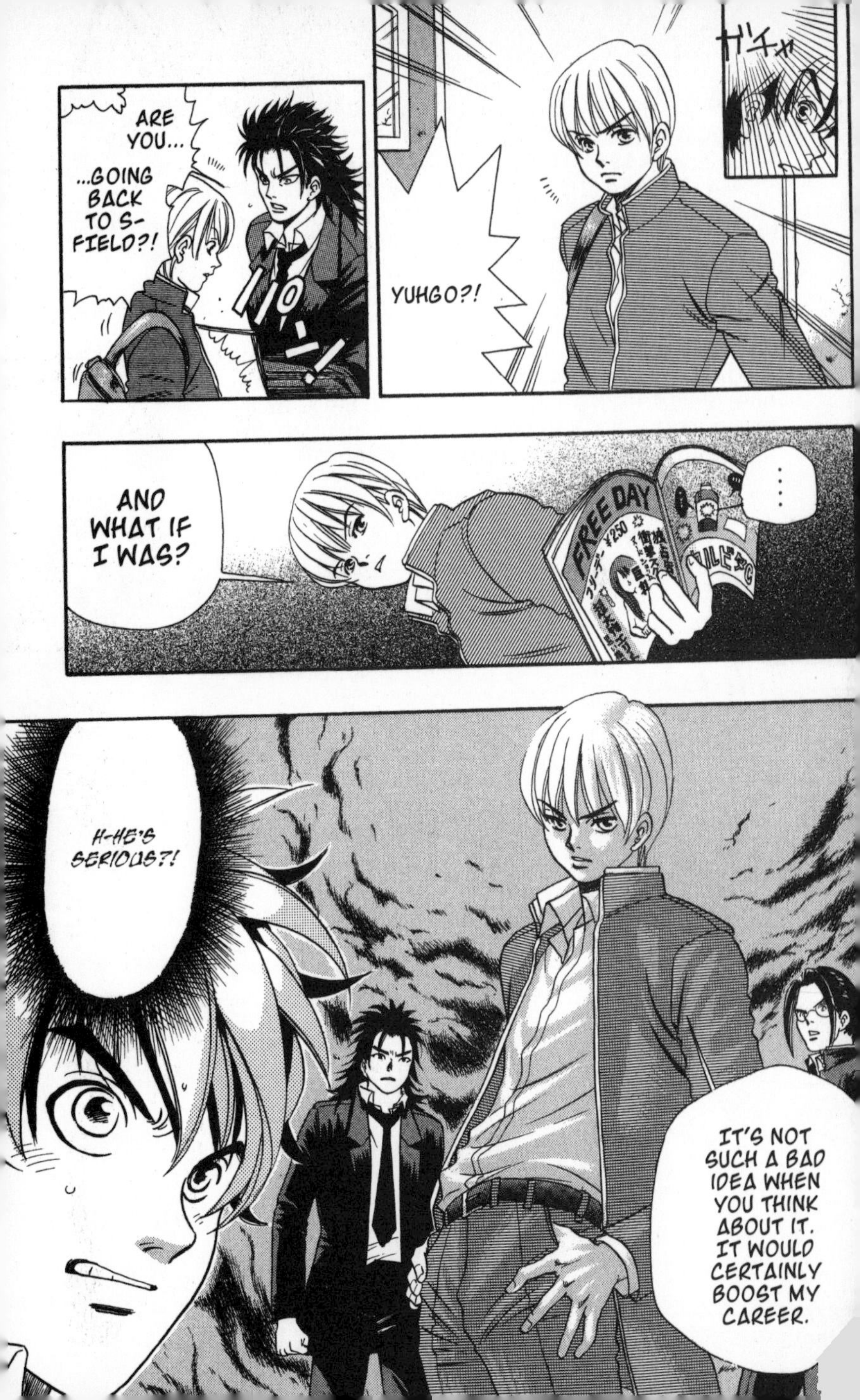
ガチャ
YUHGO?!
ARE YOU...
...GOING BACK TO S-FIELD?!
....
FREE DAY
¥250
AND WHAT IF I WAS?
H-HE'S SERIOUS?!
IT'S NOT SUCH A BAD IDEA WHEN YOU THINK ABOUT IT. IT WOULD CERTAINLY BOOST MY CAREER.

# YUHGO ETOH

THIS IS THE BEATMEN'S TOP TENOR (THE HIGHEST VOICE CATEGORY FOR A MALE), YUHGO ETOH, WHO HAS BEEN IN ENTERTAINMENT SINCE HE WAS BORN. HE MAY SEEM A LITTLE FEMININE, BUT HE DEFINITELY HAS A COOL AND FAIRLY STERN PERSONALITY. IF IT'LL HELP THE SUCCESS OF HIS CAREER, HE'LL PERFORM WHATEVER NECESSARY WITHOUT COMPLAINT. YUHGO CAN BE PRETTY COLD--"IT'S NOT NECESSARY FOR ME TO BE NICE TO PEOPLE WHO WOULD ONLY HOLD ME DOWN." HIS FAMILY SITUATION, HIS DREAMS, HIS GOALS--ALL REMAIN MYSTERIES. SHINO, GOH, AND TOSHIO PROBABLY DON'T KNOW, EITHER. MAYBE THE ARRIVAL OF RIN AMAMI WILL BREAK DOWN HIS BARRIERS.

YUHGO WASN'T ALWAYS THE WAY HE IS NOW. WHEN I FIRST STARTED PLANNING DRAGON VOICE, HE WAS A BRIGHT, YOUNG MARTIAL ARTIST (?!). BUT AFTER LISTENING TO THE ENGLISH GROUP 5IVE (THE GROUP I MENTIONED IN VOLUME ONE, UPON WHICH I BASED THE BEATMEN), I THOUGHT (FOR SOME REASON) A CHARACTER WHO SHOUTS OUT A SONG, BUT STILL MANAGES TO KEEP A COOL, COLLECTED FACE, WOULD BE A NICE ADDITION. I HOPE YOU'LL CONTINUE TO ENJOY YUHGO AS DRAGON VOICE CONTINUES!

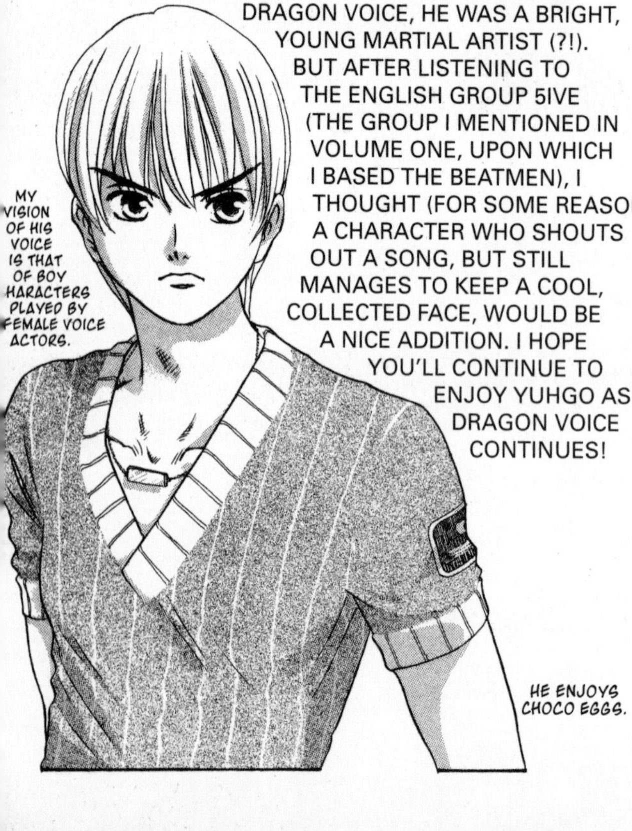
MY VISION OF HIS VOICE IS THAT OF BOY HARACTERS PLAYED BY FEMALE VOICE ACTORS.
HE ENJOYS CHOCO EGGS.

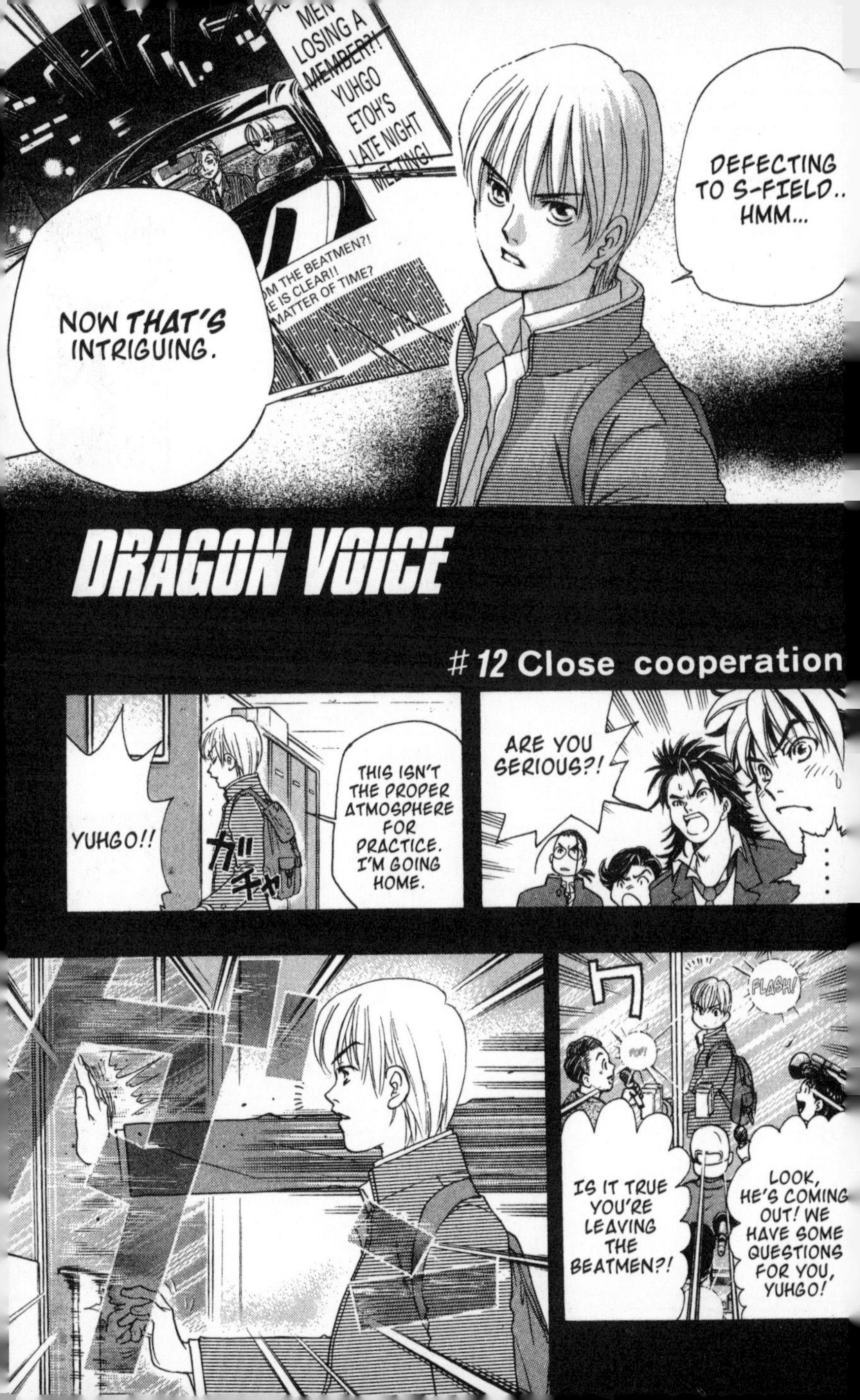
MEN LOSING A MEMBER?!! YUHGO ETOH'S LATE NIGHT MEETING!
M THE BEATMEN?! E IS CLEAR!! MATTER OF TIME?
DEFECTING TO S-FIELD.. HMM...
NOW THAT'S INTRIGUING.
DRAGON VOICE
# 12 Close cooperation
ARE YOU SERIOUS?!
...
THIS ISN'T THE PROPER ATMOSPHERE FOR PRACTICE. I'M GOING HOME.
ガチャ
YUHGO!!
FLASH!
POP!
LOOK, HE'S COMING OUT! WE HAVE SOME QUESTIONS FOR YOU, YUHGO!
IS IT TRUE YOU'RE LEAVING THE BEATMEN?!

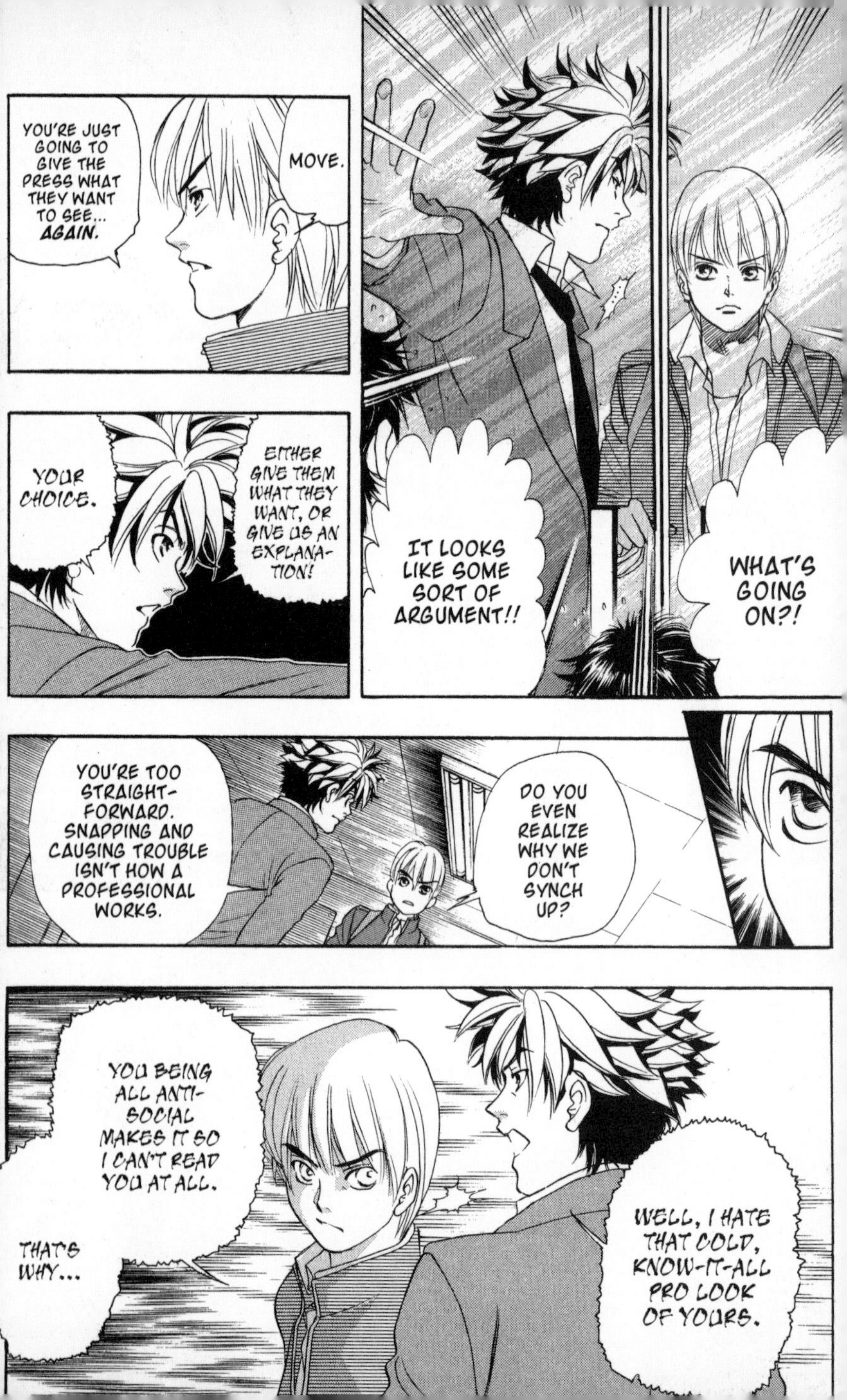
WHAT'S GOING ON?!
IT LOOKS LIKE SOME SORT OF ARGUMENT!!
MOVE.
YOU'RE JUST GOING TO GIVE THE PRESS WHAT THEY WANT TO SEE... AGAIN.
EITHER GIVE THEM WHAT THEY WANT, OR GIVE US AN EXPLANATION!
YOUR CHOICE.
DO YOU EVEN REALIZE WHY WE DON'T SYNCH UP?
YOU'RE TOO STRAIGHTFORWARD. SNAPPING AND CAUSING TROUBLE ISN'T HOW A PROFESSIONAL WORKS.
WELL, I HATE THAT COLD, KNOW-IT-ALL PRO LOOK OF YOURS.
YOU BEING ALL ANTI-SOCIAL MAKES IT SO I CAN'T READ YOU AT ALL.
THAT'S WHY...

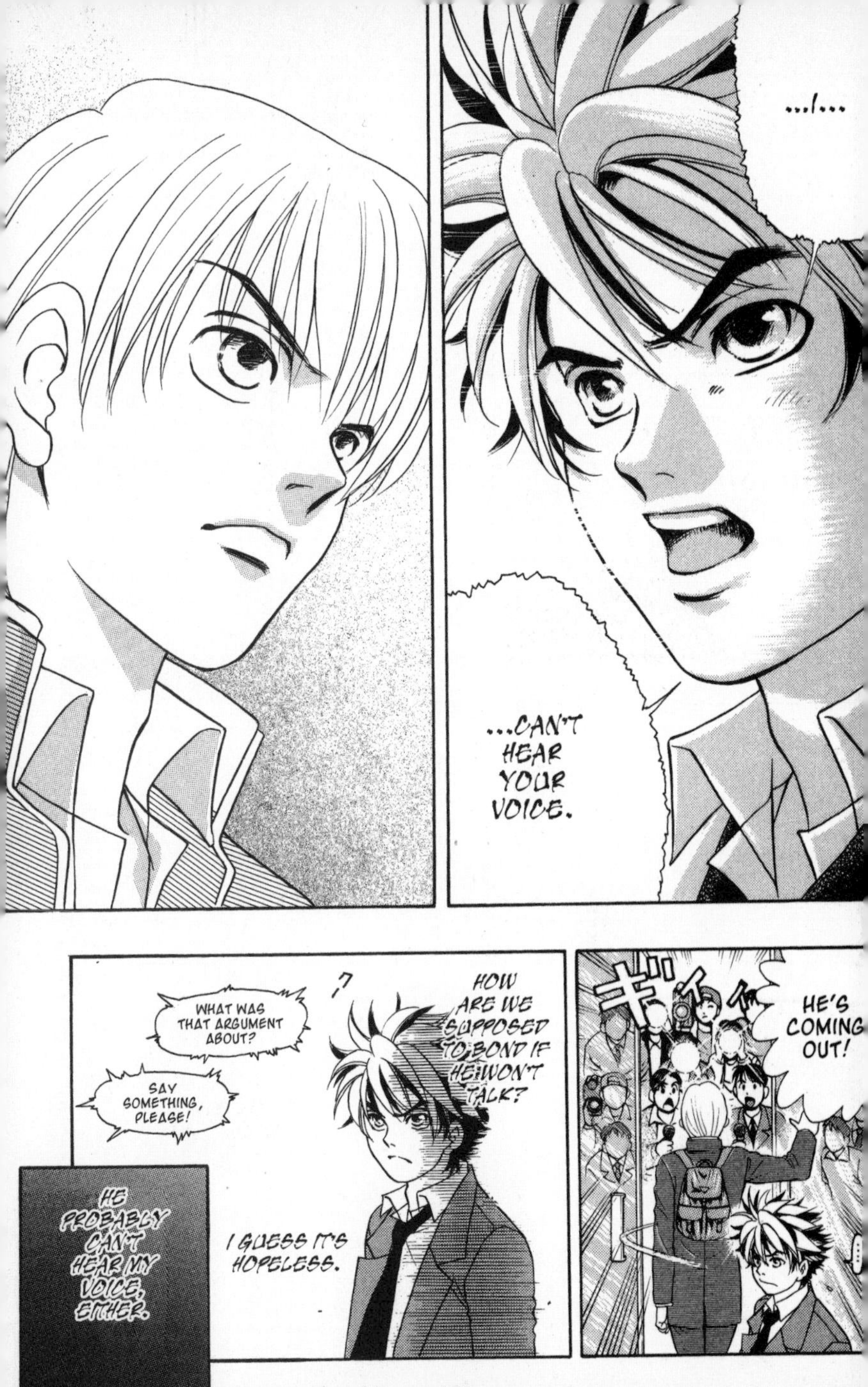
...I...
...CAN'T HEAR YOUR VOICE.
ギイィ
HE'S COMING OUT!
HOW ARE WE SUPPOSED TO BOND IF HE WON'T TALK?
?
WHAT WAS THAT ARGUMENT ABOUT?
SAY SOMETHING, PLEASE!
I GUESS IT'S HOPELESS.
HE PROBABLY CAN'T HEAR MY VOICE, EITHER.

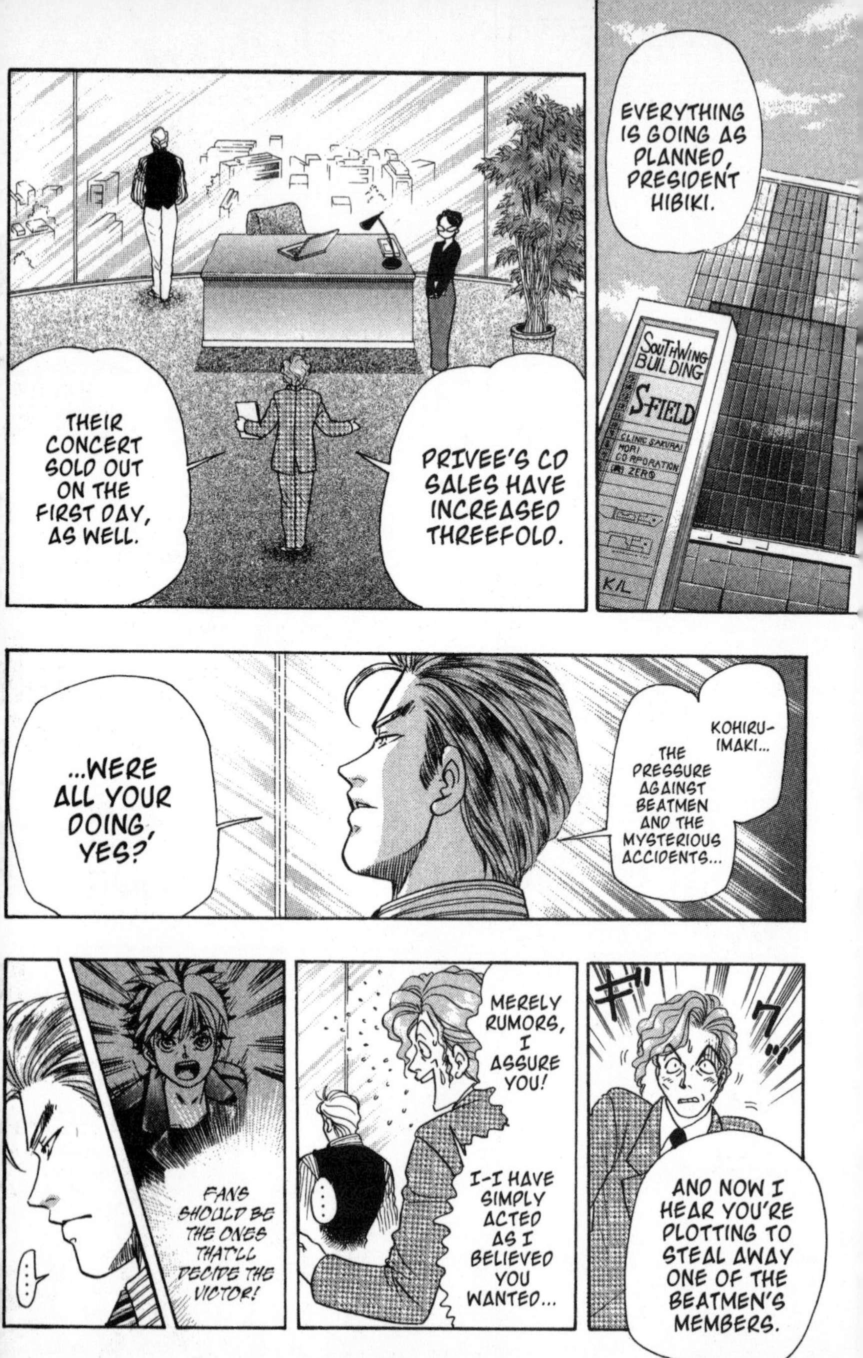
EVERYTHING IS GOING AS PLANNED, PRESIDENT HIBIKI.
SOUTH WING BUILDING
S-FIELD
CLINIC SAKURAI
MORI CORPORATION
ZERO
K/L
PRIVEE'S CD SALES HAVE INCREASED THREEFOLD.
THEIR CONCERT SOLD OUT ON THE FIRST DAY, AS WELL.
KOHIRU-IMAKI...
THE PRESSURE AGAINST BEATMEN AND THE MYSTERIOUS ACCIDENTS...
...WERE ALL YOUR DOING, YES?
ギク
AND NOW I HEAR YOU'RE PLOTTING TO STEAL AWAY ONE OF THE BEATMEN'S MEMBERS.
MERELY RUMORS, I ASSURE YOU!
I-I HAVE SIMPLY ACTED AS I BELIEVED YOU WANTED...
FANS SHOULD BE THE ONES THAT'LL DECIDE THE VICTOR!
....

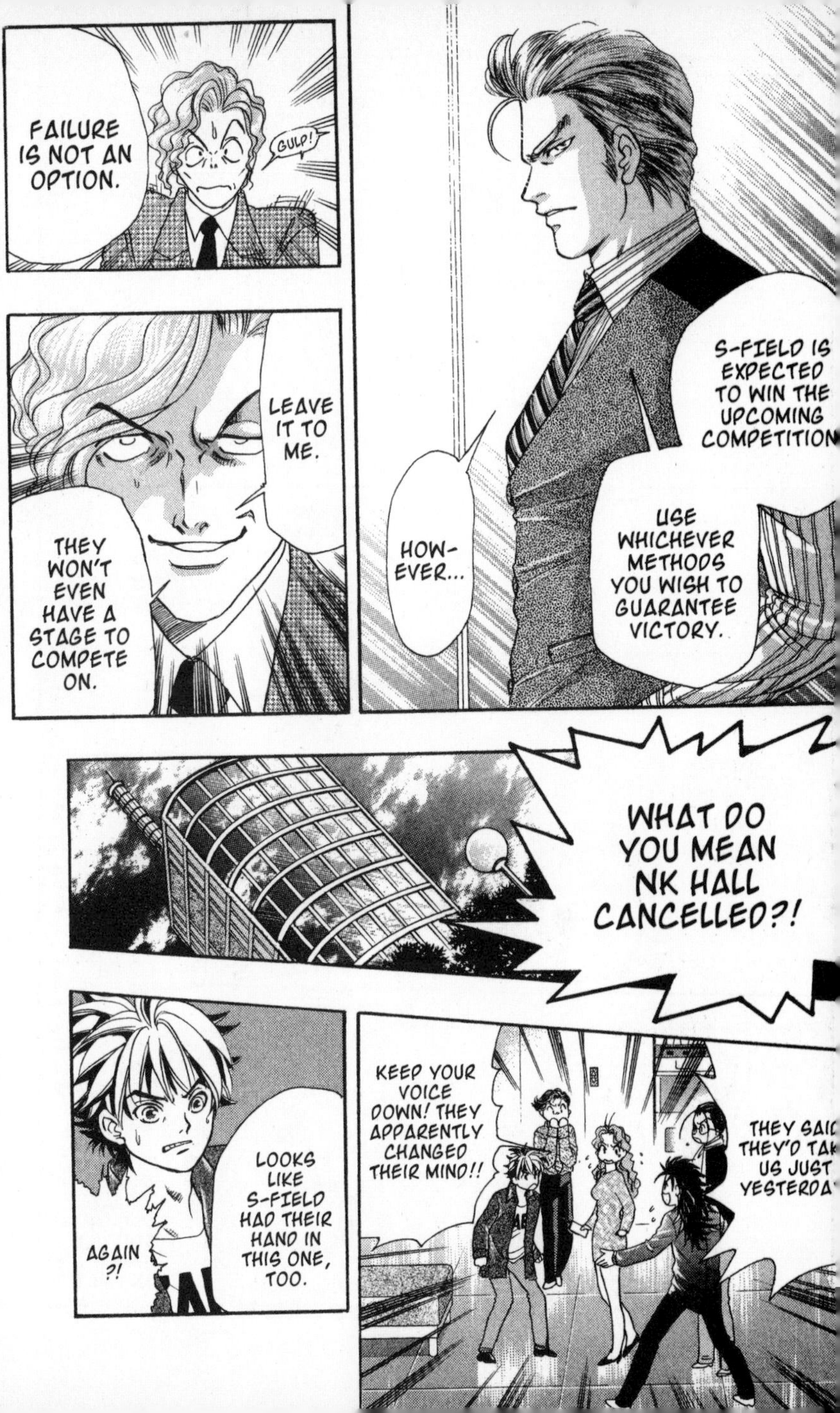
S-FIELD IS EXPECTED TO WIN THE UPCOMING COMPETITION
USE WHICHEVER METHODS YOU WISH TO GUARANTEE VICTORY.
HOW-EVER...
FAILURE IS NOT AN OPTION.
GULP!
LEAVE IT TO ME.
THEY WON'T EVEN HAVE A STAGE TO COMPETE ON.
WHAT DO YOU MEAN NK HALL CANCELLED?!
THEY SAID THEY'D TAK US JUST YESTERDA
KEEP YOUR VOICE DOWN! THEY APPARENTLY CHANGED THEIR MIND!!
LOOKS LIKE S-FIELD HAD THEIR HAND IN THIS ONE, TOO.
AGAIN ?!

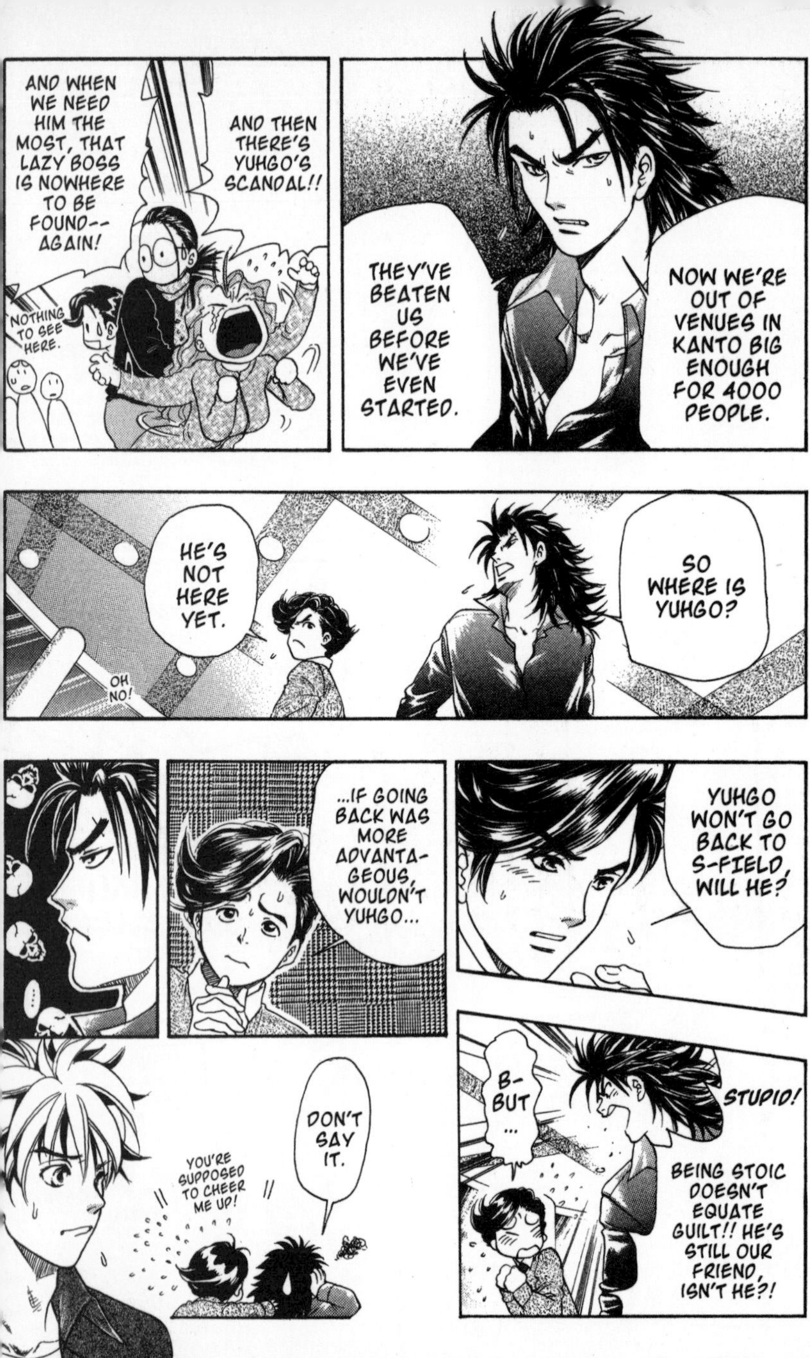
NOW WE'RE OUT OF VENUES IN KANTO BIG ENOUGH FOR 4000 PEOPLE.
THEY'VE BEATEN US BEFORE WE'VE EVEN STARTED.
AND THEN THERE'S YUHGO'S SCANDAL!!
AND WHEN WE NEED HIM THE MOST, THAT LAZY BOSS IS NOWHERE TO BE FOUND--AGAIN!
NOTHING TO SEE HERE.
SO WHERE IS YUHGO?
HE'S NOT HERE YET.
OH NO!
YUHGO WON'T GO BACK TO S-FIELD, WILL HE?
STUPID!
B-BUT...
BEING STOIC DOESN'T EQUATE GUILT!! HE'S STILL OUR FRIEND, ISN'T HE?!
...IF GOING BACK WAS MORE ADVANTA-GEOUS, WOULDN'T YUHGO...
...
DON'T SAY IT.
YOU'RE SUPPOSED TO CHEER ME UP!

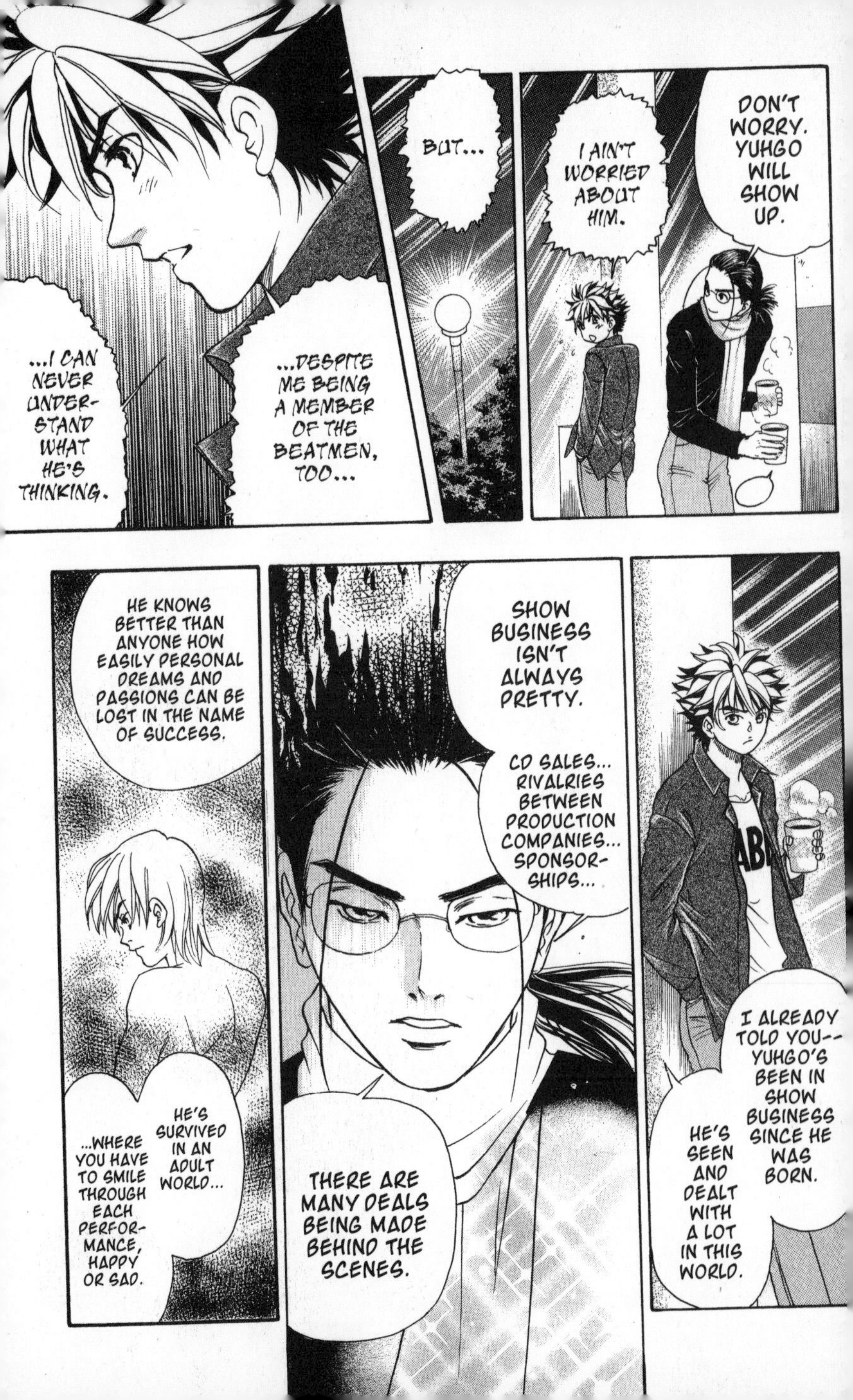
DON'T WORRY. YUHGO WILL SHOW UP.
I AIN'T WORRIED ABOUT HIM.
BUT...
...DESPITE ME BEING A MEMBER OF THE BEATMEN, TOO...
...I CAN NEVER UNDER-STAND WHAT HE'S THINKING.
I ALREADY TOLD YOU--YUHGO'S BEEN IN SHOW BUSINESS SINCE HE WAS BORN.
HE'S SEEN AND DEALT WITH A LOT IN THIS WORLD.
SHOW BUSINESS ISN'T ALWAYS PRETTY.
CD SALES... RIVALRIES BETWEEN PRODUCTION COMPANIES... SPONSOR-SHIPS...
THERE ARE MANY DEALS BEING MADE BEHIND THE SCENES.
HE KNOWS BETTER THAN ANYONE HOW EASILY PERSONAL DREAMS AND PASSIONS CAN BE LOST IN THE NAME OF SUCCESS.
HE'S SURVIVED IN AN ADULT WORLD...
...WHERE YOU HAVE TO SMILE THROUGH EACH PERFOR-MANCE, HAPPY OR SAD.

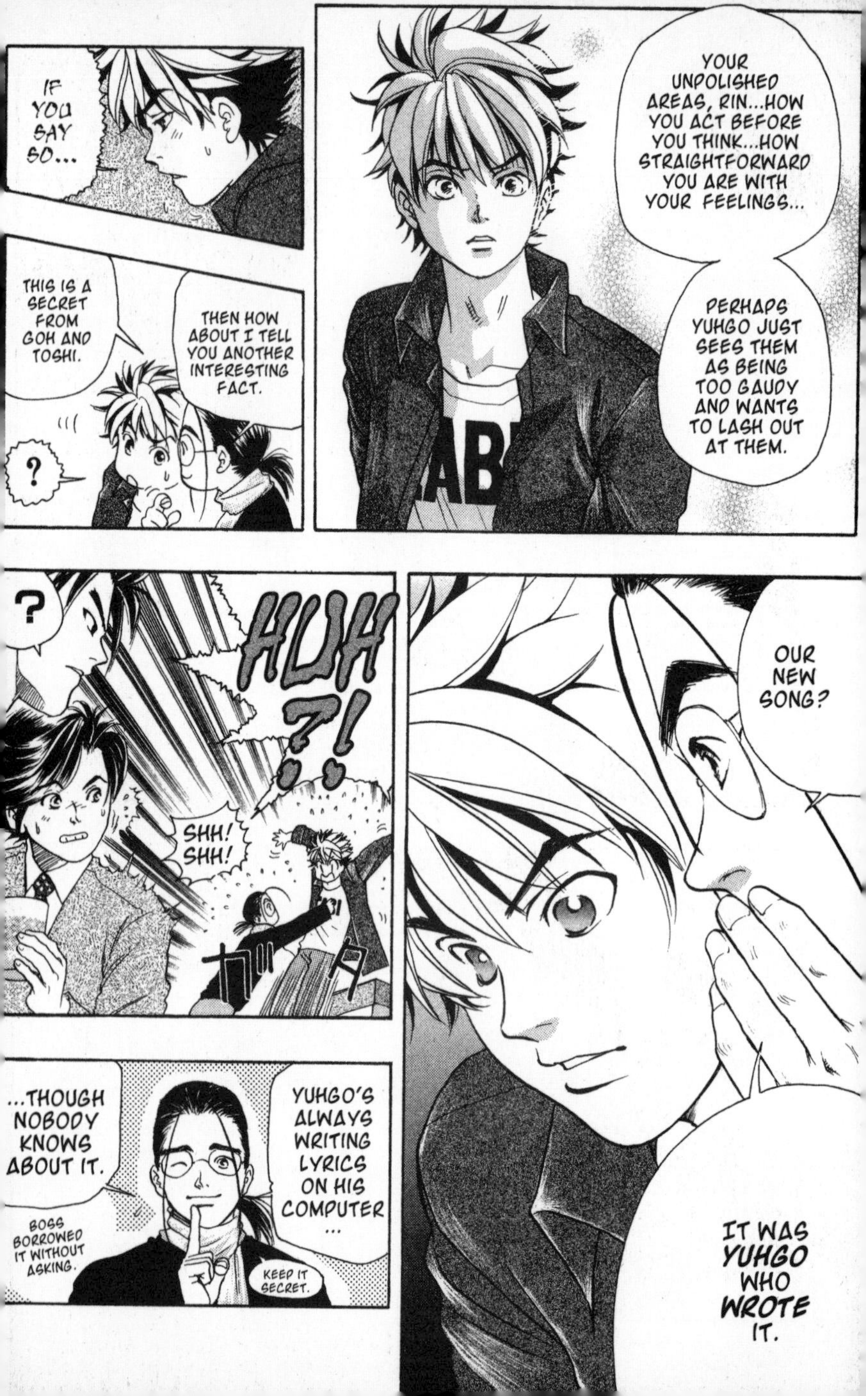
YOUR UNPOLISHED AREAS, RIN...HOW YOU ACT BEFORE YOU THINK...HOW STRAIGHTFORWARD YOU ARE WITH YOUR FEELINGS...
PERHAPS YUHGO JUST SEES THEM AS BEING TOO GAUDY AND WANTS TO LASH OUT AT THEM.
IF YOU SAY SO...
THEN HOW ABOUT I TELL YOU ANOTHER INTERESTING FACT.
THIS IS A SECRET FROM GOH AND TOSHI.
?
OUR NEW SONG?
IT WAS YUHGO WHO WROTE IT.
HUH ?!
?
SHH! SHH!
YUHGO'S ALWAYS WRITING LYRICS ON HIS COMPUTER...
...THOUGH NOBODY KNOWS ABOUT IT.
KEEP IT SECRET.
BOSS BORROWED IT WITHOUT ASKING.

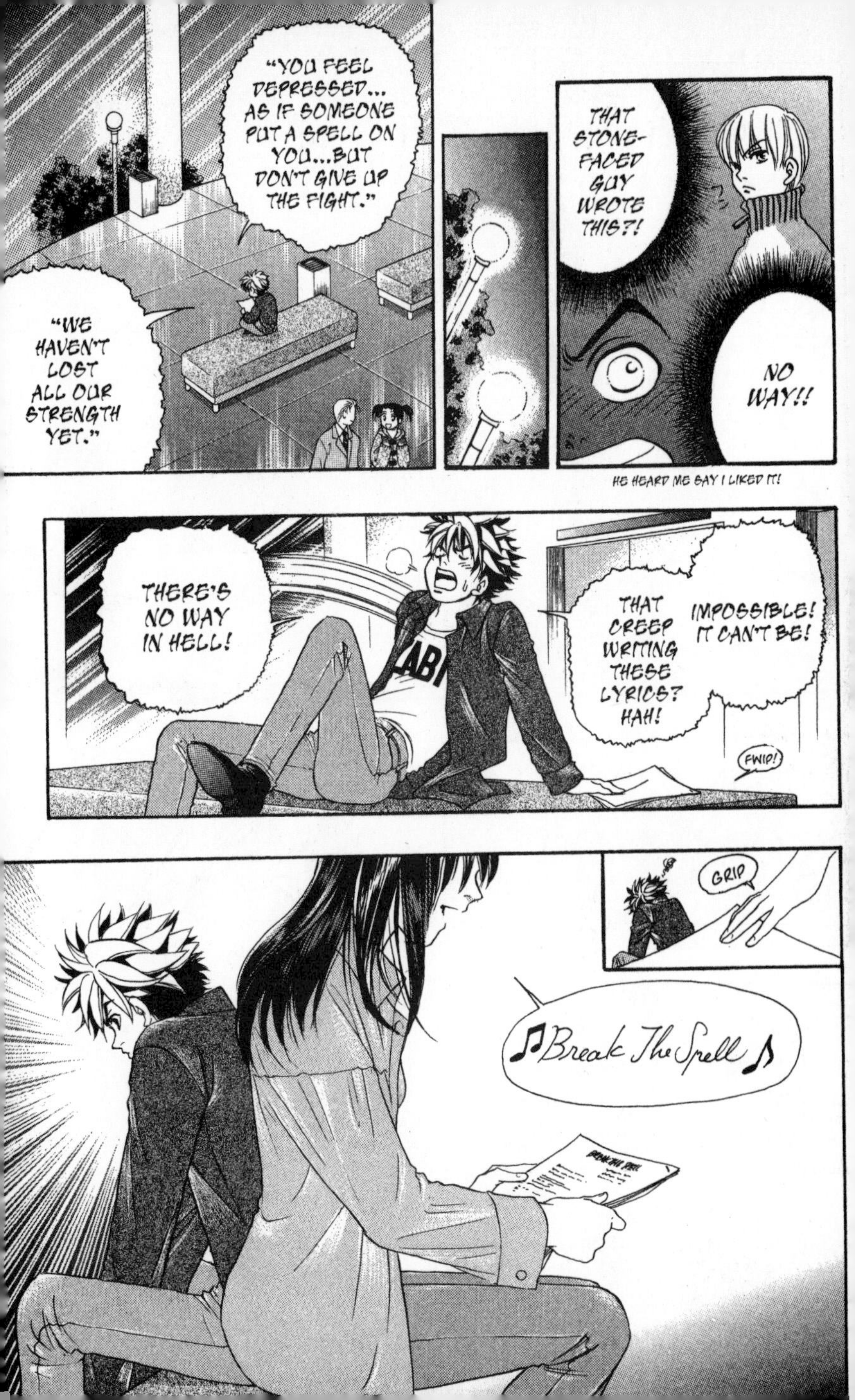
THAT STONE-FACED GUY WROTE THIS?!
NO WAY!!
"YOU FEEL DEPRESSED... AS IF SOMEONE PUT A SPELL ON YOU...BUT DON'T GIVE UP THE FIGHT."
"WE HAVEN'T LOST ALL OUR STRENGTH YET."
HE HEARD ME SAY I LIKED IT!
IMPOSSIBLE! IT CAN'T BE!
THAT CREEP WRITING THESE LYRICS? HAH!
THERE'S NO WAY IN HELL!
FWIP!
GRIP
♫Break The Spell♪

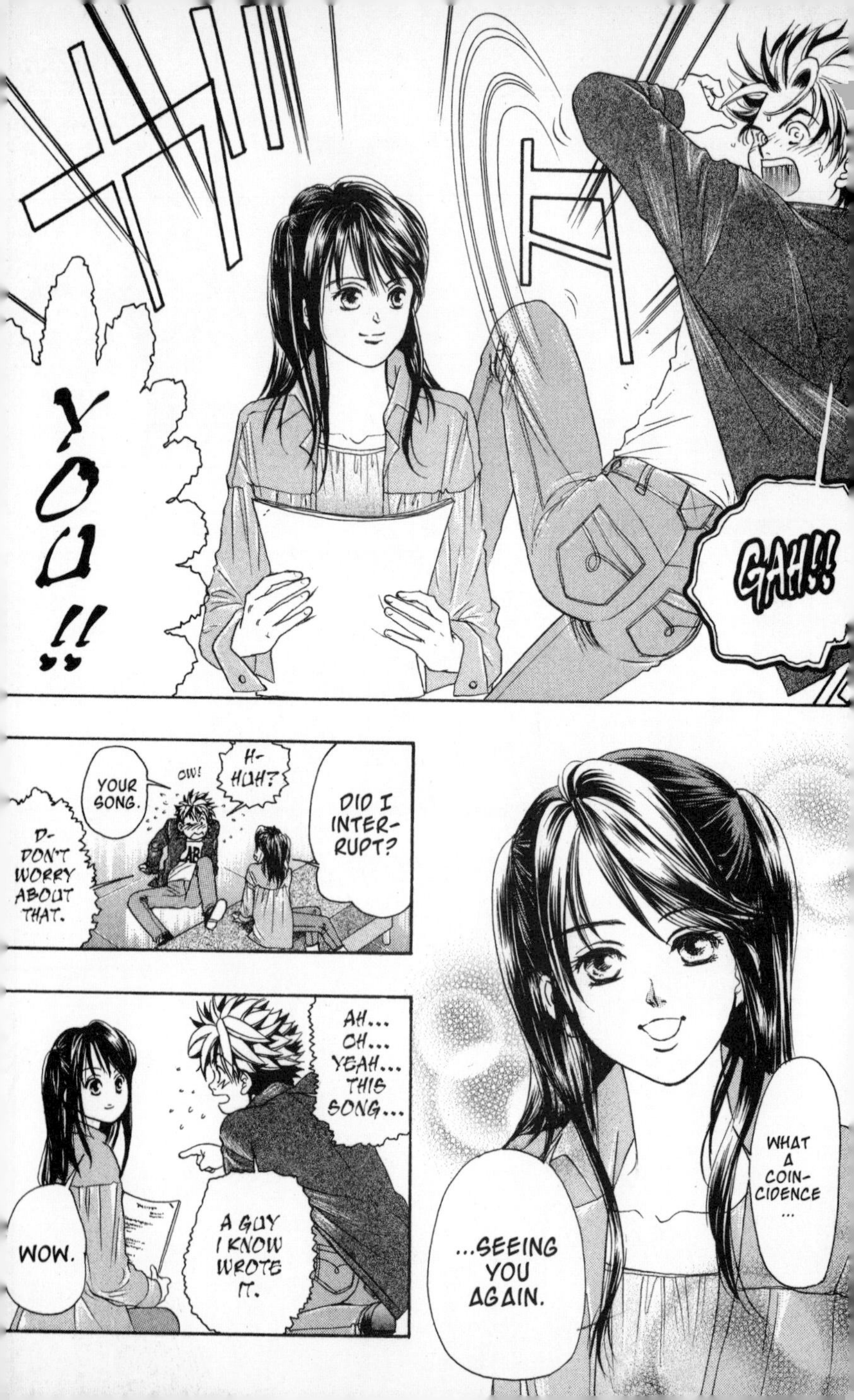
GAH!!
YOU!!
WHAT A COINCIDENCE...
...SEEING YOU AGAIN.
DID I INTERRUPT?
H-HUH?
OW!
YOUR SONG.
D-DON'T WORRY ABOUT THAT.
AH... OH... YEAH... THIS SONG...
A GUY I KNOW WROTE IT.
WOW.

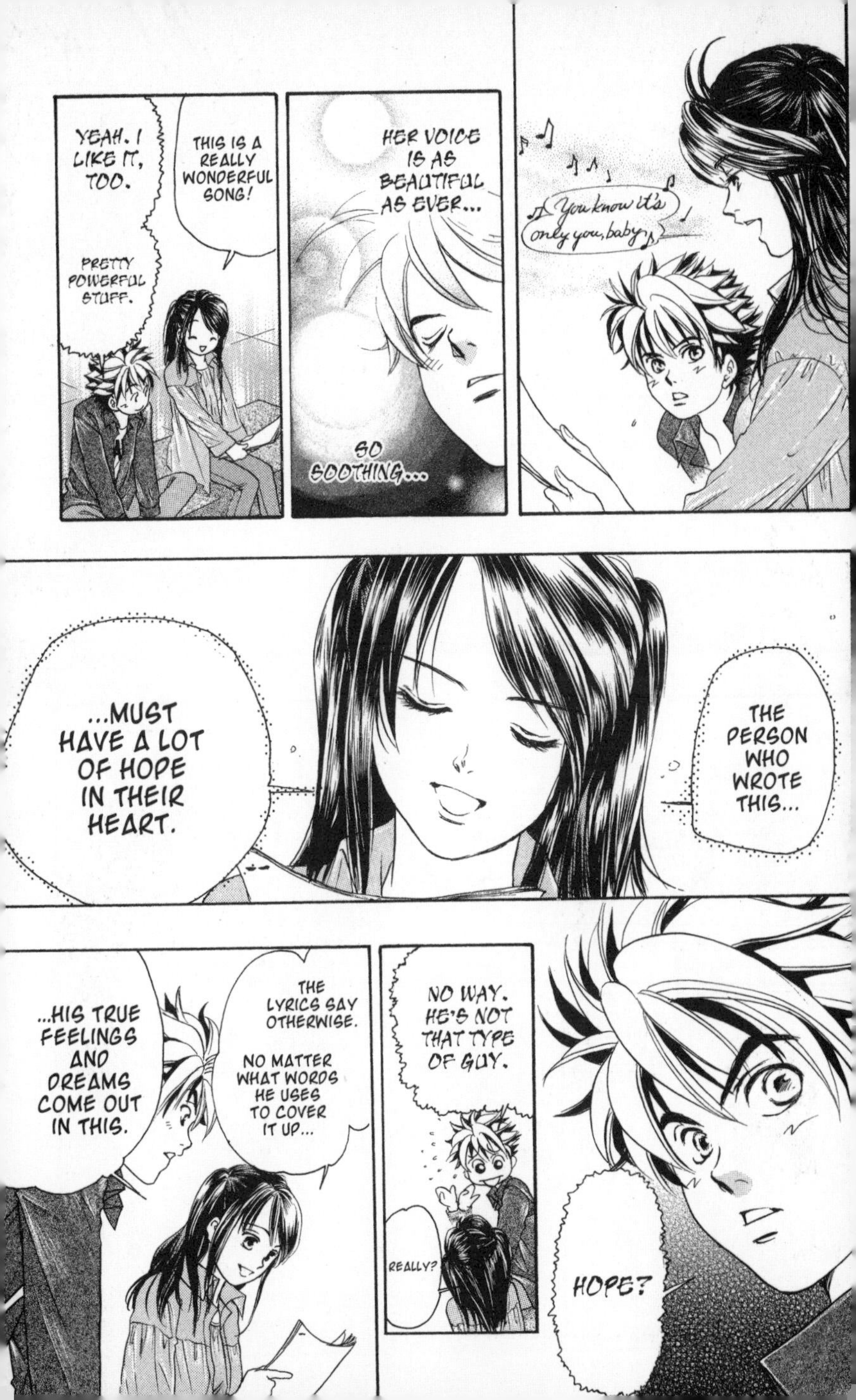
You know it's only you, baby
HER VOICE IS AS BEAUTIFUL AS EVER...
SO SOOTHING...
THIS IS A REALLY WONDERFUL SONG!
YEAH. I LIKE IT, TOO.
PRETTY POWERFUL STUFF.
THE PERSON WHO WROTE THIS...
...MUST HAVE A LOT OF HOPE IN THEIR HEART.
HOPE?
NO WAY. HE'S NOT THAT TYPE OF GUY.
REALLY?
THE LYRICS SAY OTHERWISE.
NO MATTER WHAT WORDS HE USES TO COVER IT UP...
...HIS TRUE FEELINGS AND DREAMS COME OUT IN THIS.

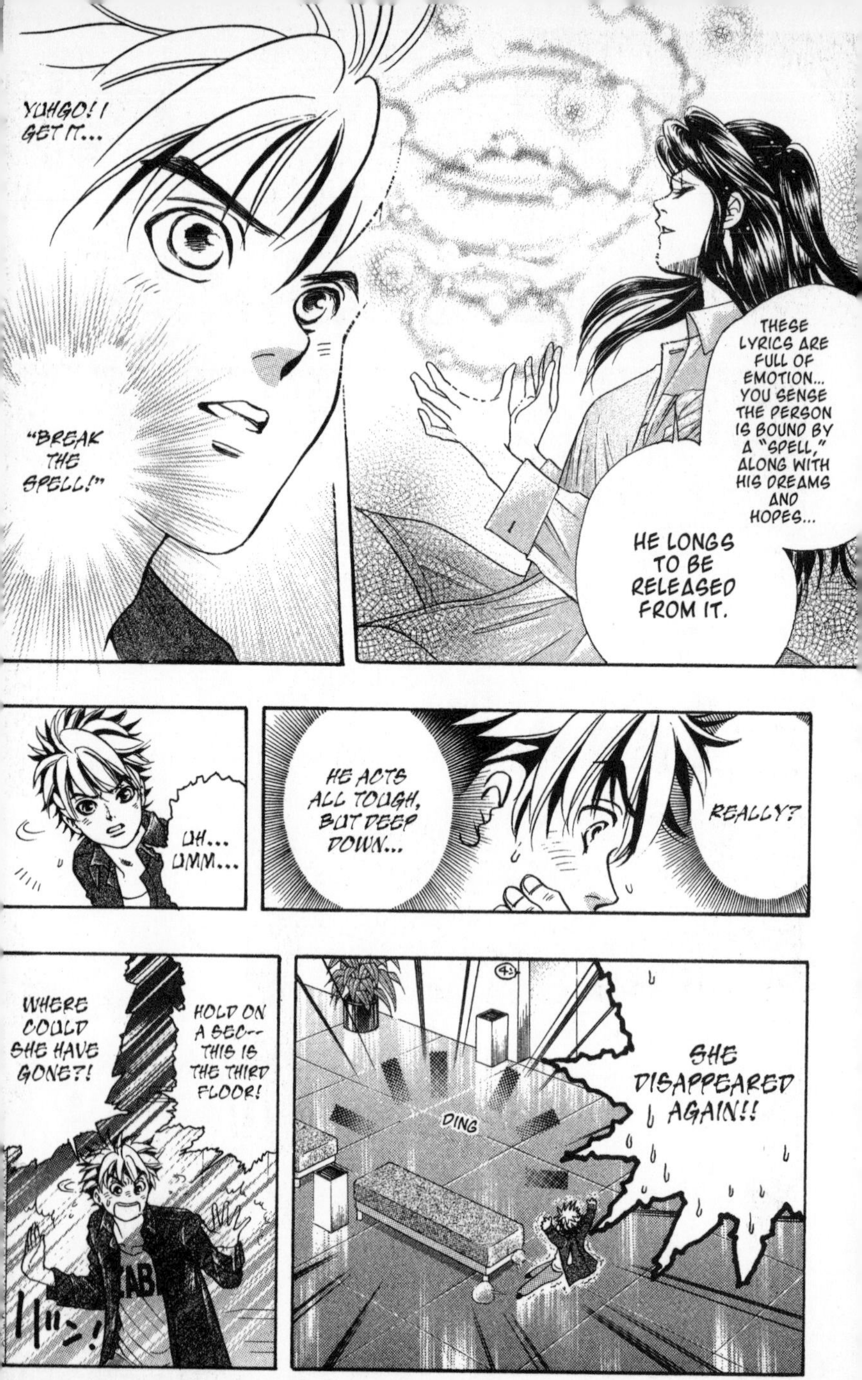
THESE LYRICS ARE FULL OF EMOTION... YOU SENSE THE PERSON IS BOUND BY A "SPELL," ALONG WITH HIS DREAMS AND HOPES...
HE LONGS TO BE RELEASED FROM IT.
YUHGO! I GET IT...
"BREAK THE SPELL!"
REALLY?
HE ACTS ALL TOUGH, BUT DEEP DOWN...
UH... UMM...
SHE DISAPPEARED AGAIN!!
DING
HOLD ON A SEC-- THIS IS THE THIRD FLOOR!
WHERE COULD SHE HAVE GONE?!

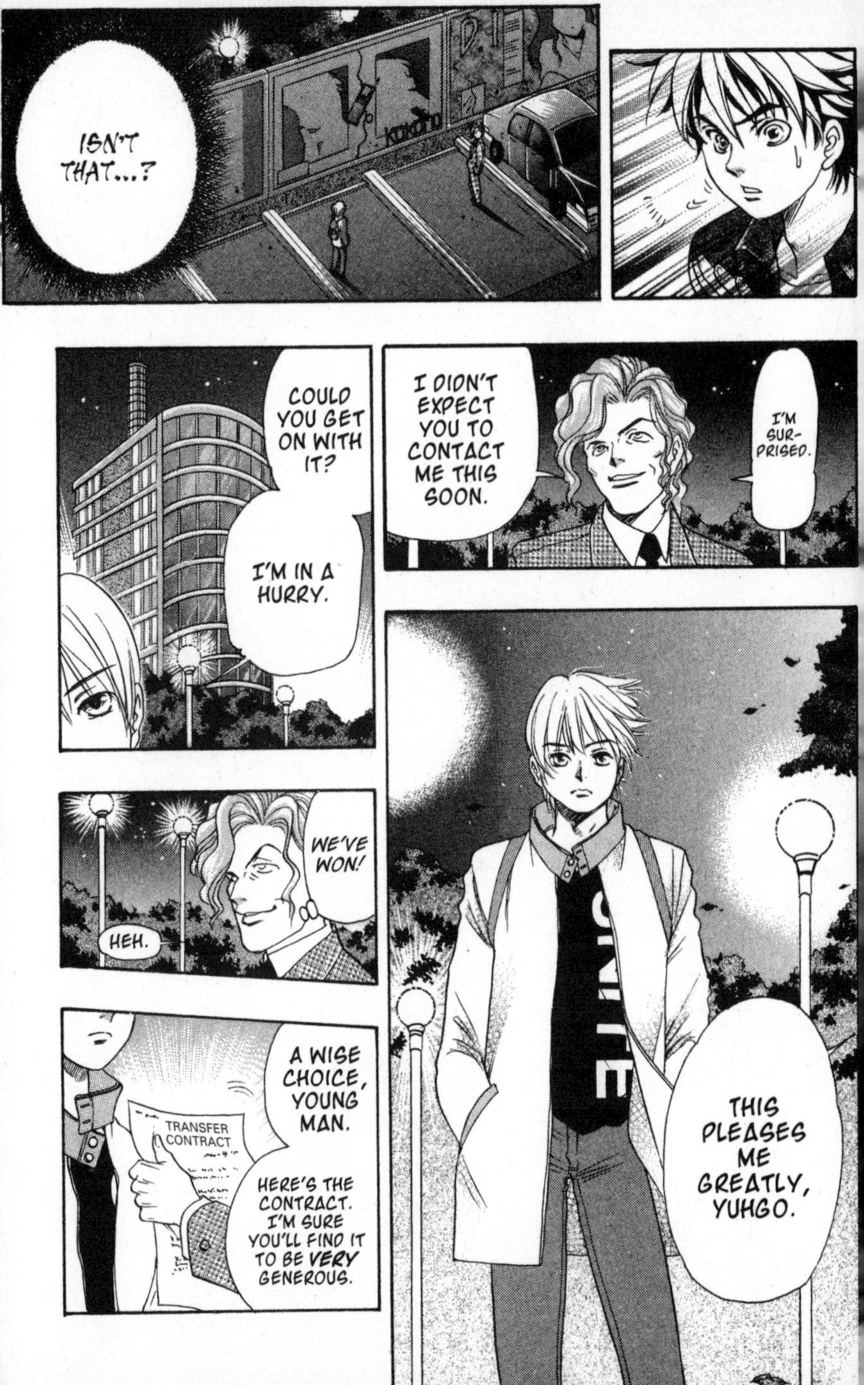

ISN'T THAT...?
I'M SUR-PRISED.
I DIDN'T EXPECT YOU TO CONTACT ME THIS SOON.
COULD YOU GET ON WITH IT?
I'M IN A HURRY.
THIS PLEASES ME GREATLY, YUHGO.
WE'VE WON!
HEH.
A WISE CHOICE, YOUNG MAN.
HERE'S THE CONTRACT. I'M SURE YOU'LL FIND IT TO BE VERY GENEROUS.
TRANSFER CONTRACT

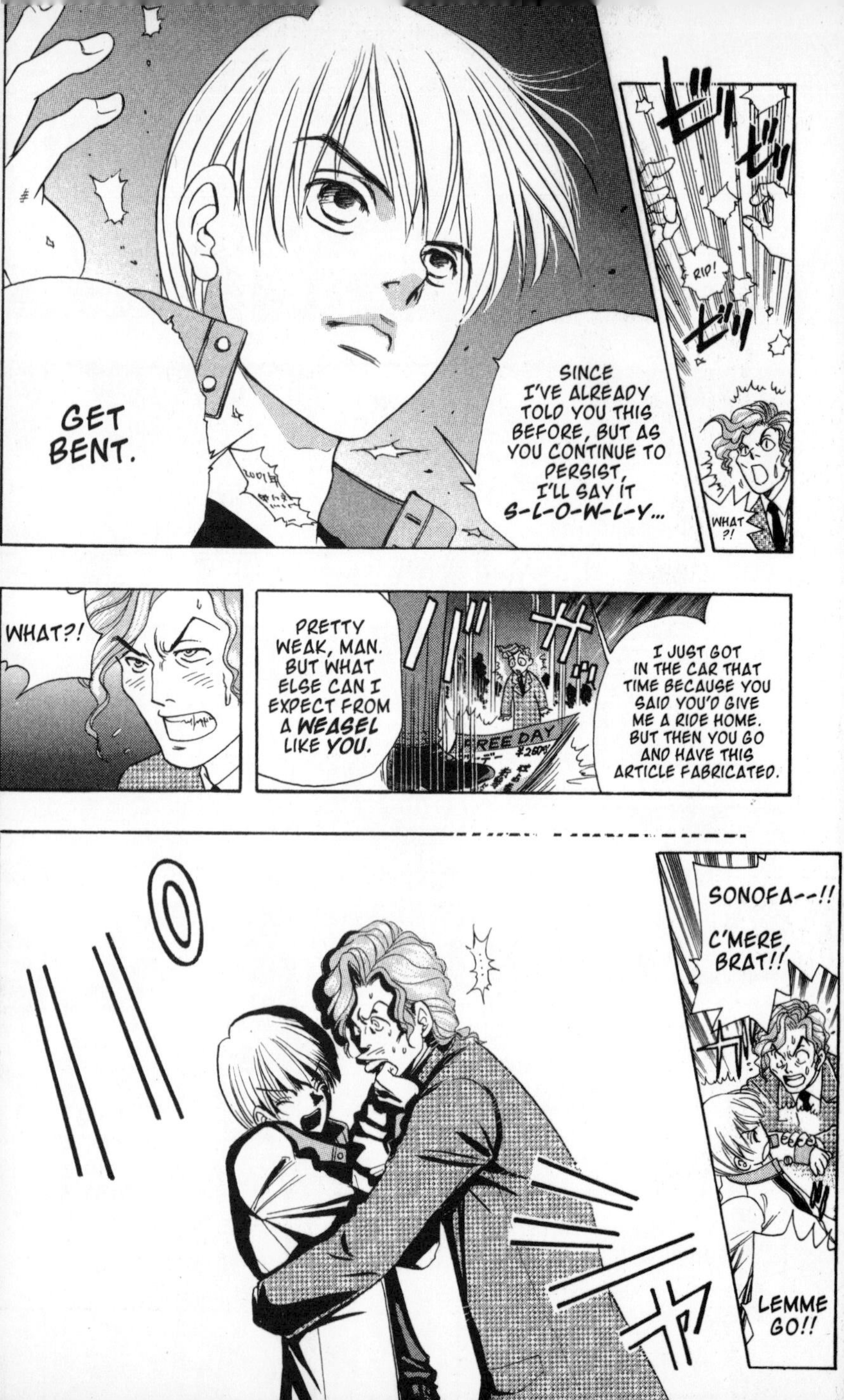
RIP!
WHAT?!
SINCE I'VE ALREADY TOLD YOU THIS BEFORE, BUT AS YOU CONTINUE TO PERSIST, I'LL SAY IT S-L-O-W-L-Y...
GET BENT.
I JUST GOT IN THE CAR THAT TIME BECAUSE YOU SAID YOU'D GIVE ME A RIDE HOME. BUT THEN YOU GO AND HAVE THIS ARTICLE FABRICATED.
PRETTY WEAK, MAN. BUT WHAT ELSE CAN I EXPECT FROM A WEASEL LIKE YOU.
WHAT?!
SONOFA--!!
C'MERE, BRAT!!
LEMME GO!!

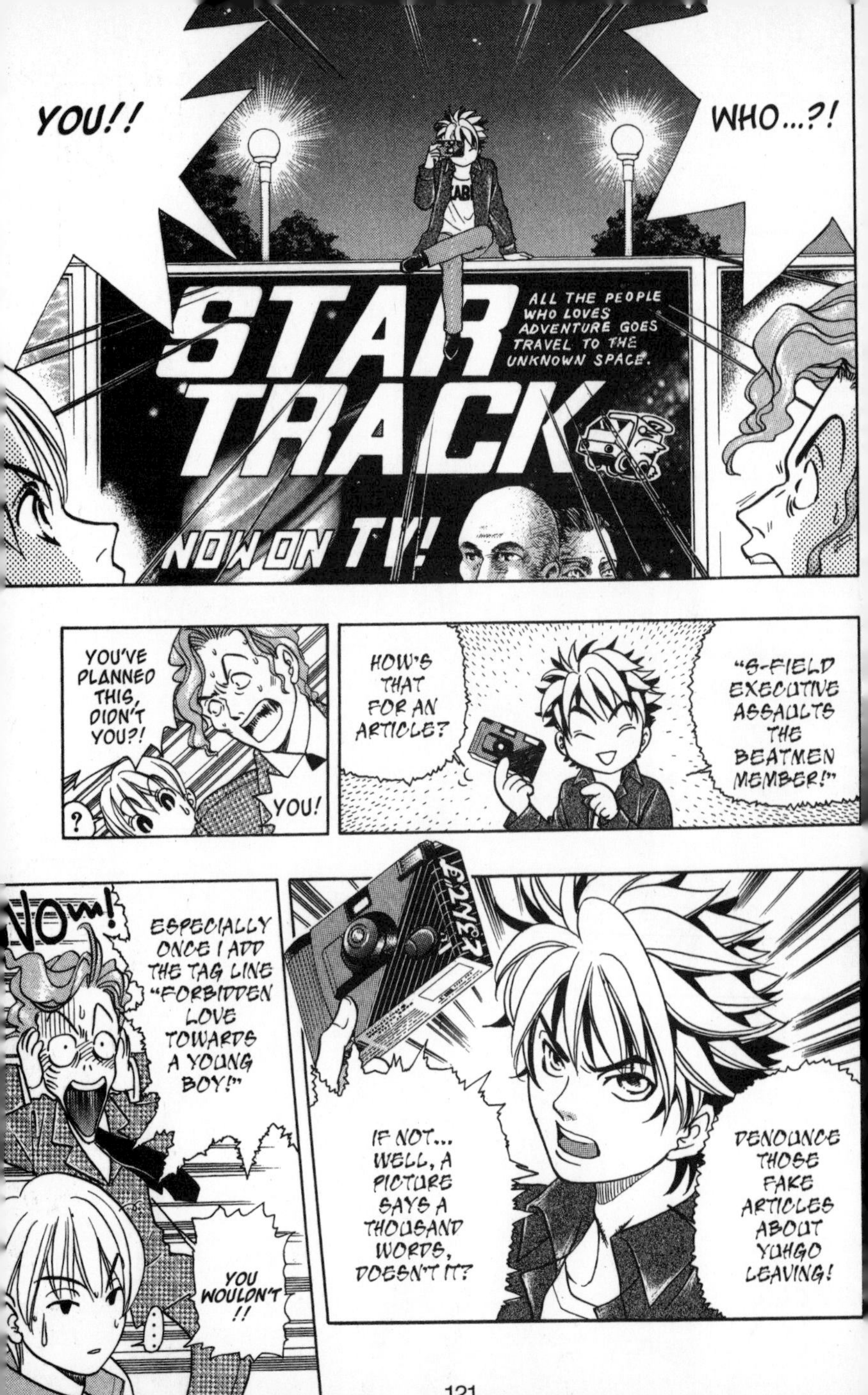
WHO...?!
YOU!!
STAR TRACK
ALL THE PEOPLE WHO LOVES ADVENTURE GOES TRAVEL TO THE UNKNOWN SPACE.
NOW ON TV!
"S-FIELD EXECUTIVE ASSAULTS THE BEATMEN MEMBER!"
HOW'S THAT FOR AN ARTICLE?
YOU'VE PLANNED THIS, DIDN'T YOU?!
YOU!
?
DENOUNCE THOSE FAKE ARTICLES ABOUT YUHGO LEAVING!
IF NOT... WELL, A PICTURE SAYS A THOUSAND WORDS, DOESN'T IT?
ESPECIALLY ONCE I ADD THE TAG LINE "FORBIDDEN LOVE TOWARDS A YOUNG BOY!"
YOU WOULDN'T !!
...

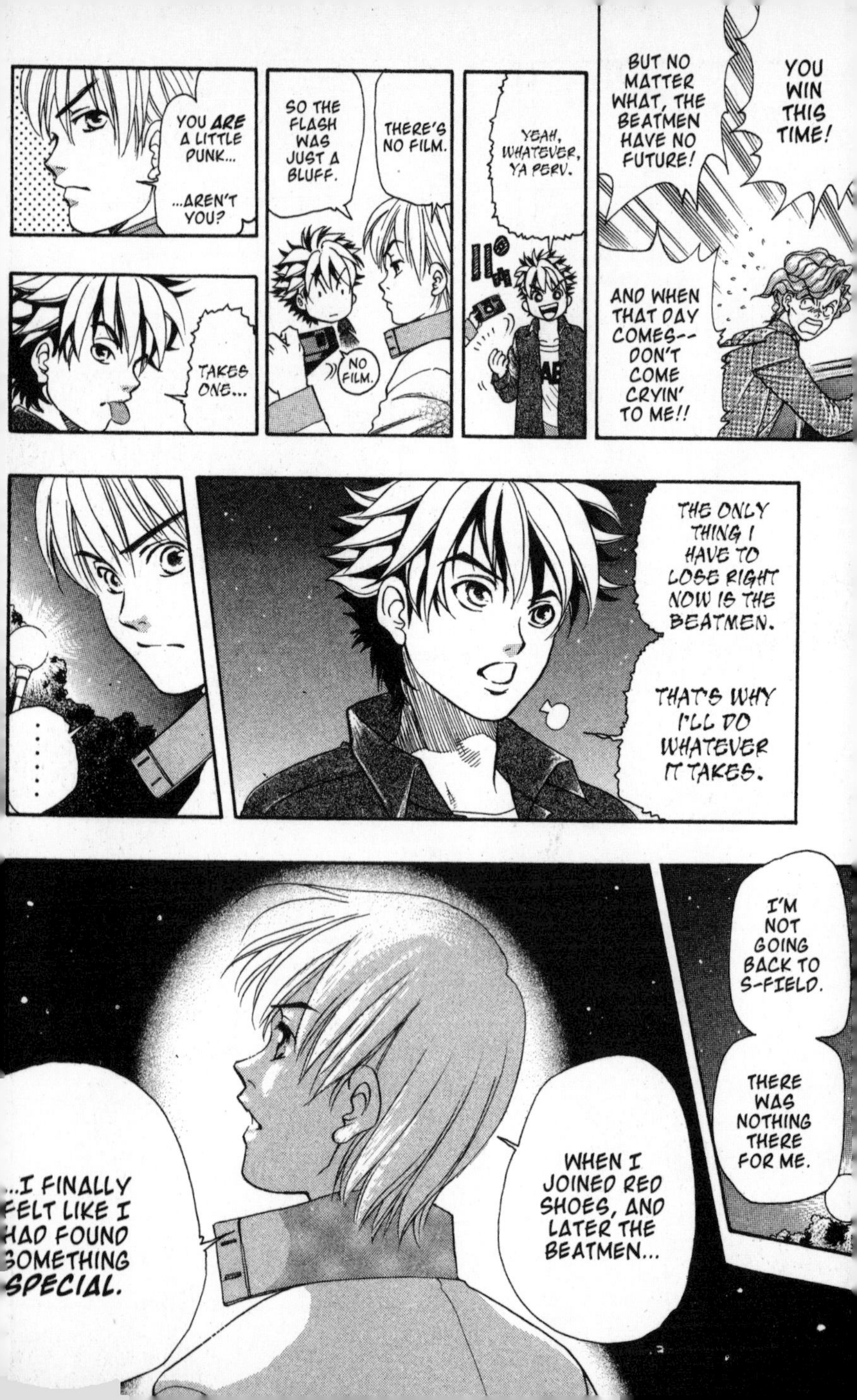
YOU WIN THIS TIME!
BUT NO MATTER WHAT, THE BEATMEN HAVE NO FUTURE!
AND WHEN THAT DAY COMES--DON'T COME CRYIN' TO ME!!
YEAH, WHATEVER, YA PERV.
THERE'S NO FILM.
SO THE FLASH WAS JUST A BLUFF.
NO FILM.
YOU ARE A LITTLE PUNK...
...AREN'T YOU?
TAKES ONE...
THE ONLY THING I HAVE TO LOSE RIGHT NOW IS THE BEATMEN.
THAT'S WHY I'LL DO WHATEVER IT TAKES.
......
I'M NOT GOING BACK TO S-FIELD.
THERE WAS NOTHING THERE FOR ME.
WHEN I JOINED RED SHOES, AND LATER THE BEATMEN...
...I FINALLY FELT LIKE I HAD FOUND SOMETHING SPECIAL.

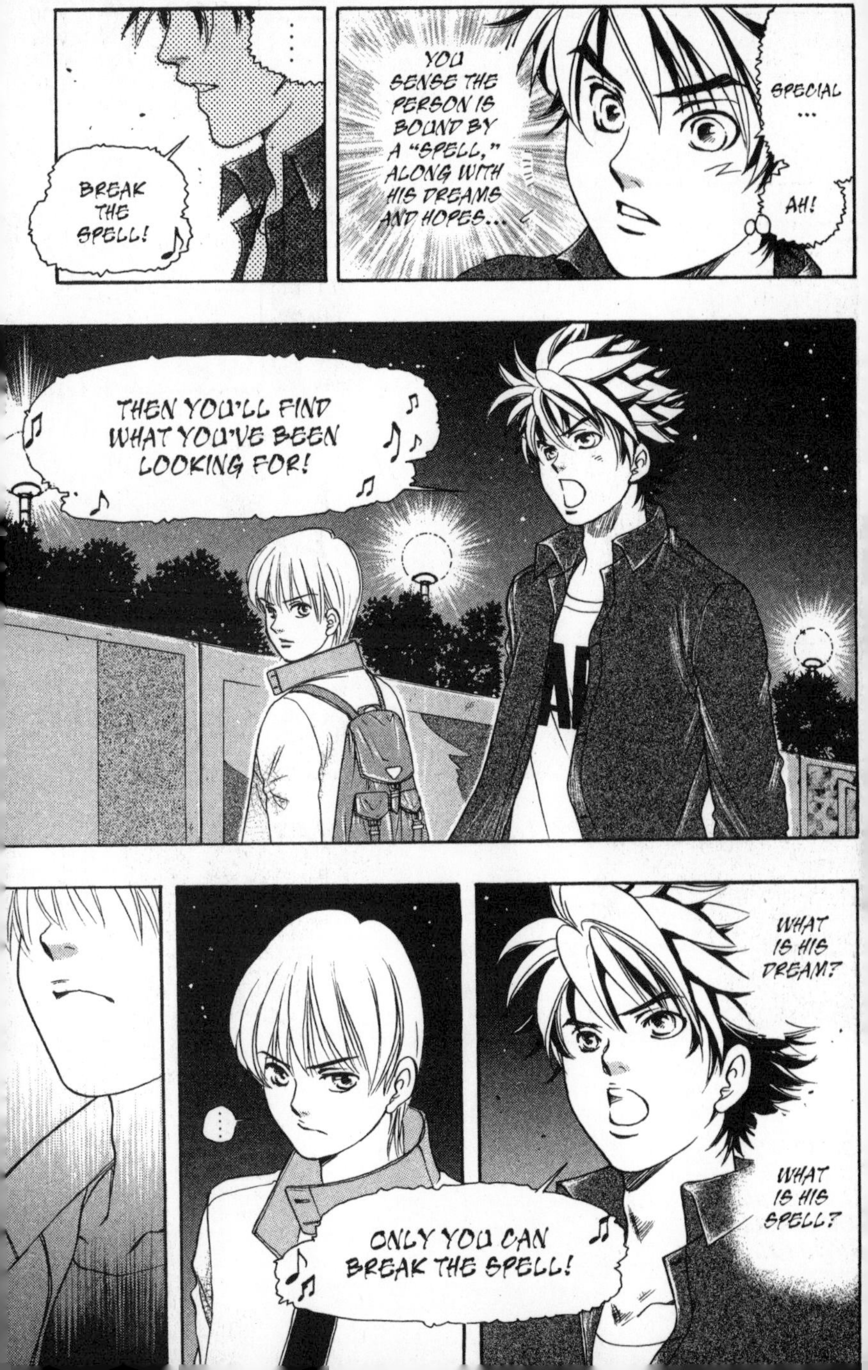
SPECIAL ...
AH!
YOU SENSE THE PERSON IS BOUND BY A "SPELL," ALONG WITH HIS DREAMS AND HOPES...
...
BREAK THE SPELL!
THEN YOU'LL FIND WHAT YOU'VE BEEN LOOKING FOR!
WHAT IS HIS DREAM?
WHAT IS HIS SPELL?
ONLY YOU CAN BREAK THE SPELL!
...

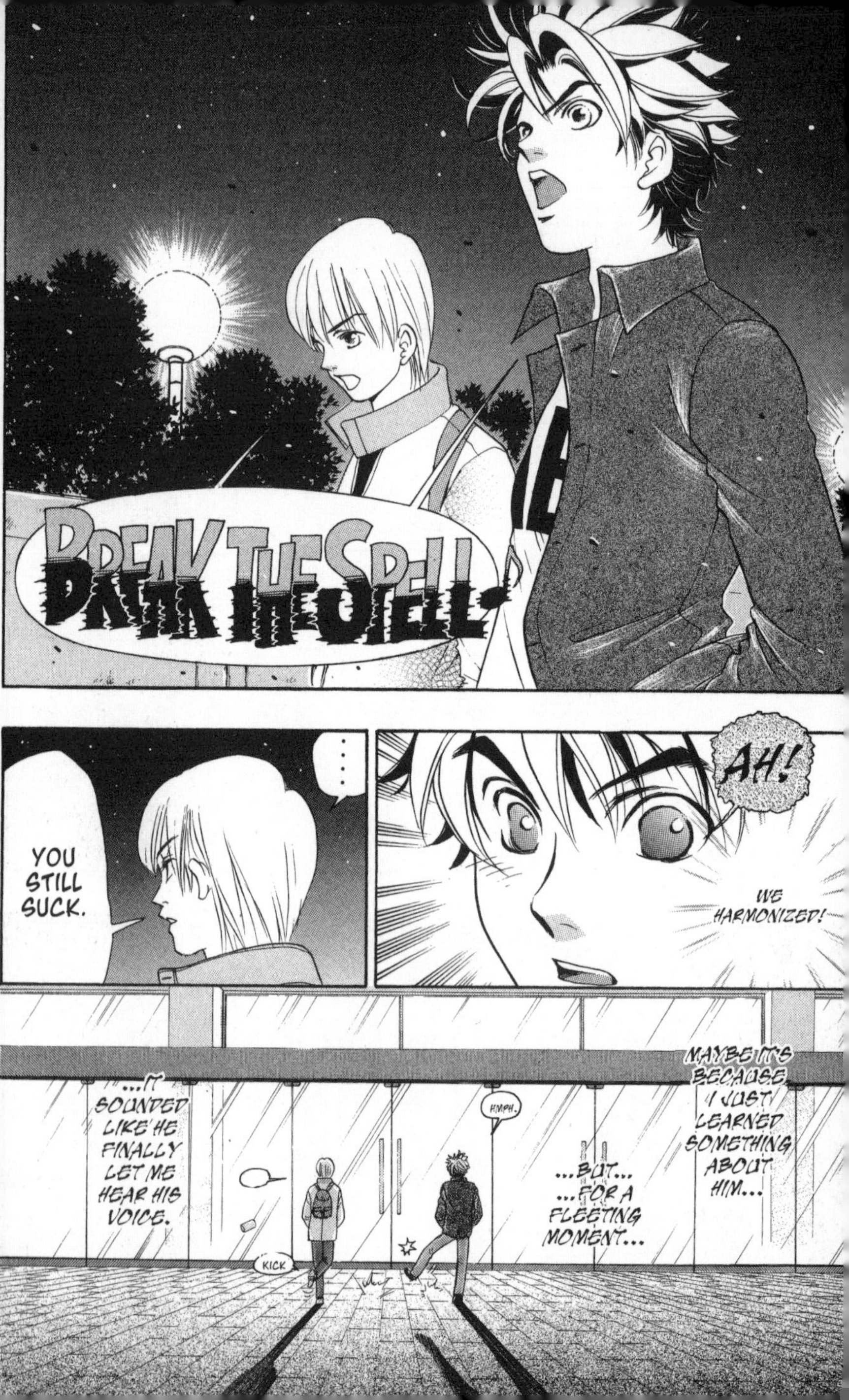
BREAK THE SPELL!
AH!
WE HARMONIZED!
...
YOU STILL SUCK.
MAYBE IT'S BECAUSE I JUST LEARNED SOMETHING ABOUT HIM...
...BUT... ...FOR A FLEETING MOMENT...
HMPH.
...IT SOUNDED LIKE HE FINALLY LET ME HEAR HIS VOICE.
KICK

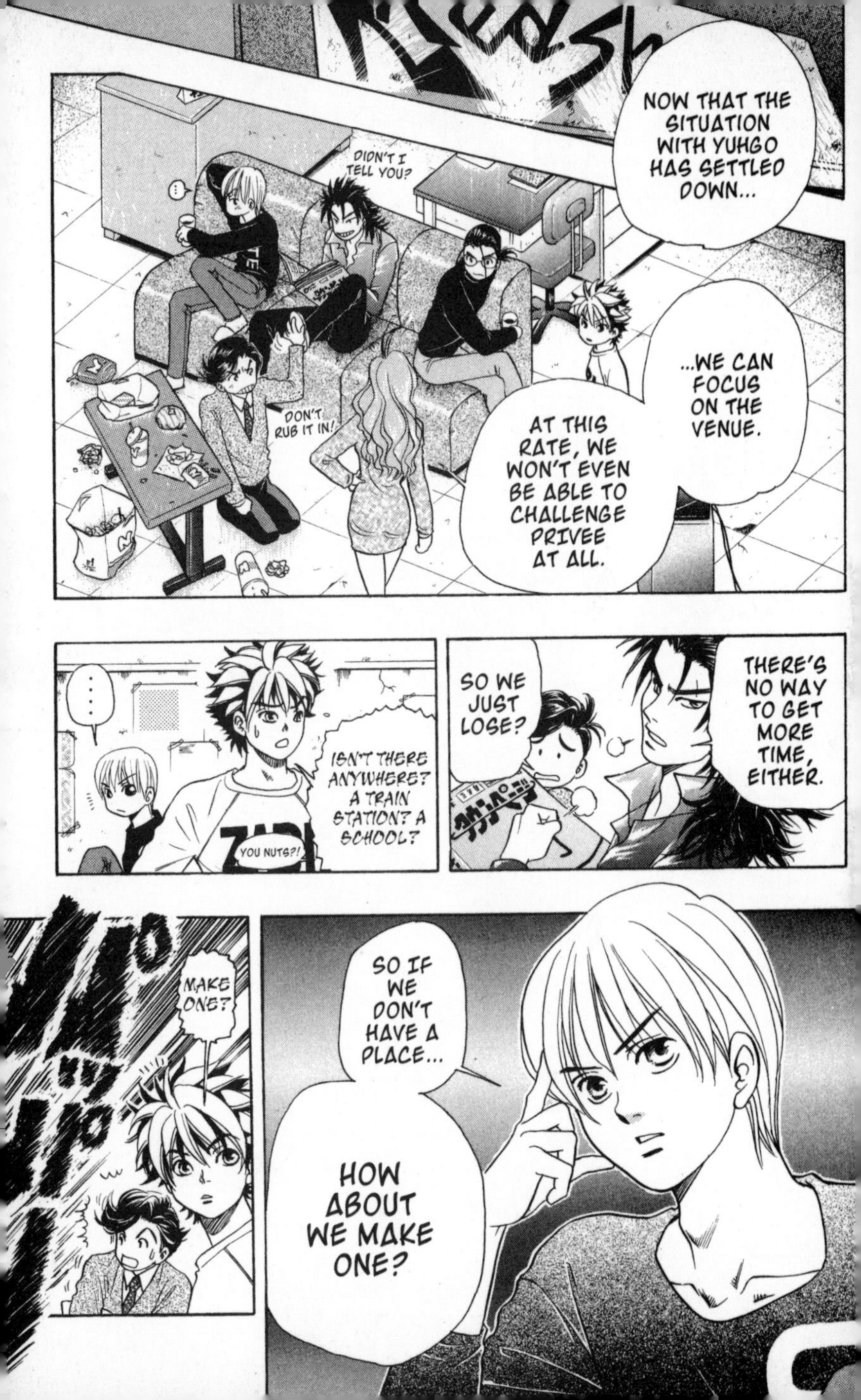
NOW THAT THE SITUATION WITH YUHGO HAS SETTLED DOWN...
...WE CAN FOCUS ON THE VENUE.
AT THIS RATE, WE WON'T EVEN BE ABLE TO CHALLENGE PRIVEE AT ALL.
DIDN'T I TELL YOU?
...
DON'T RUB IT IN!
THERE'S NO WAY TO GET MORE TIME, EITHER.
SO WE JUST LOSE?
ISN'T THERE ANYWHERE? A TRAIN STATION? A SCHOOL?
YOU NUTS?!
......
SO IF WE DON'T HAVE A PLACE...
HOW ABOUT WE MAKE ONE?
MAKE ONE?

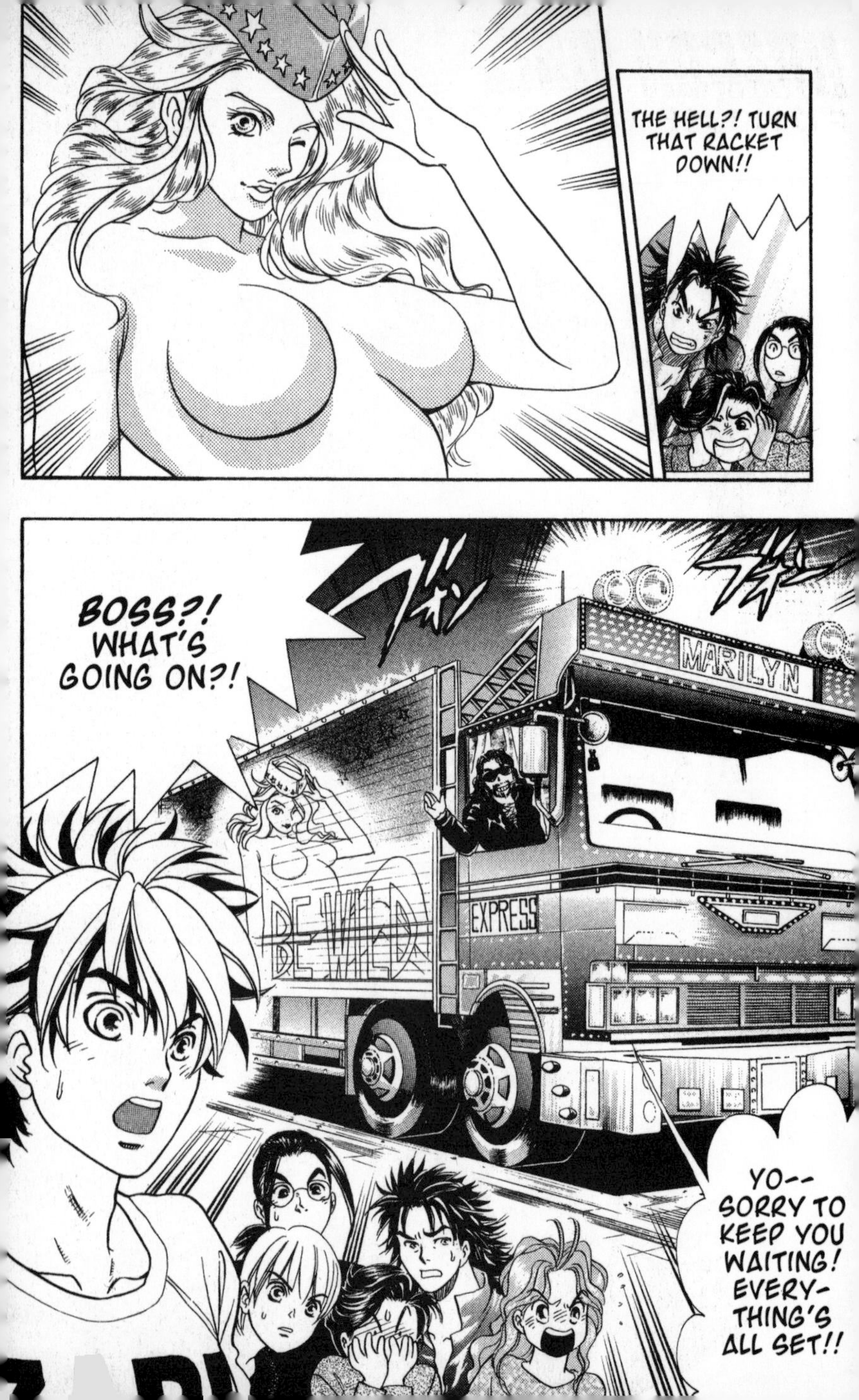
THE HELL?! TURN THAT RACKET DOWN!!
BOSS?! WHAT'S GOING ON?!
MARILYN
EXPRESS
YO-- SORRY TO KEEP YOU WAITING! EVERY-THING'S ALL SET!!

# DRAGON VOICE
## # 13 HOUSE OF SHOCK!

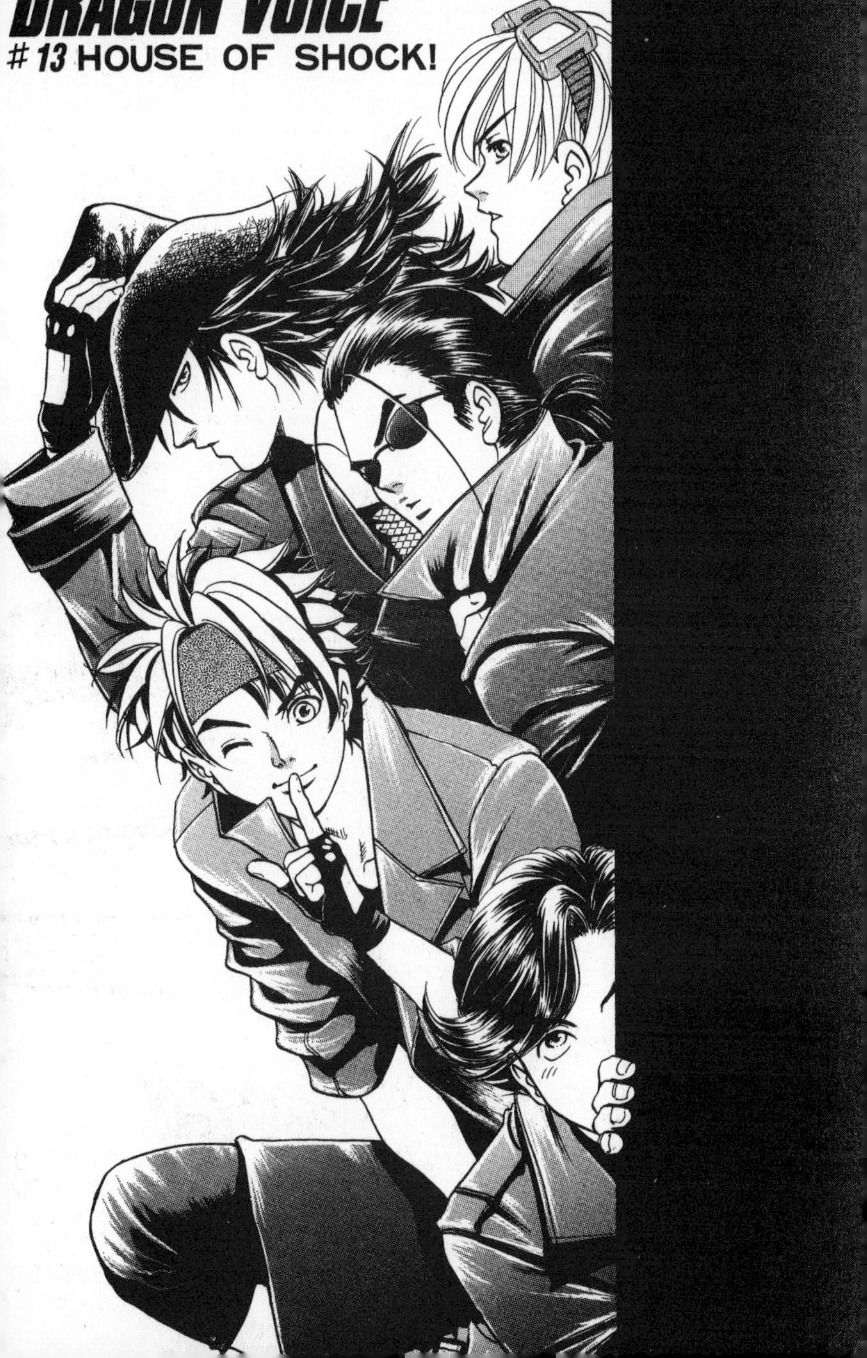

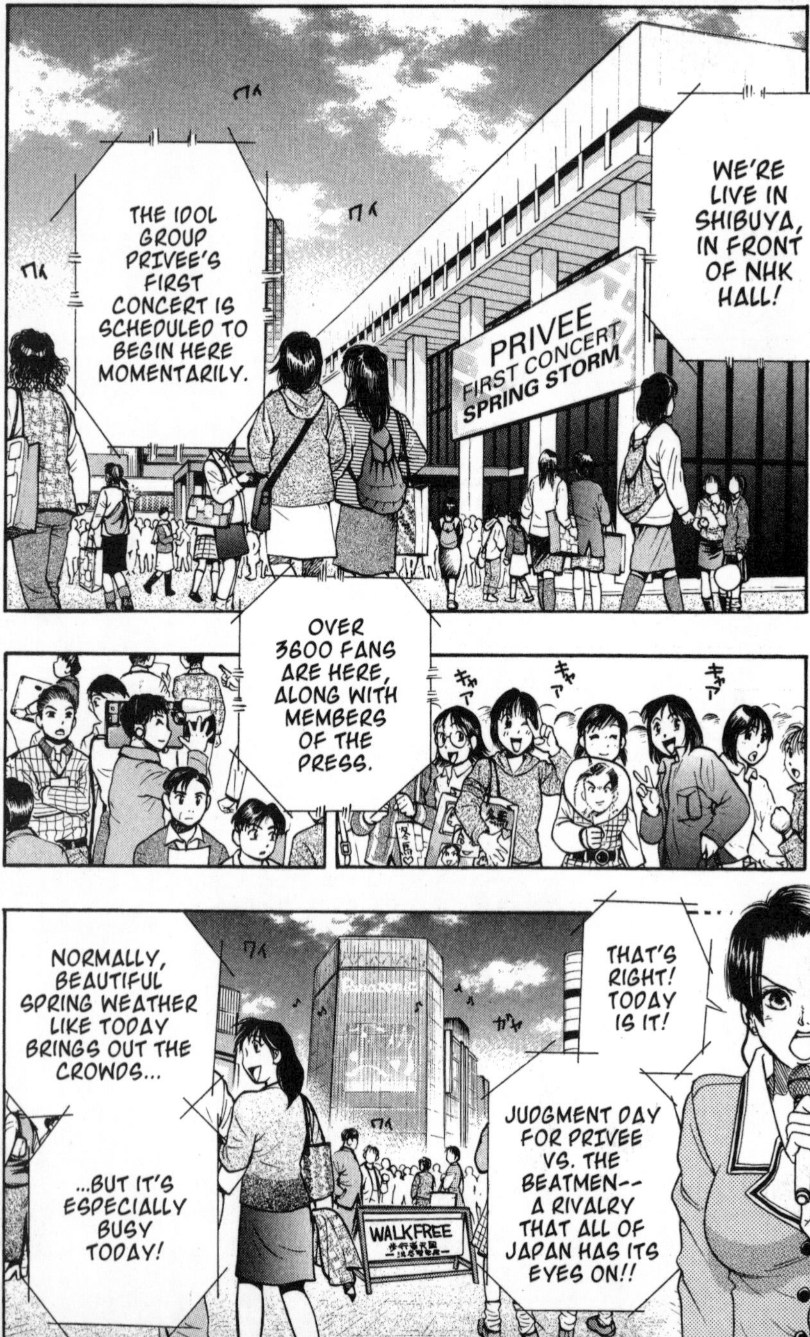
WE'RE LIVE IN SHIBUYA, IN FRONT OF NHK HALL!
PRIVEE FIRST CONCERT SPRING STORM
THE IDOL GROUP PRIVEE'S FIRST CONCERT IS SCHEDULED TO BEGIN HERE MOMENTARILY.
OVER 3600 FANS ARE HERE, ALONG WITH MEMBERS OF THE PRESS.
THAT'S RIGHT! TODAY IS IT!
JUDGMENT DAY FOR PRIVEE VS. THE BEATMEN--A RIVALRY THAT ALL OF JAPAN HAS ITS EYES ON!!
NORMALLY, BEAUTIFUL SPRING WEATHER LIKE TODAY BRINGS OUT THE CROWDS...
...BUT IT'S ESPECIALLY BUSY TODAY!
WALKFREE

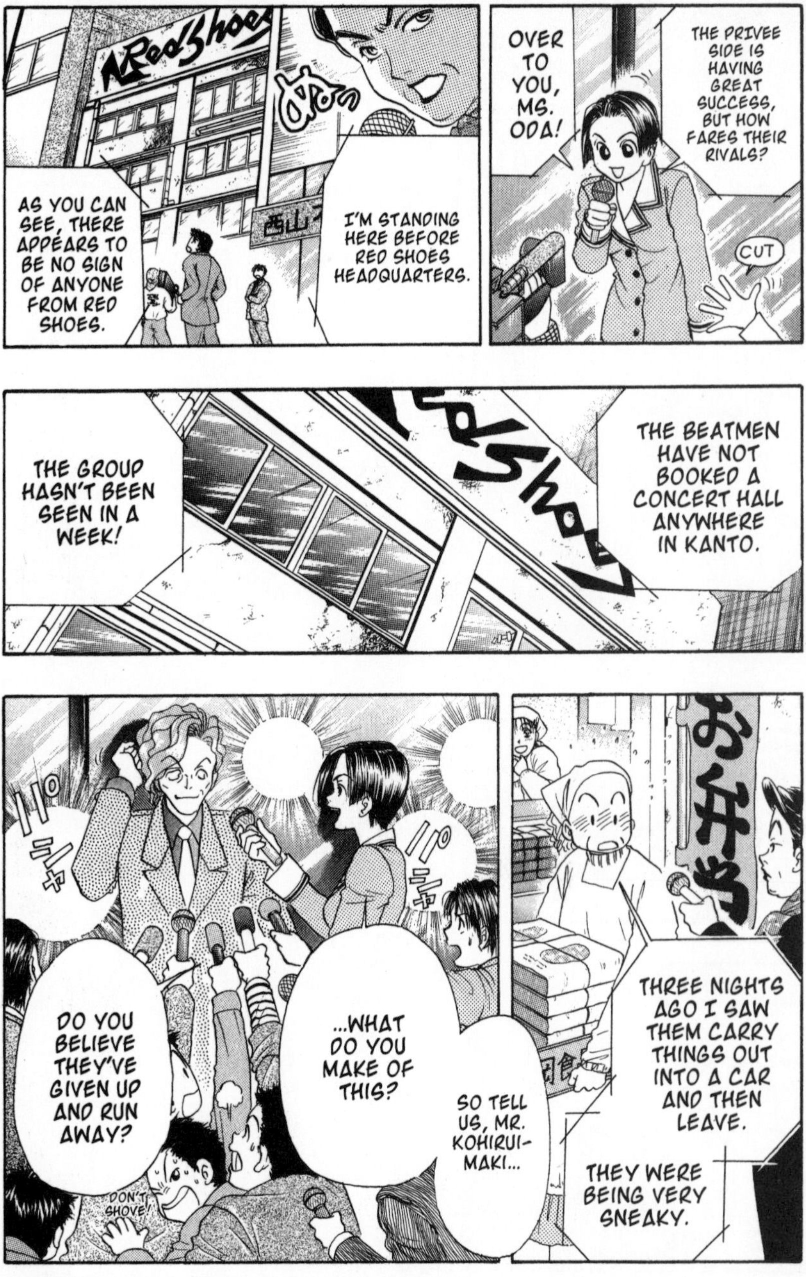
THE PRIVEE SIDE IS HAVING GREAT SUCCESS, BUT HOW FARES THEIR RIVALS?
OVER TO YOU, MS. ODA!
CUT
I'M STANDING HERE BEFORE RED SHOES HEADQUARTERS.
AS YOU CAN SEE, THERE APPEARS TO BE NO SIGN OF ANYONE FROM RED SHOES.
THE BEATMEN HAVE NOT BOOKED A CONCERT HALL ANYWHERE IN KANTO.
THE GROUP HASN'T BEEN SEEN IN A WEEK!
お弁当
THREE NIGHTS AGO I SAW THEM CARRY THINGS OUT INTO A CAR AND THEN LEAVE.
THEY WERE BEING VERY SNEAKY.
パシャ
パシャ
SO TELL US, MR. KOHIRUI-MAKI...
...WHAT DO YOU MAKE OF THIS?
DO YOU BELIEVE THEY'VE GIVEN UP AND RUN AWAY?
DON'T SHOVE!

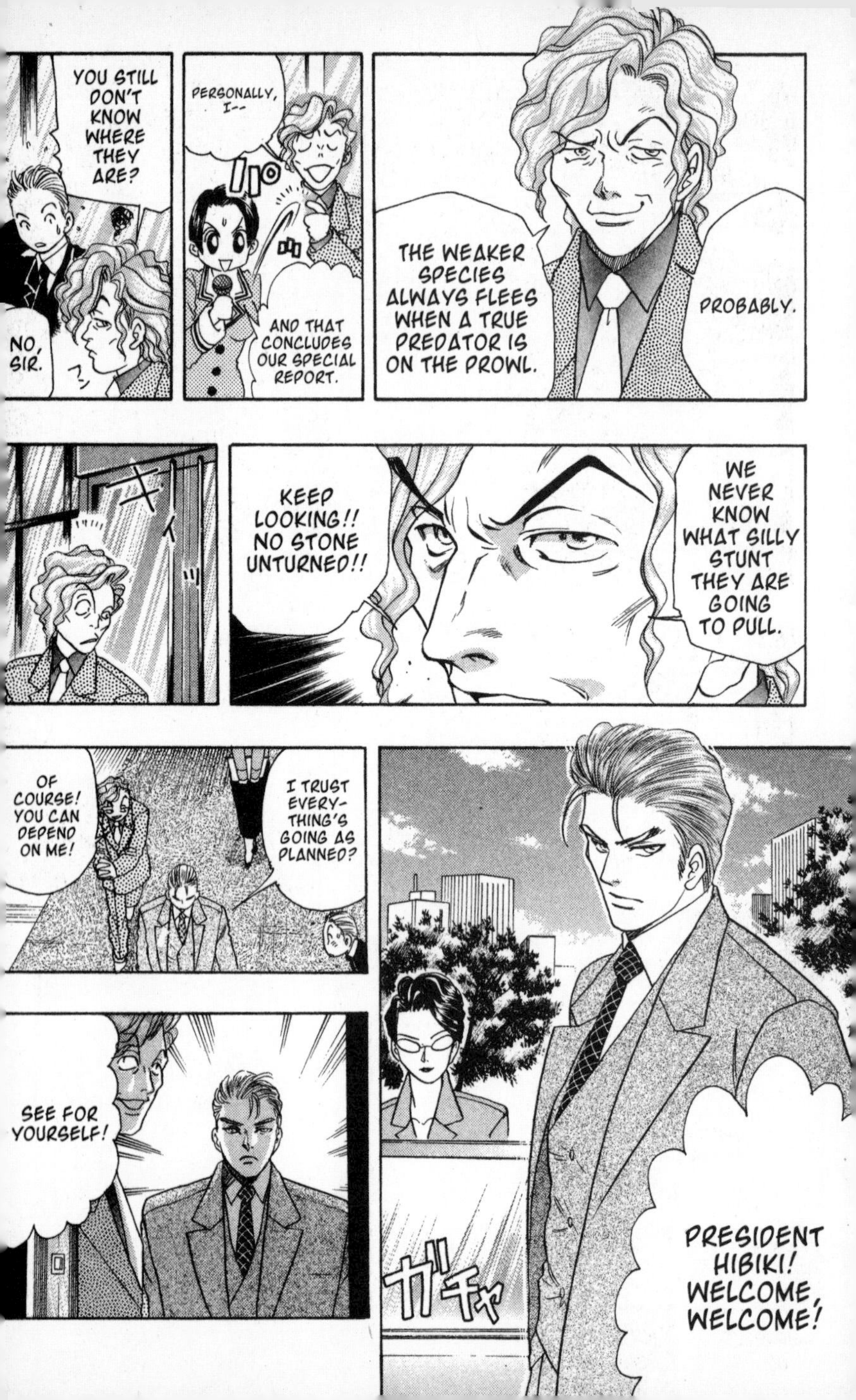
PROBABLY.
THE WEAKER SPECIES ALWAYS FLEES WHEN A TRUE PREDATOR IS ON THE PROWL.
PERSONALLY, I--
AND THAT CONCLUDES OUR SPECIAL REPORT.
YOU STILL DON'T KNOW WHERE THEY ARE?
NO, SIR.
WE NEVER KNOW WHAT SILLY STUNT THEY ARE GOING TO PULL.
KEEP LOOKING!! NO STONE UNTURNED!!
PRESIDENT HIBIKI! WELCOME, WELCOME!
ガチャ
I TRUST EVERY-THING'S GOING AS PLANNED?
OF COURSE! YOU CAN DEPEND ON ME!
SEE FOR YOURSELF!

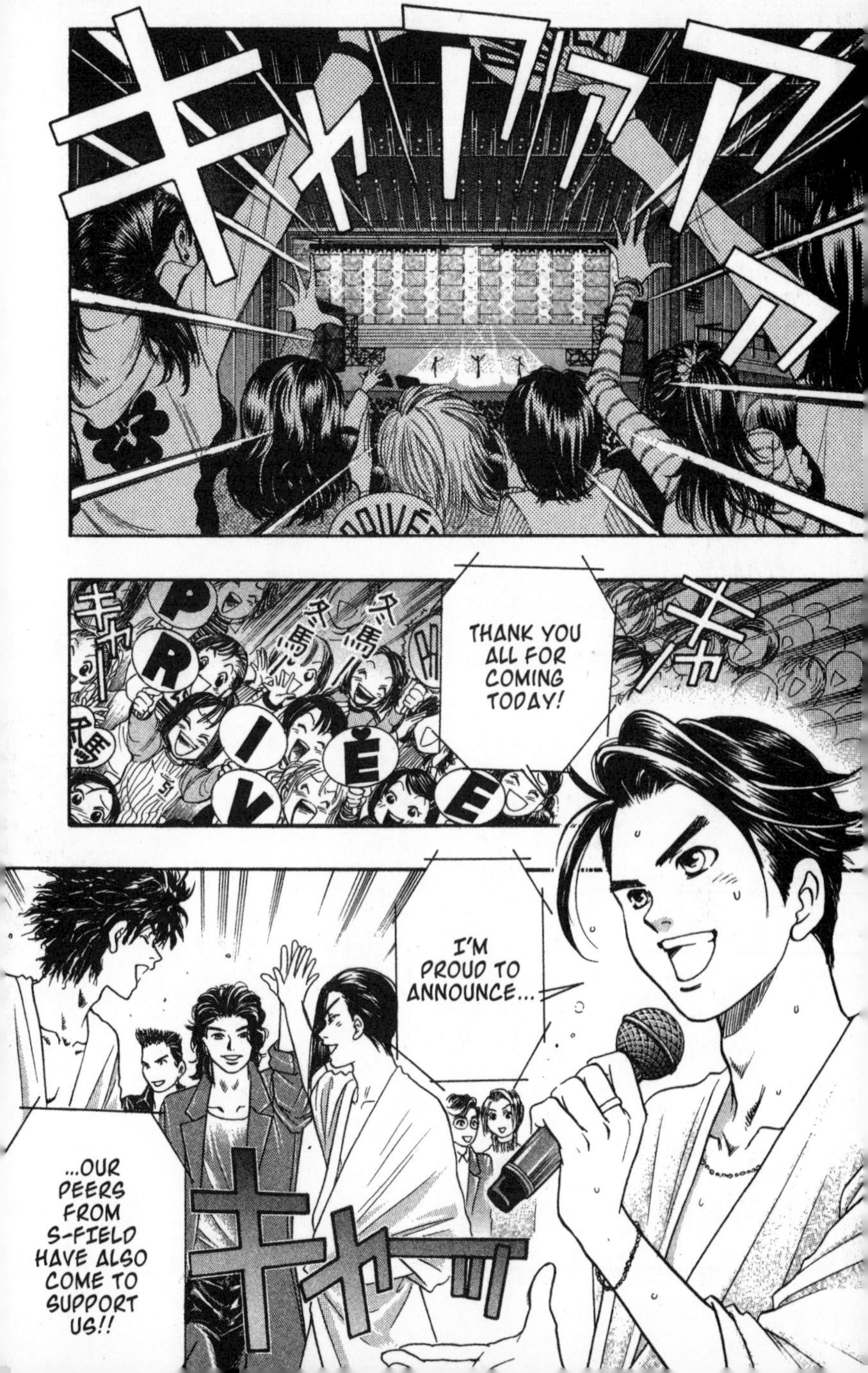

キャアアアア
THANK YOU ALL FOR COMING TODAY!
キャー
P R I V E E
I'M PROUD TO ANNOUNCE...
...OUR PEERS FROM S-FIELD HAVE ALSO COME TO SUPPORT US!!
キャー

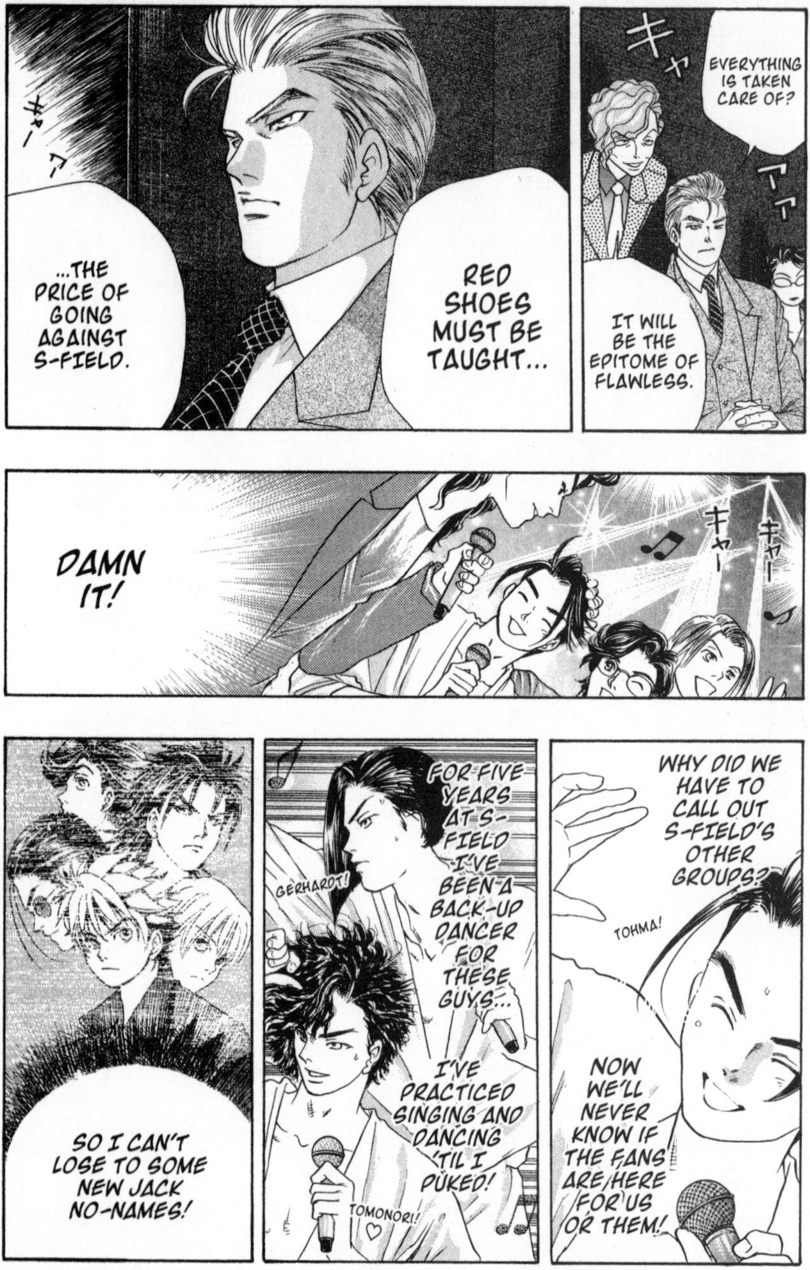
キャ
EVERYTHING IS TAKEN CARE OF?
アア
IT WILL BE THE EPITOME OF FLAWLESS.
RED SHOES MUST BE TAUGHT...
キャーア
...THE PRICE OF GOING AGAINST S-FIELD.
キャー
キャー
DAMN IT!
WHY DID WE HAVE TO CALL OUT S-FIELD'S OTHER GROUPS?
TOHMA!
NOW WE'LL NEVER KNOW IF THE FANS ARE HERE FOR US OR THEM!
FOR FIVE YEARS AT S-FIELD I'VE BEEN A BACK-UP DANCER FOR THESE GUYS...
GERHARDT!
I'VE PRACTICED SINGING AND DANCING 'TIL I PUKED!
TOMONORI! ♡
SO I CAN'T LOSE TO SOME NEW JACK NO-NAMES!

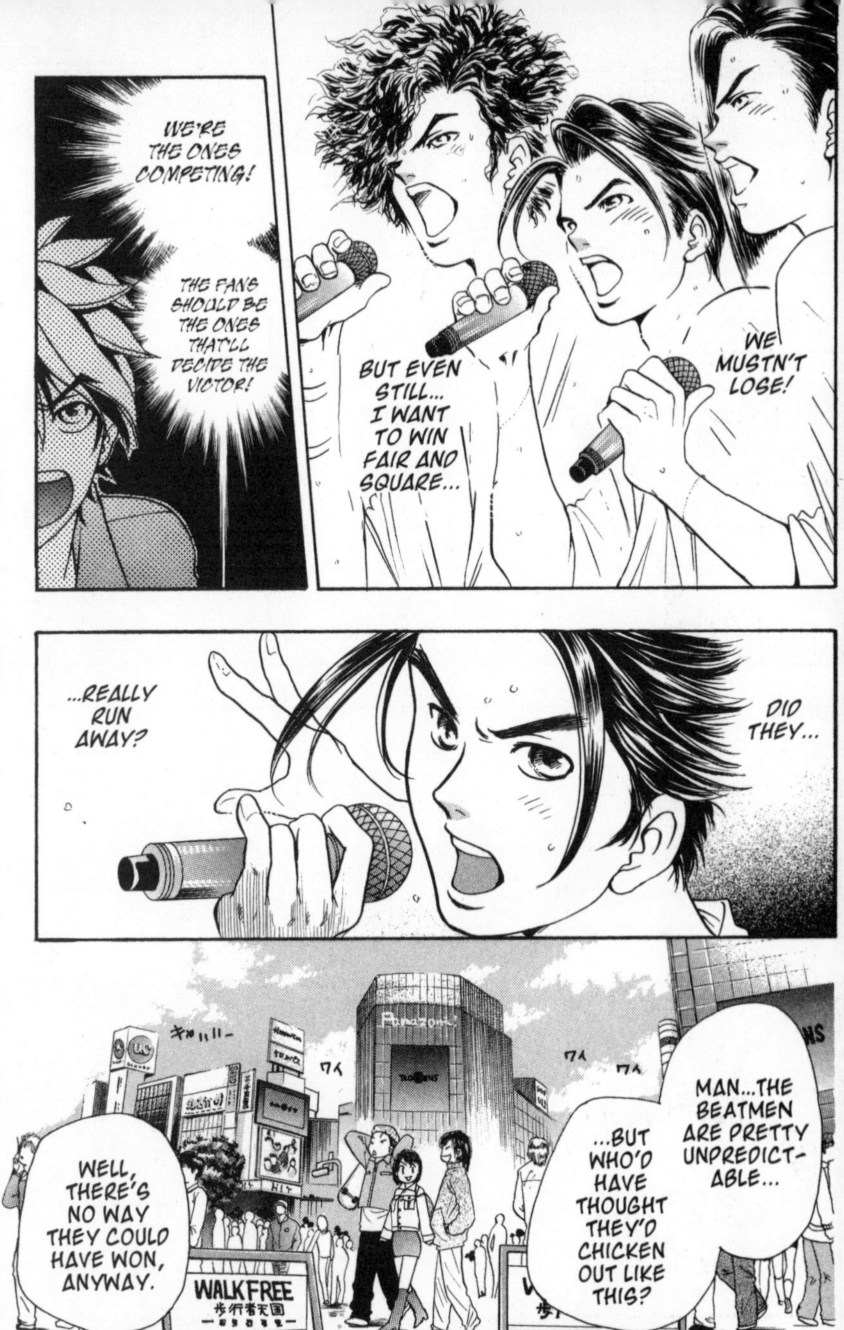
WE MUSTN'T LOSE!
BUT EVEN STILL... I WANT TO WIN FAIR AND SQUARE...
WE'RE THE ONES COMPETING!
THE FANS SHOULD BE THE ONES THAT'LL DECIDE THE VICTOR!
DID THEY...
...REALLY RUN AWAY?
MAN...THE BEATMEN ARE PRETTY UNPREDICT-ABLE...
...BUT WHO'D HAVE THOUGHT THEY'D CHICKEN OUT LIKE THIS?
WELL, THERE'S NO WAY THEY COULD HAVE WON, ANYWAY.
WALKFREE
歩行者天国

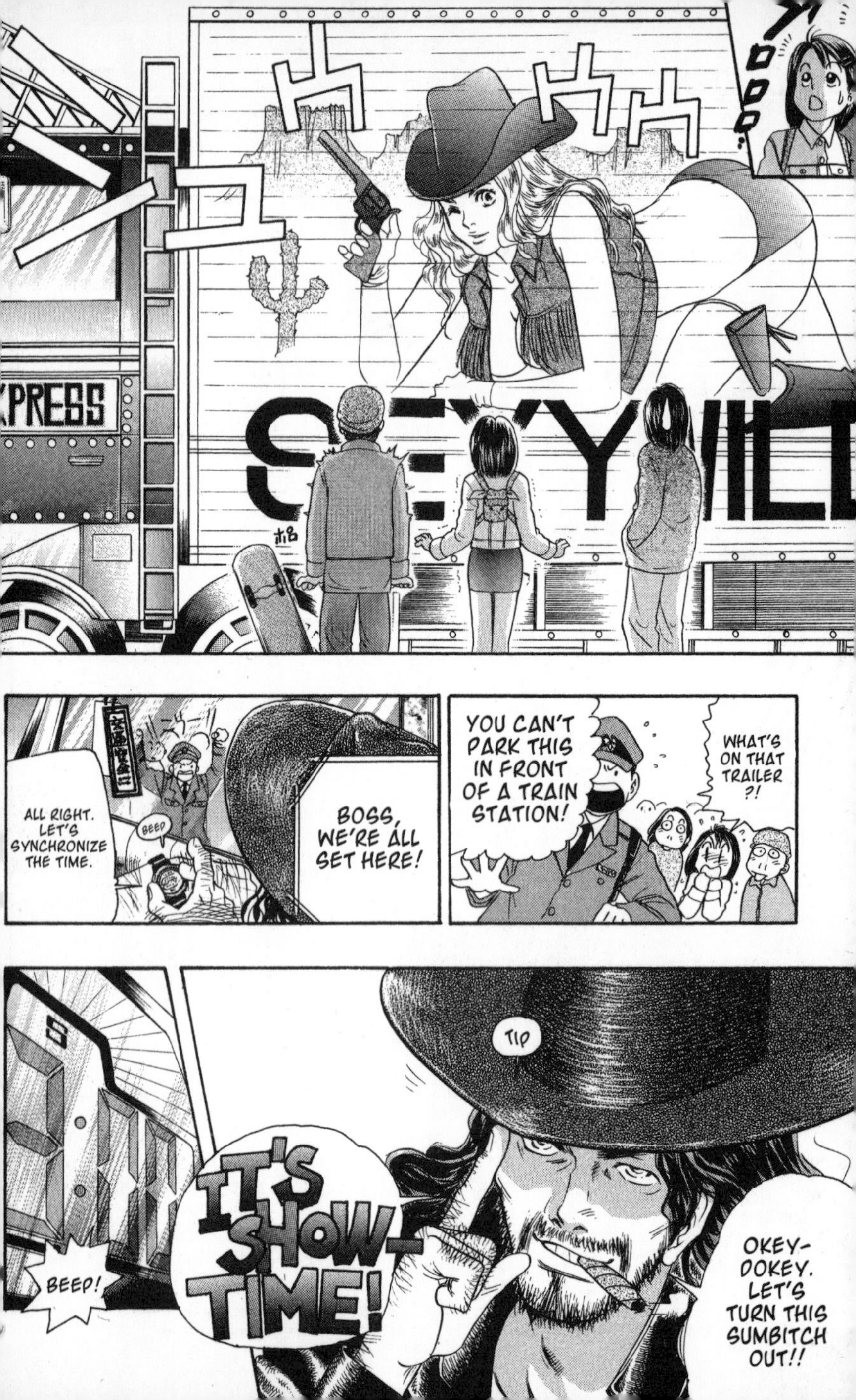
WHAT'S ON THAT TRAILER ?!
YOU CAN'T PARK THIS IN FRONT OF A TRAIN STATION!
BOSS, WE'RE ALL SET HERE!
BEEP
ALL RIGHT. LET'S SYNCHRONIZE THE TIME.
TIP
OKEY-DOKEY. LET'S TURN THIS SUMBITCH OUT!!
IT'S SHOW-TIME!
BEEP!

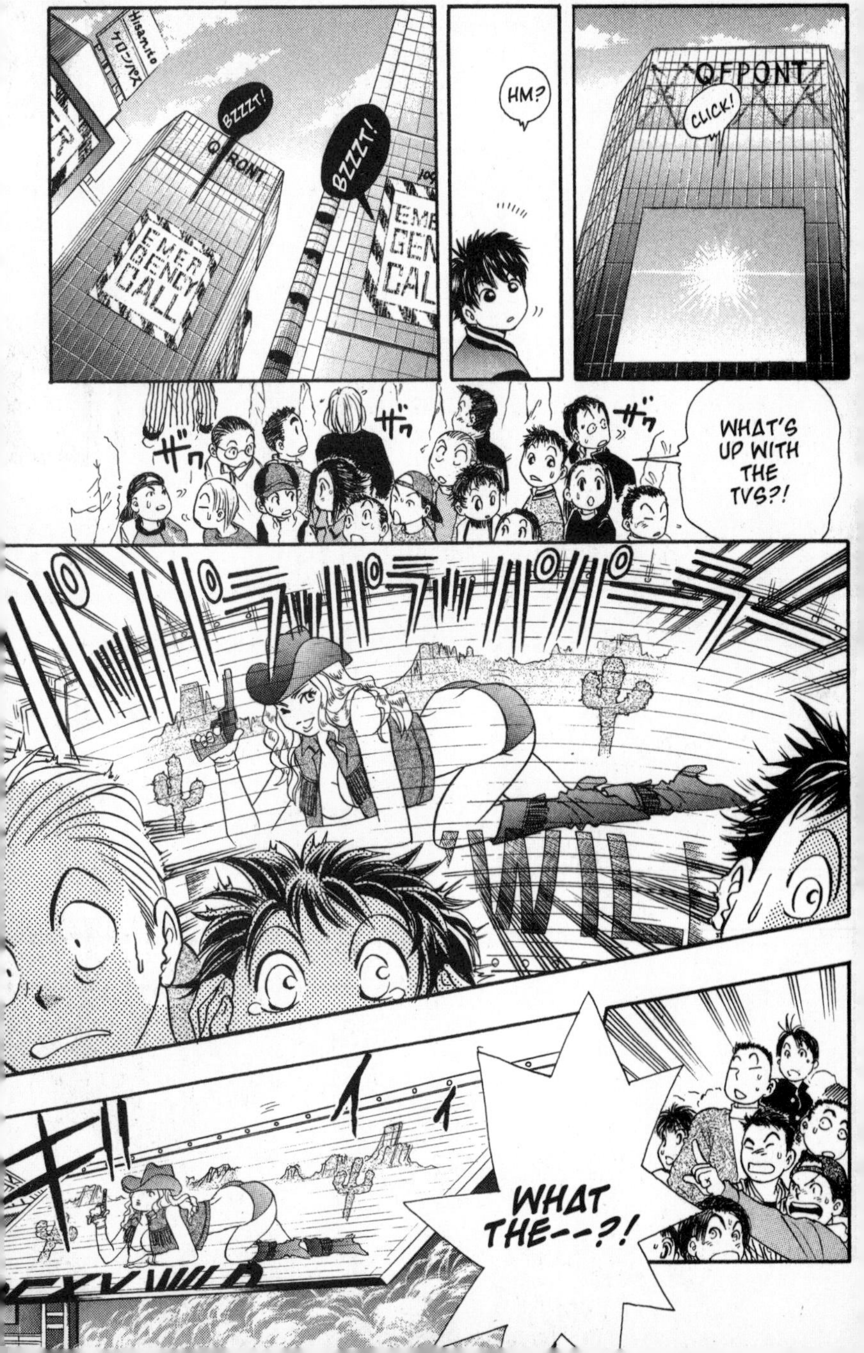
CLICK!
HM?
BZZZT!
BZZZT!
EMERGENCY CALL
EMERGENCY CALL
WHAT'S UP WITH THE TVS?!
ザワ
ザワ
ザワ
WHAT THE--?!

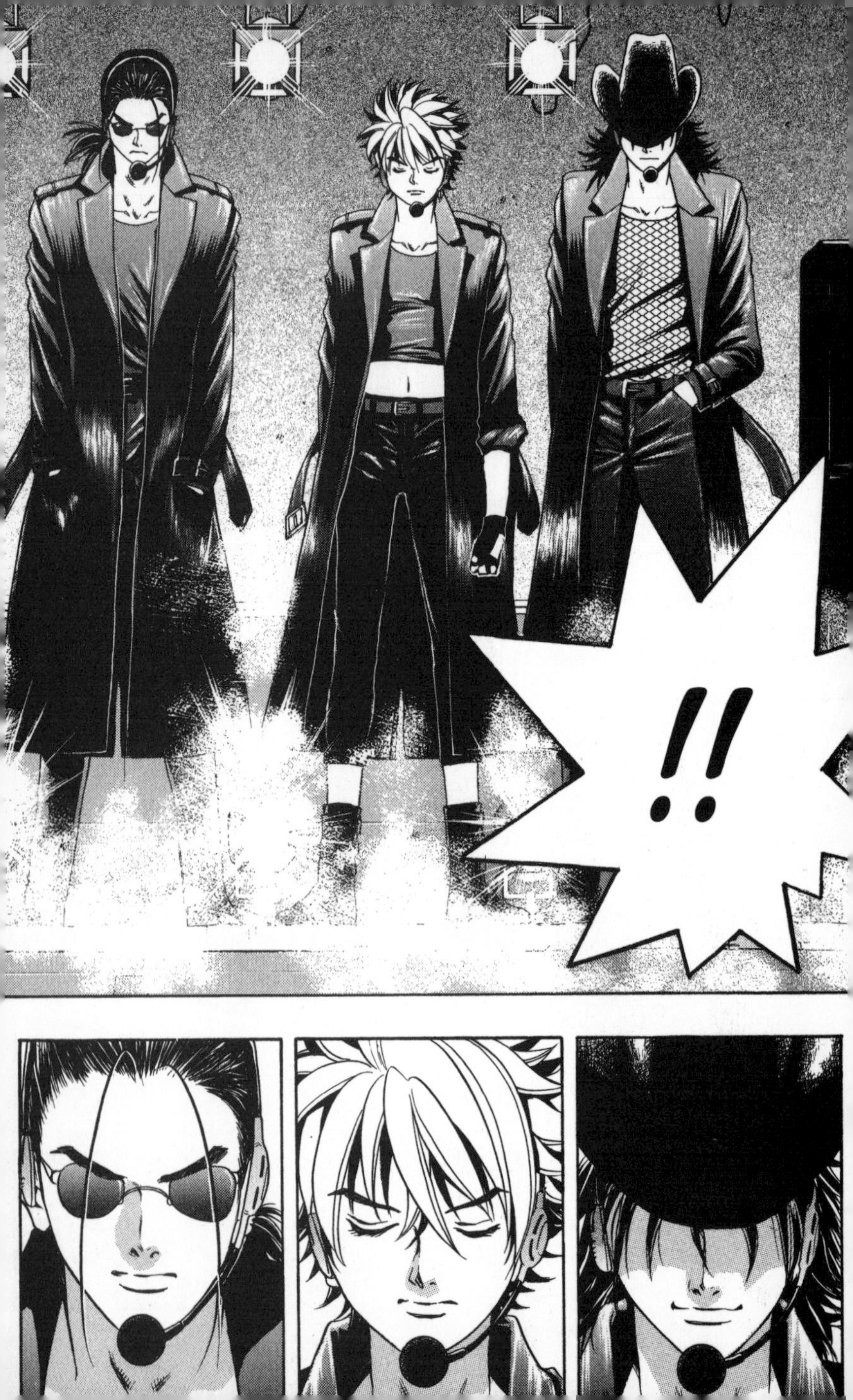
!!

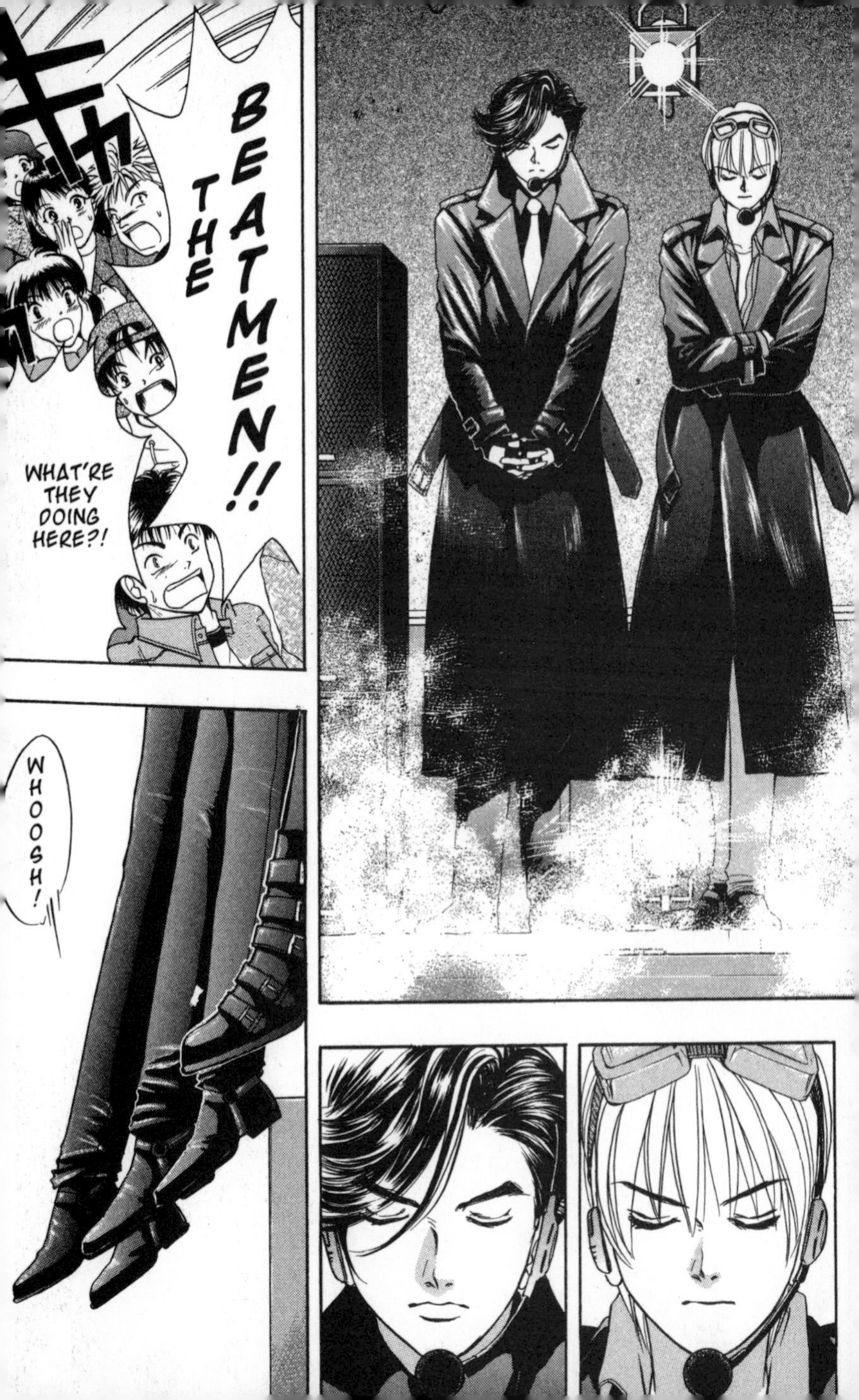
THE BEATMEN!!
WHAT'RE THEY DOING HERE?!
WHOOSH!

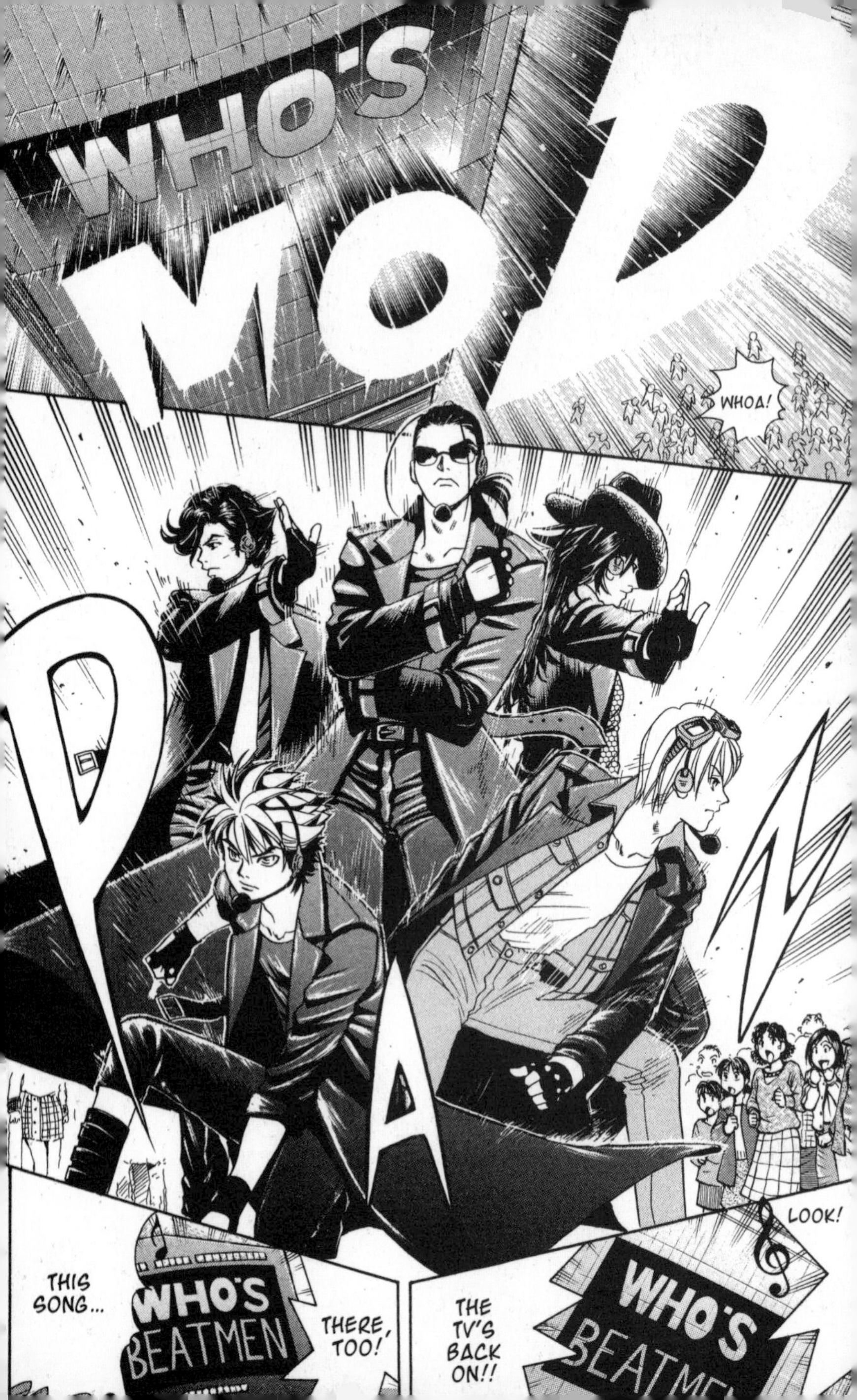
WHO'S WHO?
WHOA!
PAN
LOOK!
WHO'S BEATMEN
THE TV'S BACK ON!!
THERE, TOO!
WHO'S BEATMEN
THIS SONG...

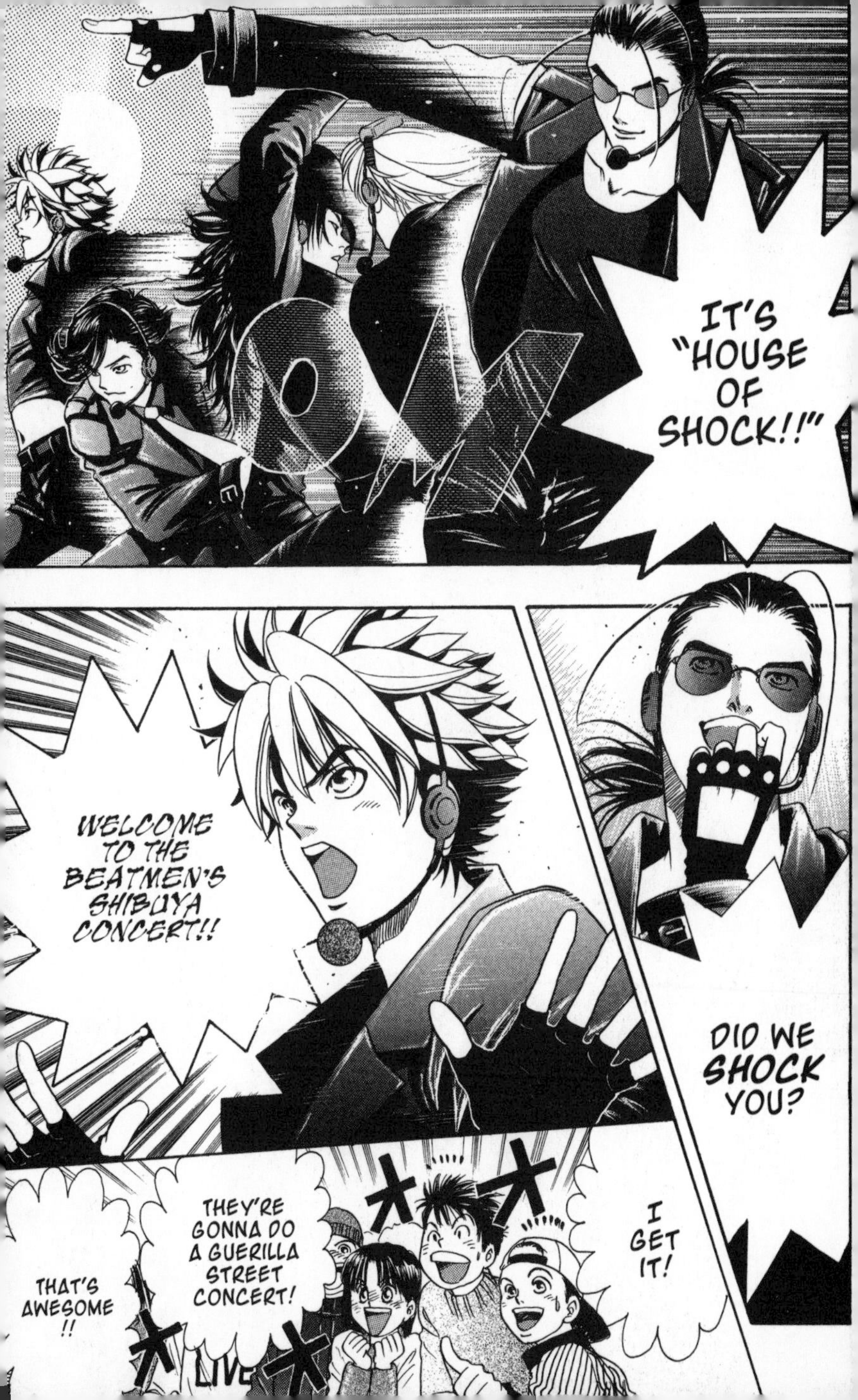
IT'S "HOUSE OF SHOCK!!"
DID WE SHOCK YOU?
WELCOME TO THE BEATMEN'S SHIBUYA CONCERT!!
I GET IT!
THEY'RE GONNA DO A GUERILLA STREET CONCERT!
THAT'S AWESOME!!

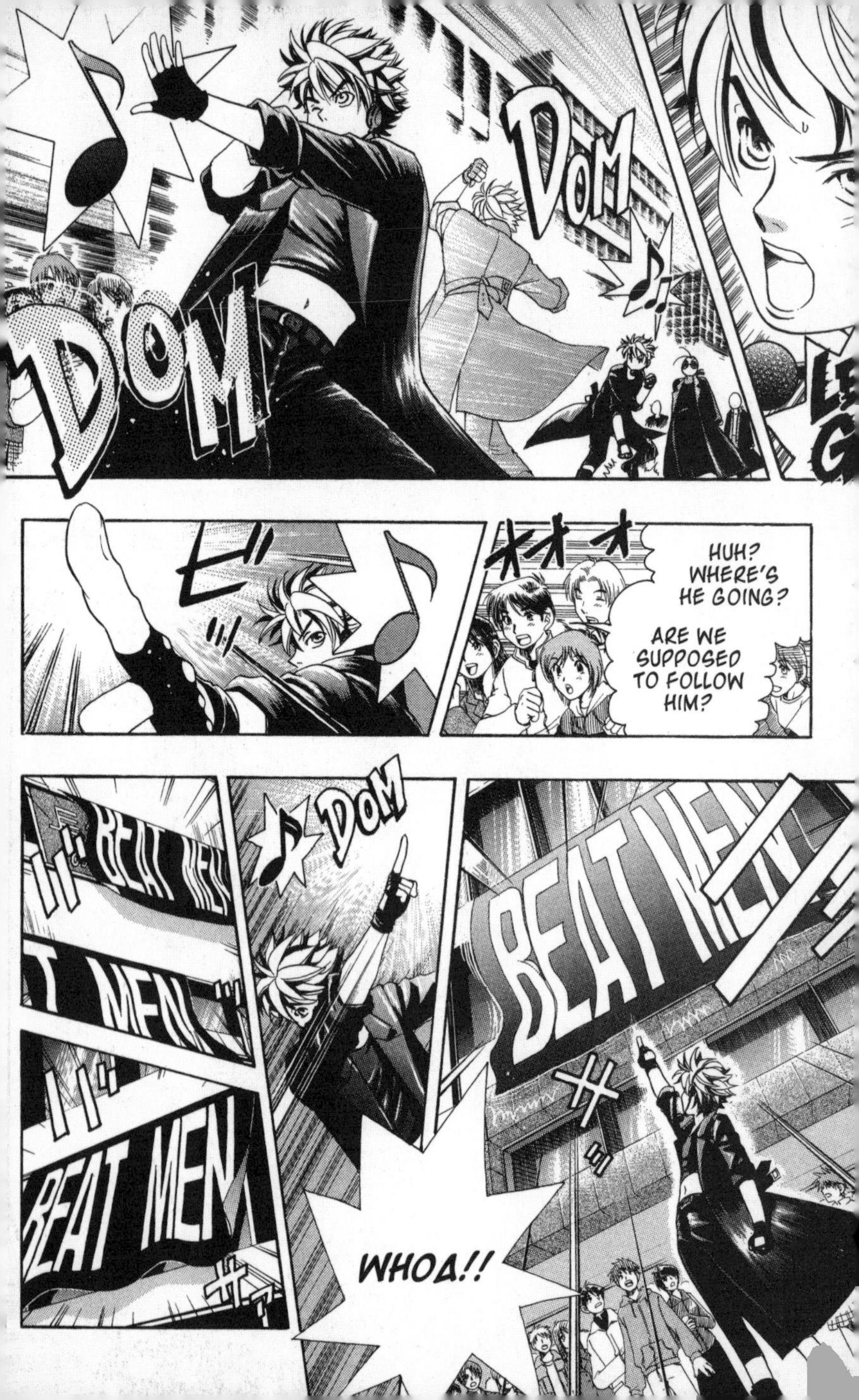

DOM
DOM
HUH? WHERE'S HE GOING?
ARE WE SUPPOSED TO FOLLOW HIM?
BEAT MEN
WHOA!!
DOM
BEAT MEN
BEAT MEN

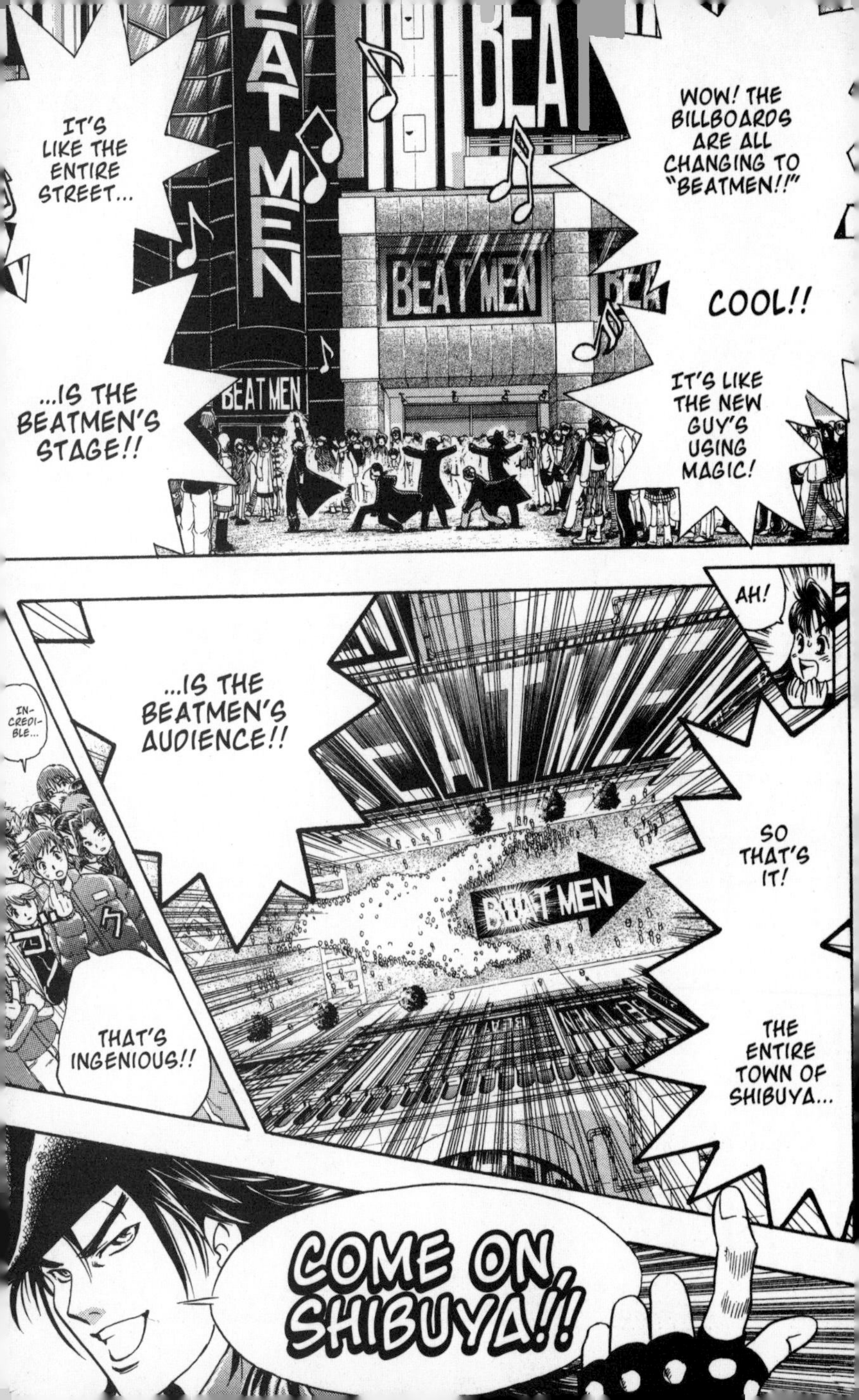
WOW! THE BILLBOARDS ARE ALL CHANGING TO "BEATMEN!!"
COOL!!
IT'S LIKE THE NEW GUY'S USING MAGIC!
IT'S LIKE THE ENTIRE STREET...
...IS THE BEATMEN'S STAGE!!
AH!
SO THAT'S IT!
THE ENTIRE TOWN OF SHIBUYA...
...IS THE BEATMEN'S AUDIENCE!!
IN-CREDI-BLE...
THAT'S INGENIOUS!!
COME ON, SHIBUYA!!!

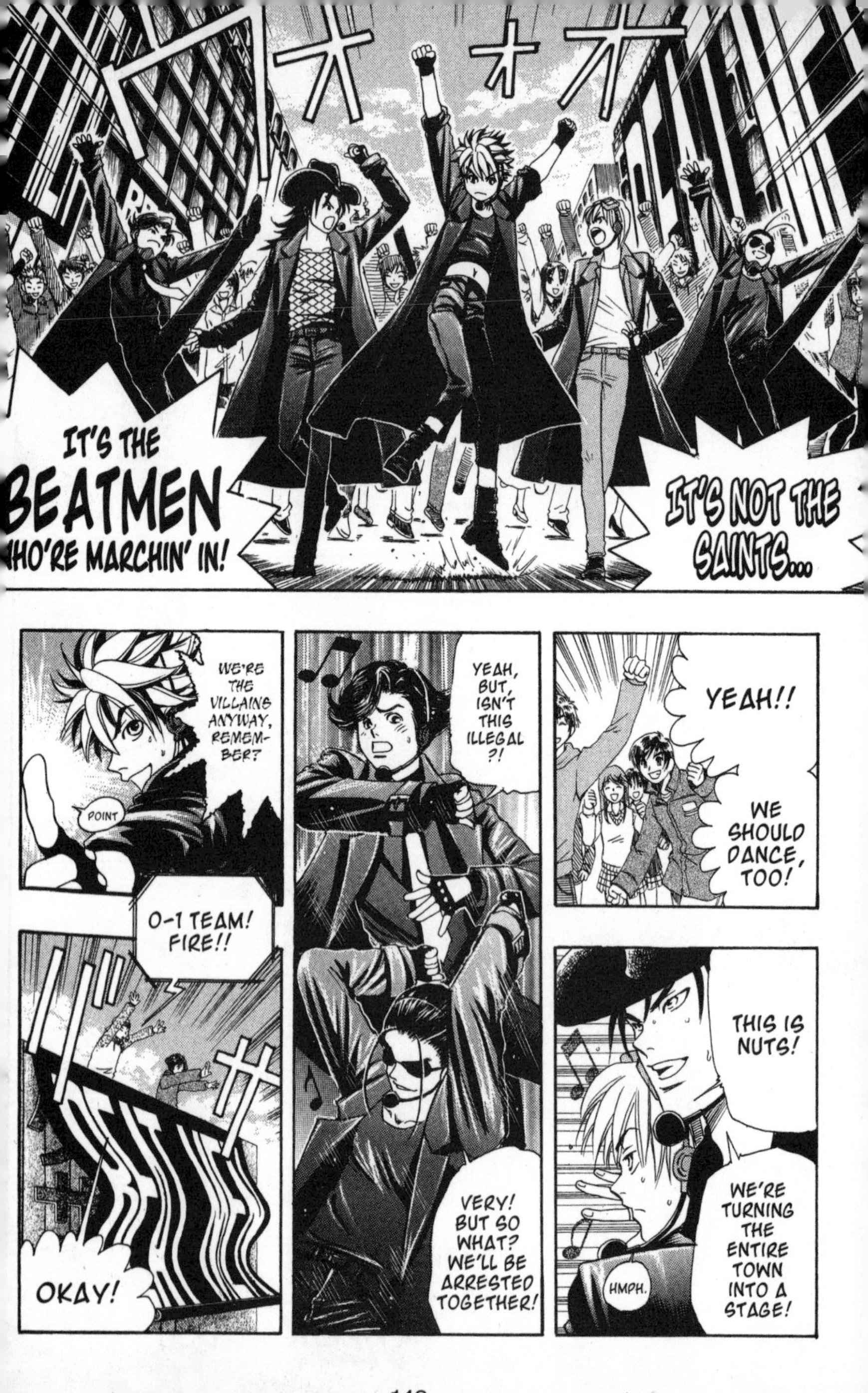

IT'S NOT THE SAINTS...
IT'S THE BEATMEN
IHO'RE MARCHIN' IN!
YEAH!!
WE SHOULD DANCE, TOO!
THIS IS NUTS!
WE'RE TURNING THE ENTIRE TOWN INTO A STAGE!
HMPH.
YEAH, BUT, ISN'T THIS ILLEGAL?!
VERY! BUT SO WHAT? WE'LL BE ARRESTED TOGETHER!
WE'RE THE VILLAINS ANYWAY, REMEMBER?
POINT
O-1 TEAM! FIRE!!
OKAY!

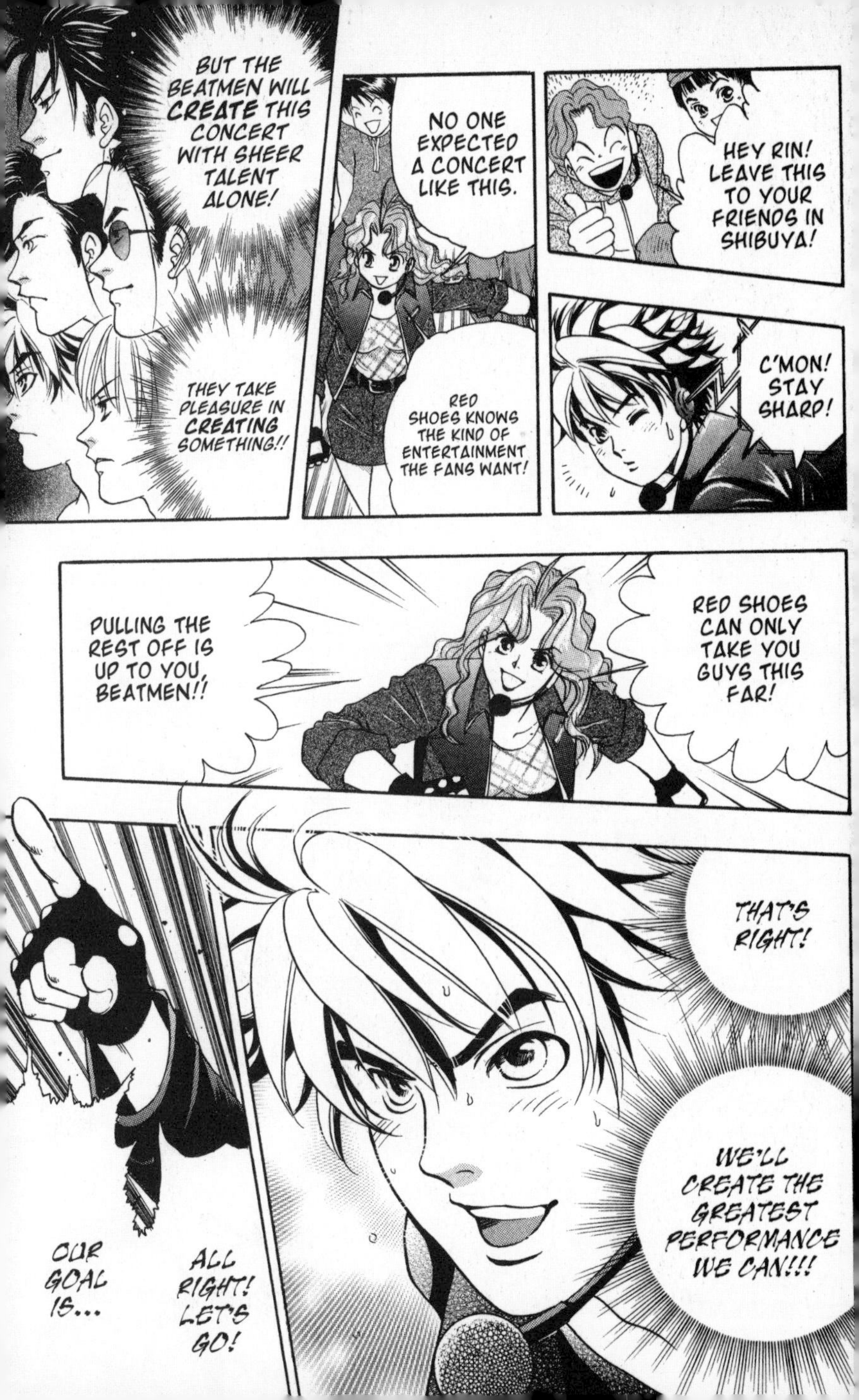
HEY RIN! LEAVE THIS TO YOUR FRIENDS IN SHIBUYA!
C'MON! STAY SHARP!
NO ONE EXPECTED A CONCERT LIKE THIS.
RED SHOES KNOWS THE KIND OF ENTERTAINMENT THE FANS WANT!
BUT THE BEATMEN WILL **CREATE** THIS CONCERT WITH SHEER TALENT ALONE!
THEY TAKE PLEASURE IN **CREATING** SOMETHING!!
RED SHOES CAN ONLY TAKE YOU GUYS THIS FAR!
PULLING THE REST OFF IS UP TO YOU, BEATMEN!!
THAT'S RIGHT!
WE'LL CREATE THE GREATEST PERFORMANCE WE CAN!!!
ALL RIGHT! LET'S GO!
OUR GOAL IS...

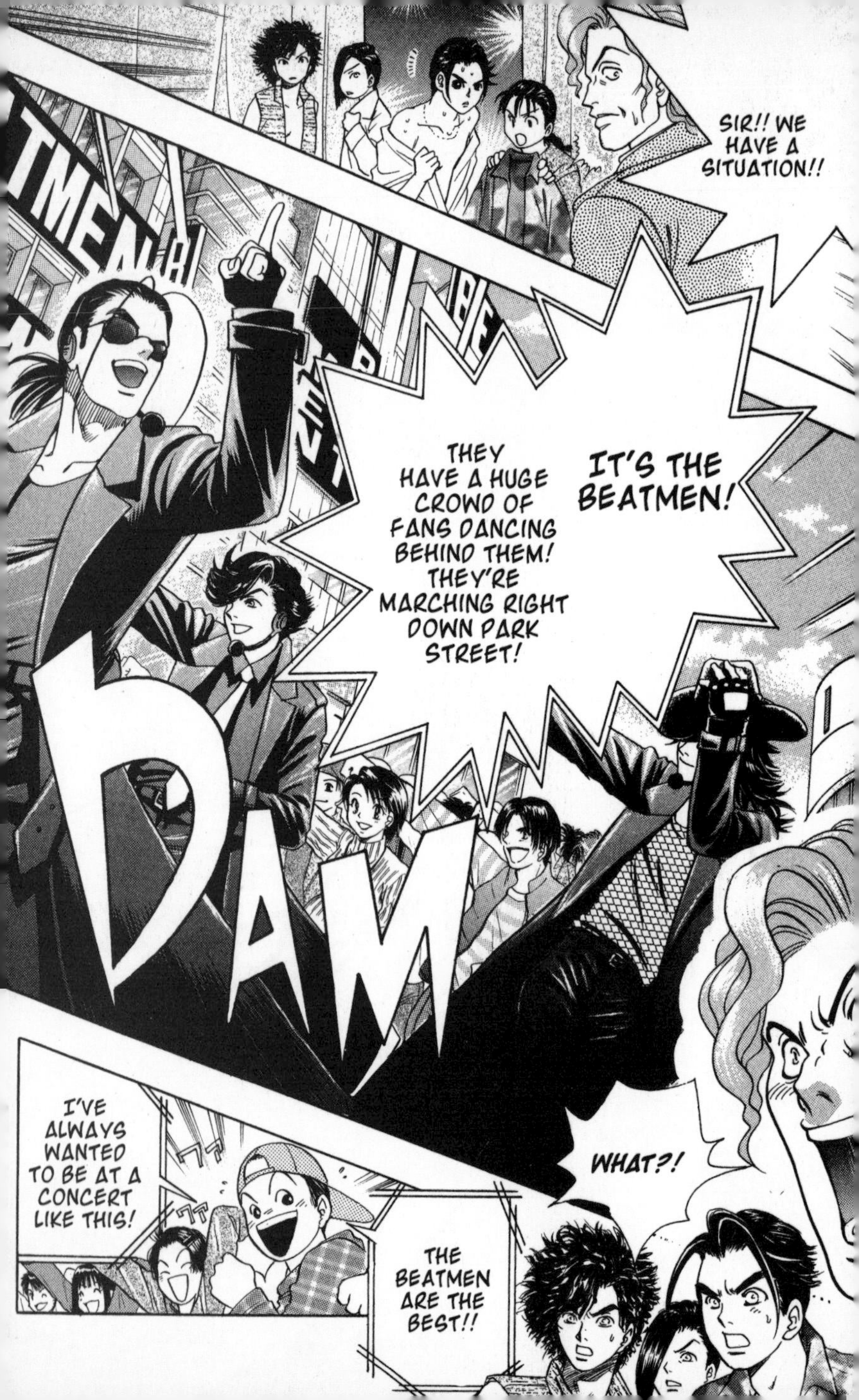
SIR!! WE HAVE A SITUATION!!
IT'S THE BEATMEN!
THEY HAVE A HUGE CROWD OF FANS DANCING BEHIND THEM! THEY'RE MARCHING RIGHT DOWN PARK STREET!
DAM
WHAT?!
THE BEATMEN ARE THE BEST!!
I'VE ALWAYS WANTED TO BE AT A CONCERT LIKE THIS!

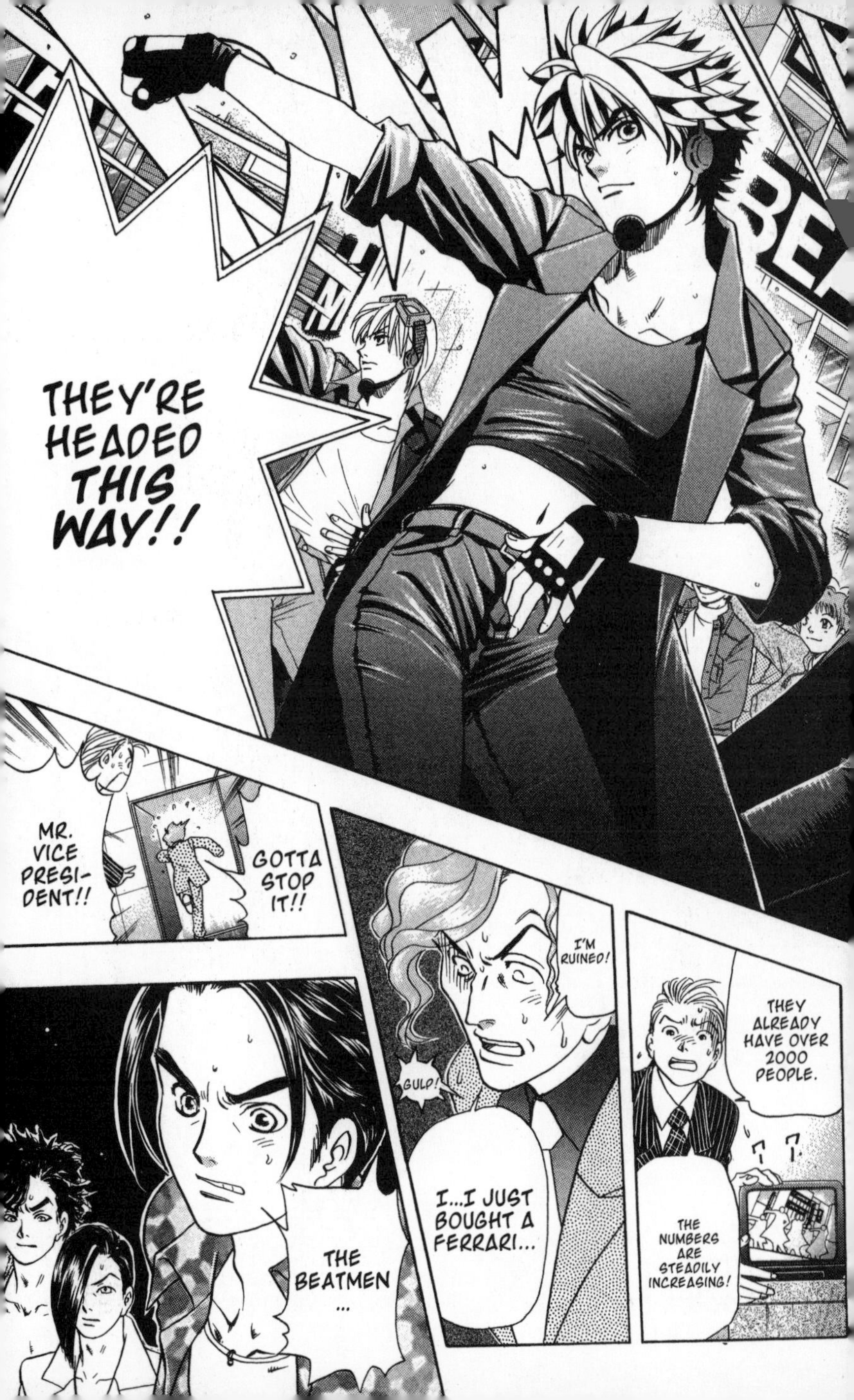
THEY'RE HEADED THIS WAY!!
THEY ALREADY HAVE OVER 2000 PEOPLE.
THE NUMBERS ARE STEADILY INCREASING!
I'M RUINED!
GULP!
I...I JUST BOUGHT A FERRARI...
GOTTA STOP IT!!
MR. VICE PRESIDENT!!
THE BEATMEN
...

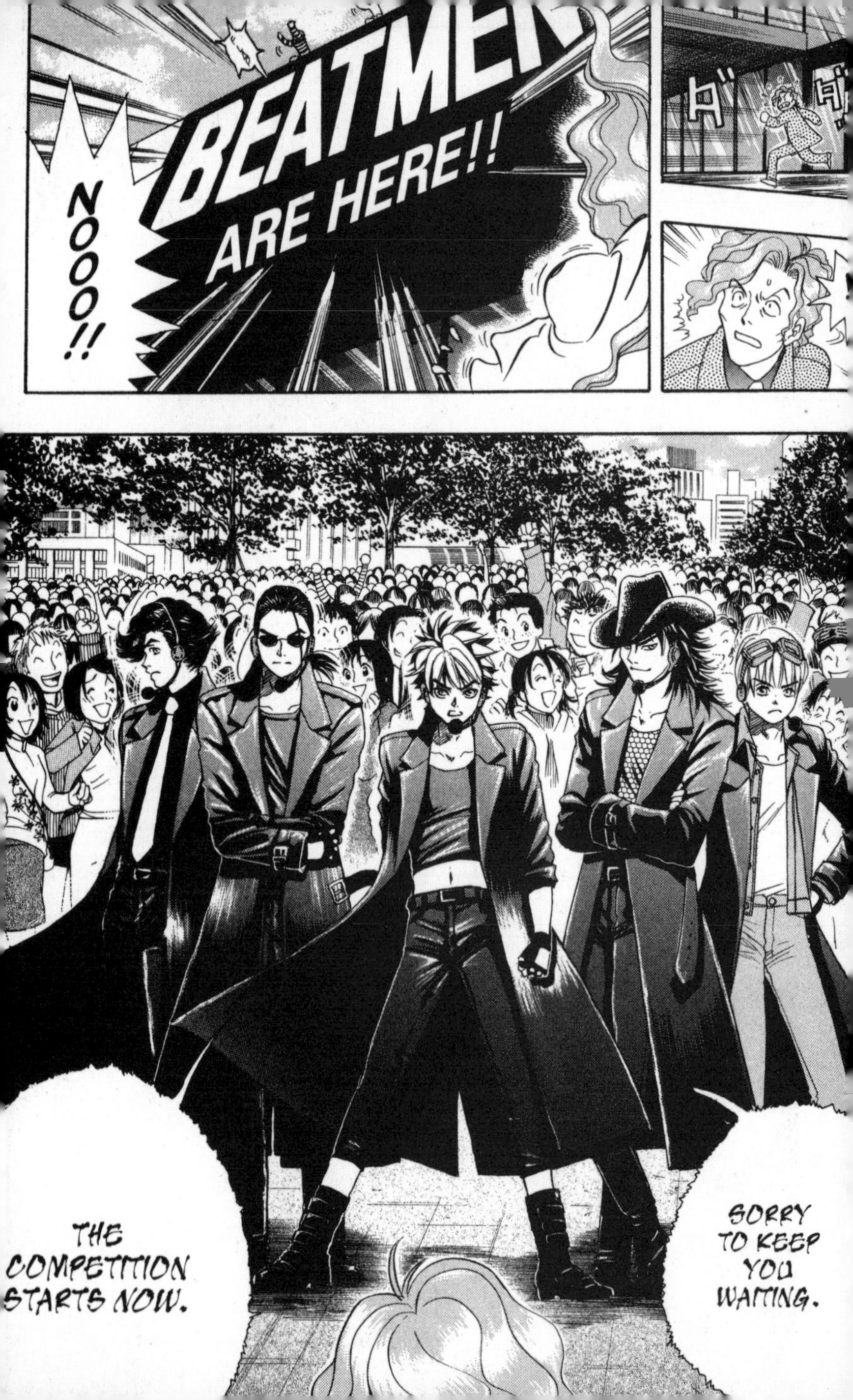
ダ ダ
BEATMEN ARE HERE!!
NOOOO!!
SORRY TO KEEP YOU WAITING.
THE COMPETITION STARTS NOW.

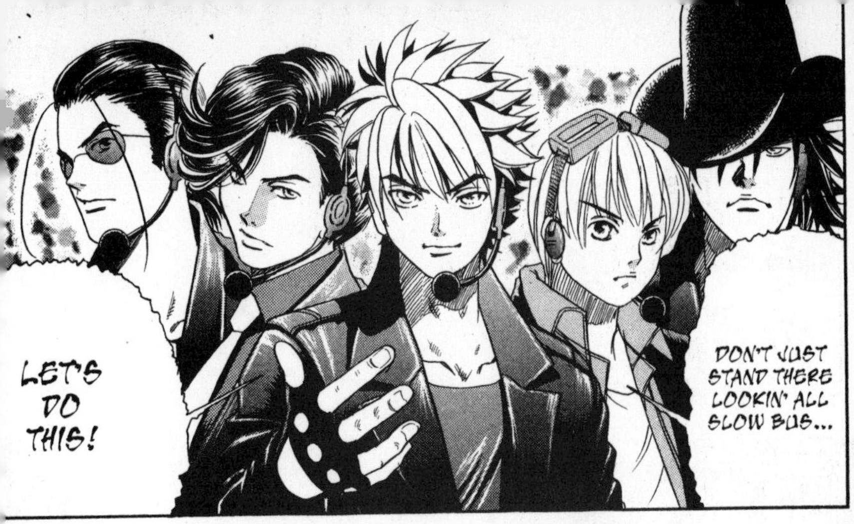
DON'T JUST STAND THERE LOOKIN' ALL SLOW BUS...
LET'S DO THIS!

# DRAGON VOICE

## # 14 Breathe Out

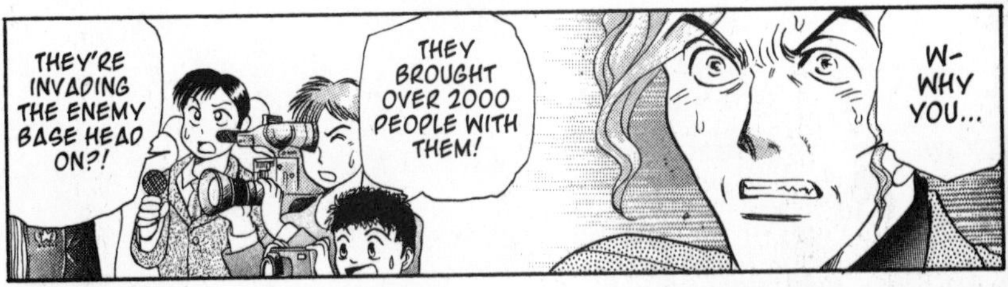
W-WHY YOU...
THEY BROUGHT OVER 2000 PEOPLE WITH THEM!
THEY'RE INVADING THE ENEMY BASE HEAD ON?!

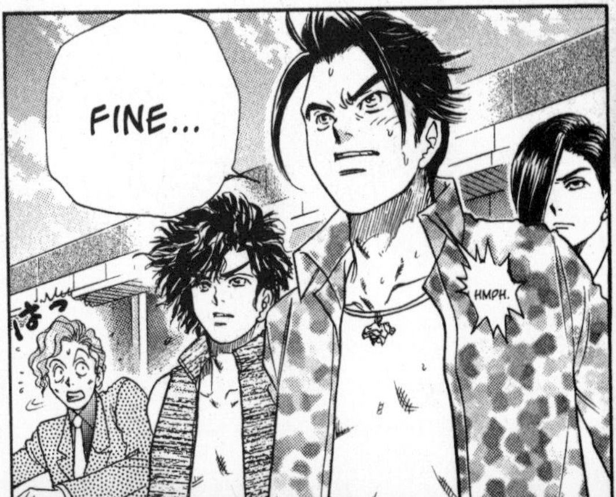
FINE...
HMPH.

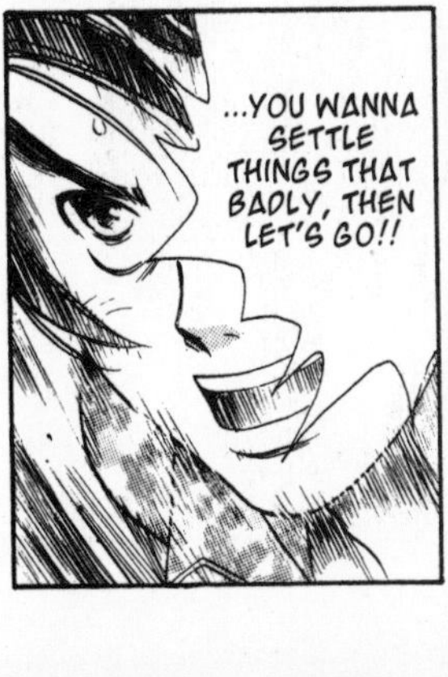
...YOU WANNA SETTLE THINGS THAT BADLY, THEN LET'S GO!!

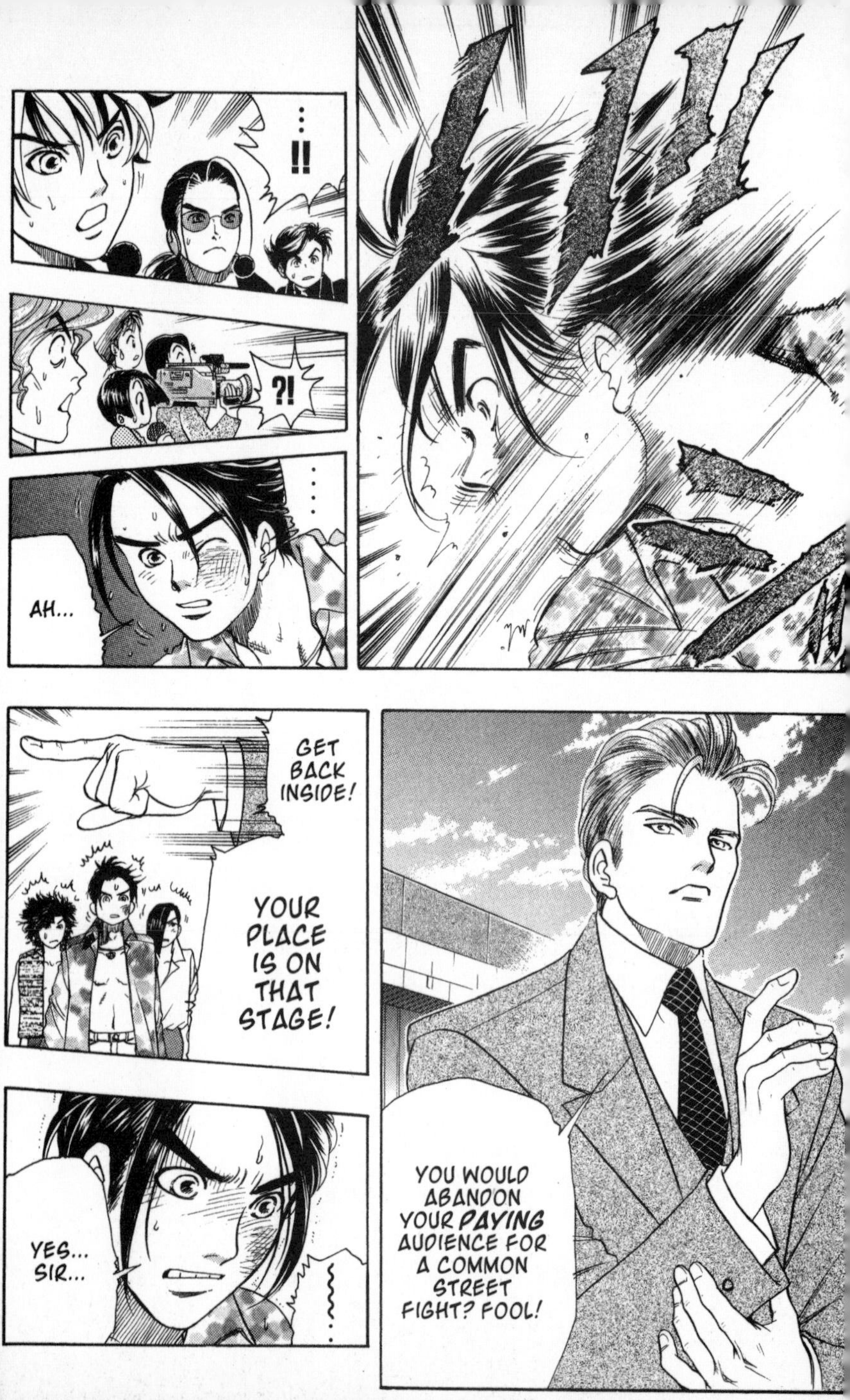
...!!
?!
.....
AH...
YOU WOULD ABANDON YOUR PAYING AUDIENCE FOR A COMMON STREET FIGHT? FOOL!
GET BACK INSIDE!
YOUR PLACE IS ON THAT STAGE!
......
YES... SIR...

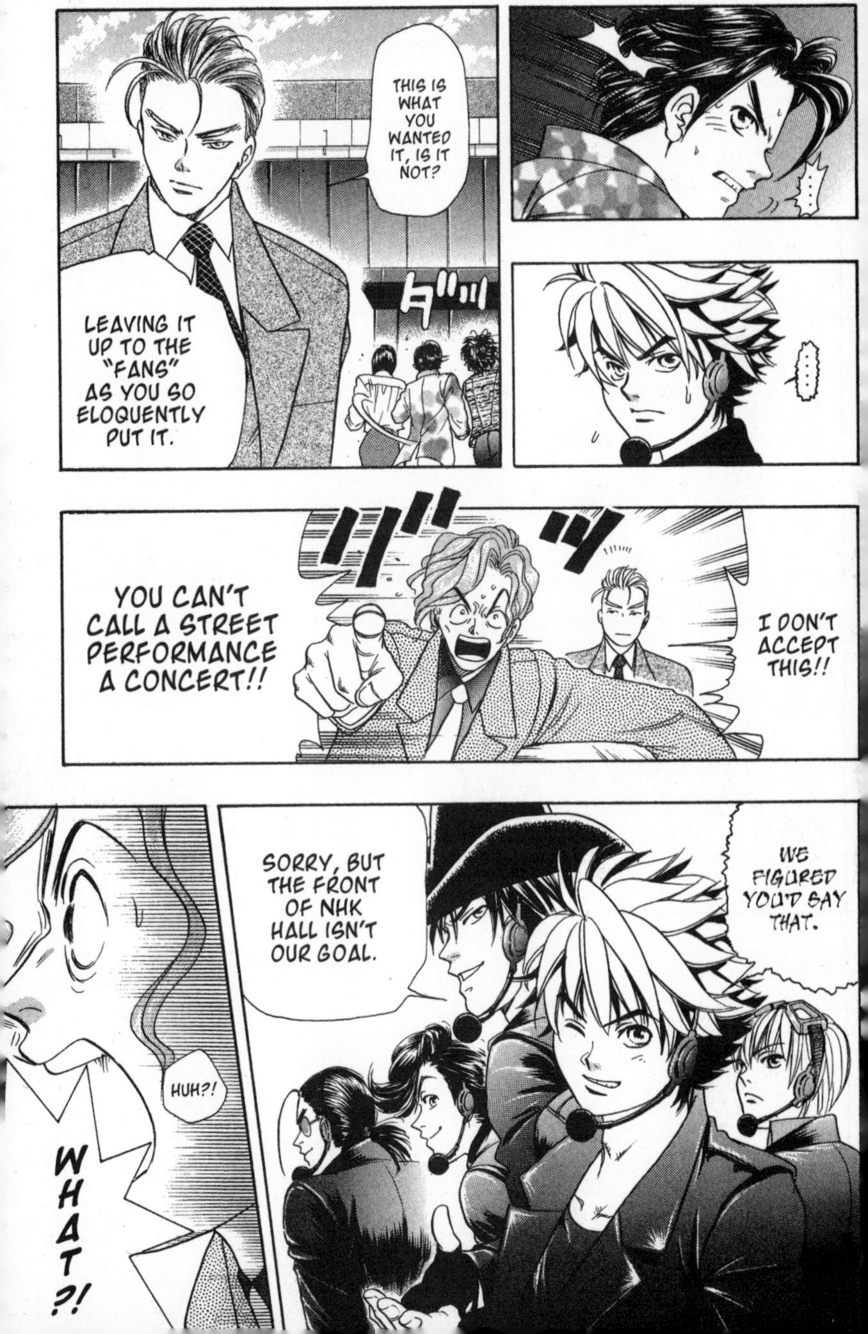
...
...
THIS IS WHAT YOU WANTED IT, IS IT NOT?
LEAVING IT UP TO THE "FANS" AS YOU SO ELOQUENTLY PUT IT.
I DON'T ACCEPT THIS!!
YOU CAN'T CALL A STREET PERFORMANCE A CONCERT!!
WE FIGURED YOU'D SAY THAT.
SORRY, BUT THE FRONT OF NHK HALL ISN'T OUR GOAL.
HUH?!
WHAT?!

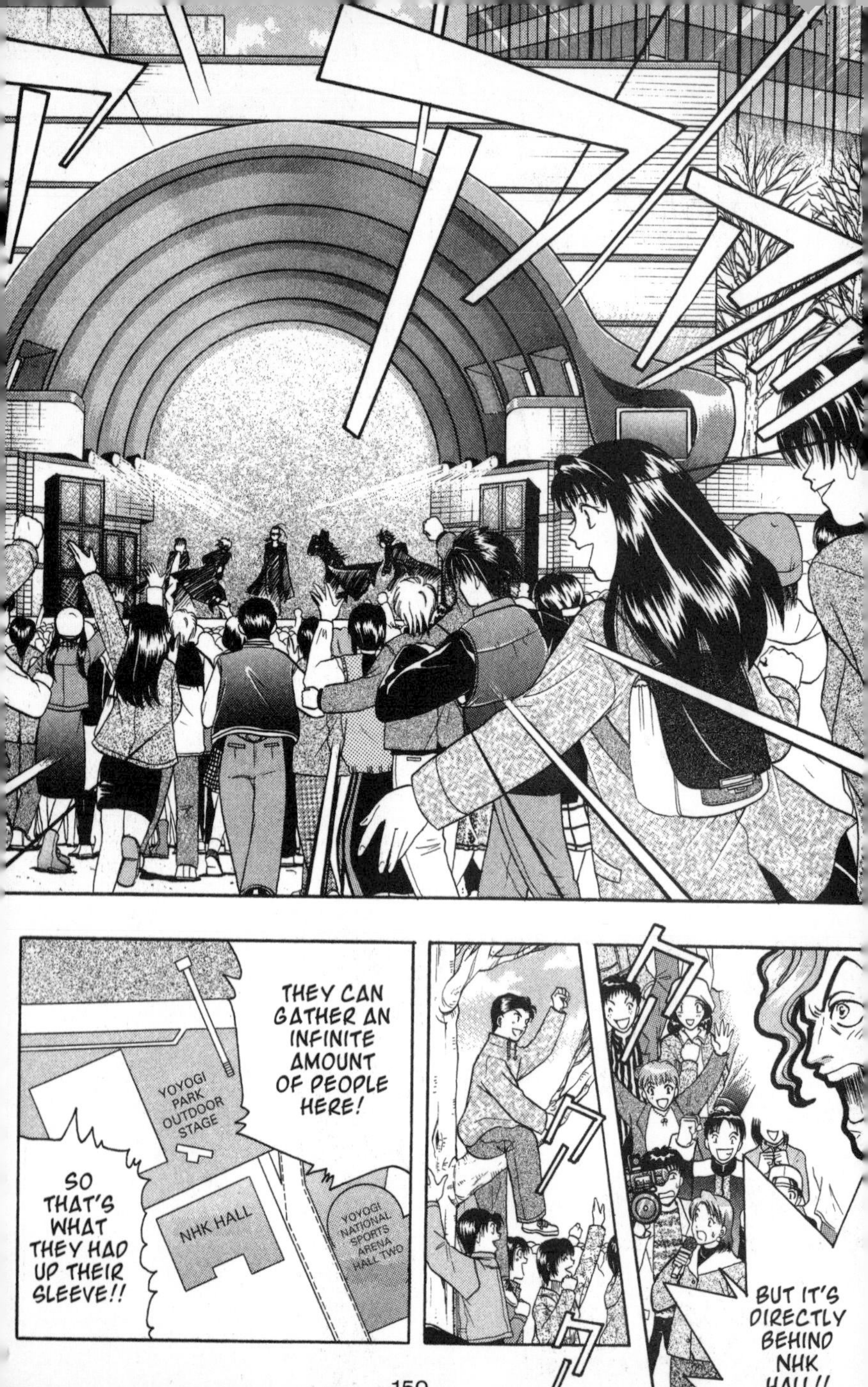
BUT IT'S DIRECTLY BEHIND NHK HALL!!
THEY CAN GATHER AN INFINITE AMOUNT OF PEOPLE HERE!
YOYOGI PARK OUTDOOR STAGE
YOYOGI NATIONAL SPORTS ARENA HALL TWO
NHK HALL
SO THAT'S WHAT THEY HAD UP THEIR SLEEVE!!

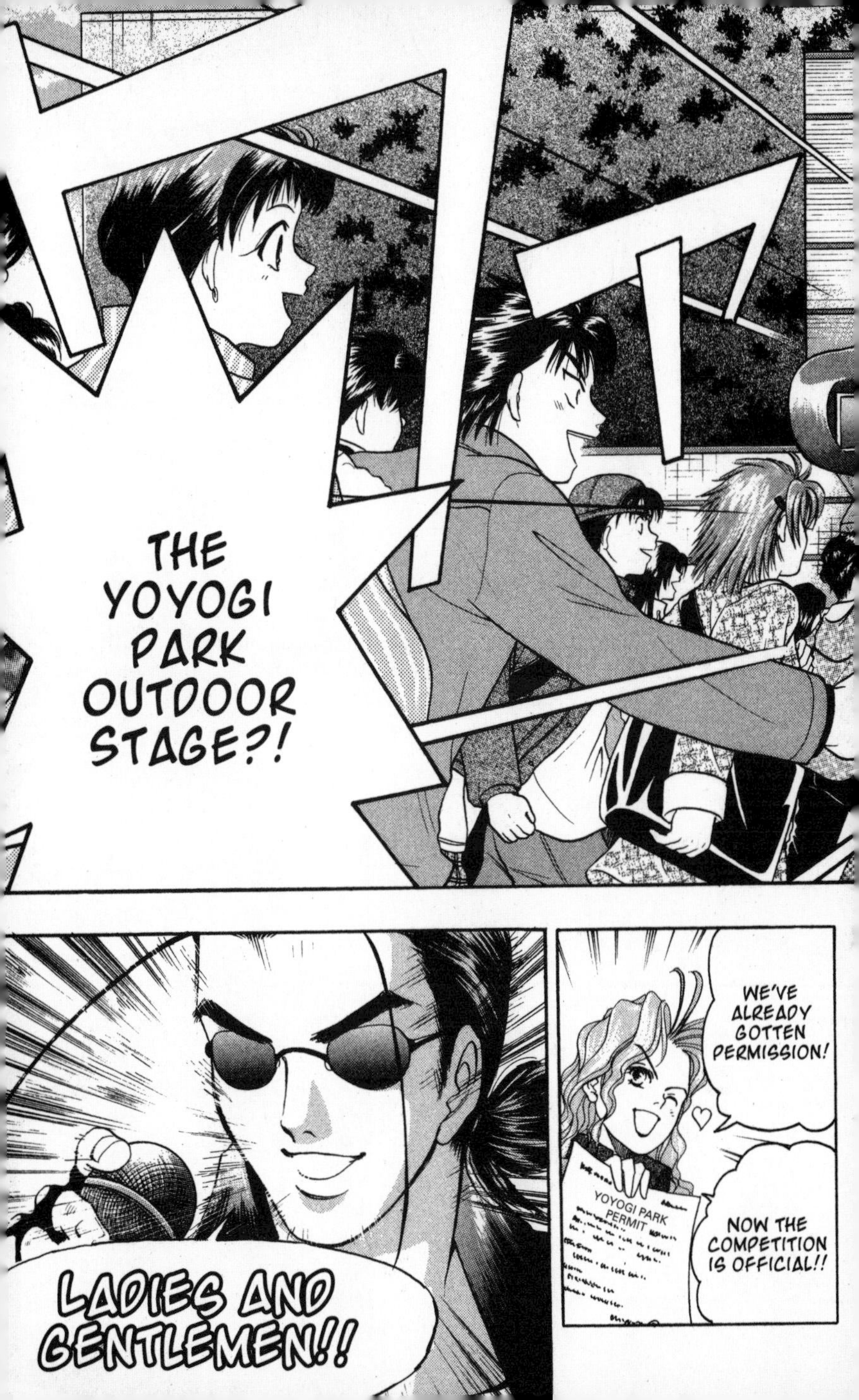
THE YOYOGI PARK OUTDOOR STAGE?!
WE'VE ALREADY GOTTEN PERMISSION!
YOYOGI PARK PERMIT
NOW THE COMPETITION IS OFFICIAL!!
LADIES AND GENTLEMEN!!

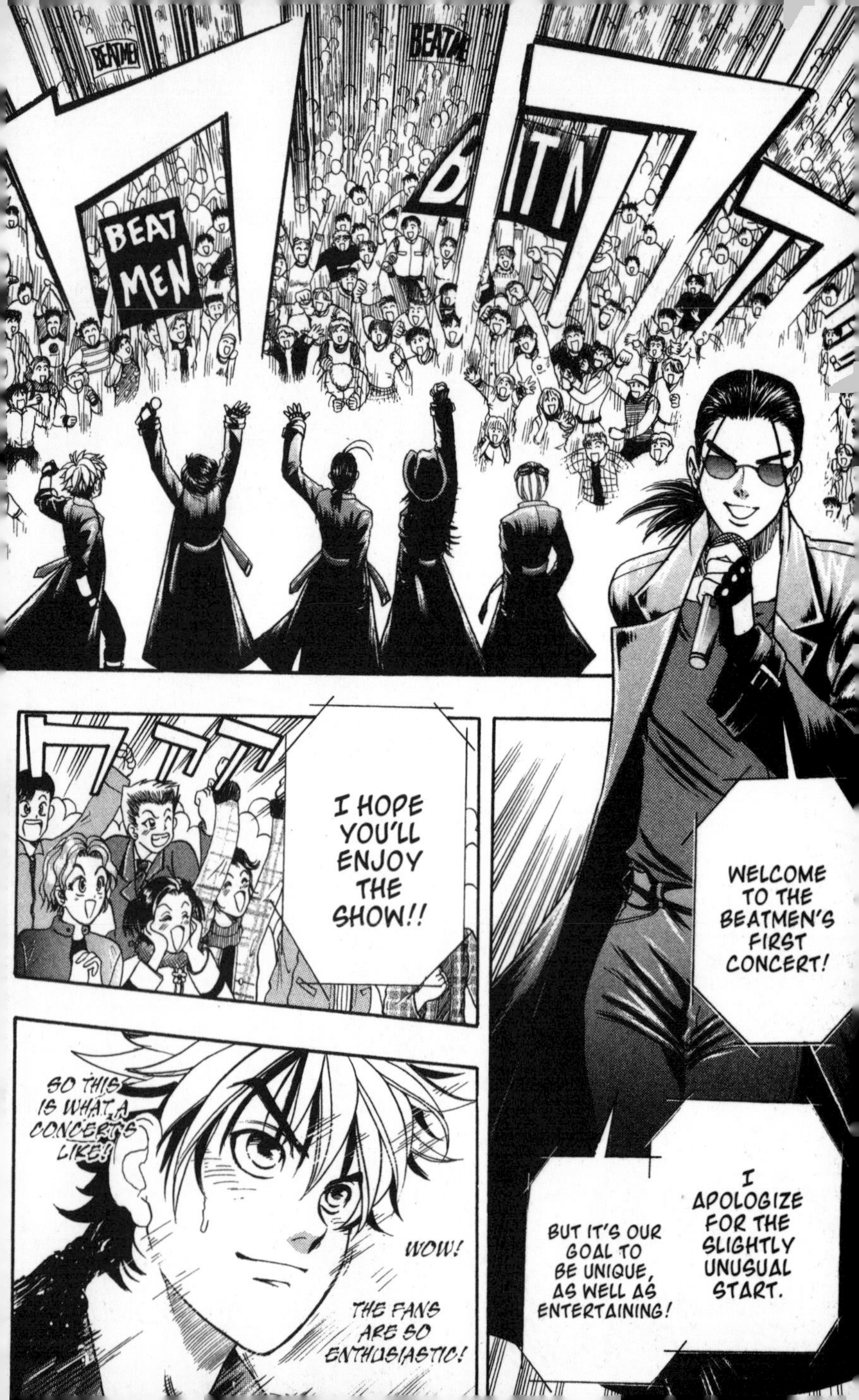
BEATMEN
BEAT MEN
WELCOME TO THE BEATMEN'S FIRST CONCERT!
I APOLOGIZE FOR THE SLIGHTLY UNUSUAL START.
BUT IT'S OUR GOAL TO BE UNIQUE, AS WELL AS ENTERTAINING!
I HOPE YOU'LL ENJOY THE SHOW!!
SO THIS IS WHAT A CONCERT'S LIKE!
WOW!
THE FANS ARE SO ENTHUSIASTIC!

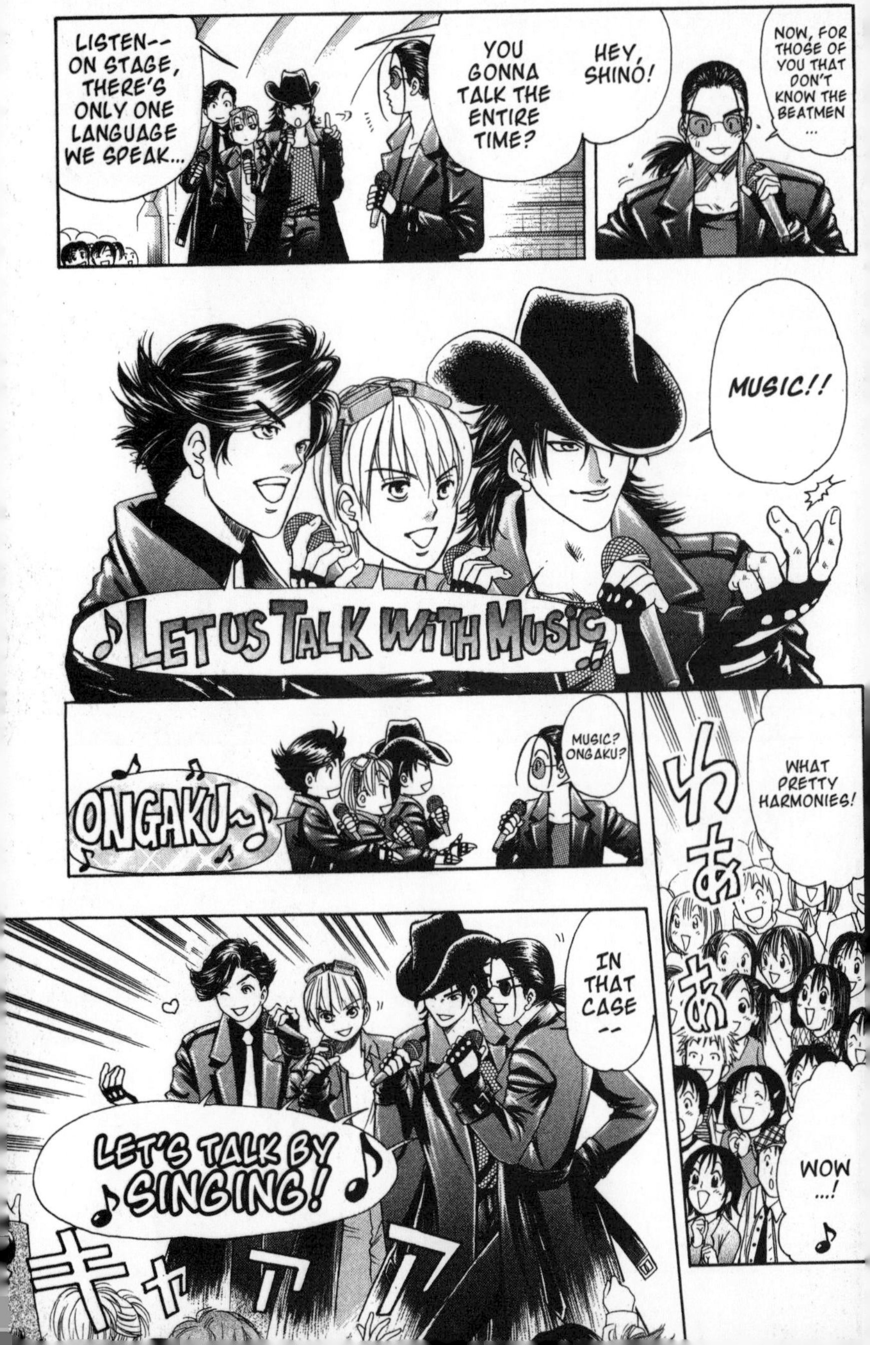
NOW, FOR THOSE OF YOU THAT DON'T KNOW THE BEATMEN ...
HEY, SHINO!
YOU GONNA TALK THE ENTIRE TIME?
LISTEN-- ON STAGE, THERE'S ONLY ONE LANGUAGE WE SPEAK...
MUSIC!!
♪LET US TALK WITH MUSIC♪
WHAT PRETTY HARMONIES!
わあああ
WOW ...!
MUSIC? ONGAKU?
ONGAKU~♪
IN THAT CASE --
LET'S TALK BY SINGING!
キャア

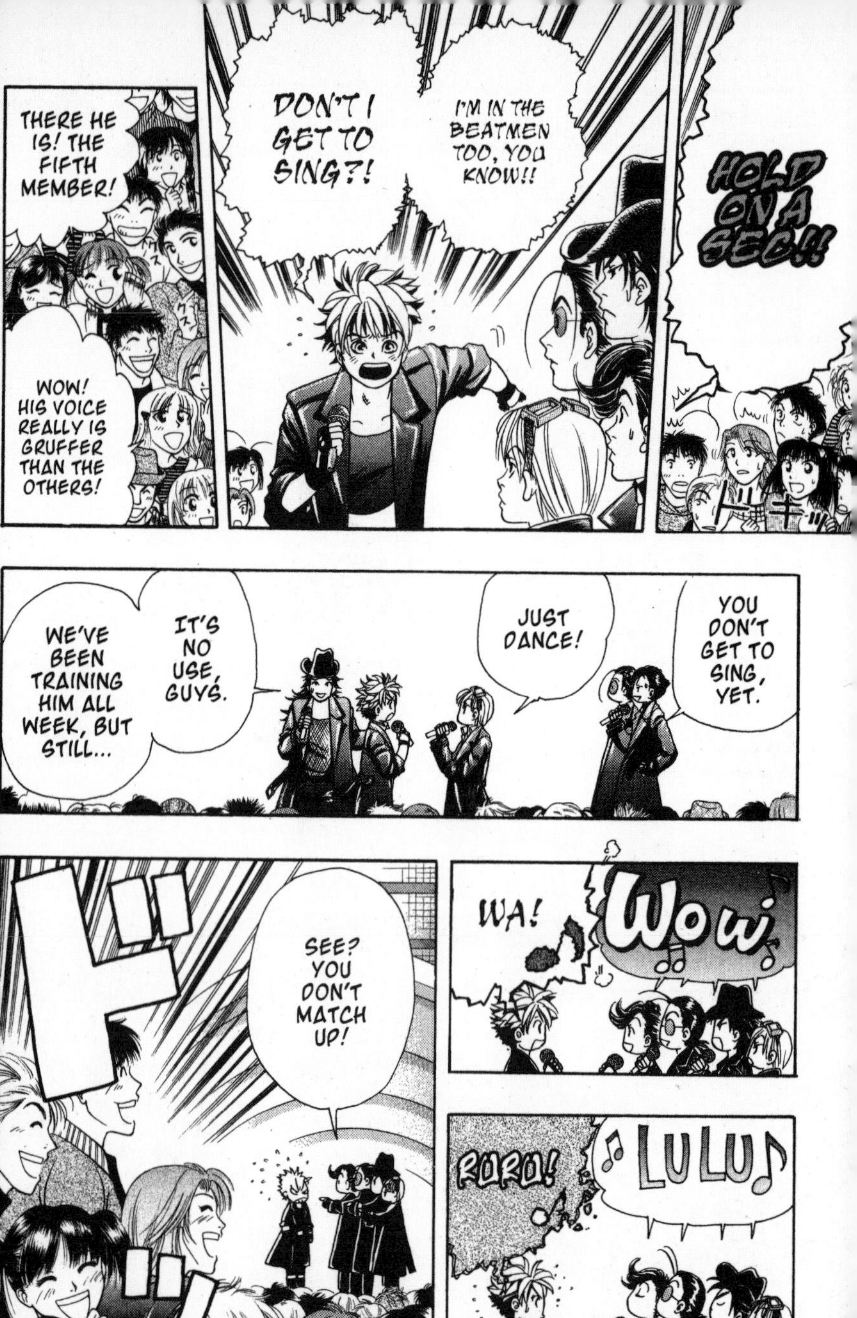
HOLD ON A SEC!!
I'M IN THE BEATMEN TOO, YOU KNOW!!
DON'T I GET TO SING?!
THERE HE IS! THE FIFTH MEMBER!
WOW! HIS VOICE REALLY IS GRUFFER THAN THE OTHERS!
YOU DON'T GET TO SING, YET.
JUST DANCE!
IT'S NO USE, GUYS.
WE'VE BEEN TRAINING HIM ALL WEEK, BUT STILL...
WOW
WA!
♪LULU♪
RURU!
SEE? YOU DON'T MATCH UP!

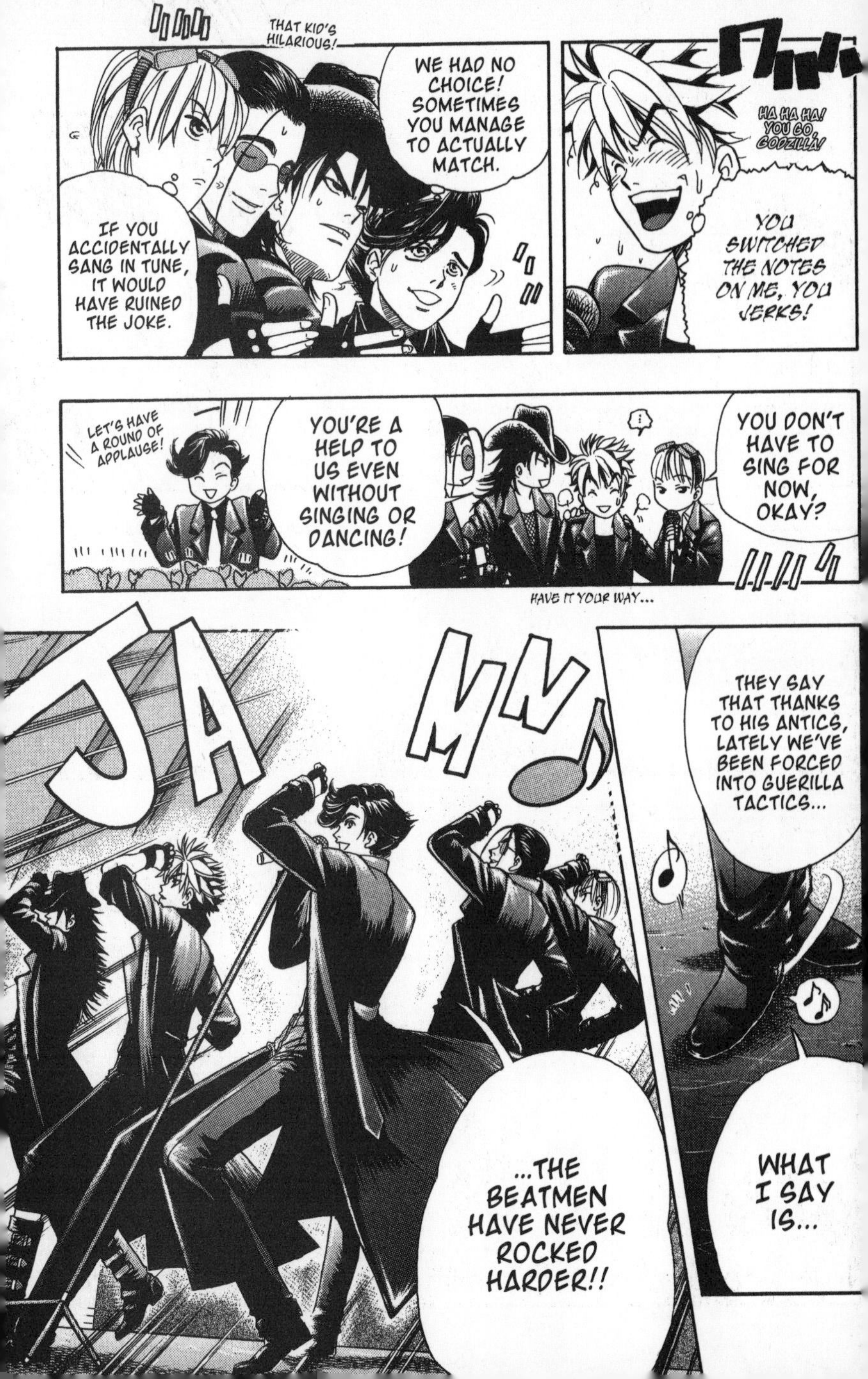
HA HA HA! YOU GO GODZILLA!
YOU SWITCHED THE NOTES ON ME, YOU JERKS!
THAT KID'S HILARIOUS!
WE HAD NO CHOICE! SOMETIMES YOU MANAGE TO ACTUALLY MATCH.
IF YOU ACCIDENTALLY SANG IN TUNE, IT WOULD HAVE RUINED THE JOKE.
YOU DON'T HAVE TO SING FOR NOW, OKAY?
HAVE IT YOUR WAY...
YOU'RE A HELP TO US EVEN WITHOUT SINGING OR DANCING!
LET'S HAVE A ROUND OF APPLAUSE!
THEY SAY THAT THANKS TO HIS ANTICS, LATELY WE'VE BEEN FORCED INTO GUERILLA TACTICS...
WHAT I SAY IS...
JA
MN
...THE BEATMEN HAVE NEVER ROCKED HARDER!!

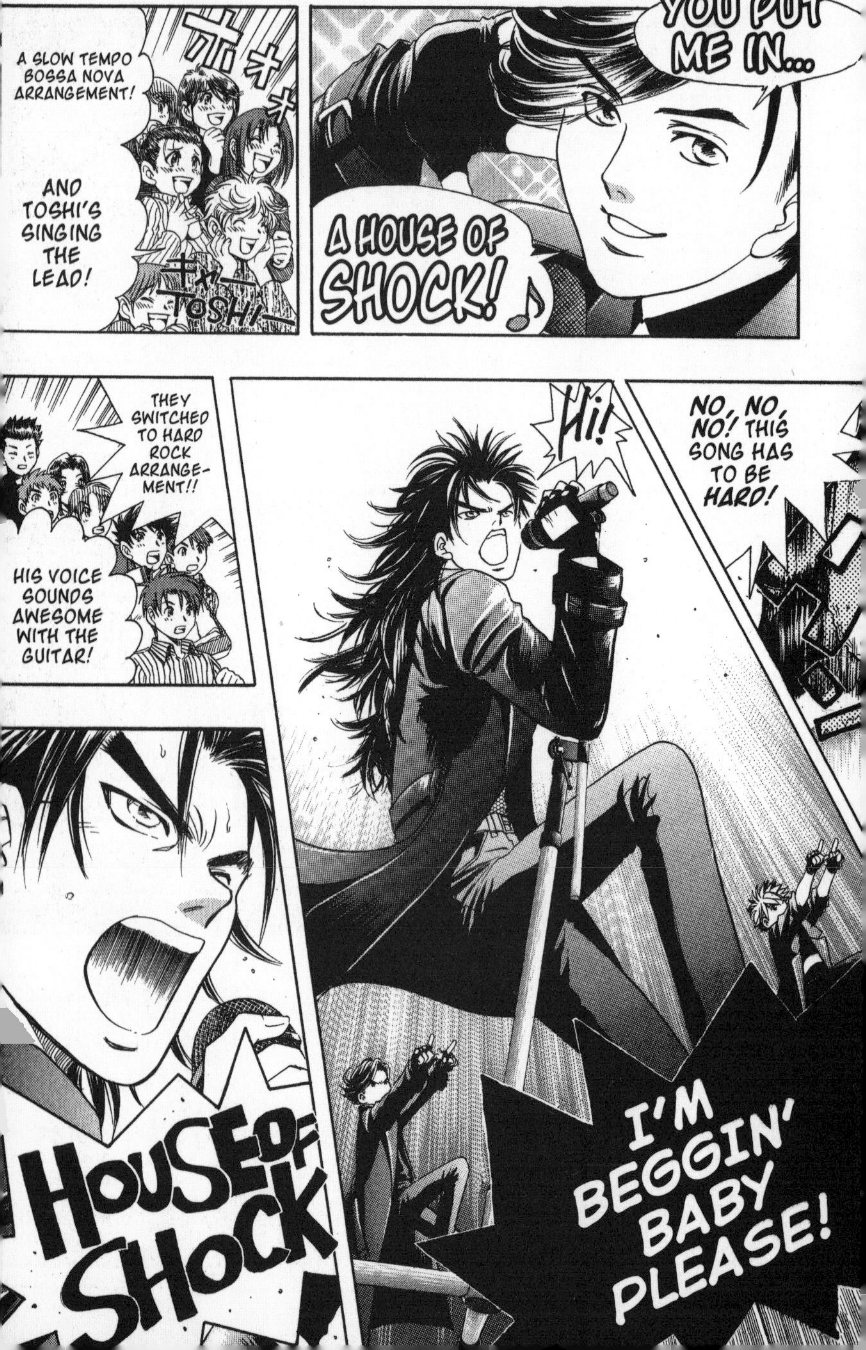
YOU PUT ME IN...
A HOUSE OF SHOCK! ♪
ホオオ
A SLOW TEMPO BOSSA NOVA ARRANGEMENT!
AND TOSHI'S SINGING THE LEAD!
キャー TOSHI ー
NO, NO, NO! THIS SONG HAS TO BE HARD!
Hi!
I'M BEGGIN' BABY PLEASE!
THEY SWITCHED TO HARD ROCK ARRANGE-MENT!!
HIS VOICE SOUNDS AWESOME WITH THE GUITAR!
HOUSE OF SHOCK

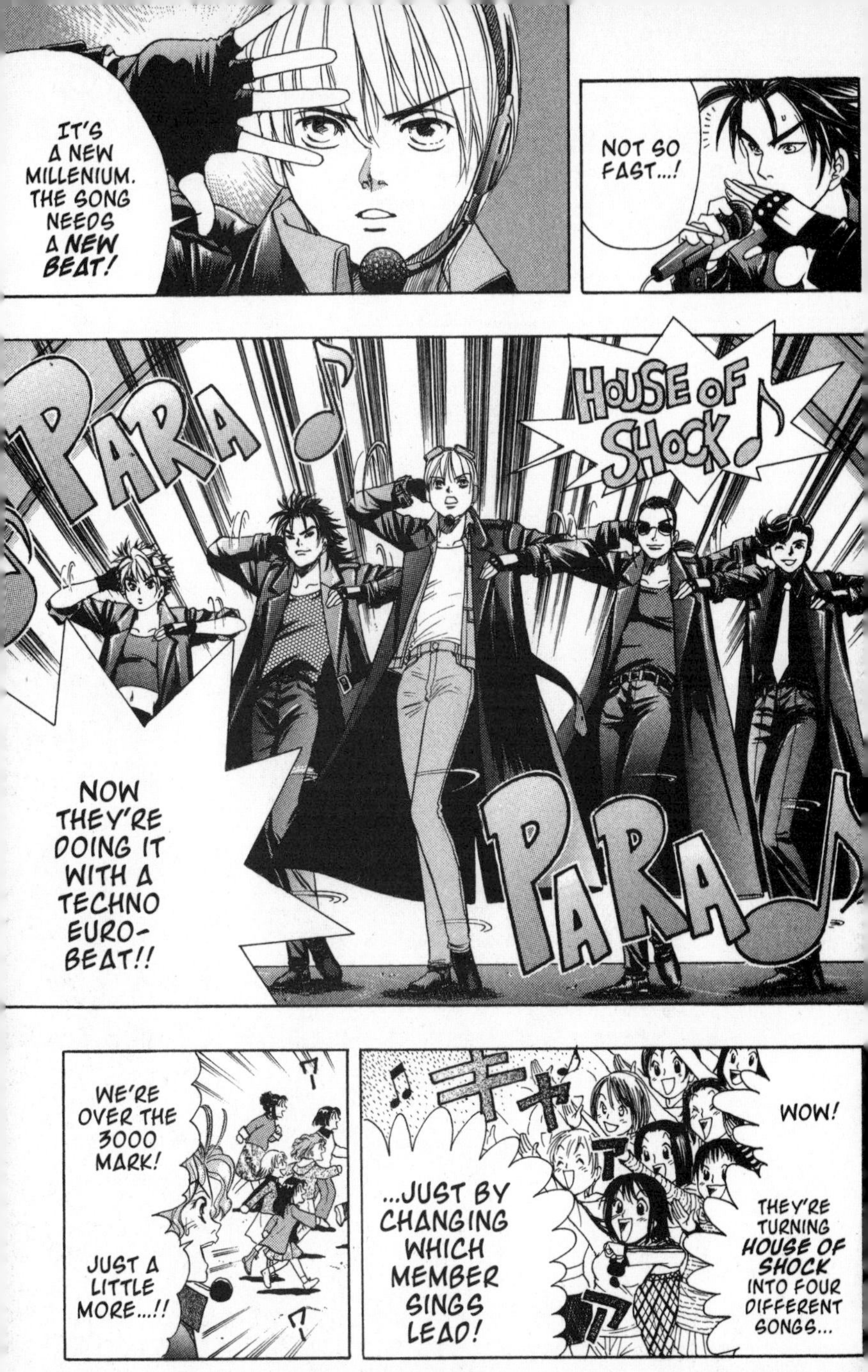
NOT SO FAST...!
IT'S A NEW MILLENIUM. THE SONG NEEDS A NEW BEAT!
HOUSE OF SHOCK
PARA
PARA
NOW THEY'RE DOING IT WITH A TECHNO EURO-BEAT!!
WOW!
THEY'RE TURNING HOUSE OF SHOCK INTO FOUR DIFFERENT SONGS...
...JUST BY CHANGING WHICH MEMBER SINGS LEAD!
WE'RE OVER THE 3000 MARK!
JUST A LITTLE MORE...!!

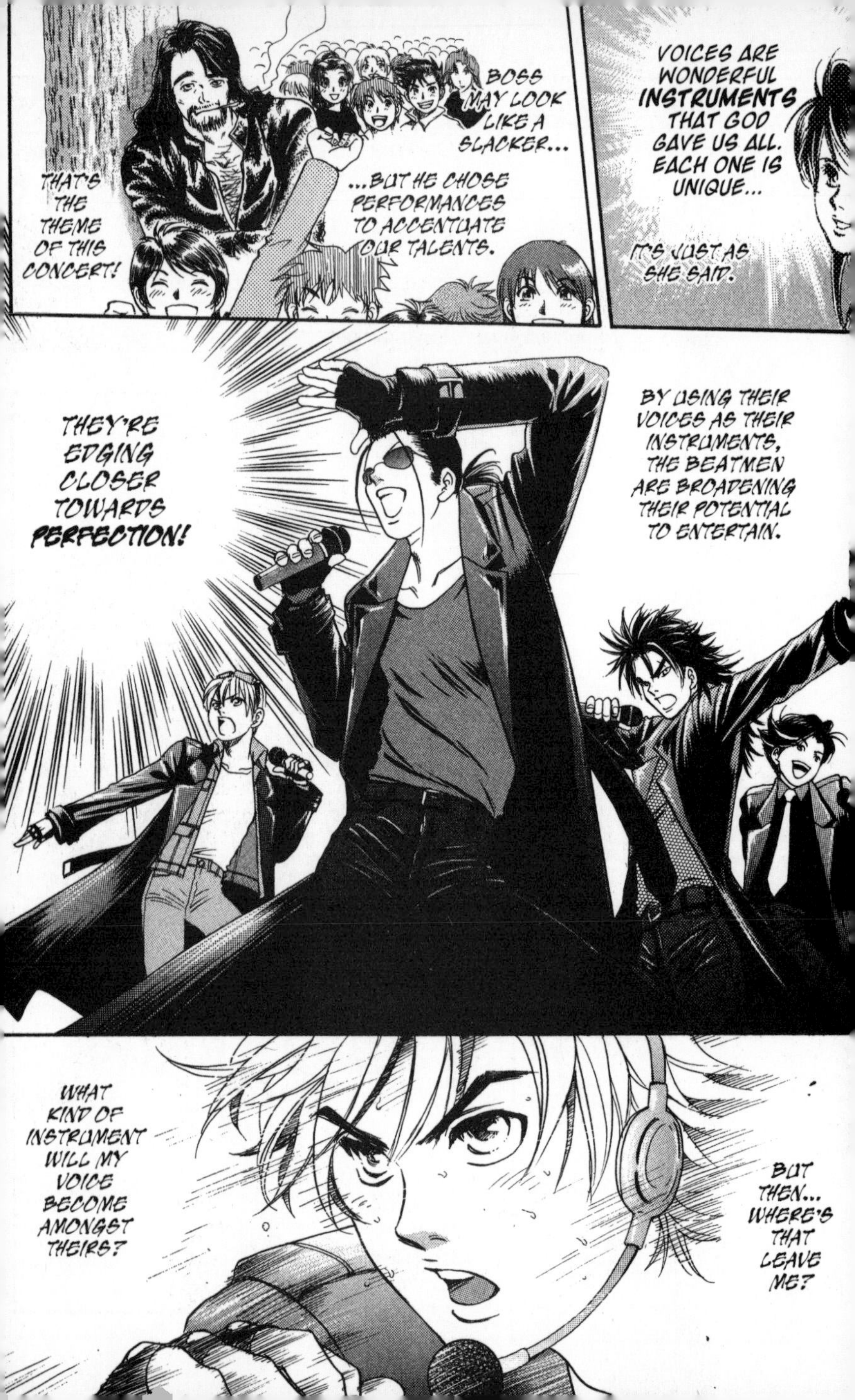

VOICES ARE WONDERFUL INSTRUMENTS THAT GOD GAVE US ALL. EACH ONE IS UNIQUE...
IT'S JUST AS SHE SAID.
BOSS MAY LOOK LIKE A SLACKER...
...BUT HE CHOSE PERFORMANCES TO ACCENTUATE OUR TALENTS.
THAT'S THE THEME OF THIS CONCERT!
BY USING THEIR VOICES AS THEIR INSTRUMENTS, THE BEATMEN ARE BROADENING THEIR POTENTIAL TO ENTERTAIN.
THEY'RE EDGING CLOSER TOWARDS PERFECTION!
BUT THEN... WHERE'S THAT LEAVE ME?
WHAT KIND OF INSTRUMENT WILL MY VOICE BECOME AMONGST THEIRS?

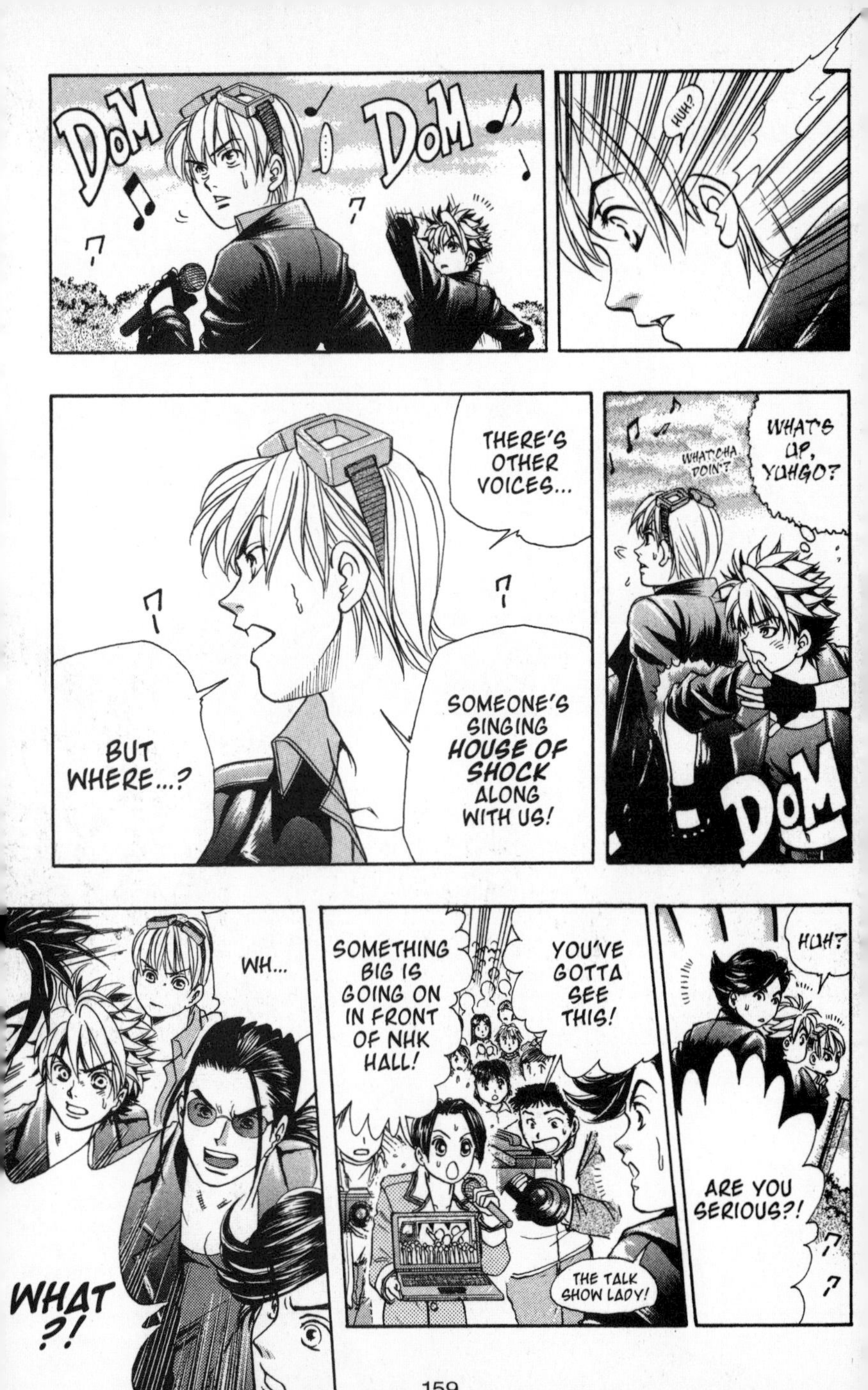
HUH?
DOM
...
DOM
WHAT'S UP, YUHGO?
WHAT'CHA DOIN'?
DOM
THERE'S OTHER VOICES...
SOMEONE'S SINGING HOUSE OF SHOCK ALONG WITH US!
BUT WHERE...?
HUH?
ARE YOU SERIOUS?!
YOU'VE GOTTA SEE THIS!
SOMETHING BIG IS GOING ON IN FRONT OF NHK HALL!
THE TALK SHOW LADY!
WH...
WHAT ?!

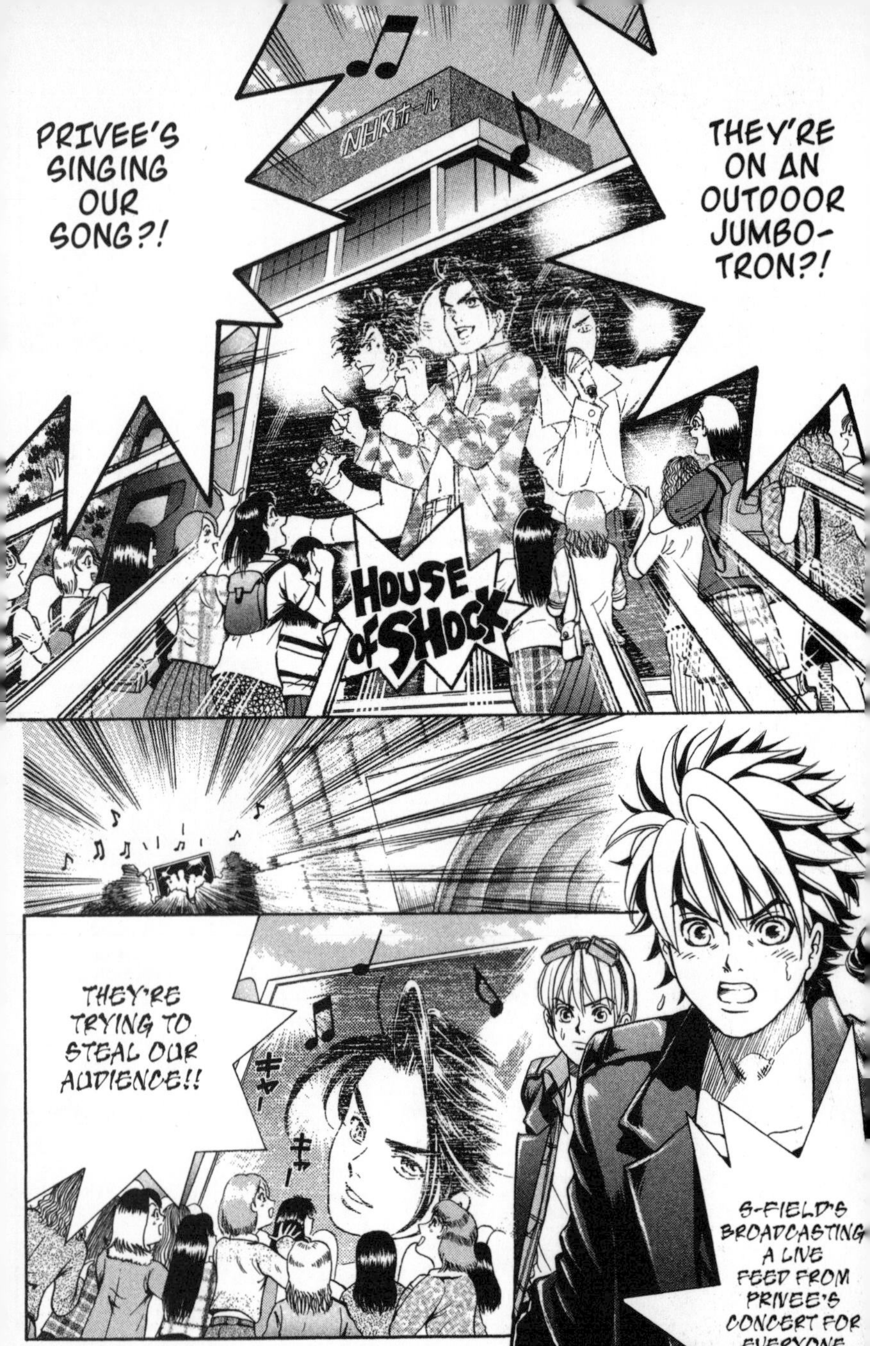
NHKホール
THEY'RE ON AN OUTDOOR JUMBOTRON?!
PRIVEE'S SINGING OUR SONG?!
HOUSE OF SHOCK
S-FIELD'S BROADCASTING A LIVE FEED FROM PRIVEE'S CONCERT FOR EVERYONE TO SEE!
THEY'RE TRYING TO STEAL OUR AUDIENCE!!
キャー
キャー

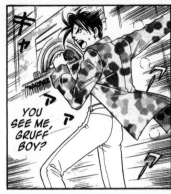

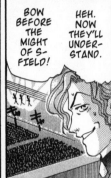

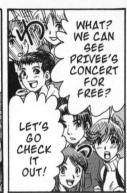

WHAT? WE CAN SEE PRIVEE'S CONCERT FOR FREE?
LET'S GO CHECK IT OUT!
HEH. NOW THEY'LL UNDER-STAND.
BOW BEFORE THE MIGHT OF S-FIELD!
YOU SEE ME, GRUFF BOY?
WE CAN SEE YOUR LITTLE CONCERT FROM HERE, TOO.
WE'RE GONNA WIN OVER YOUR AUDIENCE...
...WITH OUR OWN VOICES!!
NOW THE BAR'S BEEN RAISED OVER EVEN THE 3600 MARK!
WHAT DO WE DO?
HOUSE OF SHOCK
I NEVER EXPECTED THEM TO SING OUR OWN SONG!
NOT TO MENTION CHALLENGING US ON SHEER SINGING ABILITY?!
TOHMA... YOU JERK!
WELL, IF THAT'S YOUR GAME...

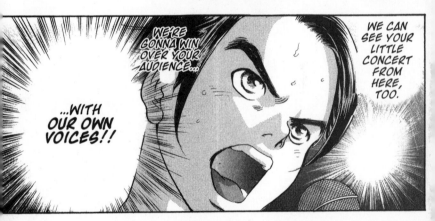

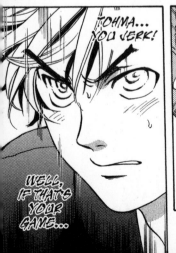

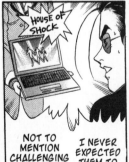

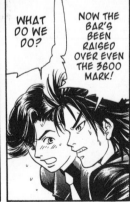

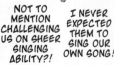

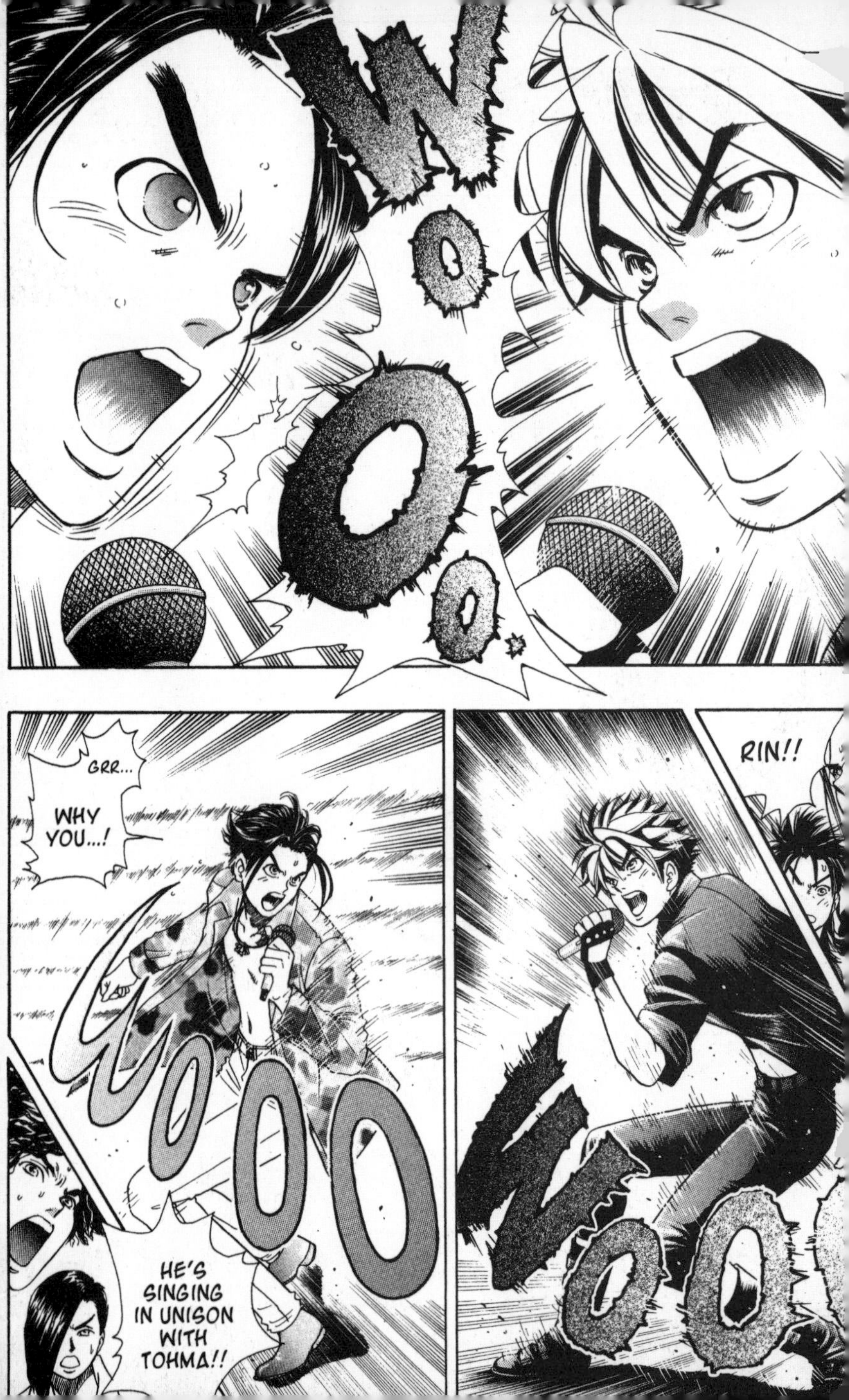

WOOO
RIN!!
WOO
GRR...
WHY YOU...!
WOOO
HE'S SINGING IN UNISON WITH TOHMA!!

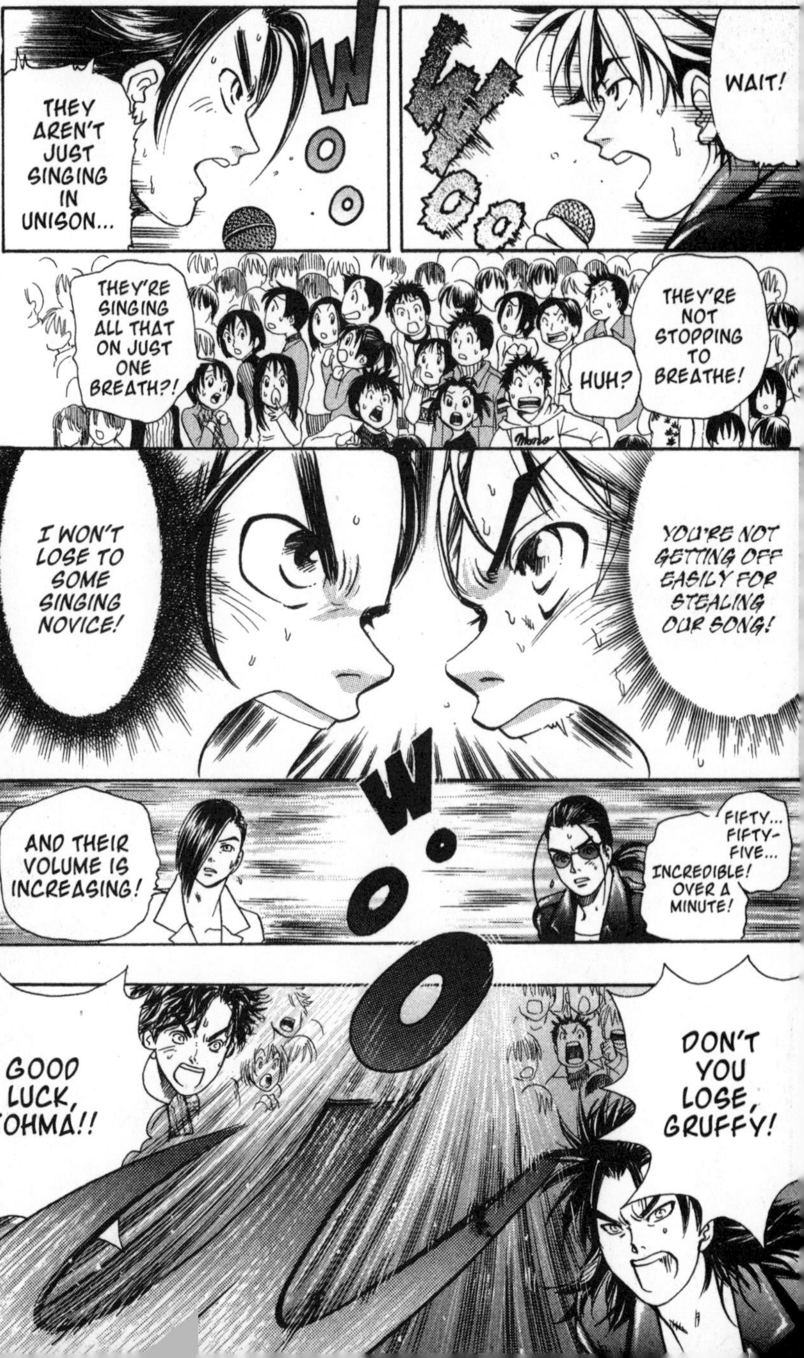

WOO
WAIT!
THEY AREN'T JUST SINGING IN UNISON...
WOO
THEY'RE NOT STOPPING TO BREATHE!
HUH?
THEY'RE SINGING ALL THAT ON JUST ONE BREATH?!
YOU'RE NOT GETTING OFF EASILY FOR STEALING OUR SONG!
I WON'T LOSE TO SOME SINGING NOVICE!
WOOO
FIFTY... FIFTY-FIVE... INCREDIBLE! OVER A MINUTE!
AND THEIR VOLUME IS INCREASING!
DON'T YOU LOSE, GRUFFY!
GOOD LUCK, TOHMA!!


* UNISON: SINGING THE SAME NOTE AT THE SAME TIME WITH ANOTHER PERSON.

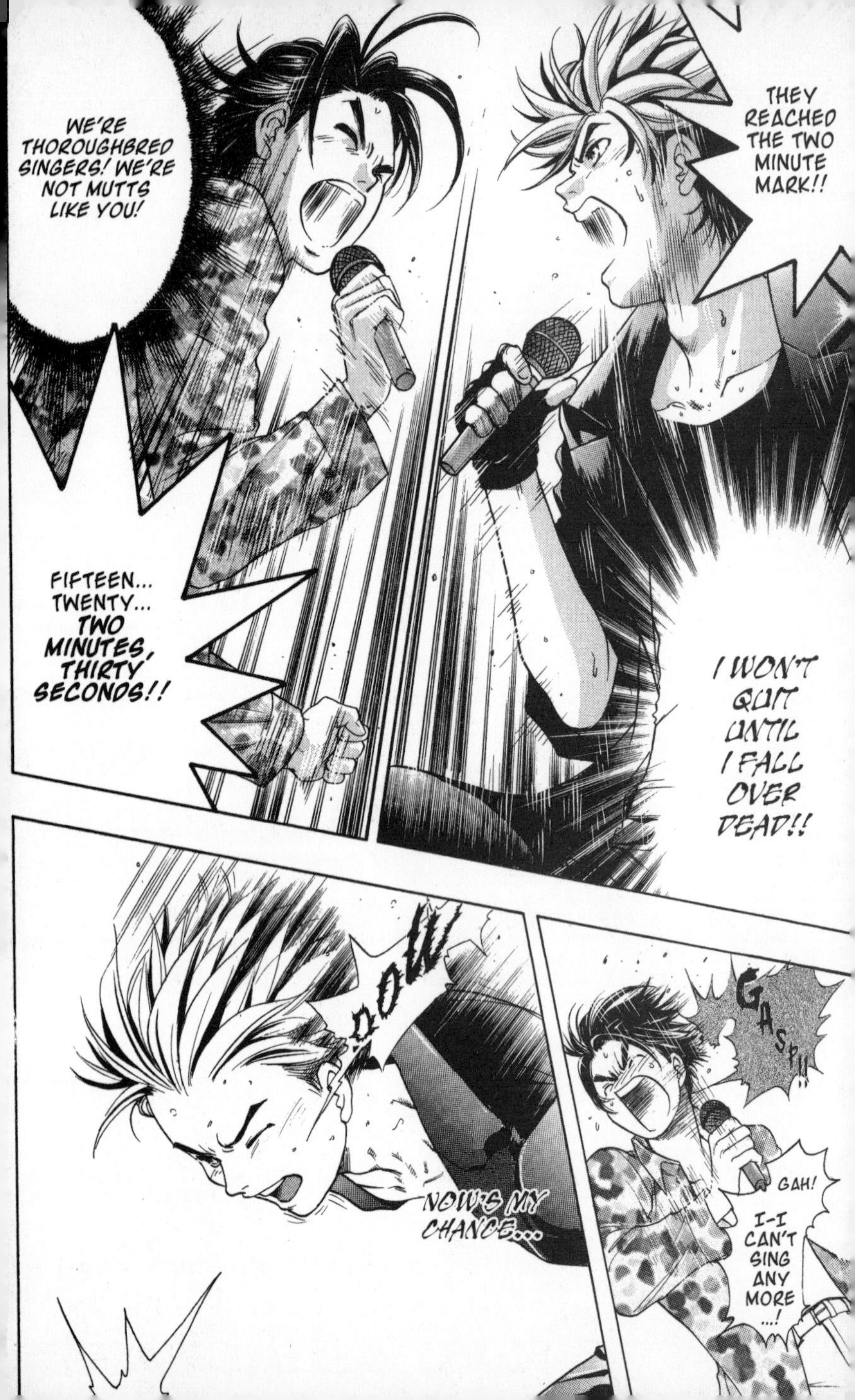
THEY REACHED THE TWO MINUTE MARK!!
WE'RE THOROUGHBRED SINGERS! WE'RE NOT MUTTS LIKE YOU!
FIFTEEN... TWENTY... TWO MINUTES, THIRTY SECONDS!!
I WON'T QUIT UNTIL I FALL OVER DEAD!!
GASP!!
GAH!
I-I CAN'T SING ANY MORE ...!
DOW
NOW'S MY CHANCE...

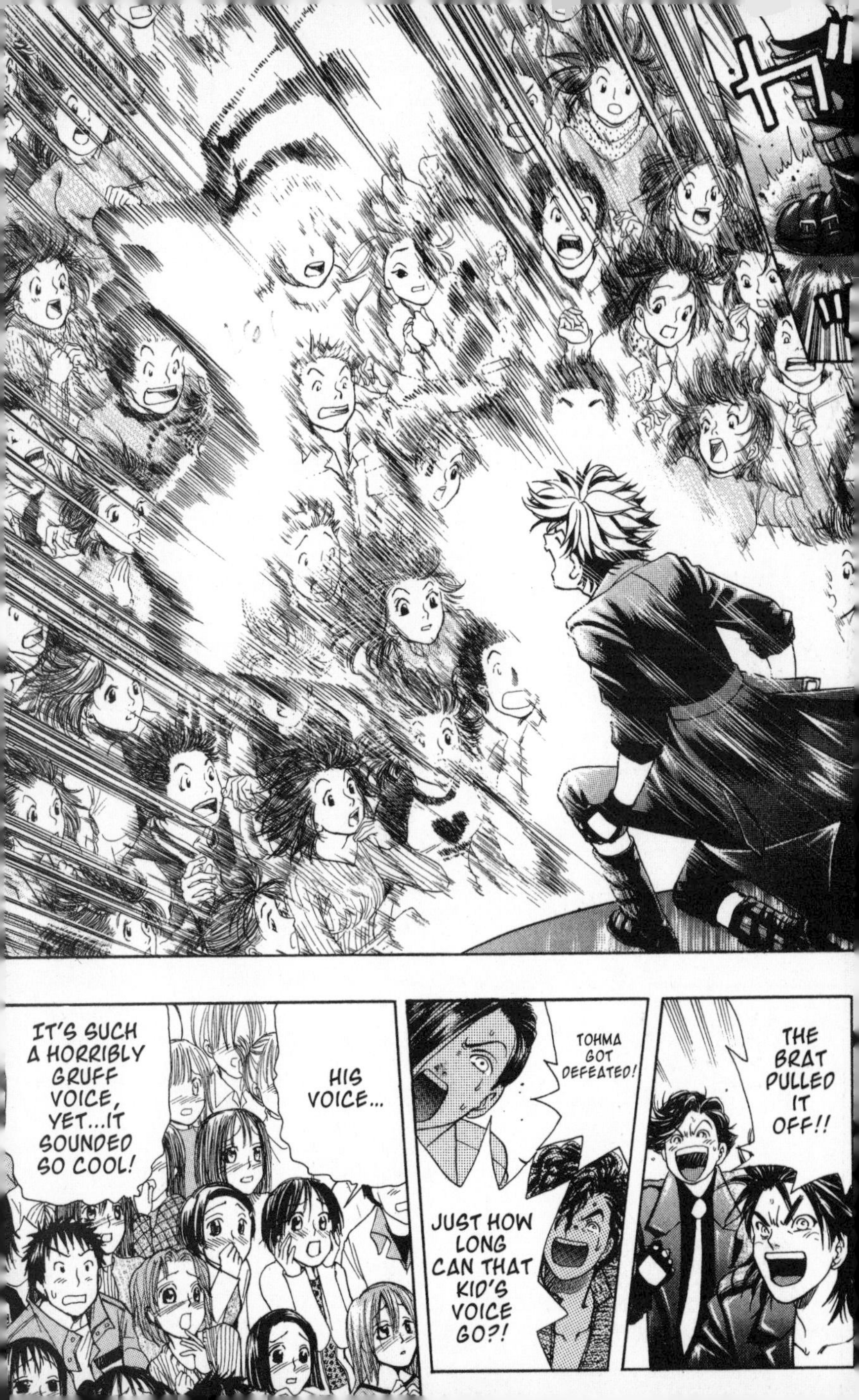
THE BRAT PULLED IT OFF!!
TOHMA GOT DEFEATED!
JUST HOW LONG CAN THAT KID'S VOICE GO?!
HIS VOICE...
IT'S SUCH A HORRIBLY GRUFF VOICE, YET...IT SOUNDED SO COOL!

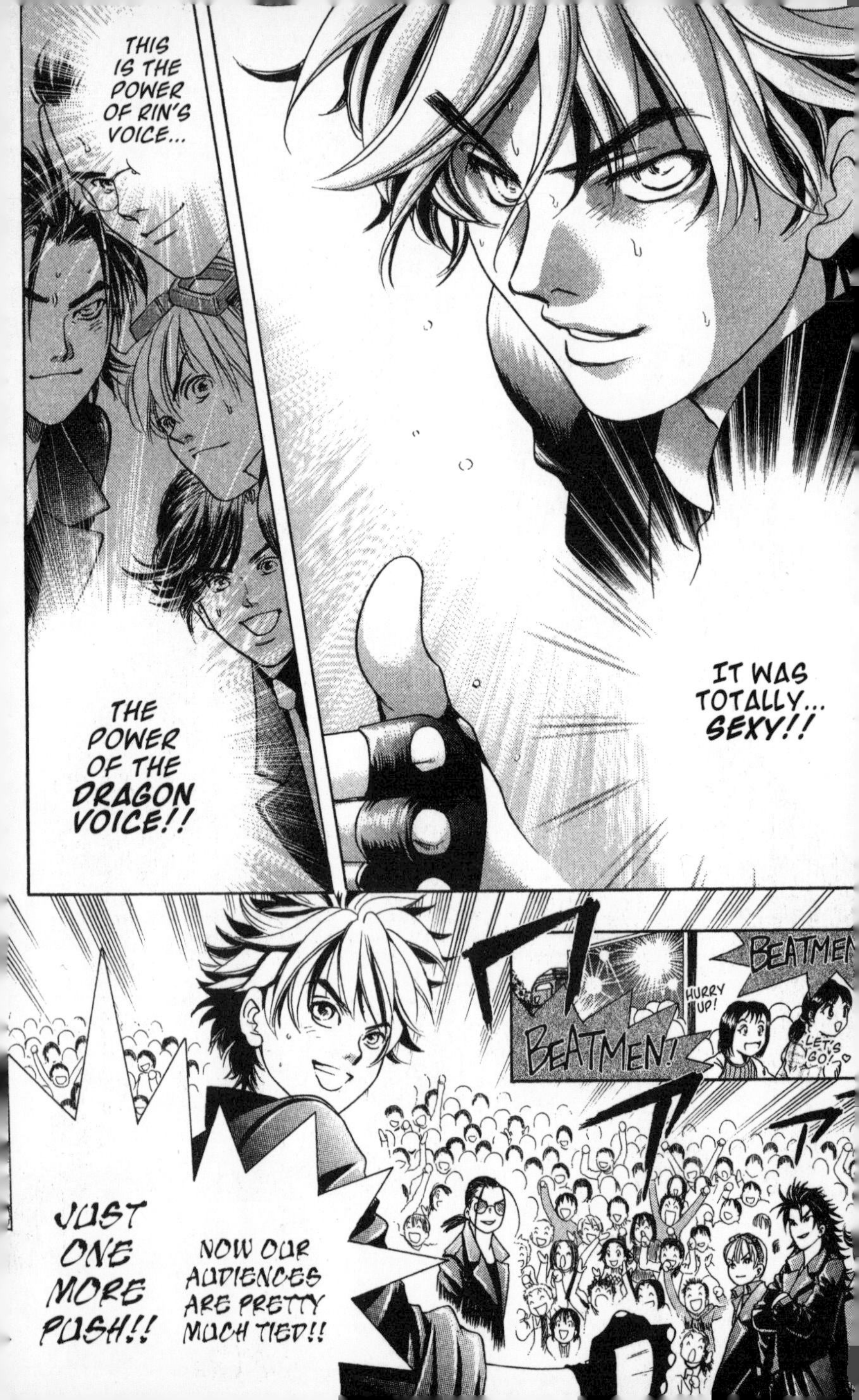
IT WAS TOTALLY... SEXY!!
THIS IS THE POWER OF RIN'S VOICE...
THE POWER OF THE DRAGON VOICE!!
BEATMEN
HURRY UP!
LET'S GO!
BEATMEN!
NOW OUR AUDIENCES ARE PRETTY MUCH TIED!!
JUST ONE MORE PUSH!!

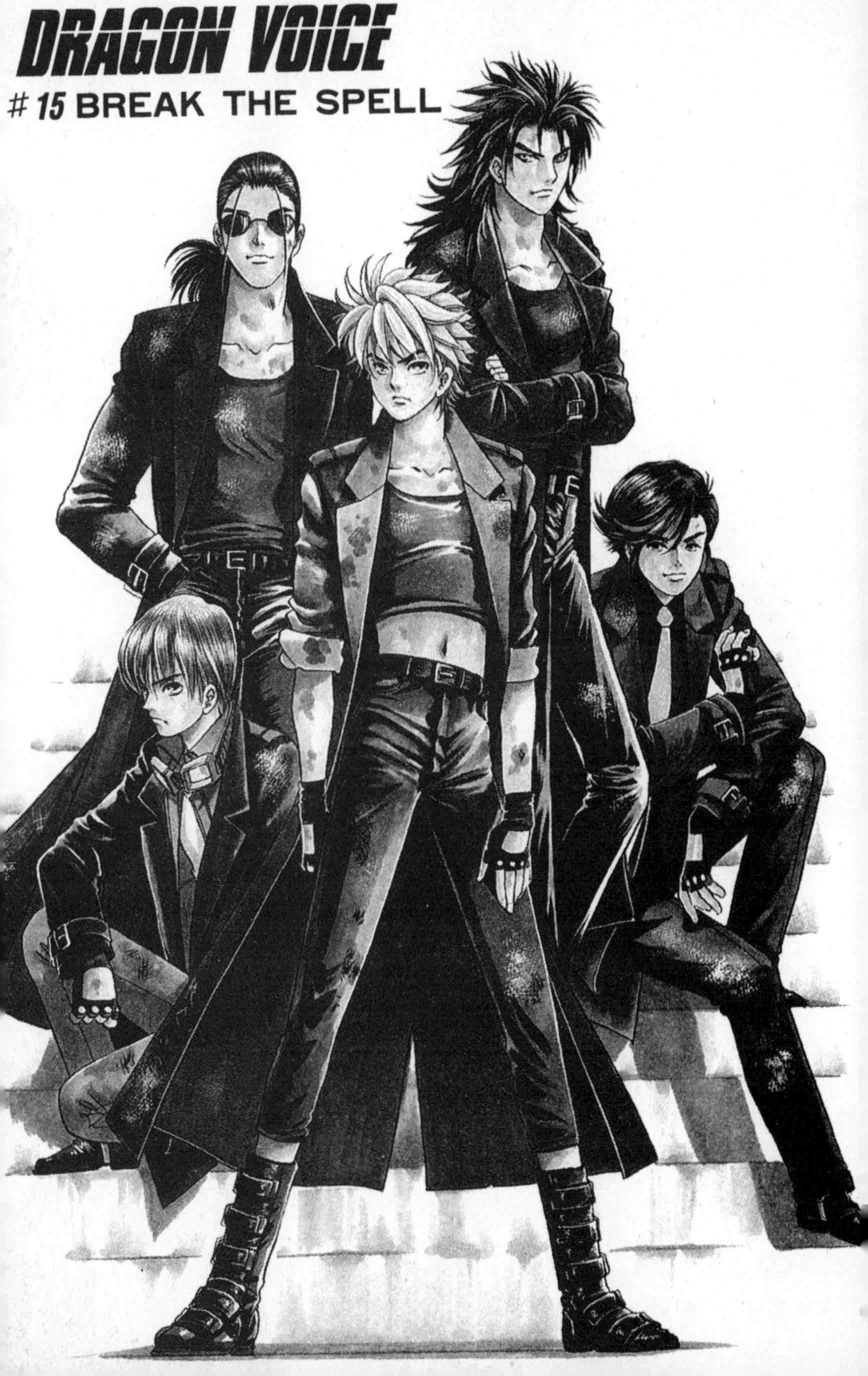
DRAGON VOICE
# 15 BREAK THE SPELL

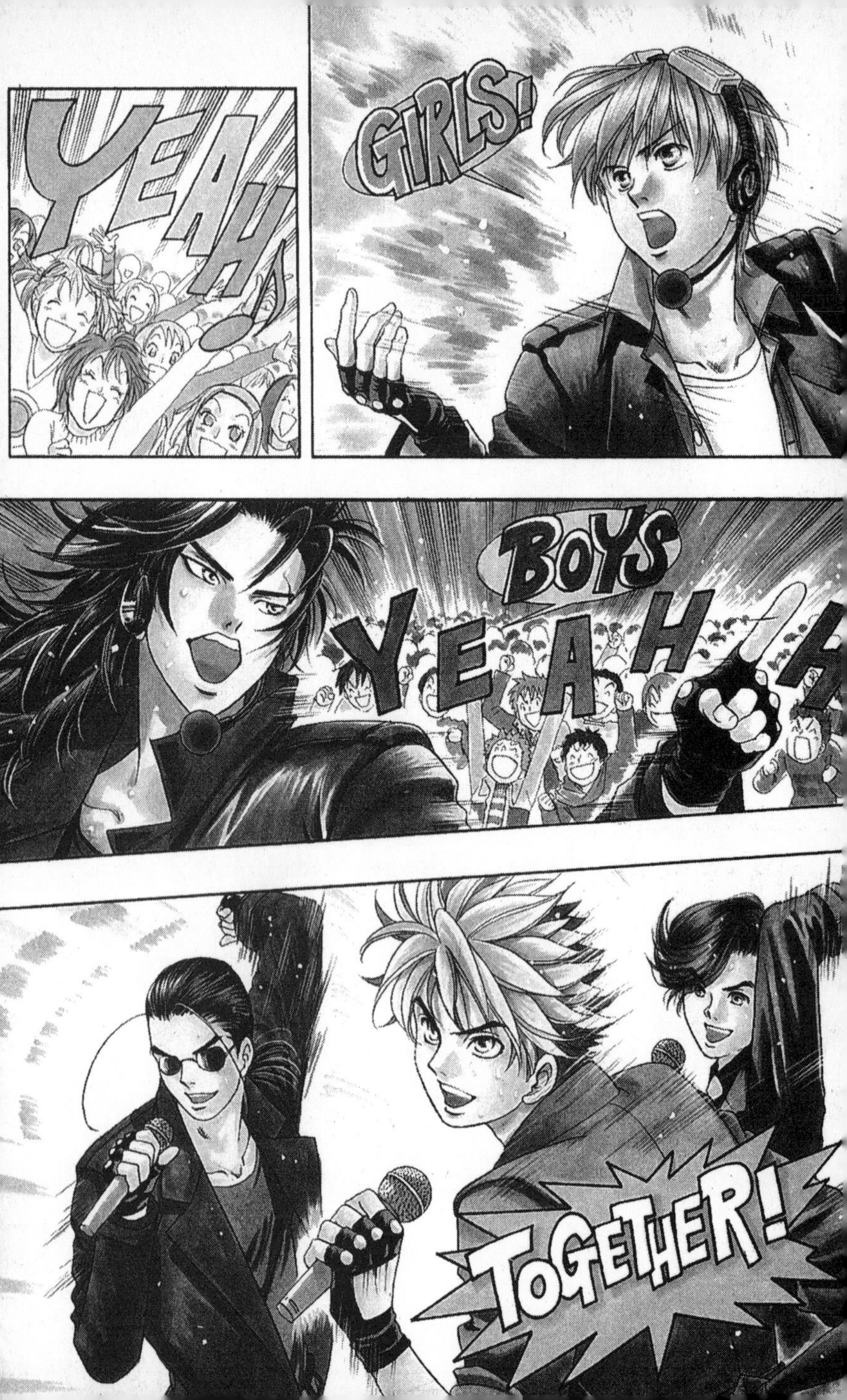
GIRLS!
YEAH
BOYS
YEAHH
TOGETHER!

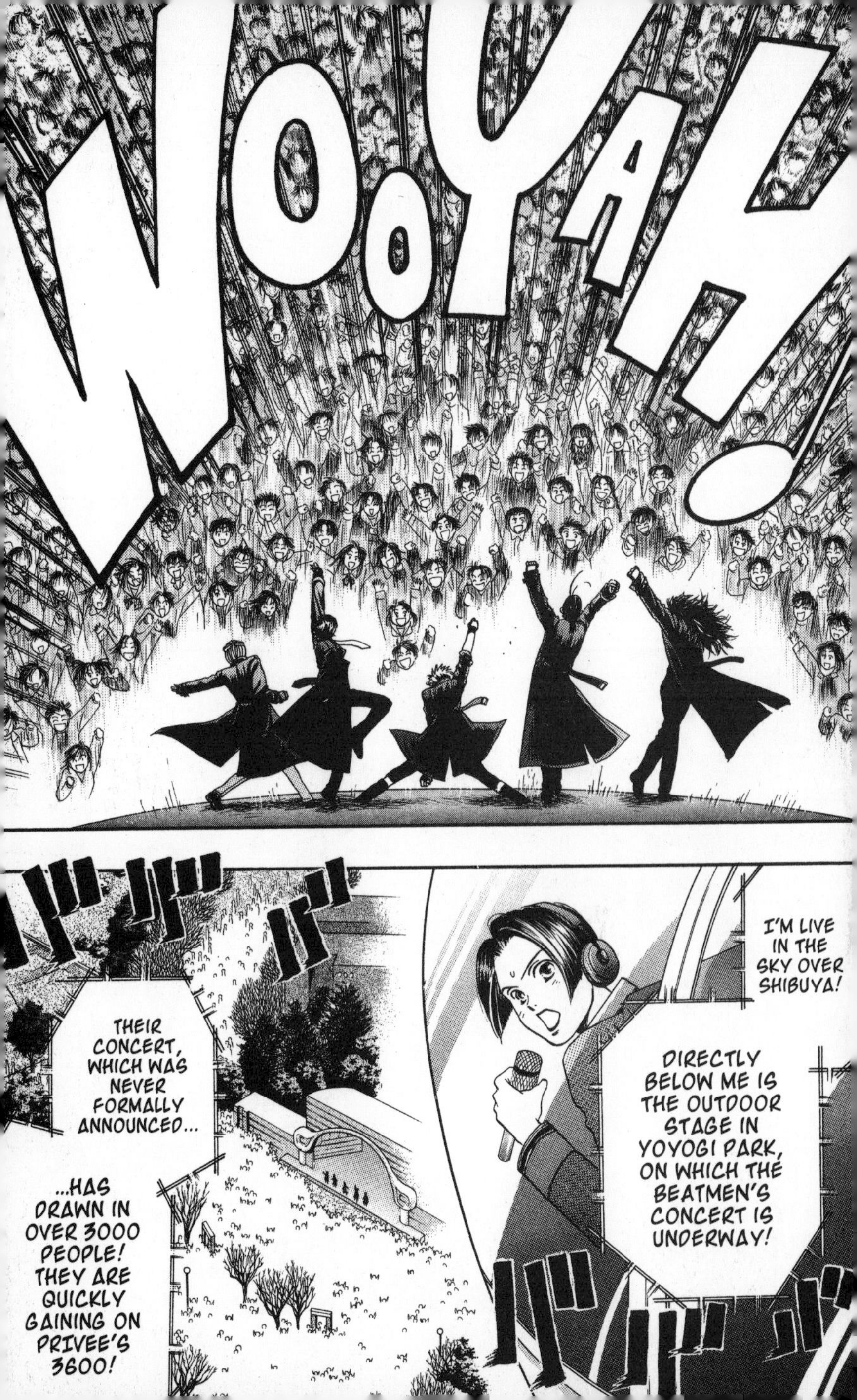
WOOYAH!
I'M LIVE IN THE SKY OVER SHIBUYA!
DIRECTLY BELOW ME IS THE OUTDOOR STAGE IN YOYOGI PARK, ON WHICH THE BEATMEN'S CONCERT IS UNDERWAY!
THEIR CONCERT, WHICH WAS NEVER FORMALLY ANNOUNCED...
...HAS DRAWN IN OVER 3000 PEOPLE! THEY ARE QUICKLY GAINING ON PRIVEE'S 3600!

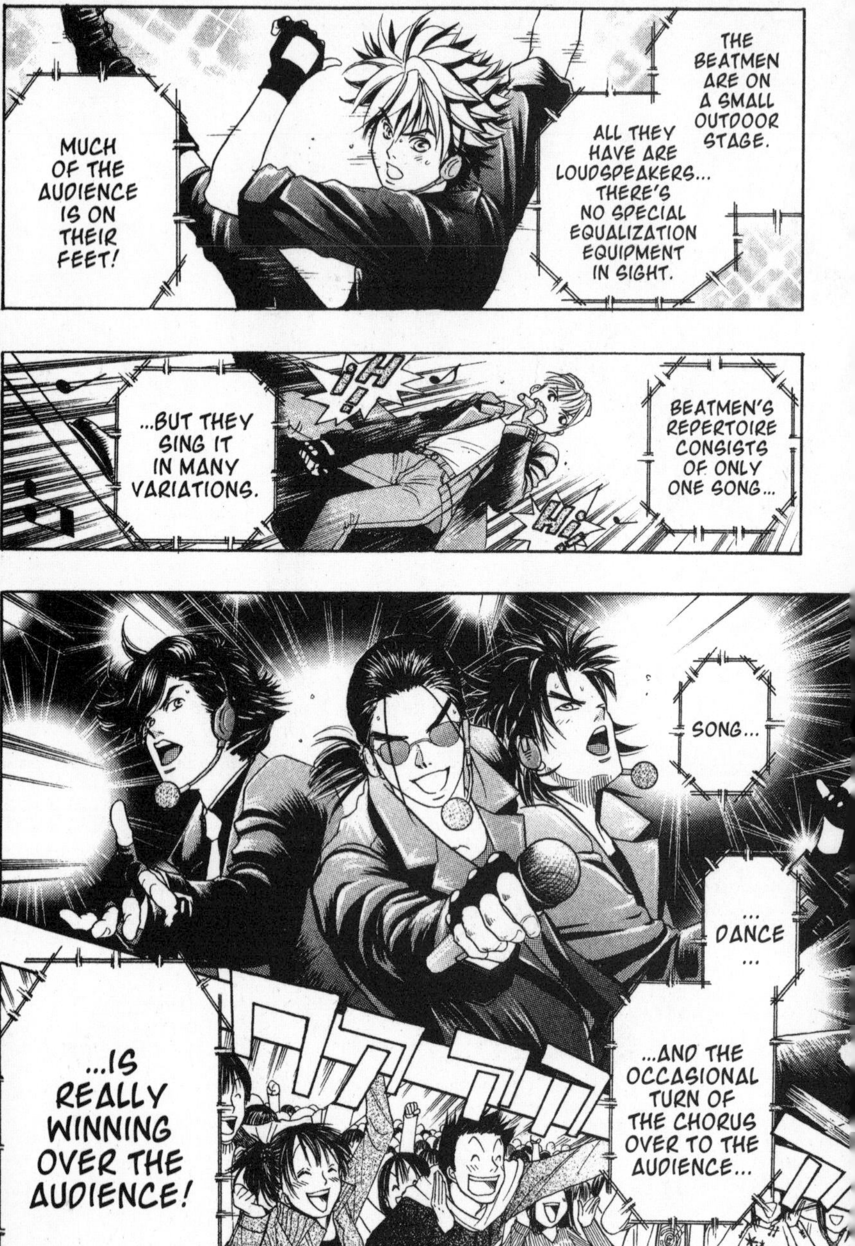
THE BEATMEN ARE ON A SMALL OUTDOOR STAGE.
ALL THEY HAVE ARE LOUDSPEAKERS... THERE'S NO SPECIAL EQUALIZATION EQUIPMENT IN SIGHT.
MUCH OF THE AUDIENCE IS ON THEIR FEET!
BEATMEN'S REPERTOIRE CONSISTS OF ONLY ONE SONG...
HI!
HI!
...BUT THEY SING IT IN MANY VARIATIONS.
SONG...
... DANCE ...
...AND THE OCCASIONAL TURN OF THE CHORUS OVER TO THE AUDIENCE...
...IS REALLY WINNING OVER THE AUDIENCE!

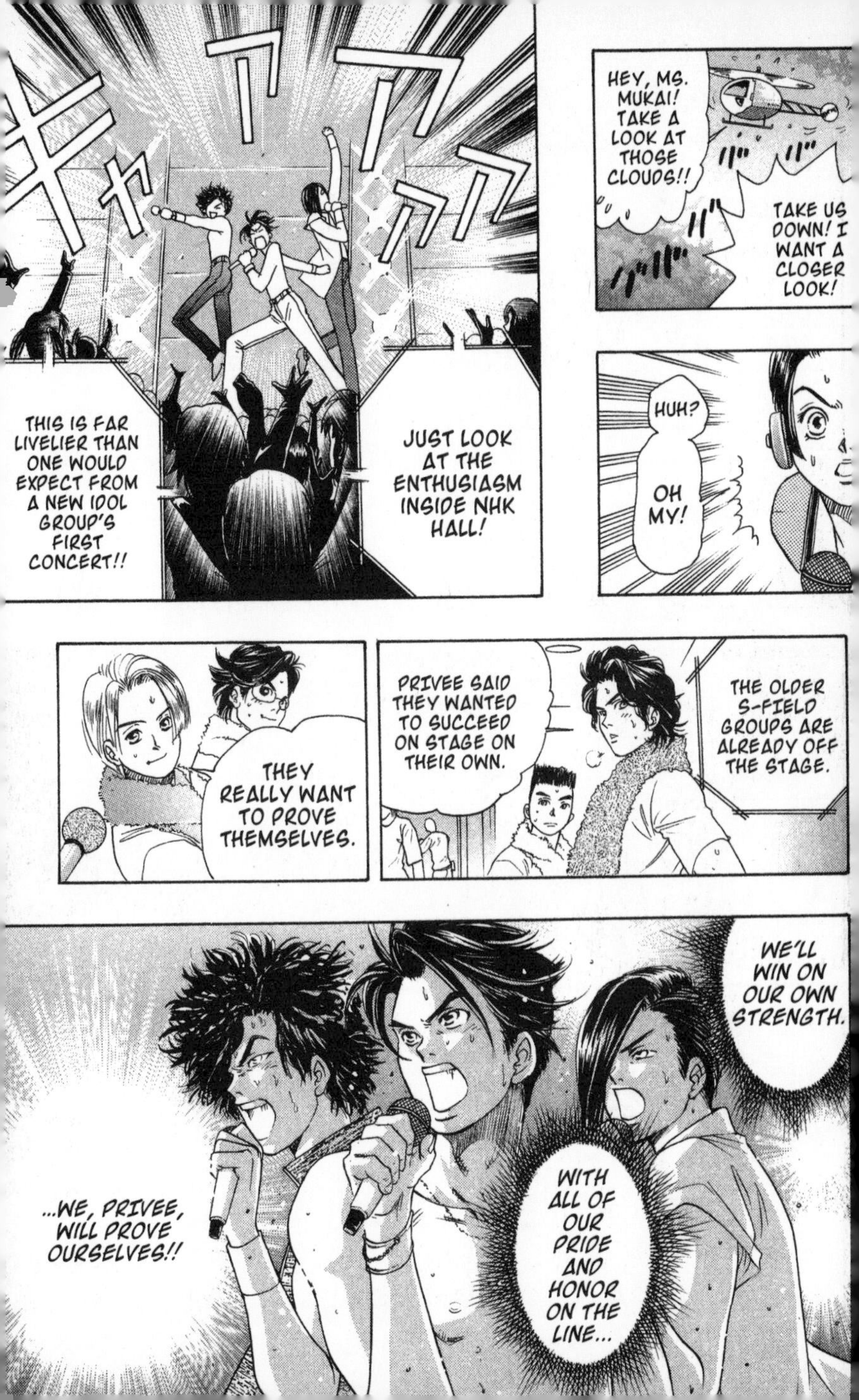
HEY, MS. MUKAI! TAKE A LOOK AT THOSE CLOUDS!!
TAKE US DOWN! I WANT A CLOSER LOOK!
HUH?
OH MY!
キャアアアア
JUST LOOK AT THE ENTHUSIASM INSIDE NHK HALL!
THIS IS FAR LIVELIER THAN ONE WOULD EXPECT FROM A NEW IDOL GROUP'S FIRST CONCERT!!
THE OLDER S-FIELD GROUPS ARE ALREADY OFF THE STAGE.
PRIVEE SAID THEY WANTED TO SUCCEED ON STAGE ON THEIR OWN.
THEY REALLY WANT TO PROVE THEMSELVES.
WE'LL WIN ON OUR OWN STRENGTH.
WITH ALL OF OUR PRIDE AND HONOR ON THE LINE...
...WE, PRIVEE, WILL PROVE OURSELVES!!

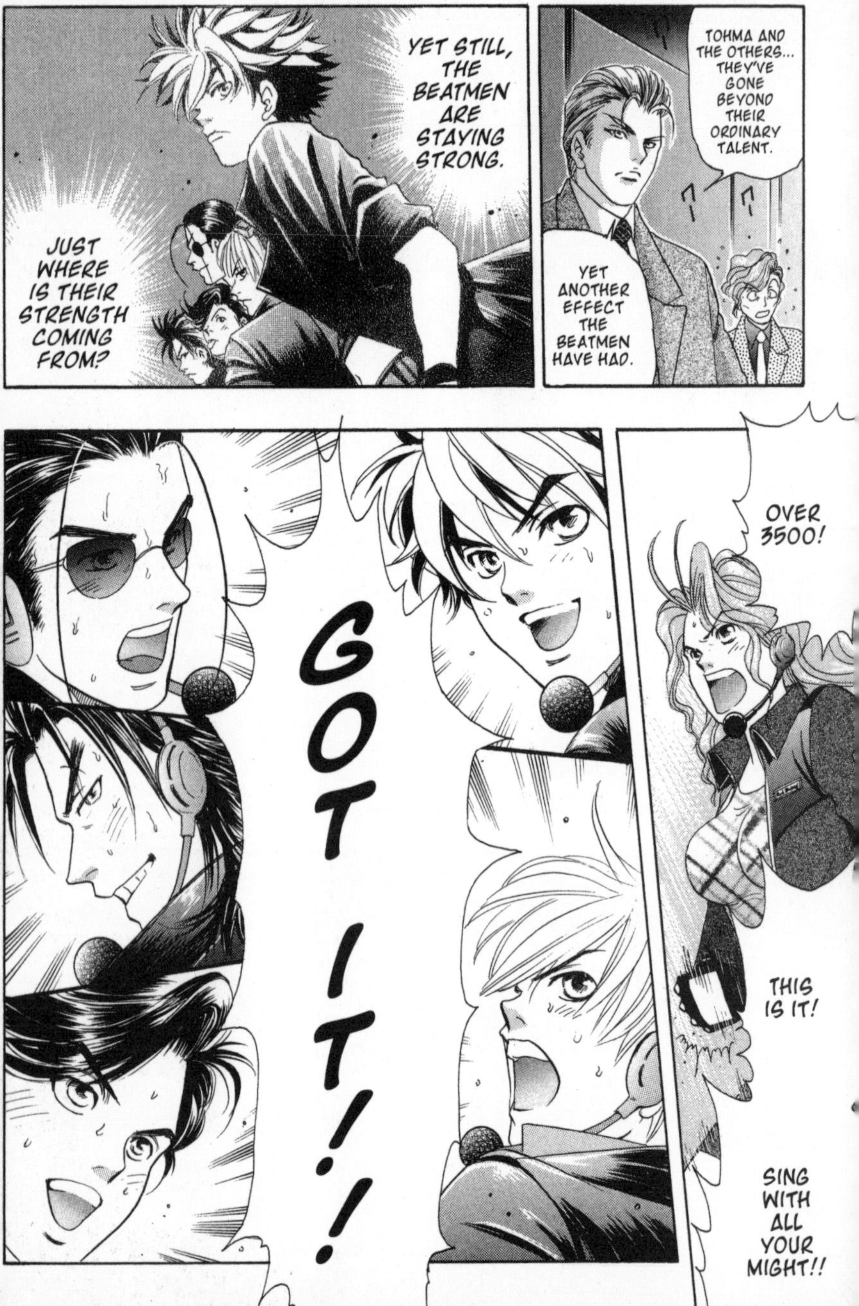
TOHMA AND THE OTHERS... THEY'VE GONE BEYOND THEIR ORDINARY TALENT.
YET ANOTHER EFFECT THE BEATMEN HAVE HAD.
YET STILL, THE BEATMEN ARE STAYING STRONG.
JUST WHERE IS THEIR STRENGTH COMING FROM?
OVER 3500!
THIS IS IT!
SING WITH ALL YOUR MIGHT!!
GOT IT!!

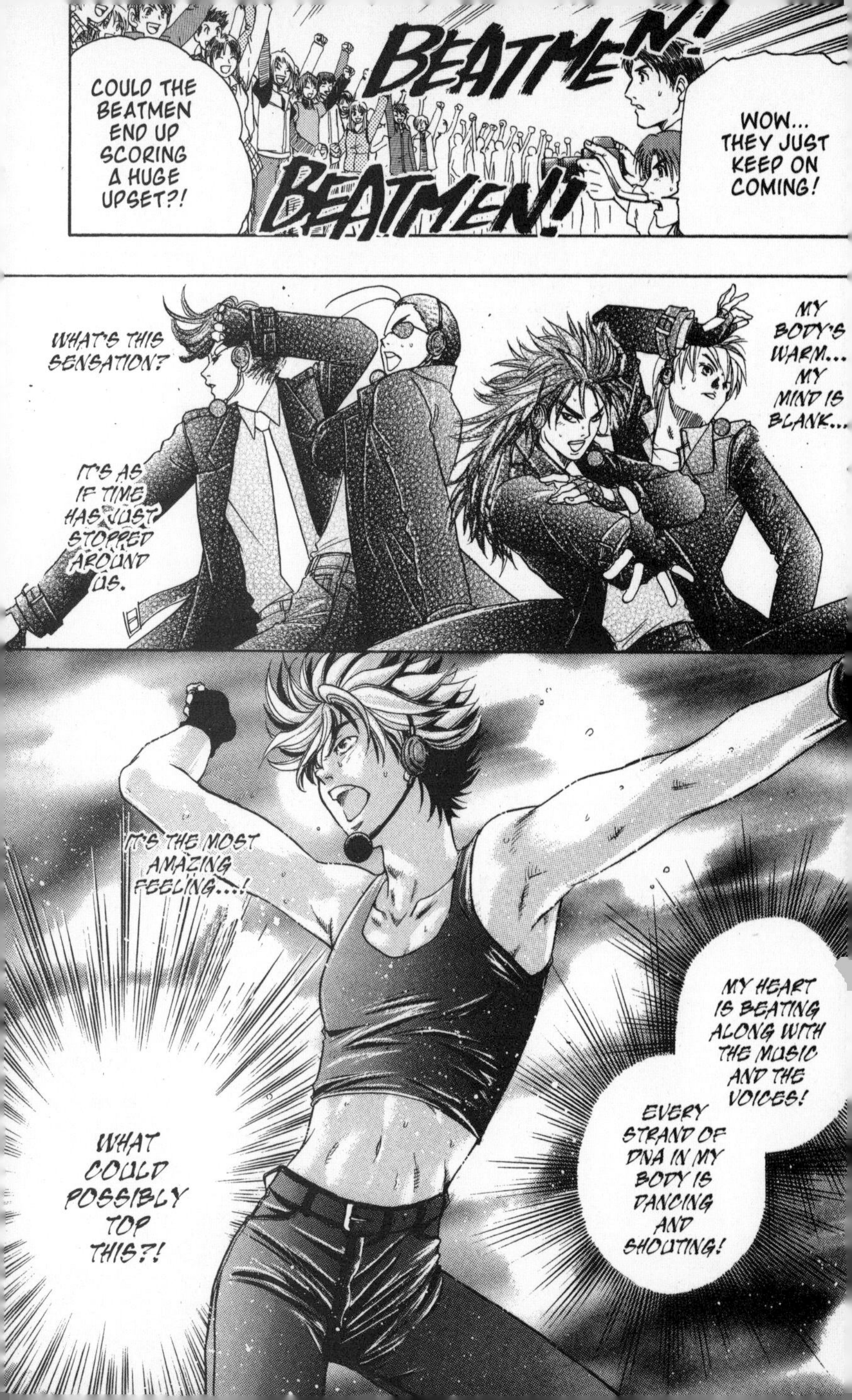

WOW... THEY JUST KEEP ON COMING!
BEATMEN!
COULD THE BEATMEN END UP SCORING A HUGE UPSET?!
BEATMEN!
MY BODY'S WARM... MY MIND IS BLANK...
WHAT'S THIS SENSATION?
IT'S AS IF TIME HAS JUST STOPPED AROUND US.
MY HEART IS BEATING ALONG WITH THE MUSIC AND THE VOICES!
EVERY STRAND OF DNA IN MY BODY IS DANCING AND SHOUTING!
IT'S THE MOST AMAZING FEELING...!
WHAT COULD POSSIBLY TOP THIS?!

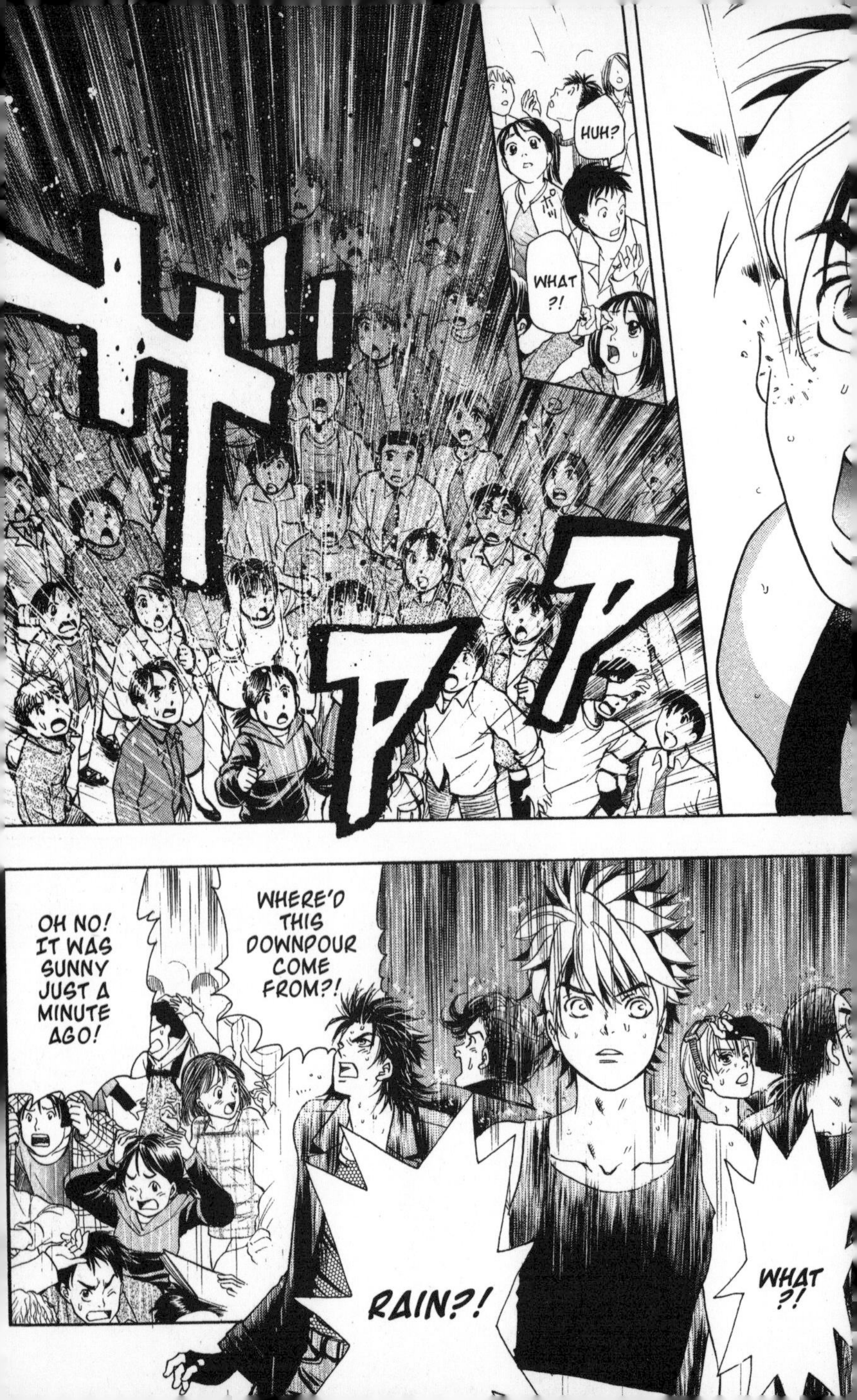
HUH?
WHAT ?!
WHAT ?!
RAIN?!
WHERE'D THIS DOWNPOUR COME FROM?!
OH NO! IT WAS SUNNY JUST A MINUTE AGO!

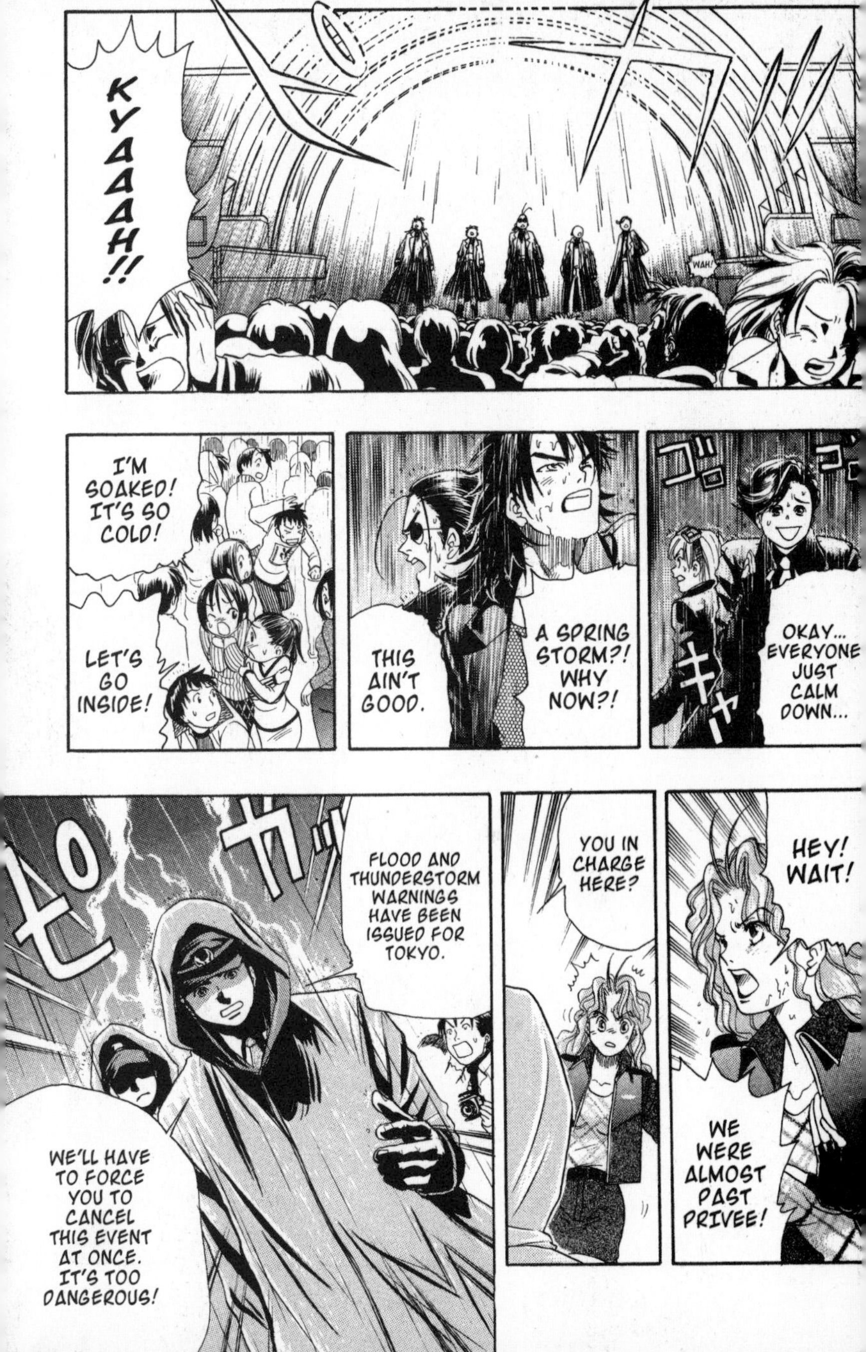
KYAAAAH!!
WAH!
OKAY... EVERYONE JUST CALM DOWN...
A SPRING STORM?! WHY NOW?!
THIS AIN'T GOOD.
I'M SOAKED! IT'S SO COLD!
LET'S GO INSIDE!
HEY! WAIT!
WE WERE ALMOST PAST PRIVEE!
YOU IN CHARGE HERE?
FLOOD AND THUNDERSTORM WARNINGS HAVE BEEN ISSUED FOR TOKYO.
WE'LL HAVE TO FORCE YOU TO CANCEL THIS EVENT AT ONCE. IT'S TOO DANGEROUS!

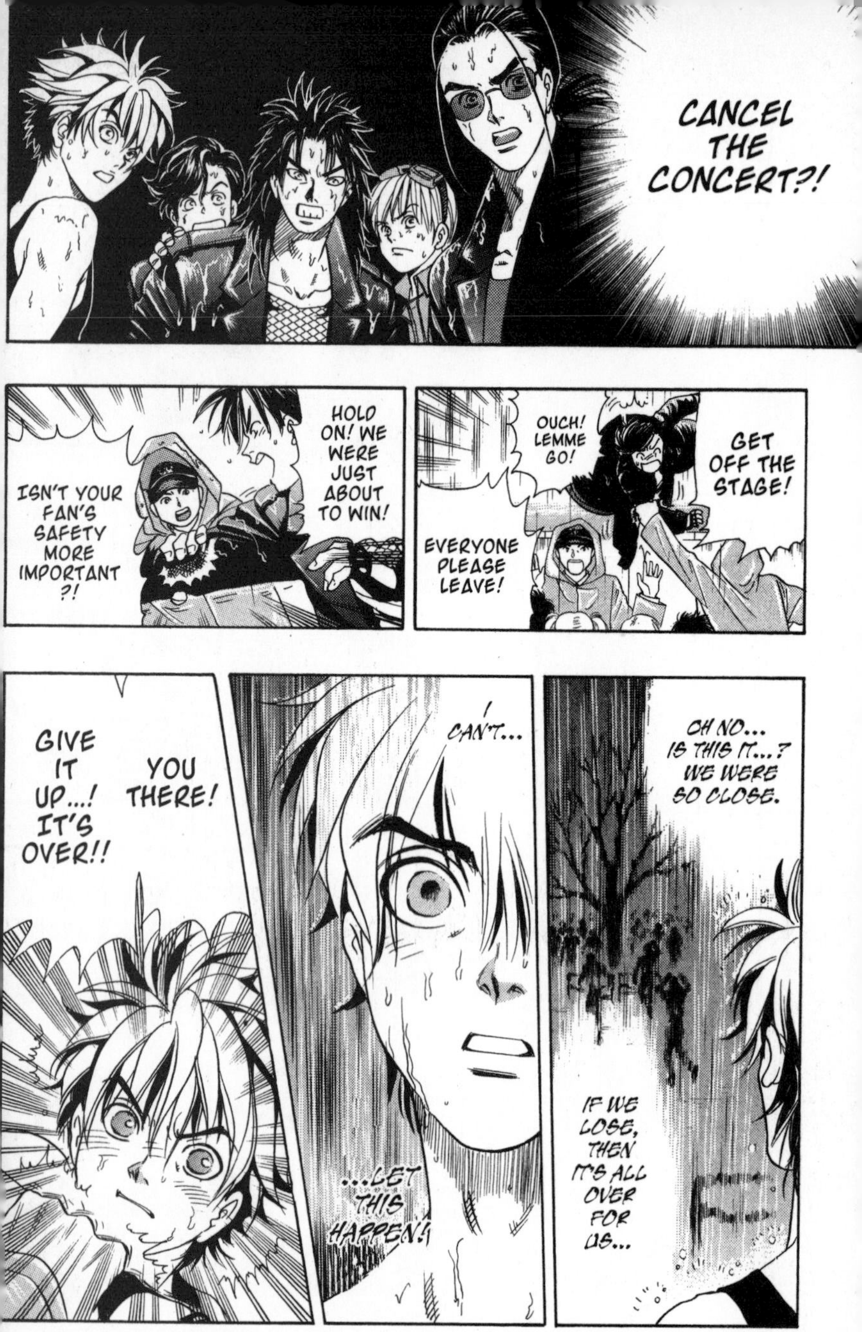
CANCEL THE CONCERT?!
GET OFF THE STAGE!
OUCH! LEMME GO!
EVERYONE PLEASE LEAVE!
HOLD ON! WE WERE JUST ABOUT TO WIN!
ISN'T YOUR FAN'S SAFETY MORE IMPORTANT?!
OH NO... IS THIS IT...? WE WERE SO CLOSE.
IF WE LOSE, THEN IT'S ALL OVER FOR US...
I CAN'T...
...LET THIS HAPPEN!
YOU THERE!
GIVE IT UP...! IT'S OVER!!

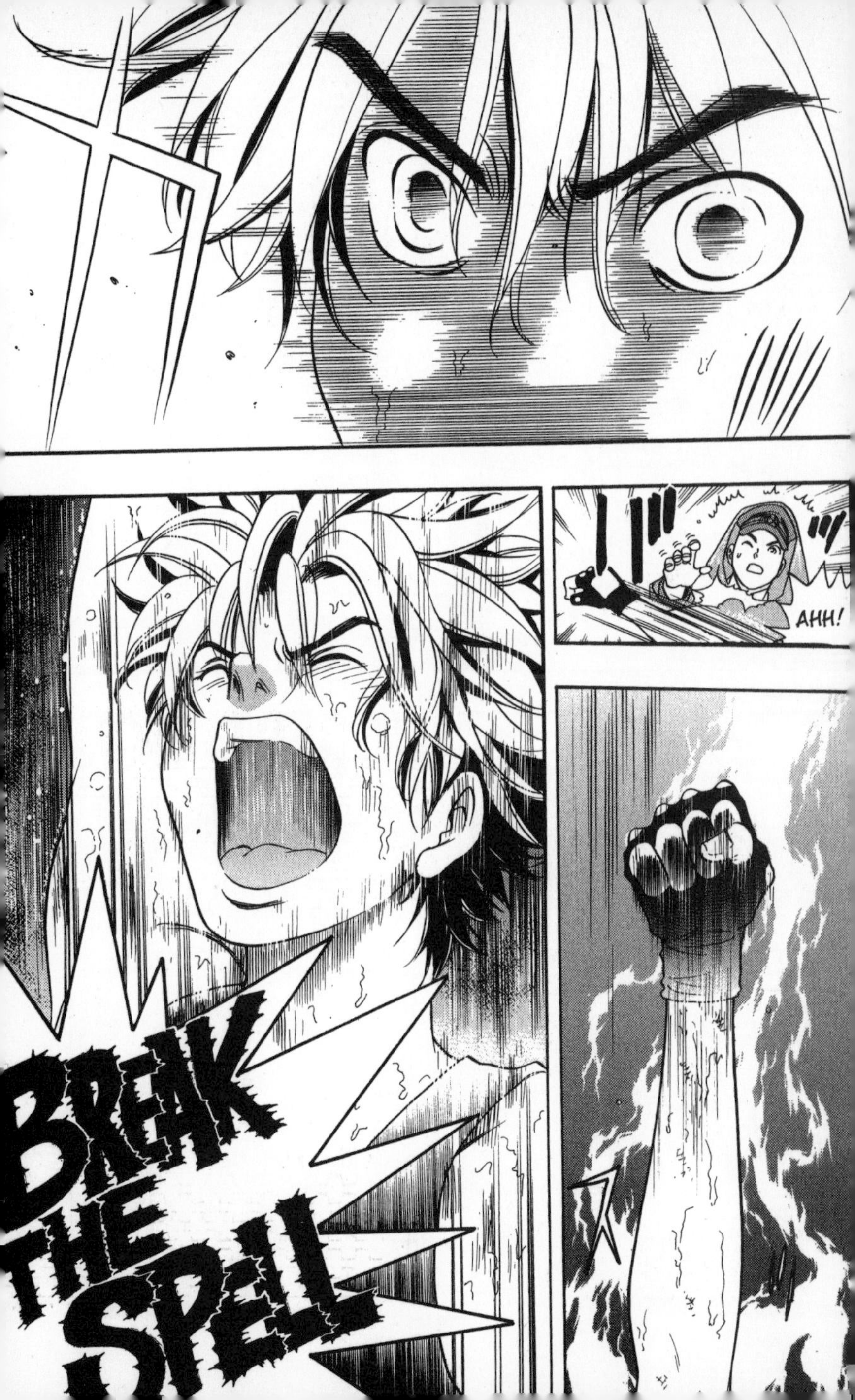
AHH!
BREAK THE SPELL

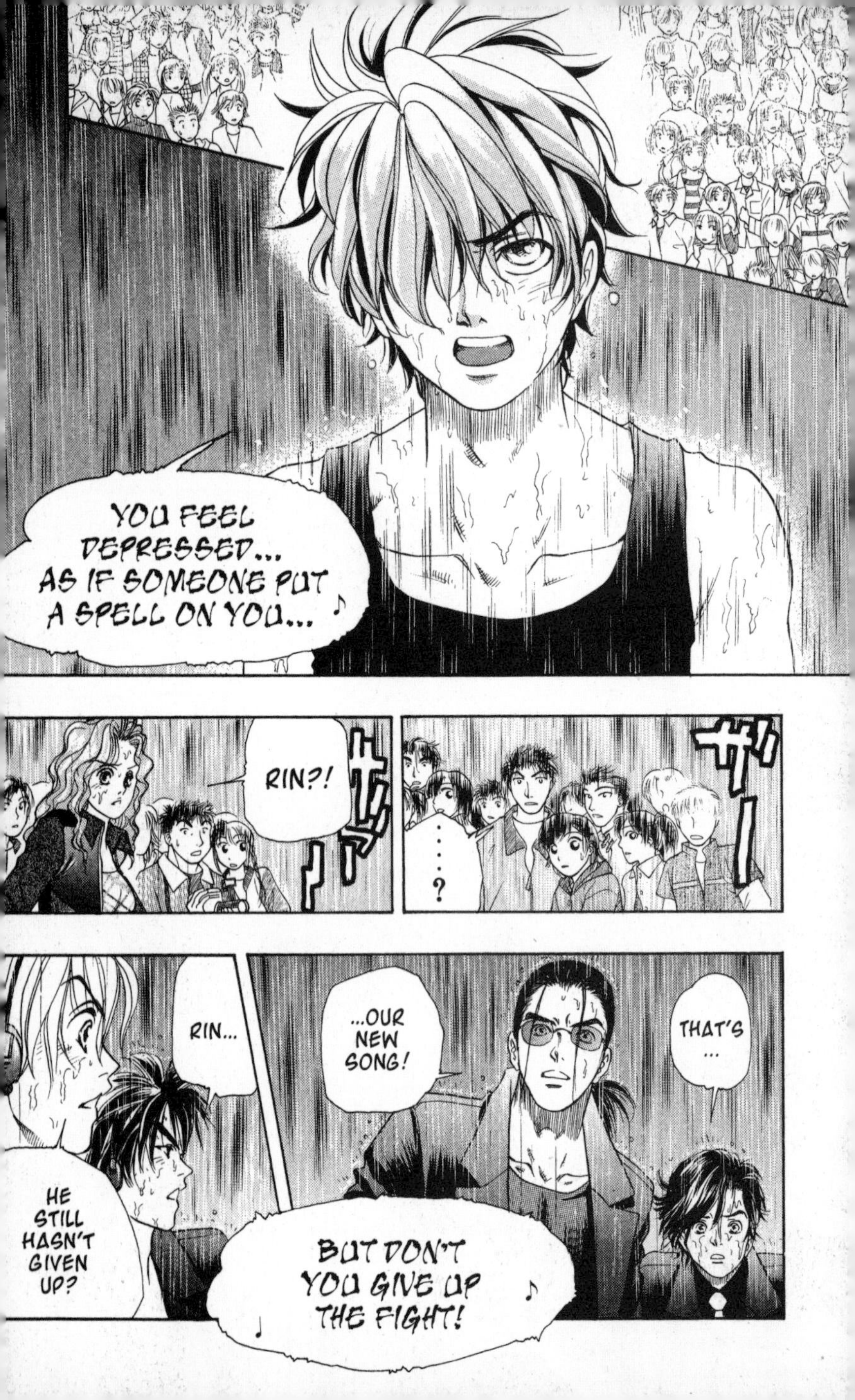
YOU FEEL DEPRESSED... AS IF SOMEONE PUT A SPELL ON YOU... ♪
...?
RIN?!
THAT'S ...
...OUR NEW SONG!
BUT DON'T YOU GIVE UP THE FIGHT! ♪
RIN...
HE STILL HASN'T GIVEN UP?

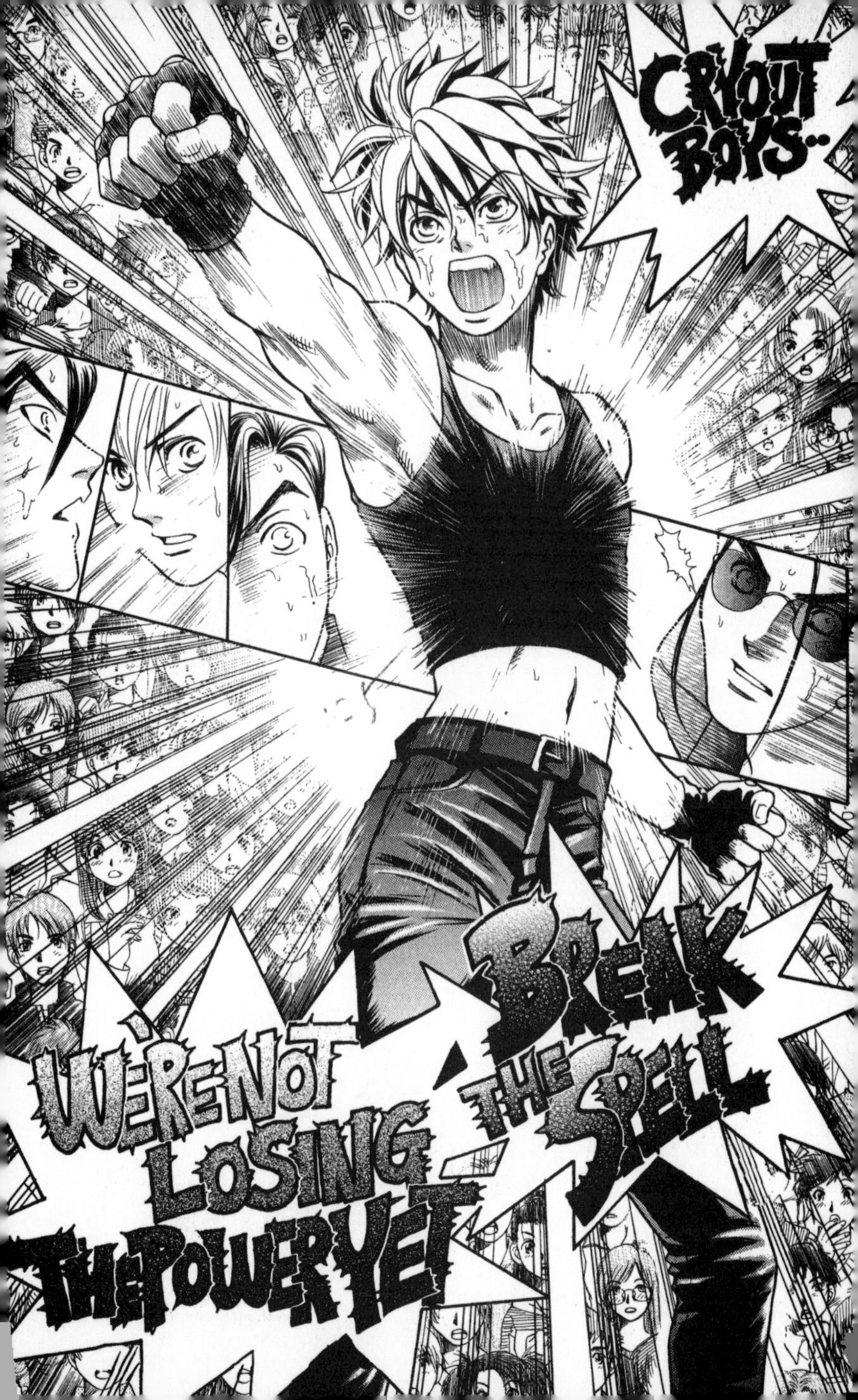
CRYOUT BOYS..
BREAK THE SPELL
WE'RE NOT LOSING THE POWER YET

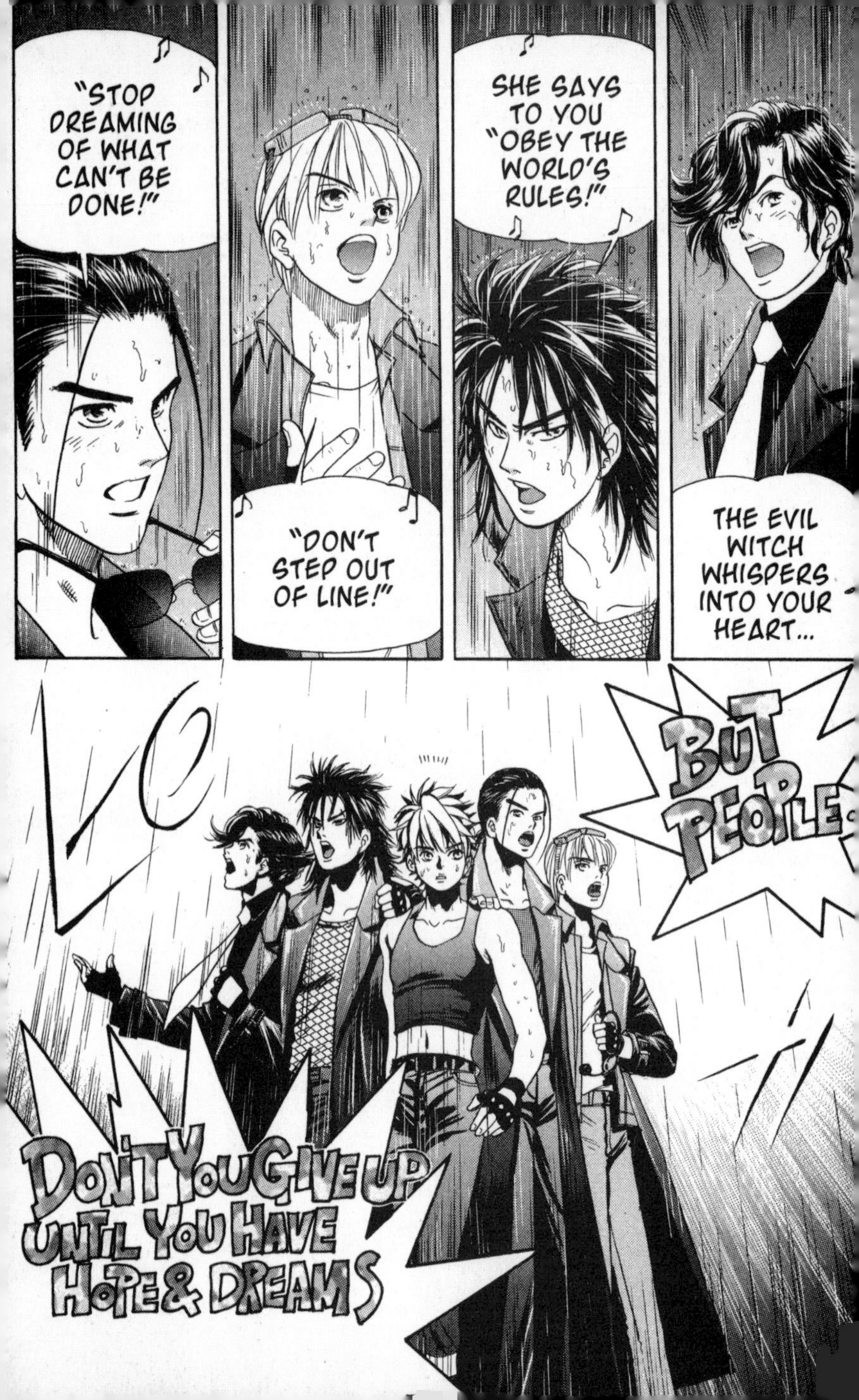
THE EVIL WITCH WHISPERS INTO YOUR HEART...
SHE SAYS TO YOU "OBEY THE WORLD'S RULES!"
"DON'T STEP OUT OF LINE!"
"STOP DREAMING OF WHAT CAN'T BE DONE!"
BUT PEOPLE,
DON'T YOU GIVE UP UNTIL YOU HAVE HOPE & DREAMS

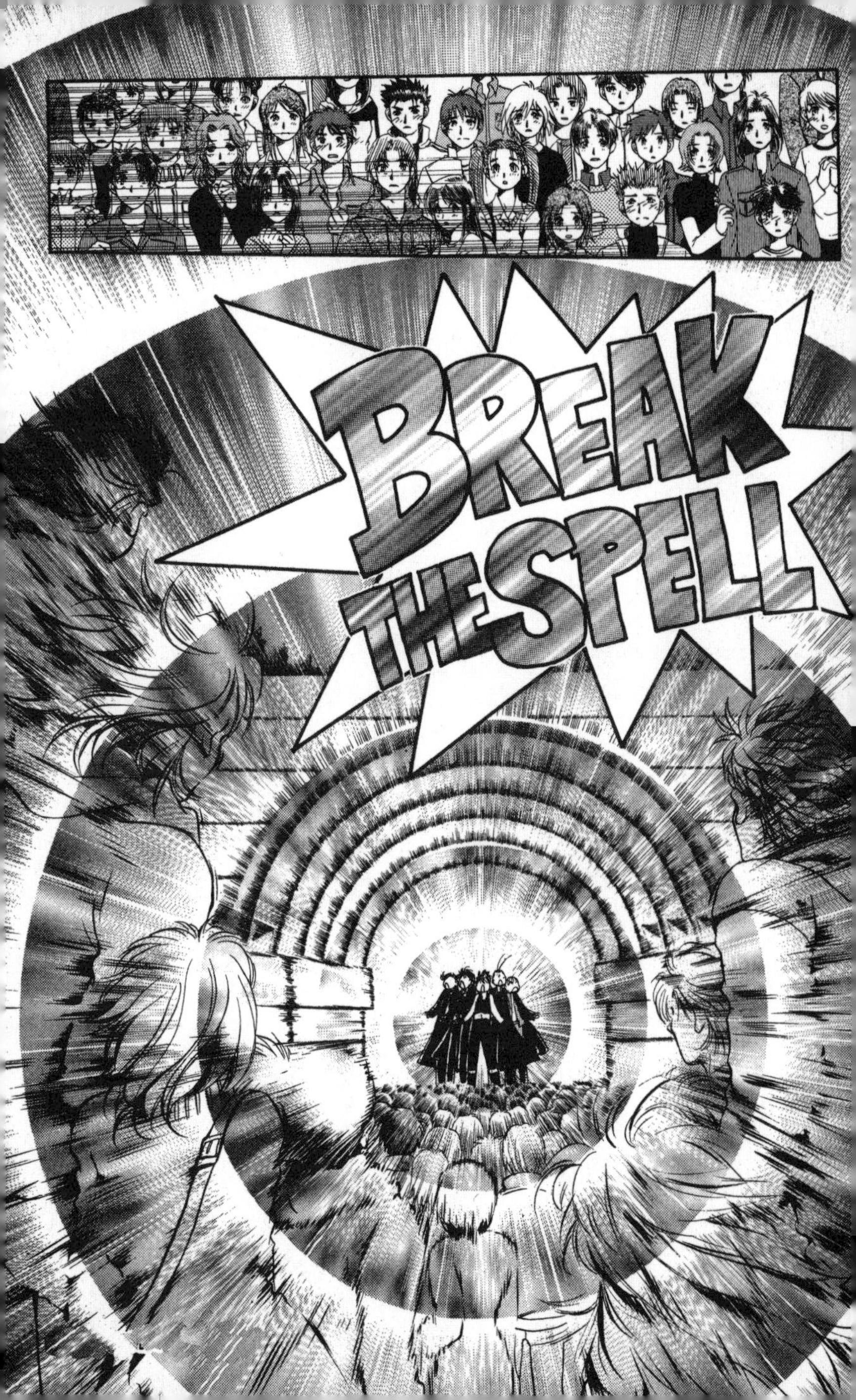
BREAK THE SPELL

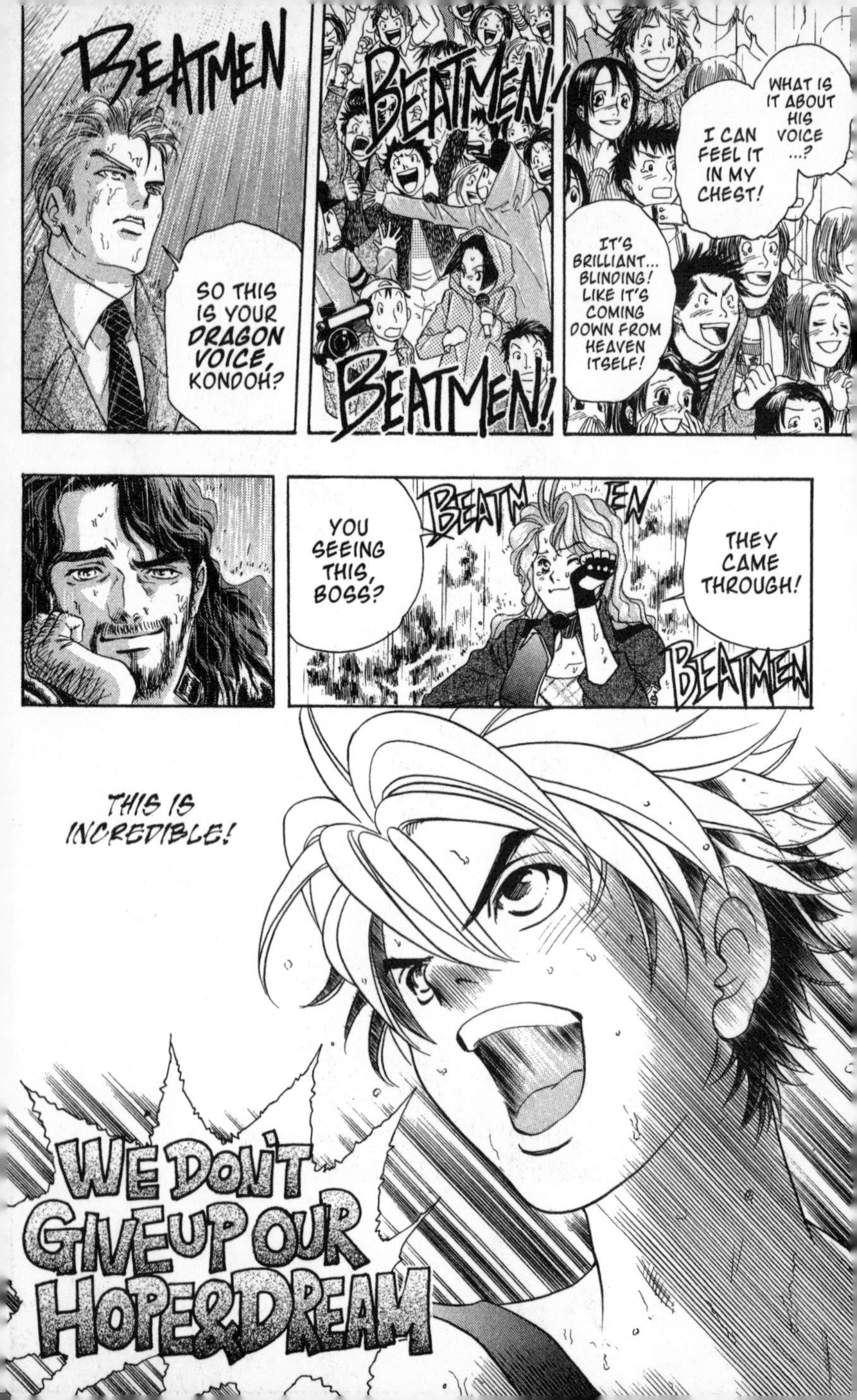
WHAT IS IT ABOUT HIS VOICE ...?
I CAN FEEL IT IN MY CHEST!
IT'S BRILLIANT... BLINDING! LIKE IT'S COMING DOWN FROM HEAVEN ITSELF!
BEATMEN!
BEATMEN!
BEATMEN
SO THIS IS YOUR DRAGON VOICE, KONDOH?
BEATM EN
THEY CAME THROUGH!
YOU SEEING THIS, BOSS?
BEATMEN
THIS IS INCREDIBLE!
WE DON'T GIVE UP OUR HOPE&DREAM

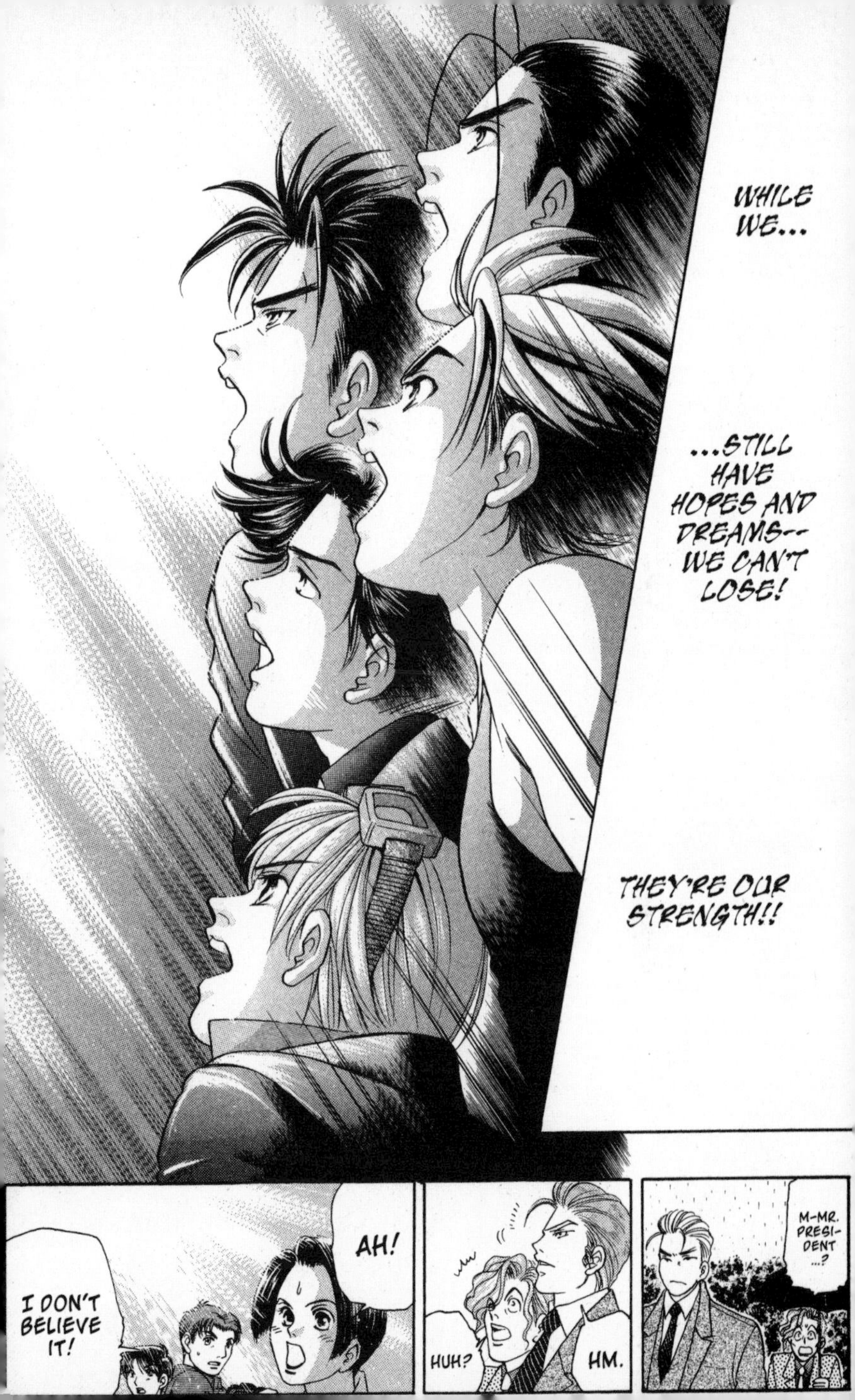
WHILE WE...
...STILL HAVE HOPES AND DREAMS-- WE CAN'T LOSE!
THEY'RE OUR STRENGTH!!
M-MR. PRESI-DENT ...?
HM.
HUH?
AH!
I DON'T BELIEVE IT!

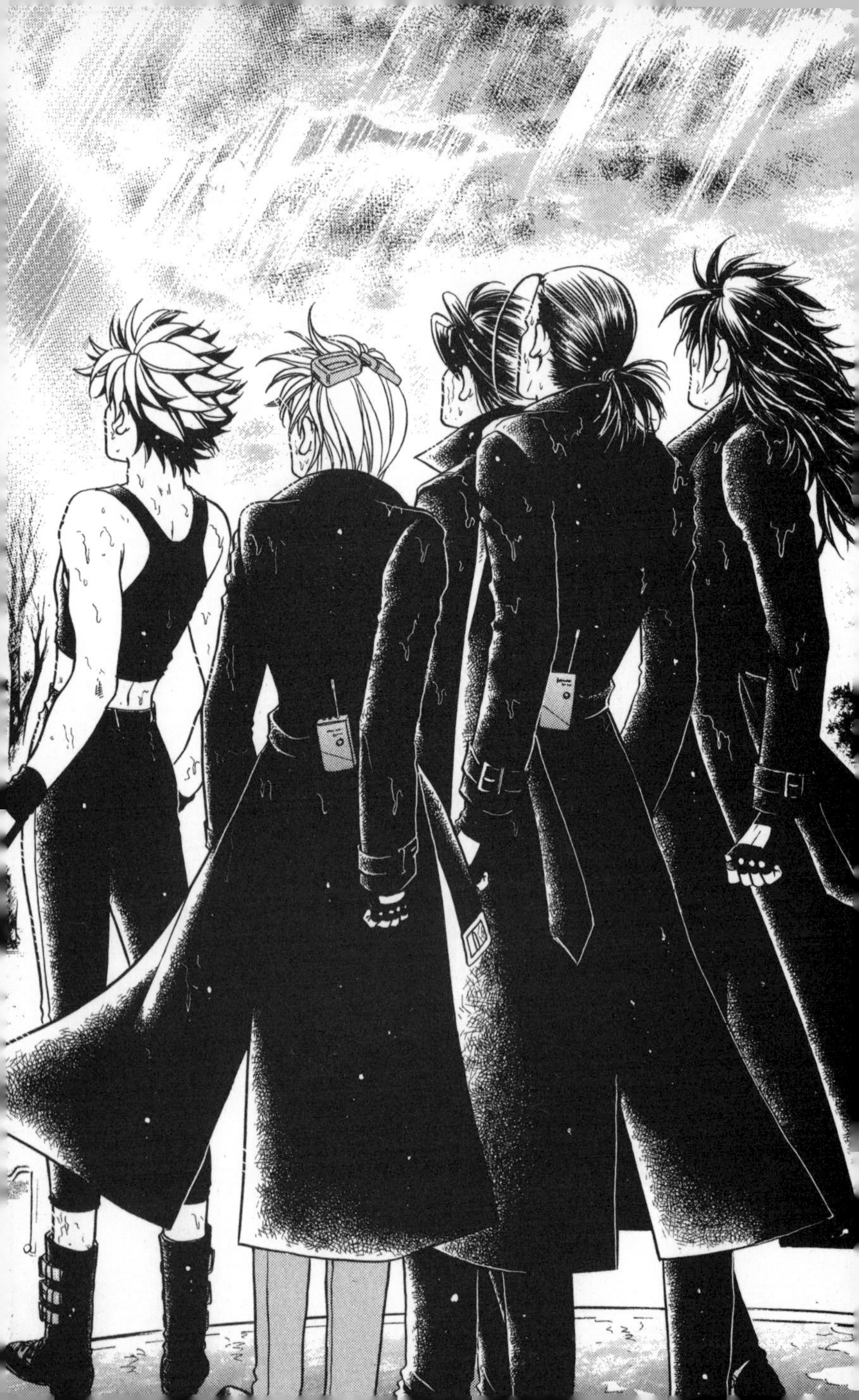

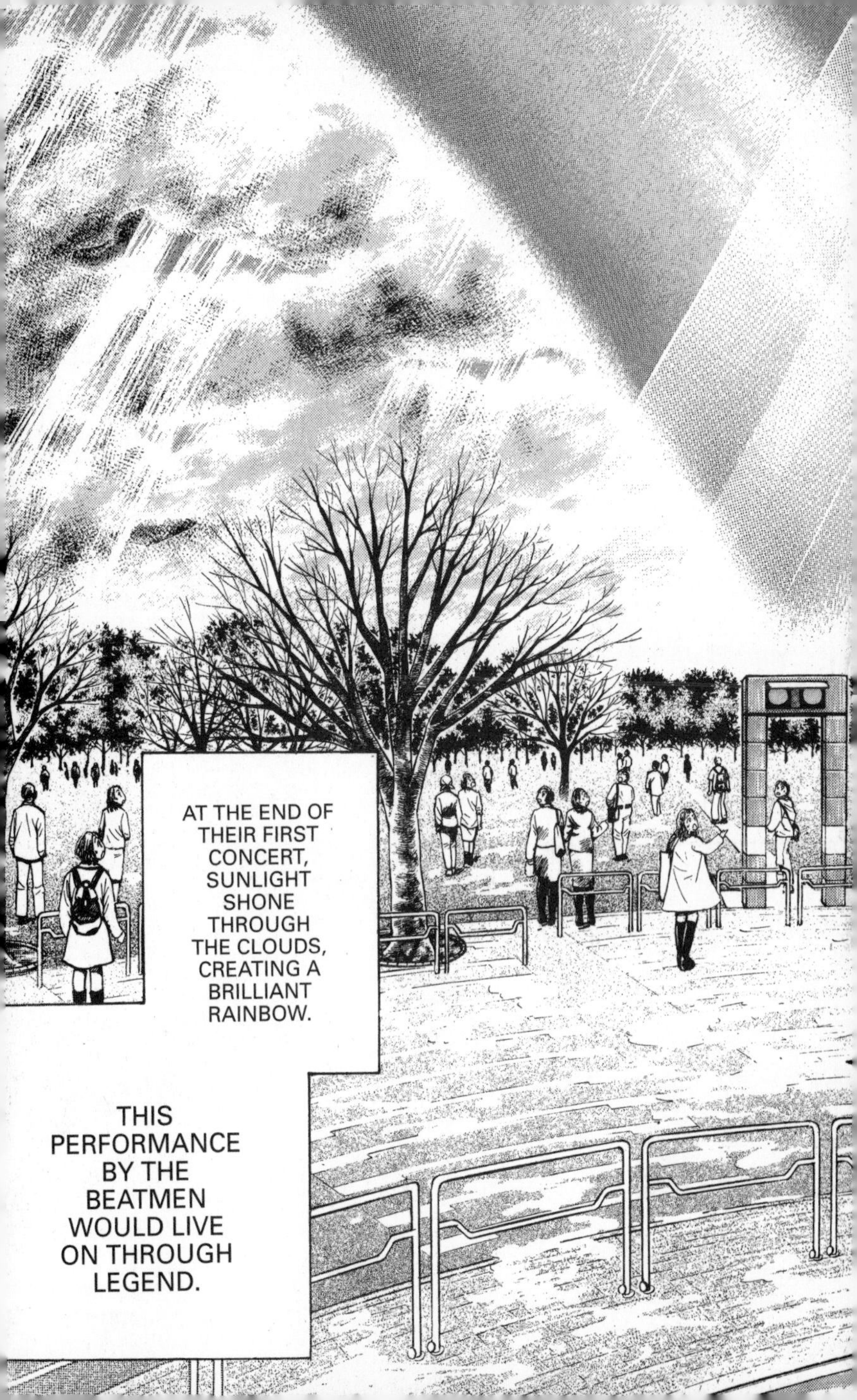
AT THE END OF THEIR FIRST CONCERT, SUNLIGHT SHONE THROUGH THE CLOUDS, CREATING A BRILLIANT RAINBOW.
THIS PERFORMANCE BY THE BEATMEN WOULD LIVE ON THROUGH LEGEND.

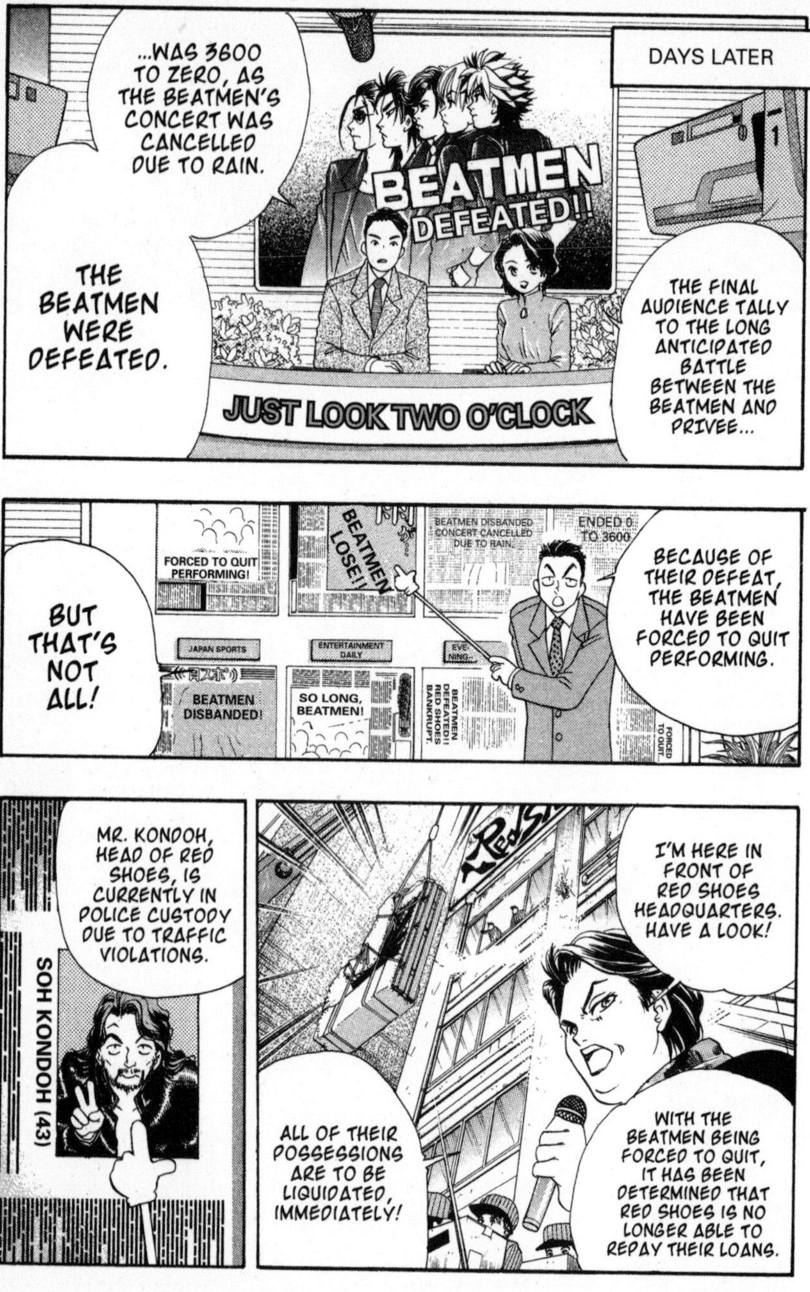
DAYS LATER
BEATMEN DEFEATED!!
JUST LOOK TWO O'CLOCK
THE FINAL AUDIENCE TALLY TO THE LONG ANTICIPATED BATTLE BETWEEN THE BEATMEN AND PRIVEE...
...WAS 3600 TO ZERO, AS THE BEATMEN'S CONCERT WAS CANCELLED DUE TO RAIN.
THE BEATMEN WERE DEFEATED.
BECAUSE OF THEIR DEFEAT, THE BEATMEN HAVE BEEN FORCED TO QUIT PERFORMING.
ENDED 0 TO 3600
BEATMEN DISBANDED CONCERT CANCELLED DUE TO RAIN.
BEATMEN LOSE!!
FORCED TO QUIT PERFORMING!
EVE-NING...
ENTERTAINMENT DAILY
JAPAN SPORTS
FORCED TO QUIT...
BEATMEN DEFEATED!! RED SHOES BANKRUPT.
SO LONG, BEATMEN!
BEATMEN DISBANDED!
BUT THAT'S NOT ALL!
I'M HERE IN FRONT OF RED SHOES HEADQUARTERS. HAVE A LOOK!
WITH THE BEATMEN BEING FORCED TO QUIT, IT HAS BEEN DETERMINED THAT RED SHOES IS NO LONGER ABLE TO REPAY THEIR LOANS.
ALL OF THEIR POSSESSIONS ARE TO BE LIQUIDATED, IMMEDIATELY!
MR. KONDOH, HEAD OF RED SHOES, IS CURRENTLY IN POLICE CUSTODY DUE TO TRAFFIC VIOLATIONS.
SOH KONDOH (43)

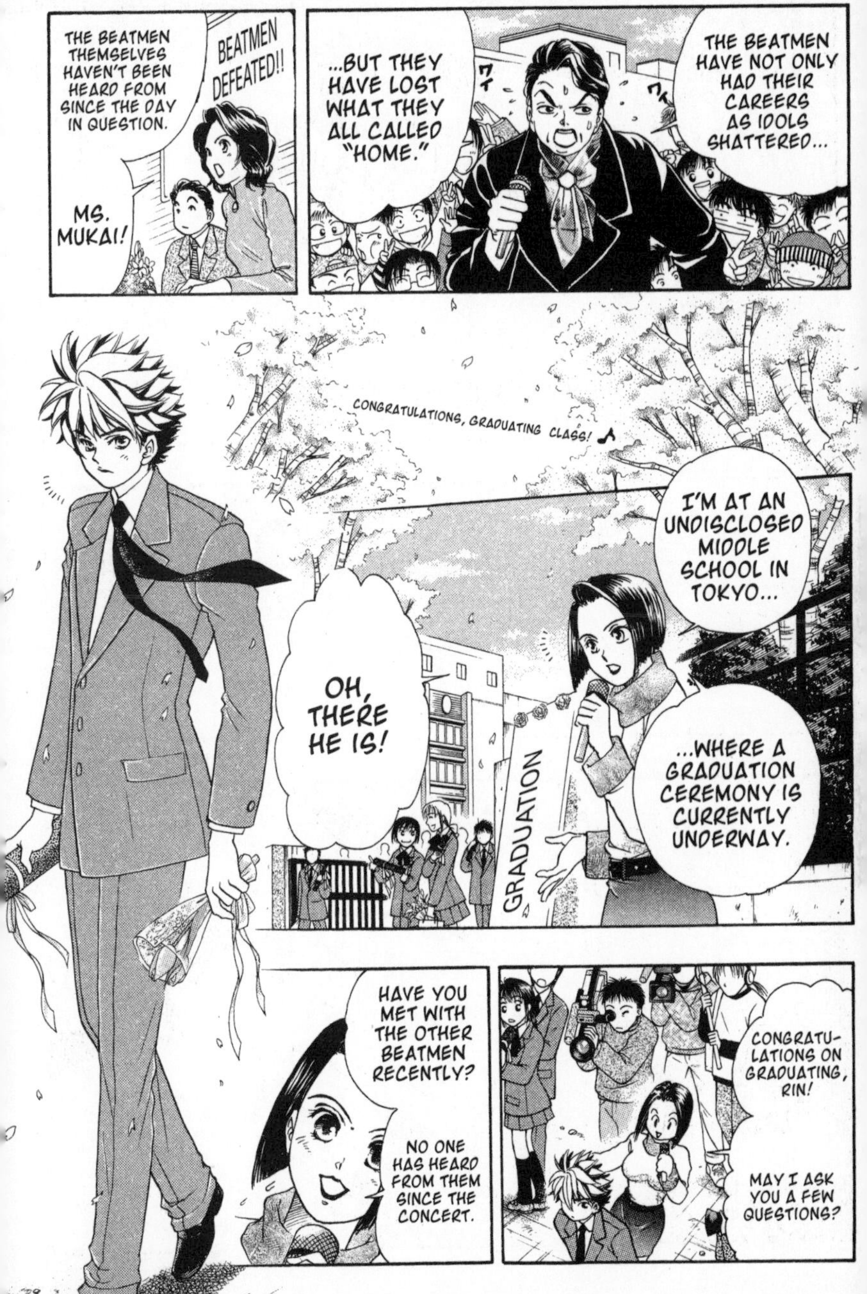
THE BEATMEN HAVE NOT ONLY HAD THEIR CAREERS AS IDOLS SHATTERED...
...BUT THEY HAVE LOST WHAT THEY ALL CALLED "HOME."
BEATMEN DEFEATED!!
THE BEATMEN THEMSELVES HAVEN'T BEEN HEARD FROM SINCE THE DAY IN QUESTION.
MS. MUKAI!
CONGRATULATIONS, GRADUATING CLASS! ♪
I'M AT AN UNDISCLOSED MIDDLE SCHOOL IN TOKYO...
...WHERE A GRADUATION CEREMONY IS CURRENTLY UNDERWAY.
GRADUATION
OH, THERE HE IS!
CONGRATU-LATIONS ON GRADUATING, RIN!
MAY I ASK YOU A FEW QUESTIONS?
HAVE YOU MET WITH THE OTHER BEATMEN RECENTLY?
NO ONE HAS HEARD FROM THEM SINCE THE CONCERT.

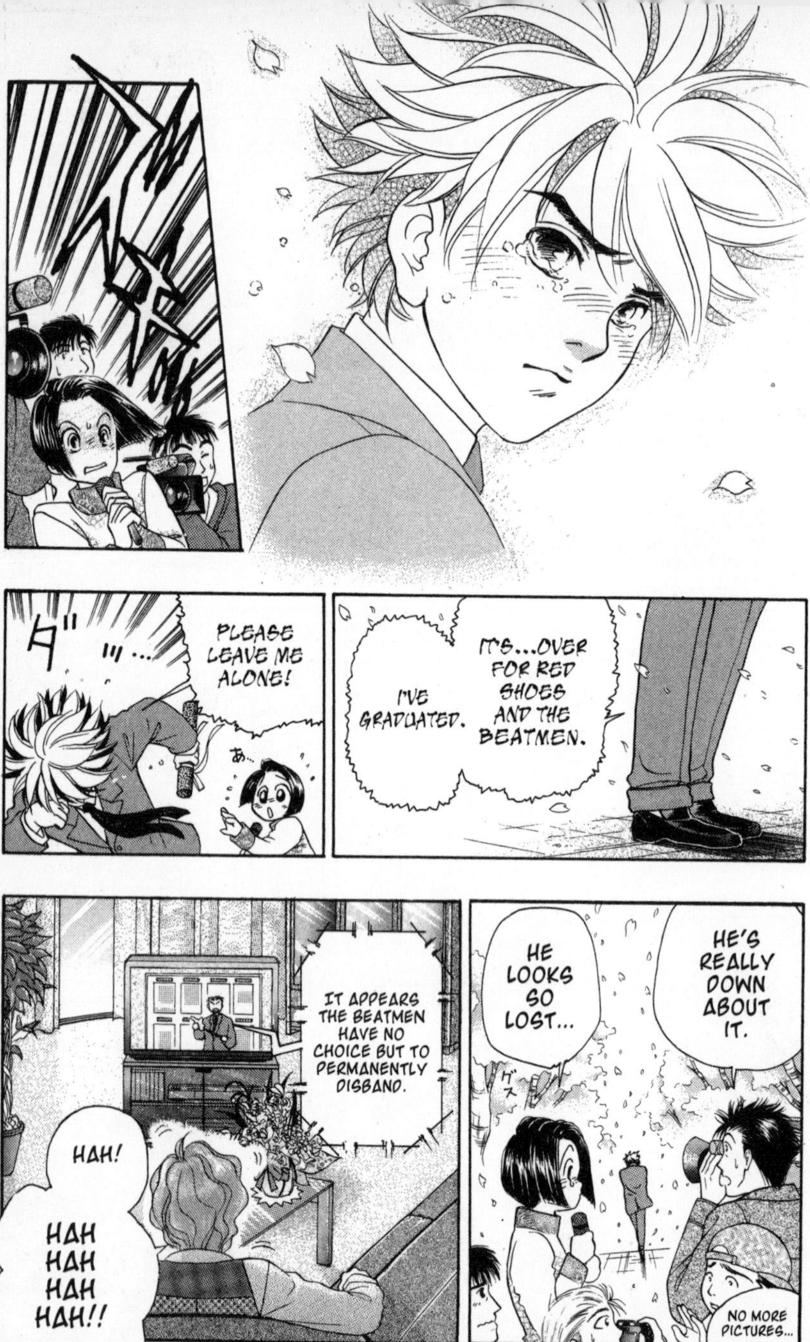

I'VE GRADUATED. IT'S...OVER FOR RED SHOES AND THE BEATMEN.
タ"...
PLEASE LEAVE ME ALONE!
あ...
HE'S REALLY DOWN ABOUT IT.
HE LOOKS SO LOST...
NO MORE PICTURES...
IT APPEARS THE BEATMEN HAVE NO CHOICE BUT TO PERMANENTLY DISBAND.
HAH!
HAH HAH HAH HAH!!

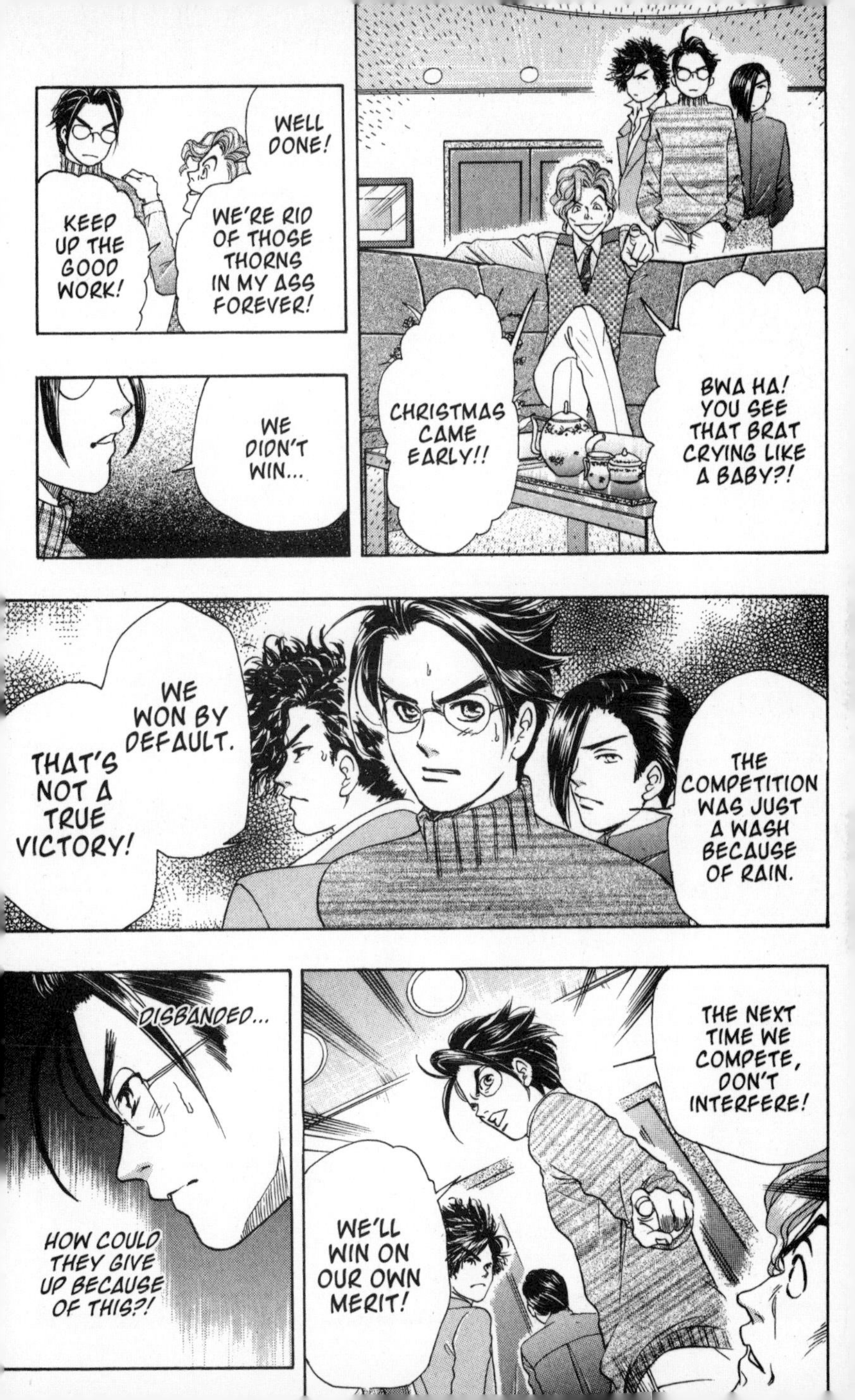
BWA HA! YOU SEE THAT BRAT CRYING LIKE A BABY?!
CHRISTMAS CAME EARLY!!
WELL DONE!
WE'RE RID OF THOSE THORNS IN MY ASS FOREVER!
KEEP UP THE GOOD WORK!
WE DIDN'T WIN...
THE COMPETITION WAS JUST A WASH BECAUSE OF RAIN.
WE WON BY DEFAULT.
THAT'S NOT A TRUE VICTORY!
THE NEXT TIME WE COMPETE, DON'T INTERFERE!
WE'LL WIN ON OUR OWN MERIT!
DISBANDED...
HOW COULD THEY GIVE UP BECAUSE OF THIS?!

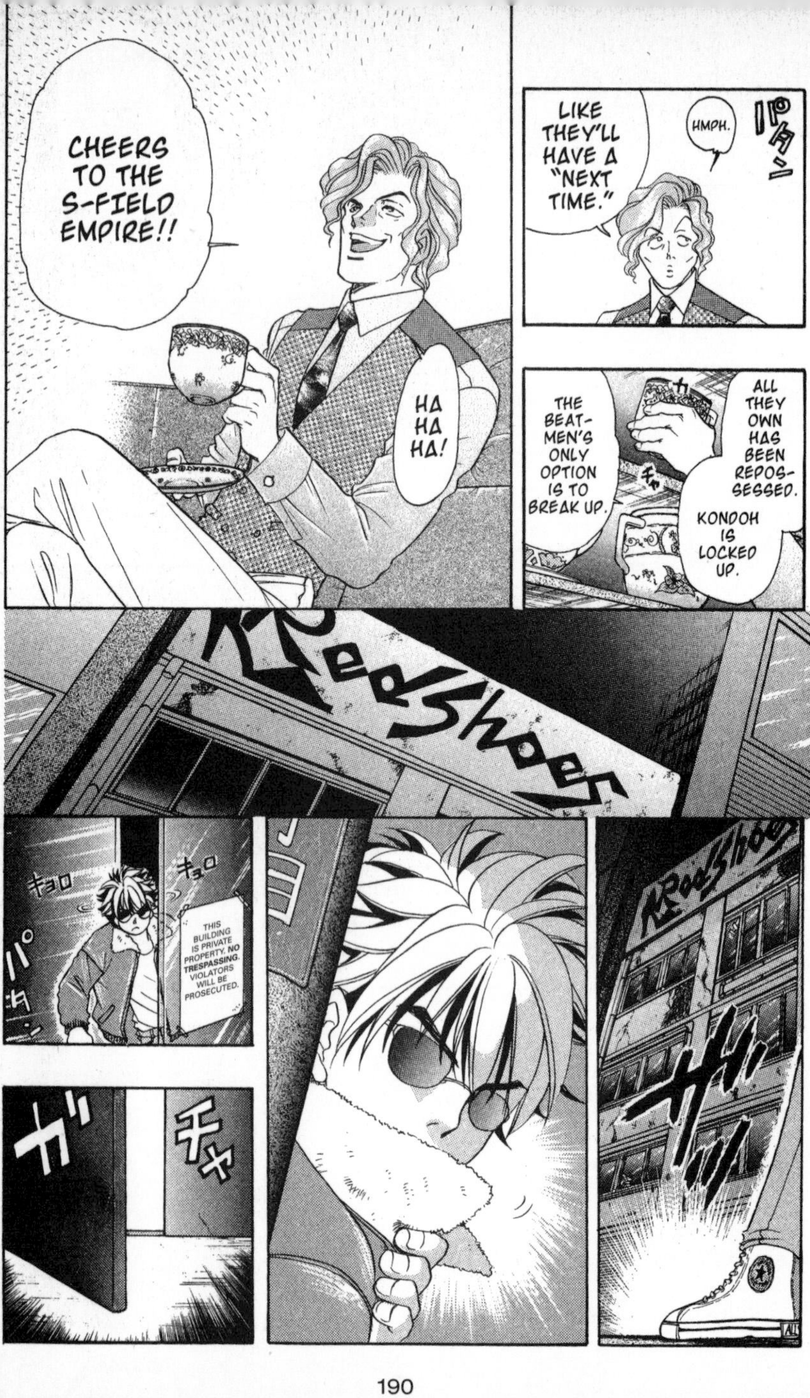
HMPH.
LIKE THEY'LL HAVE A "NEXT TIME."
ALL THEY OWN HAS BEEN REPOS-SESSED.
KONDOH IS LOCKED UP.
THE BEAT-MEN'S ONLY OPTION IS TO BREAK UP.
CHEERS TO THE S-FIELD EMPIRE!!
HA HA HA!
RedShoes
RedShoes
キョロ
キョロ
THIS BUILDING IS PRIVATE PROPERTY. NO TRESPASSING. VIOLATORS WILL BE PROSECUTED.
ガチャ

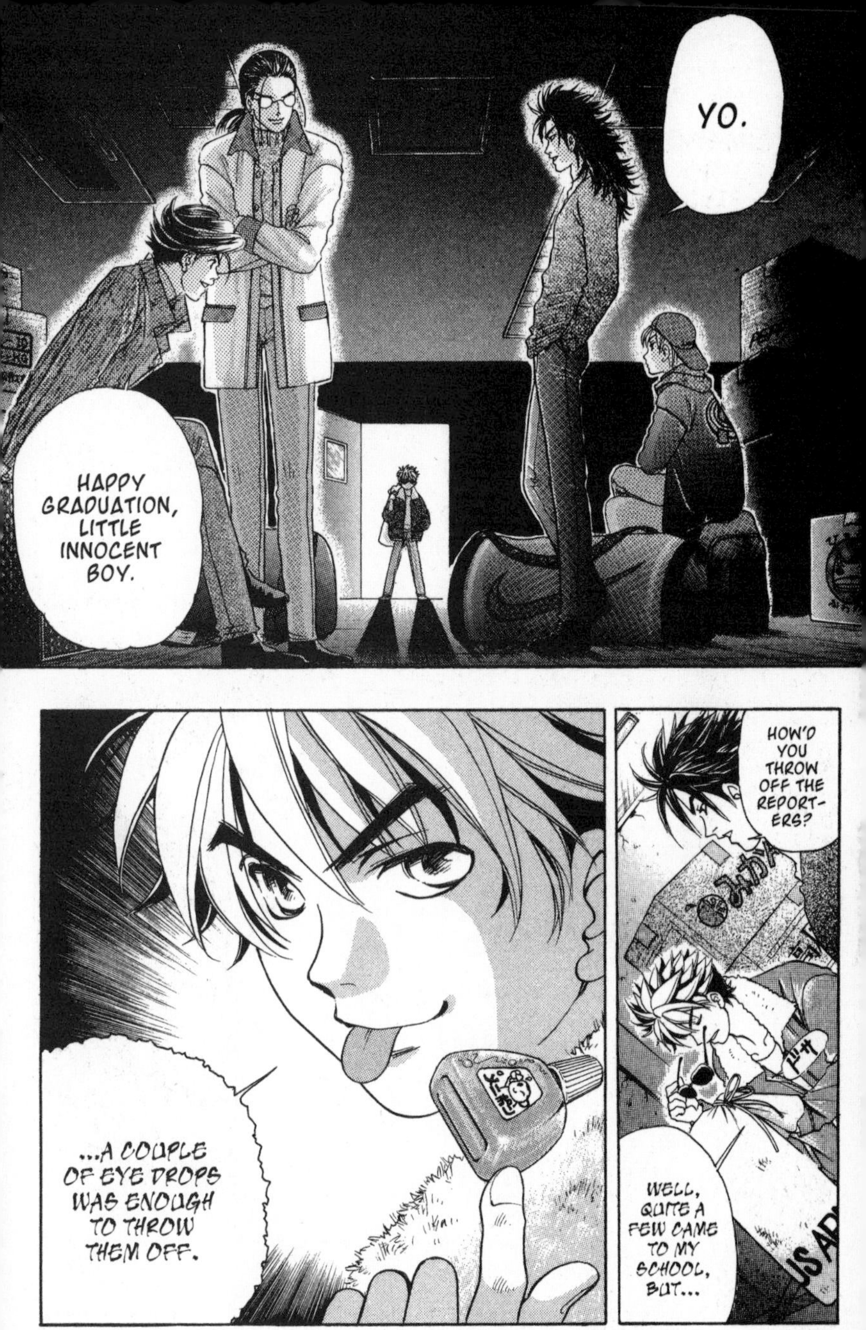
YO.
HAPPY GRADUATION, LITTLE INNOCENT BOY.
HOW'D YOU THROW OFF THE REPORTERS?
WELL, QUITE A FEW CAME TO MY SCHOOL, BUT...
...A COUPLE OF EYE DROPS WAS ENOUGH TO THROW THEM OFF.

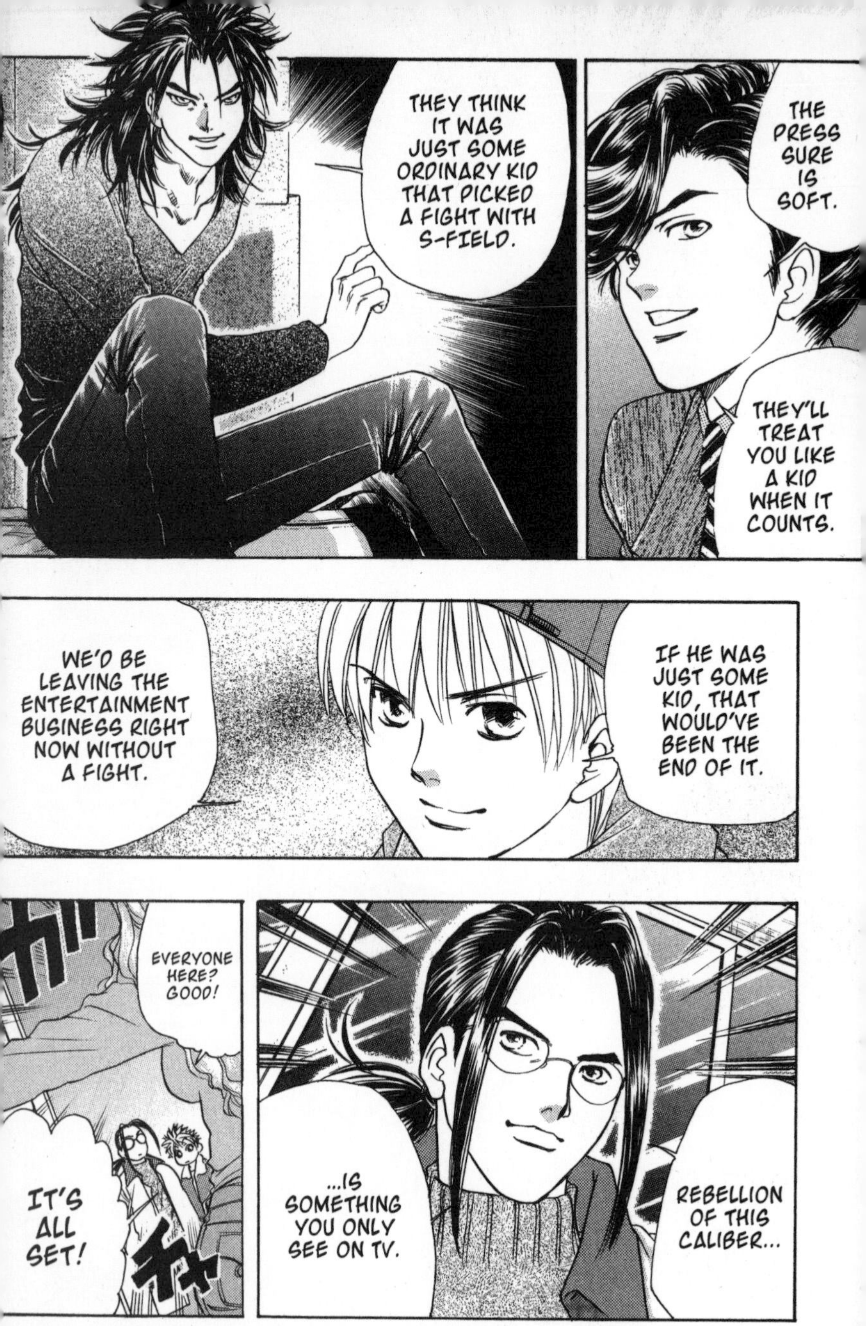
THE PRESS SURE IS SOFT.
THEY'LL TREAT YOU LIKE A KID WHEN IT COUNTS.
THEY THINK IT WAS JUST SOME ORDINARY KID THAT PICKED A FIGHT WITH S-FIELD.
IF HE WAS JUST SOME KID, THAT WOULD'VE BEEN THE END OF IT.
WE'D BE LEAVING THE ENTERTAINMENT BUSINESS RIGHT NOW WITHOUT A FIGHT.
REBELLION OF THIS CALIBER...
...IS SOMETHING YOU ONLY SEE ON TV.
EVERYONE HERE? GOOD!
IT'S ALL SET!

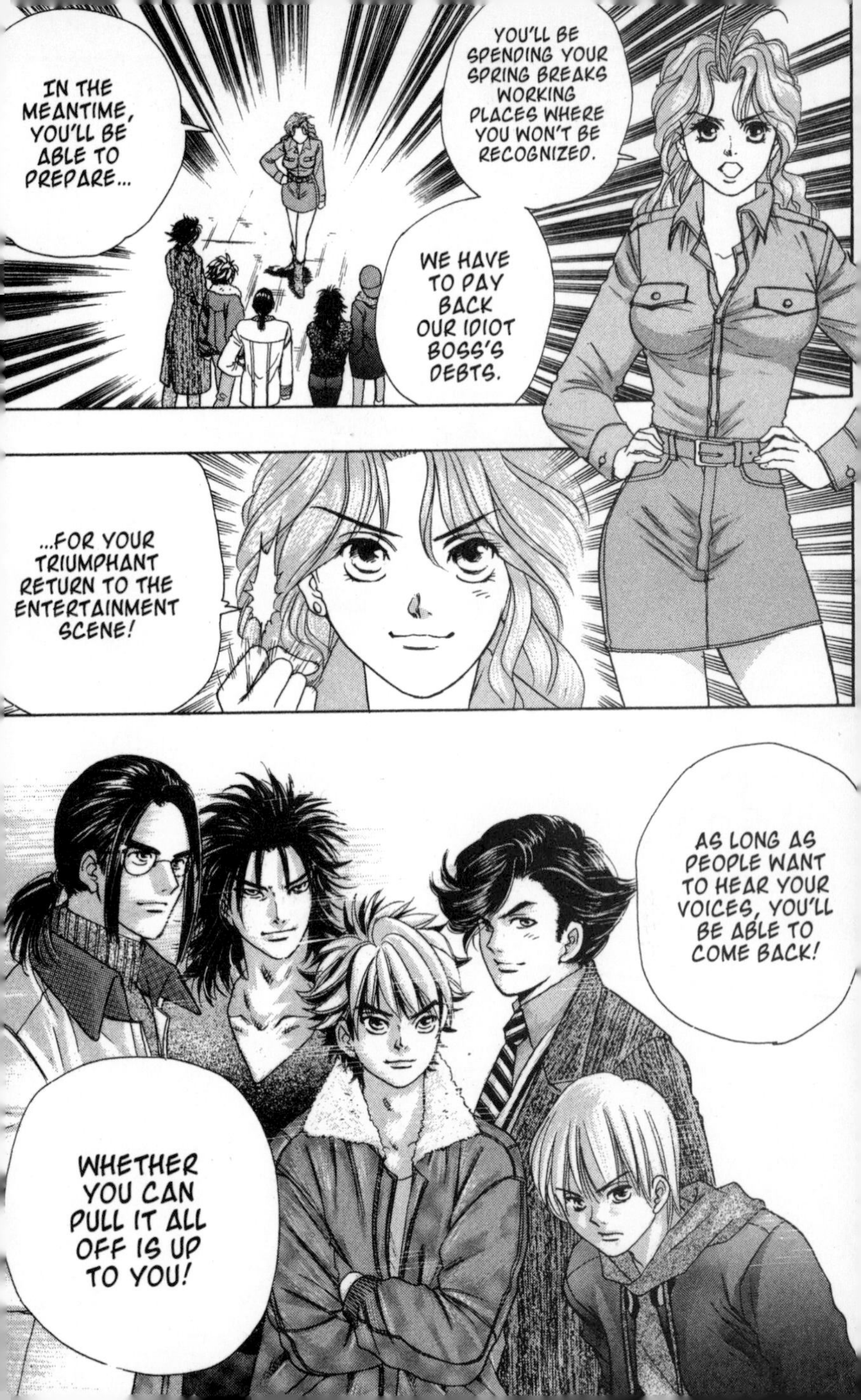
YOU'LL BE SPENDING YOUR SPRING BREAKS WORKING PLACES WHERE YOU WON'T BE RECOGNIZED.
WE HAVE TO PAY BACK OUR IDIOT BOSS'S DEBTS.
IN THE MEANTIME, YOU'LL BE ABLE TO PREPARE...
...FOR YOUR TRIUMPHANT RETURN TO THE ENTERTAINMENT SCENE!
AS LONG AS PEOPLE WANT TO HEAR YOUR VOICES, YOU'LL BE ABLE TO COME BACK!
WHETHER YOU CAN PULL IT ALL OFF IS UP TO YOU!

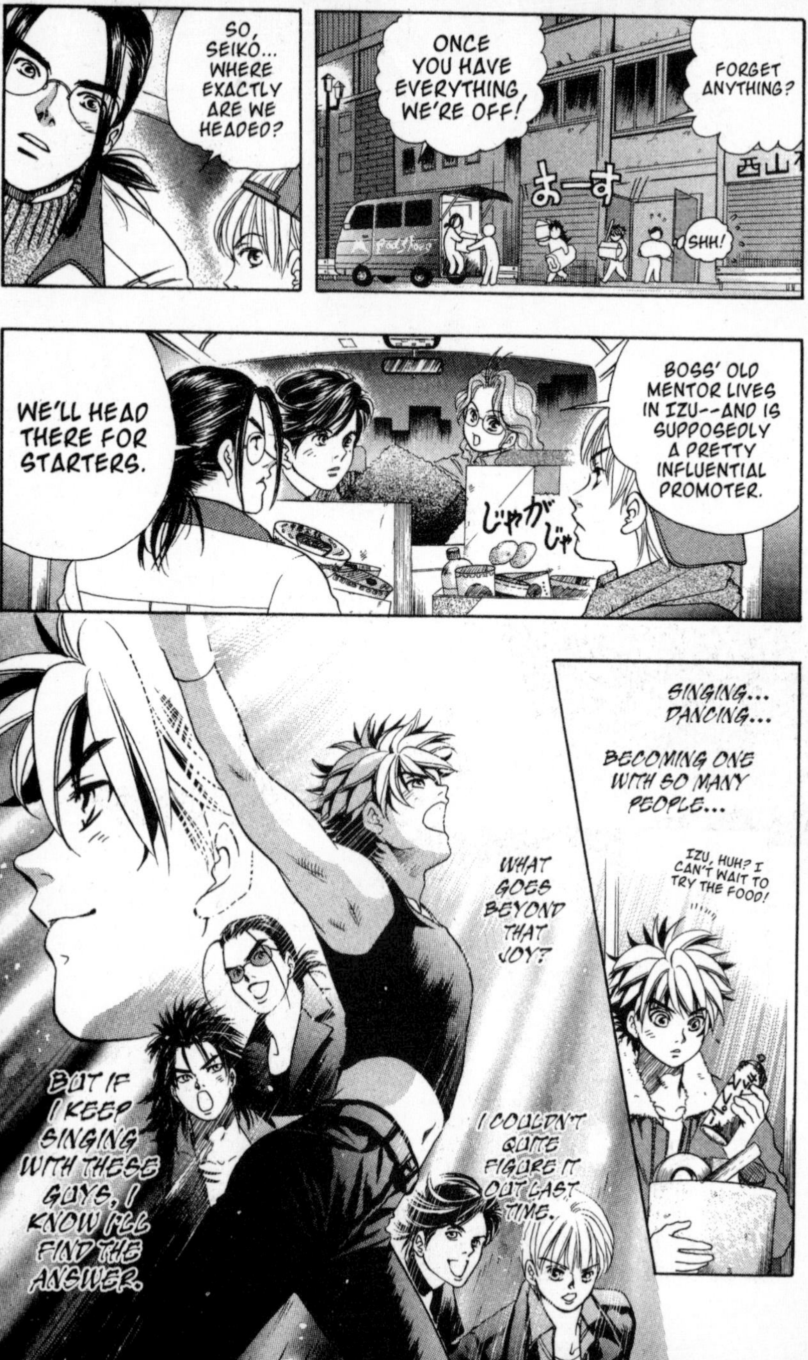
FORGET ANYTHING?
ONCE YOU HAVE EVERYTHING, WE'RE OFF!
西山
おーす
SHH!
SO, SEIKŌ... WHERE EXACTLY ARE WE HEADED?
BOSS' OLD MENTOR LIVES IN IZU--AND IS SUPPOSEDLY A PRETTY INFLUENTIAL PROMOTER.
じゃがじゃ
WE'LL HEAD THERE FOR STARTERS.
SINGING... DANCING...
BECOMING ONE WITH SO MANY PEOPLE...
IZU, HUH? I CAN'T WAIT TO TRY THE FOOD!
WHAT GOES BEYOND THAT JOY?
I COULDN'T QUITE FIGURE IT OUT LAST TIME.
BUT IF I KEEP SINGING WITH THESE GUYS, I KNOW I'LL FIND THE ANSWER.

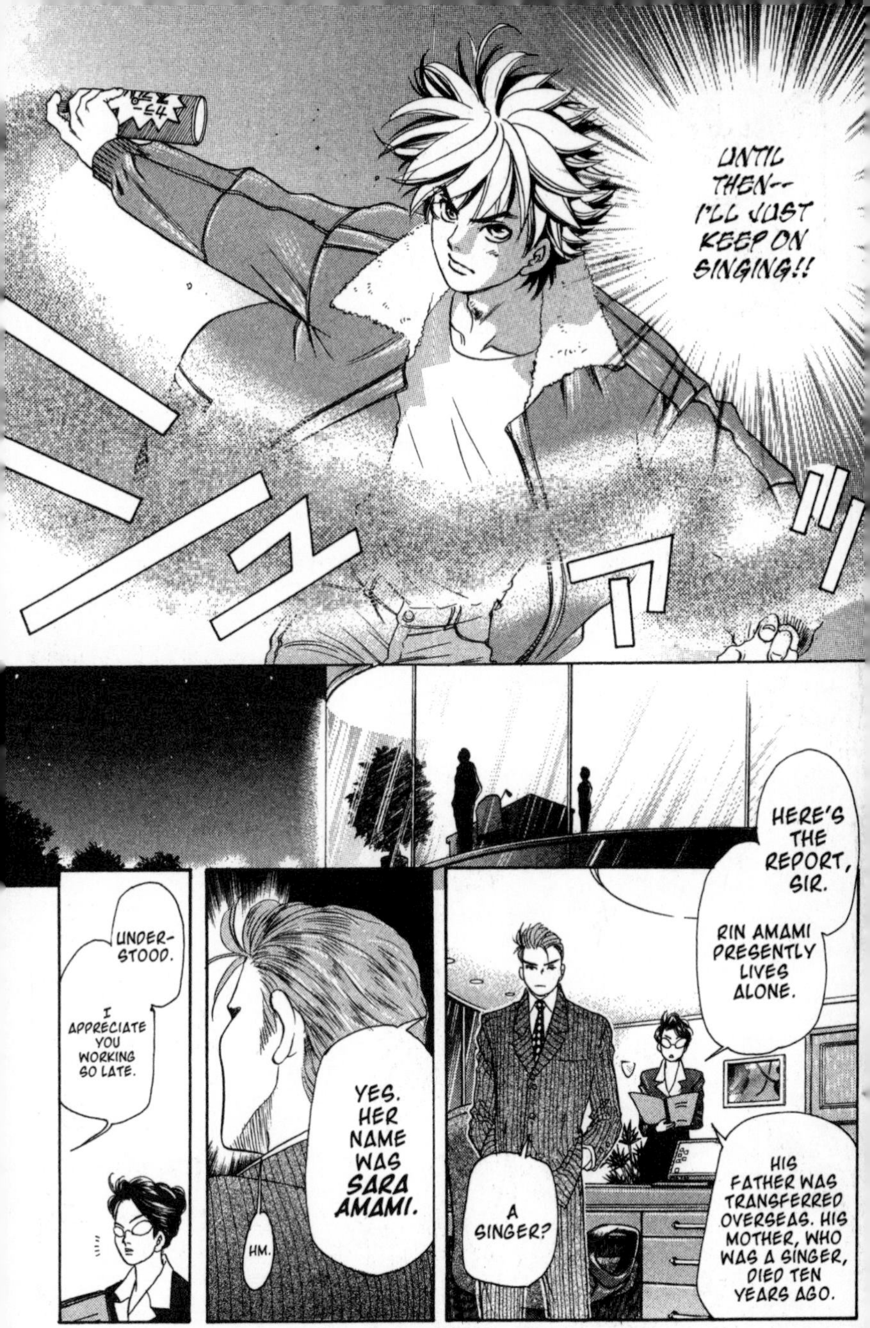
UNTIL THEN-- I'LL JUST KEEP ON SINGING!!
HERE'S THE REPORT, SIR.
RIN AMAMI PRESENTLY LIVES ALONE.
HIS FATHER WAS TRANSFERRED OVERSEAS. HIS MOTHER, WHO WAS A SINGER, DIED TEN YEARS AGO.
A SINGER?
YES. HER NAME WAS **SARA AMAMI.**
HM.
UNDER-STOOD.
I APPRECIATE YOU WORKING SO LATE.

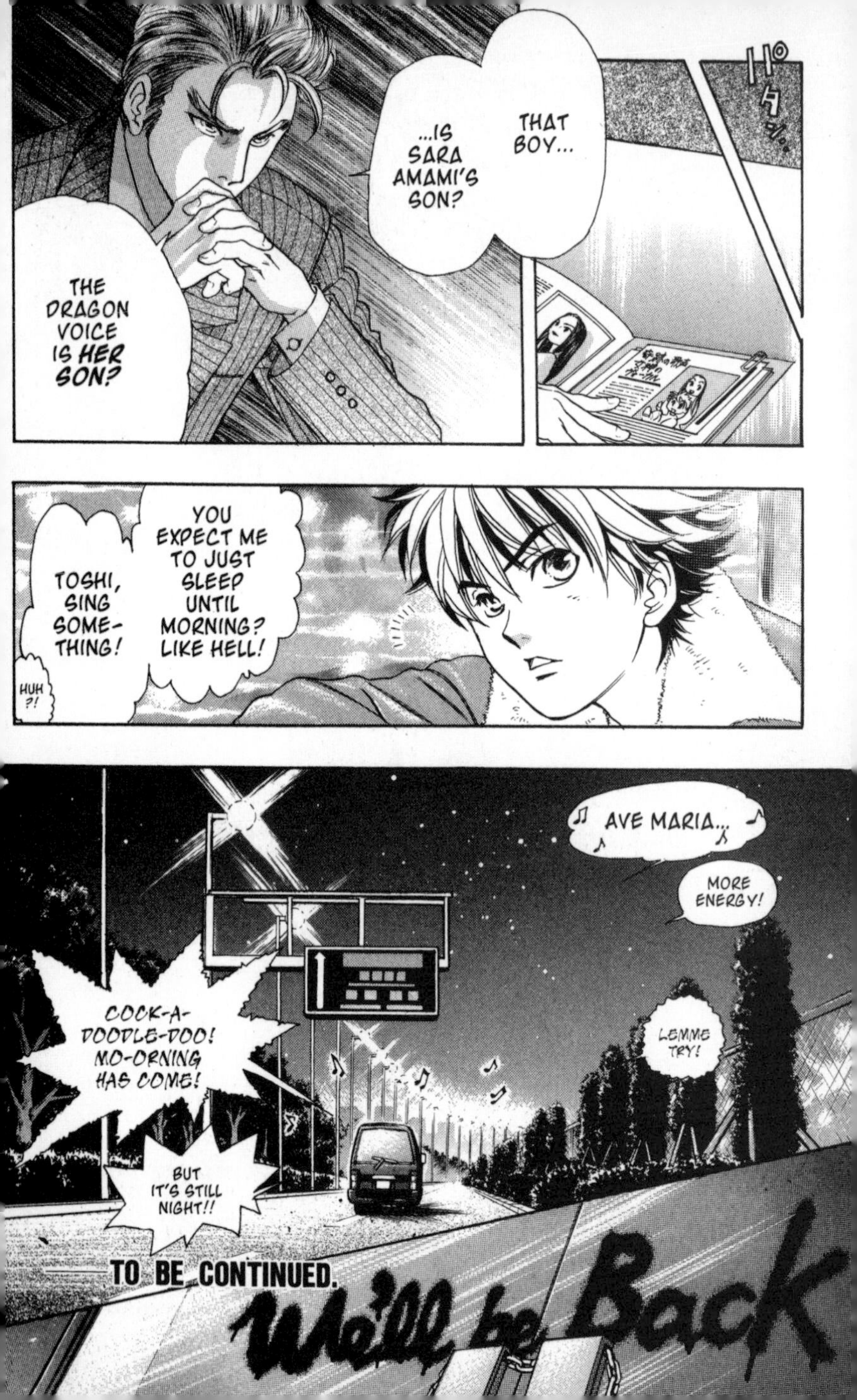
THAT BOY...
...IS SARA AMAMI'S SON?
THE DRAGON VOICE IS HER SON?
YOU EXPECT ME TO JUST SLEEP UNTIL MORNING? LIKE HELL!
TOSHI, SING SOME-THING!
HUH ?!
AVE MARIA...
MORE ENERGY!
LEMME TRY!
COCK-A-DOODLE-DOO! MO-ORNING HAS COME!
BUT IT'S STILL NIGHT!!
TO BE CONTINUED.
We'll be Back

A NEW BONUS MANGA BEGINS!!

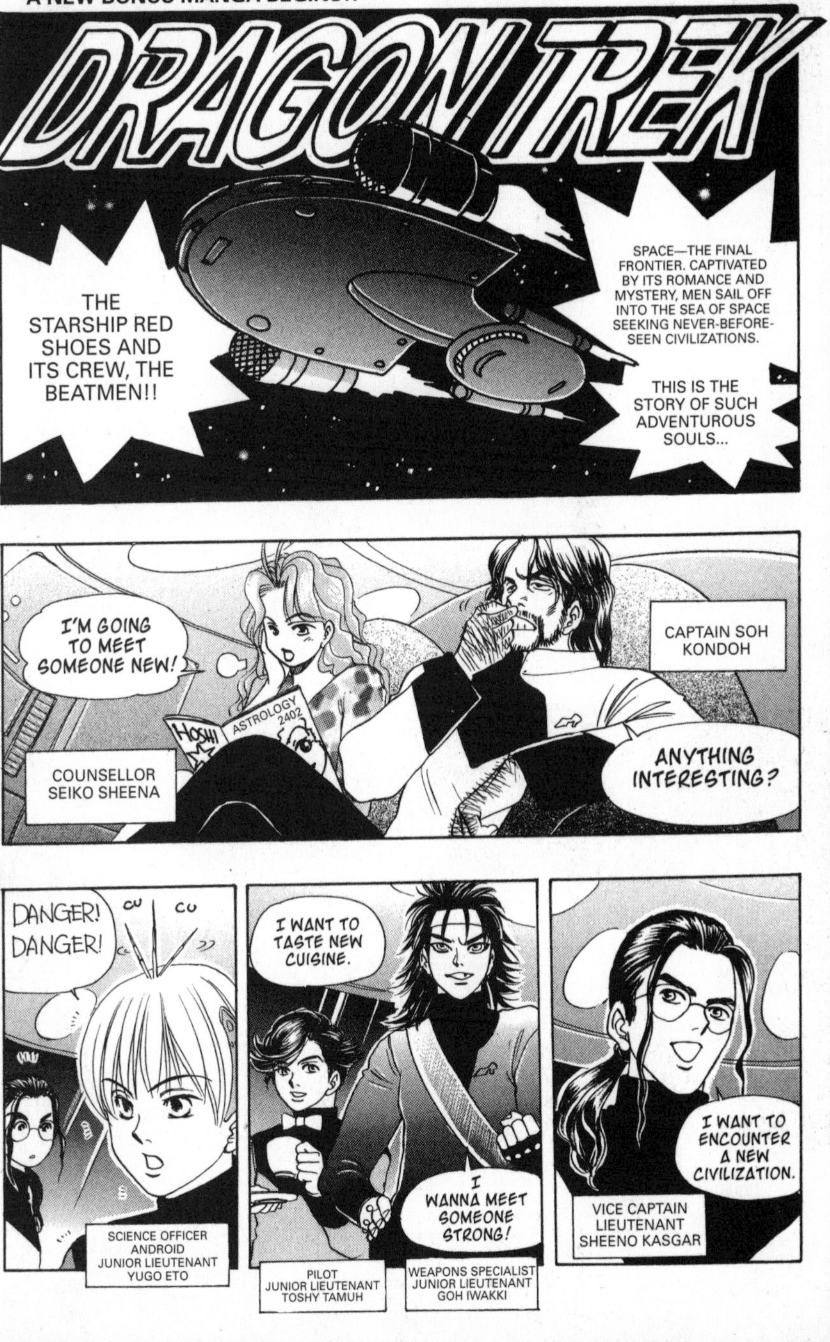
DRAGON TREK
SPACE—THE FINAL FRONTIER. CAPTIVATED BY ITS ROMANCE AND MYSTERY, MEN SAIL OFF INTO THE SEA OF SPACE SEEKING NEVER-BEFORE-SEEN CIVILIZATIONS.
THIS IS THE STORY OF SUCH ADVENTUROUS SOULS...
THE STARSHIP RED SHOES AND ITS CREW, THE BEATMEN!!
CAPTAIN SOH KONDOH
ANYTHING INTERESTING?
I'M GOING TO MEET SOMEONE NEW!
HOSHI
ASTROLOGY 2402
COUNSELLOR SEIKO SHEENA
I WANT TO ENCOUNTER A NEW CIVILIZATION.
VICE CAPTAIN LIEUTENANT SHEENO KASGAR
I WANNA MEET SOMEONE STRONG!
WEAPONS SPECIALIST JUNIOR LIEUTENANT GOH IWAKKI
I WANT TO TASTE NEW CUISINE.
PILOT JUNIOR LIEUTENANT TOSHY TAMUH
CU
CU
DANGER! DANGER!
SCIENCE OFFICER ANDROID JUNIOR LIEUTENANT YUGO ETO

DRAGON TREK SHOULD BE ABLE TO SERVE AS A QUICK SUMMARY OF THE EVENTS IN DRAGON VOICE! I HOPE YOU'LL ENJOY IT! (NISHIYAMA)

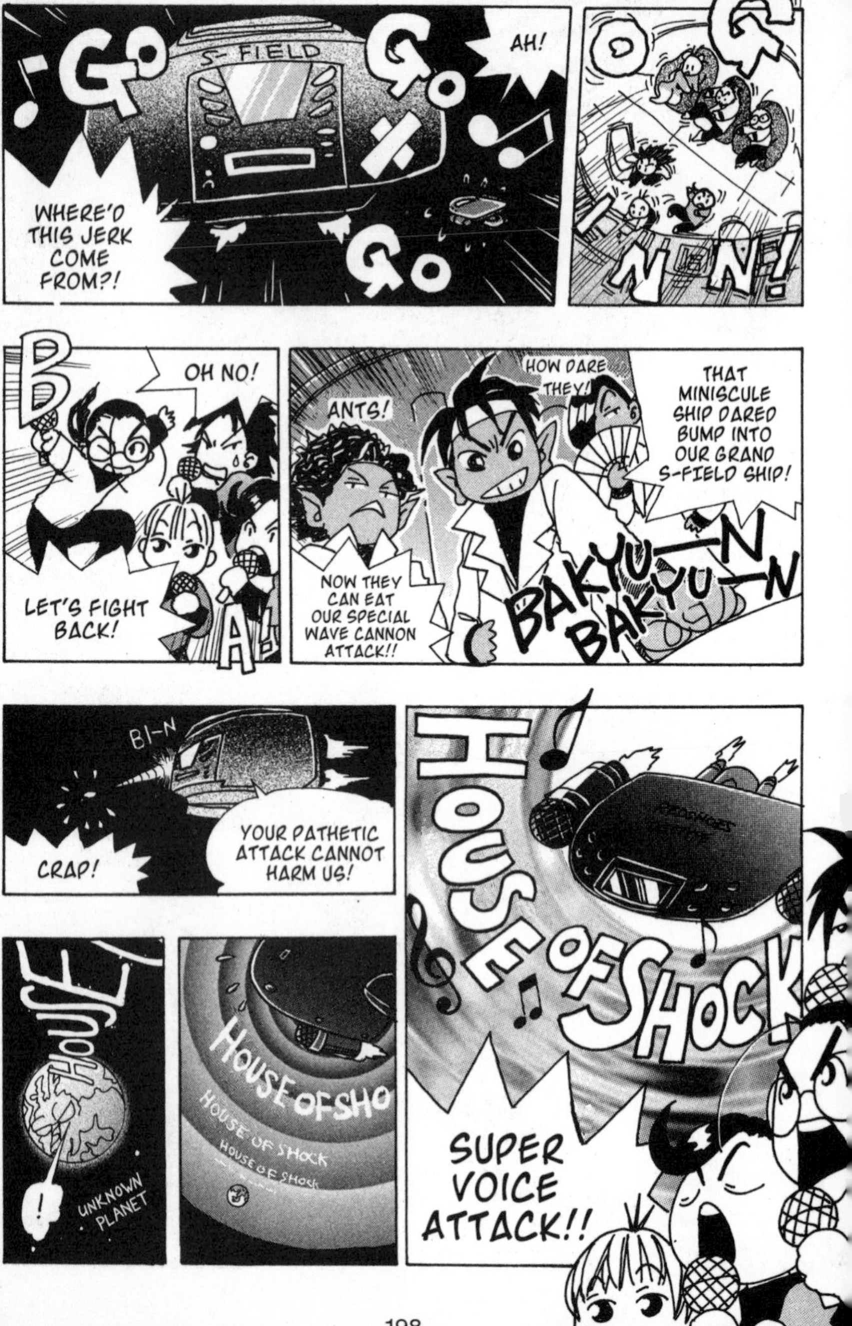
AH!
GO
GO
GO
WHERE'D THIS JERK COME FROM?!
THAT MINISCULE SHIP DARED BUMP INTO OUR GRAND S-FIELD SHIP!
HOW DARE THEY!
ANTS!
BAKYU-N BAKYU-N
NOW THEY CAN EAT OUR SPECIAL WAVE CANNON ATTACK!!
OH NO!
LET'S FIGHT BACK!
HOUSE OF SHOCK
SUPER VOICE ATTACK!!
BI-N
YOUR PATHETIC ATTACK CANNOT HARM US!
CRAP!
HOUSE OF SHO
HOUSE OF SHOCK
HOUSE OF SHOCK
HOUSE
UNKNOWN PLANET
!

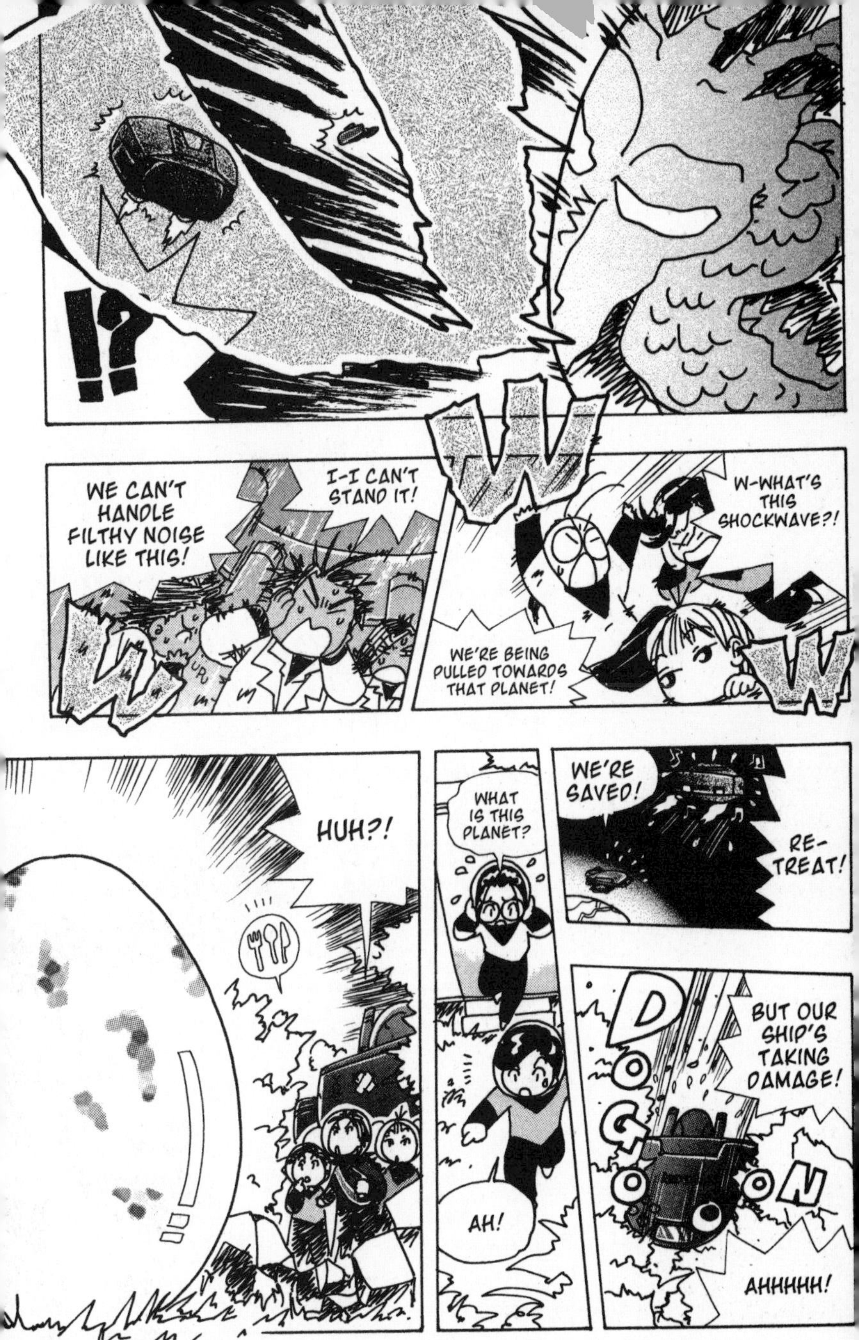
!?
W
W-WHAT'S THIS SHOCKWAVE?!
WE'RE BEING PULLED TOWARDS THAT PLANET!
W
I-I CAN'T STAND IT!
WE CAN'T HANDLE FILTHY NOISE LIKE THIS!
W
WE'RE SAVED!
RE-TREAT!
BUT OUR SHIP'S TAKING DAMAGE!
DOGOON
AHHHHH!
WHAT IS THIS PLANET?
AH!
HUH?!

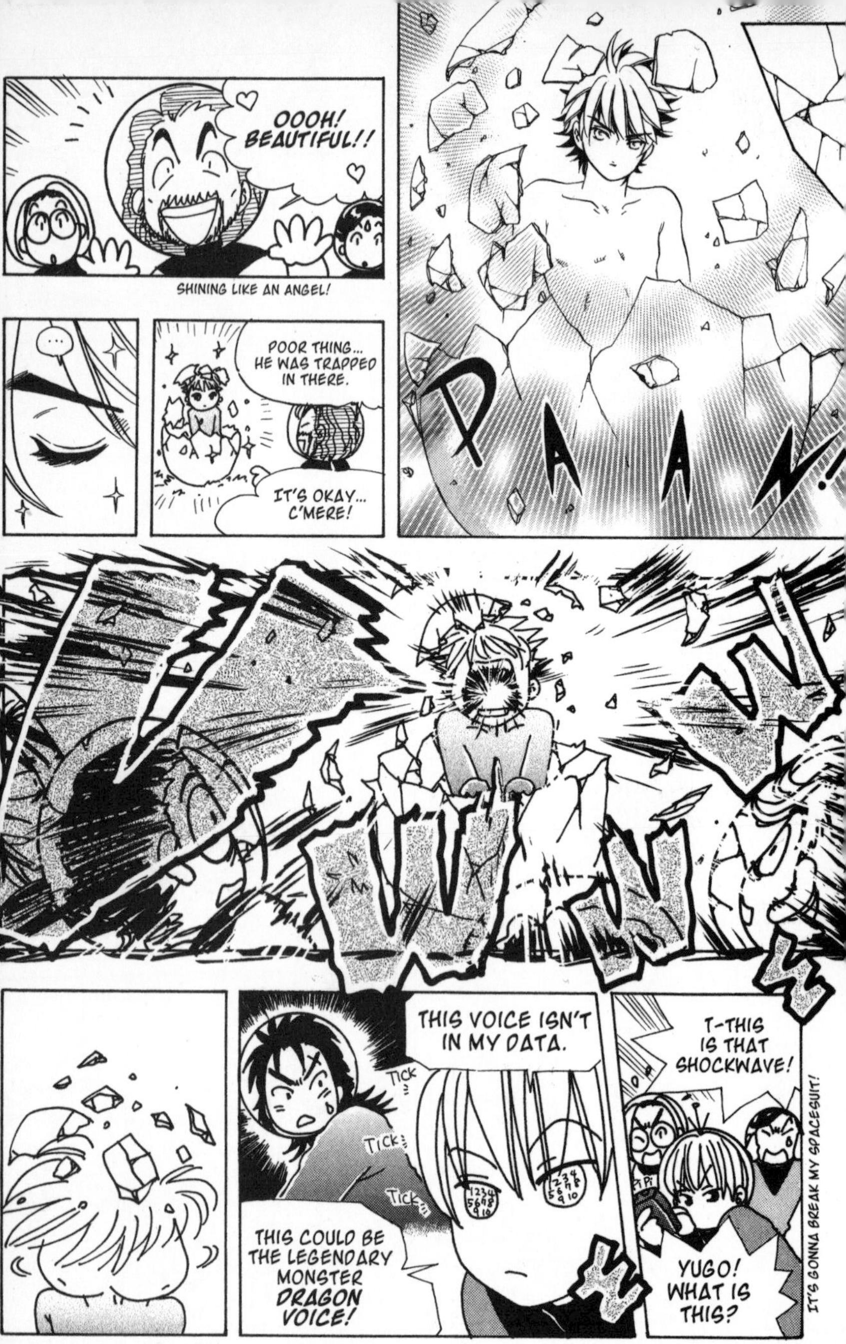
PAAAN!!
OOOH! BEAUTIFUL!!
SHINING LIKE AN ANGEL!
POOR THING... HE WAS TRAPPED IN THERE.
IT'S OKAY... C'MERE!
...
T-THIS IS THAT SHOCKWAVE!
IT'S GONNA BREAK MY SPACESUIT!
YUGO! WHAT IS THIS?
THIS VOICE ISN'T IN MY DATA.
TICK
TICK
TICK
THIS COULD BE THE LEGENDARY MONSTER DRAGON VOICE!

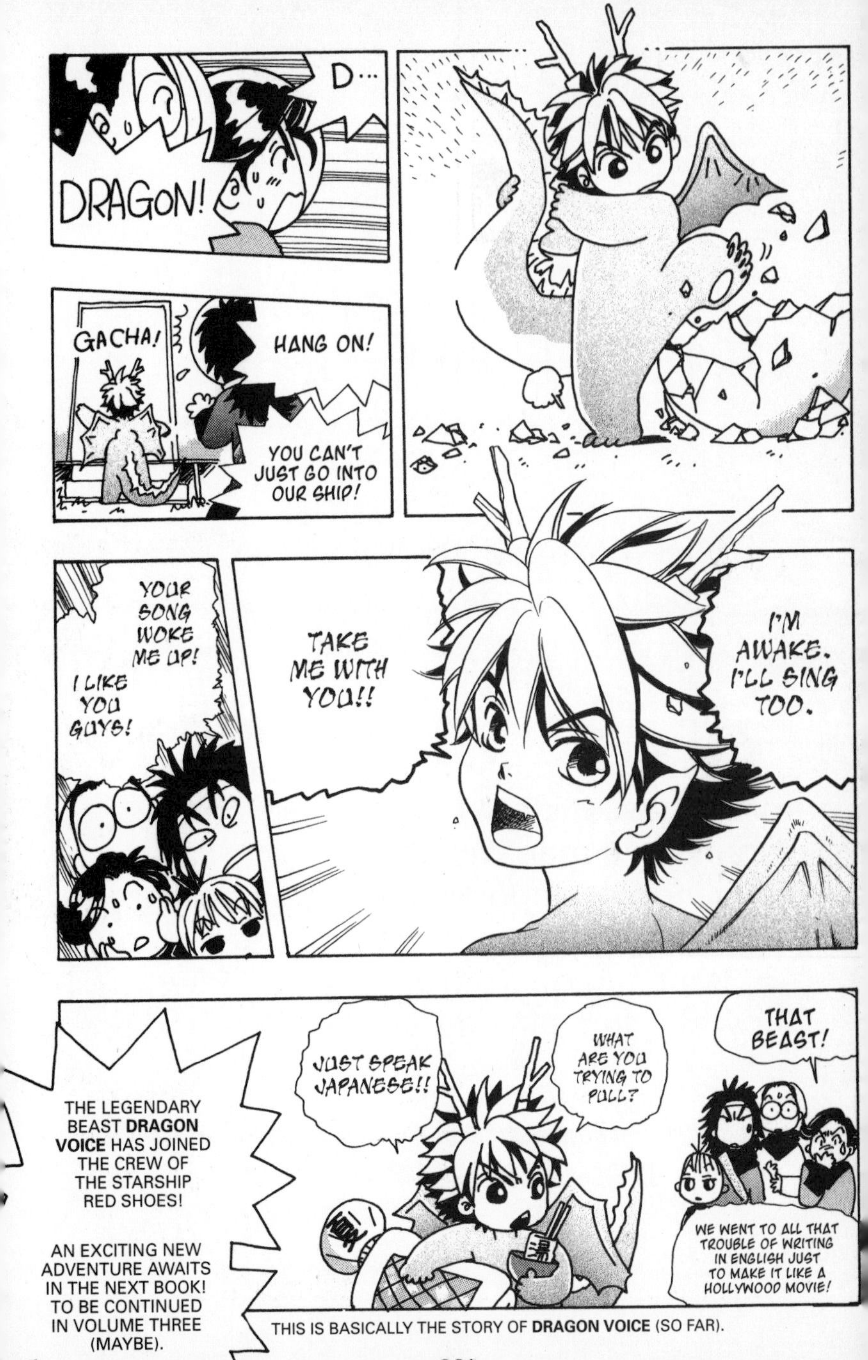
D...
DRAGON!
GACHA!
HANG ON!
YOU CAN'T JUST GO INTO OUR SHIP!
I'M AWAKE. I'LL SING TOO.
TAKE ME WITH YOU!!
YOUR SONG WOKE ME UP!
I LIKE YOU GUYS!
THAT BEAST!
WHAT ARE YOU TRYING TO PULL?
JUST SPEAK JAPANESE!!
WE WENT TO ALL THAT TROUBLE OF WRITING IN ENGLISH JUST TO MAKE IT LIKE A HOLLYWOOD MOVIE!
THE LEGENDARY BEAST **DRAGON VOICE** HAS JOINED THE CREW OF THE STARSHIP RED SHOES!
AN EXCITING NEW ADVENTURE AWAITS IN THE NEXT BOOK! TO BE CONTINUED IN VOLUME THREE (MAYBE).
THIS IS BASICALLY THE STORY OF **DRAGON VOICE** (SO FAR).

## Next in

# DRAGON VOICE

Things have never been worse for The Beatmen. RedShoes is bankrupt. Their boss is in jail. And to make ends meet, Rin, Shino, Goh, Toshi, and Yuhgo have to work in an amusement park wearing humiliating costumes while enduring voice lessons on their off-hours from a cranky old man. When the group finally gets another opportunity to step back into the spotlights, they're sidetracked by a lame gig on a kid's sci-fi TV show! Show Biz sure ain't all it's cracked up to be!

**Get a front row seat for the show in DRAGON VOICE vol. 3!**

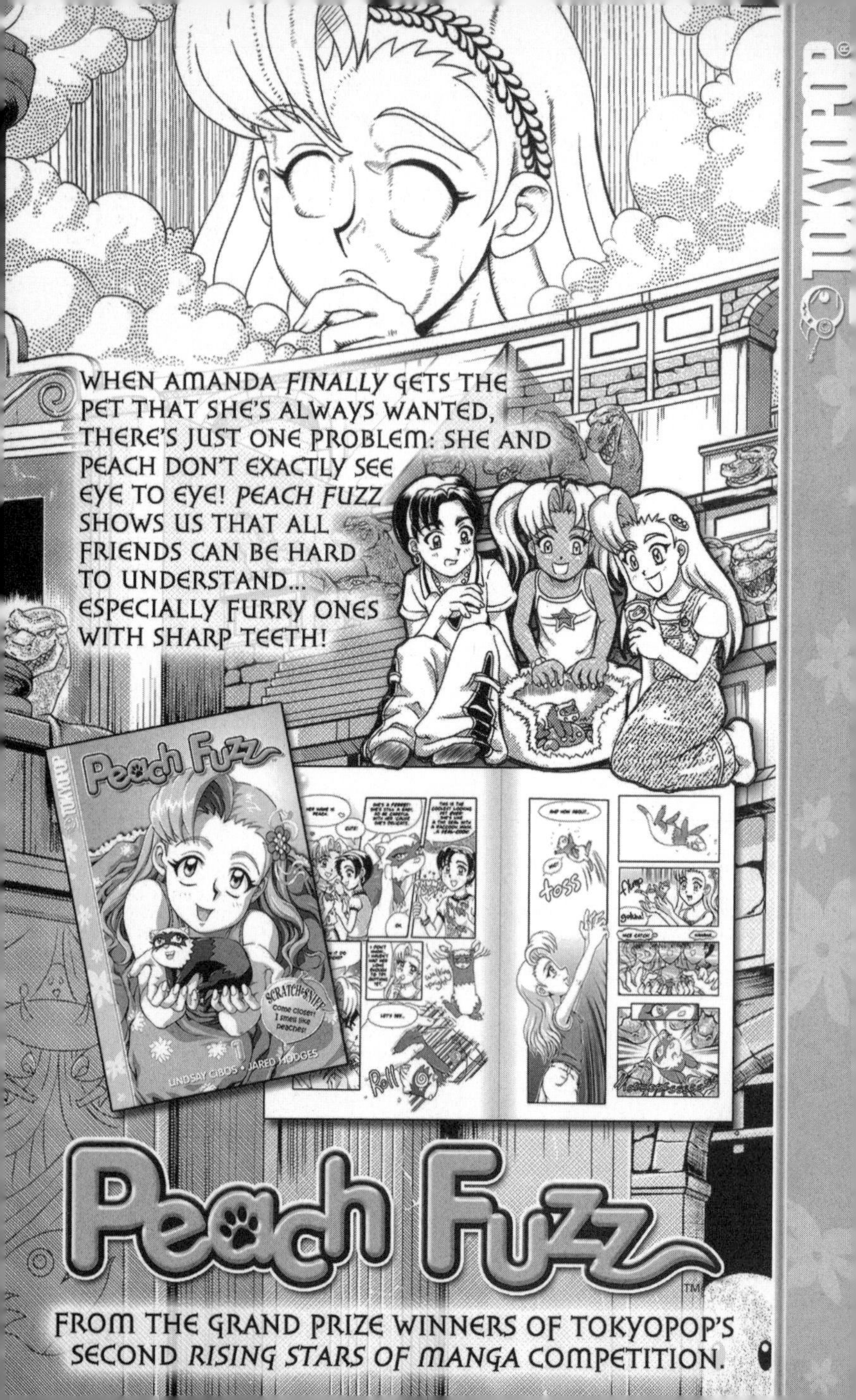
TOKYOPOP
WHEN AMANDA *FINALLY* GETS THE PET THAT SHE'S ALWAYS WANTED, THERE'S JUST ONE PROBLEM: SHE AND PEACH DON'T EXACTLY SEE EYE TO EYE! *PEACH FUZZ* SHOWS US THAT ALL FRIENDS CAN BE HARD TO UNDERSTAND... ESPECIALLY FURRY ONES WITH SHARP TEETH!
Peach Fuzz
TOKYOPOP
SCRATCH & SNIFF
Come closer! I smell like peaches!
1
LINDSAY CIBOS • JARED HODGES
toss
Roll
Peach Fuzz™
FROM THE GRAND PRIZE WINNERS OF TOKYOPOP'S SECOND *RISING STARS OF MANGA* COMPETITION.

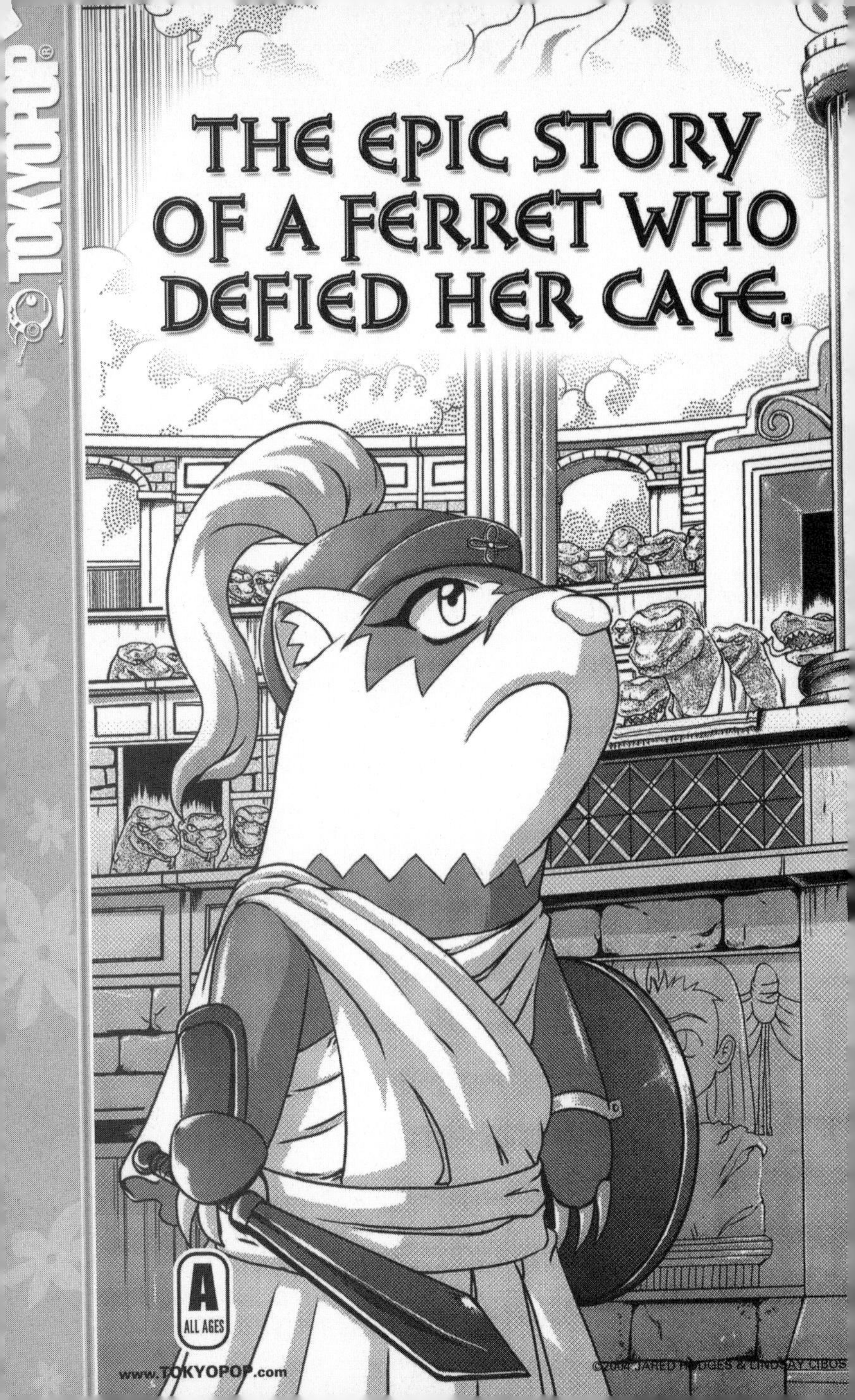
TOKYOPOP
THE EPIC STORY OF A FERRET WHO DEFIED HER CAGE.
A
ALL AGES
www.TOKYOPOP.com
©2004 JARED HODGES & LINDSAY CIBOS

# ALSO AVAILABLE FROM TOKYOPOP®

## MANGA

.HACK//LEGEND OF THE TWILIGHT
@LARGE
ABENOBASHI: MAGICAL SHOPPING ARCADE
A.I. LOVE YOU
AI YORI AOSHI
ALICHINO
ANGELIC LAYER
ARM OF KANNON
BABY BIRTH
BATTLE ROYALE
BATTLE VIXENS
BOYS BE...
BRAIN POWERED
BRIGADOON
B'TX
CANDIDATE FOR GODDESS, THE
CARDCAPTOR SAKURA
CARDCAPTOR SAKURA - MASTER OF THE CLOW
CHOBITS
CHRONICLES OF THE CURSED SWORD
CLAMP SCHOOL DETECTIVES
CLOVER
COMIC PARTY
CONFIDENTIAL CONFESSIONS
CORRECTOR YUI
COWBOY BEBOP
COWBOY BEBOP: SHOOTING STAR
CRAZY LOVE STORY
CRESCENT MOON
CROSS
CULDCEPT
CYBORG 009
D•N•ANGEL
DEARS
DEMON DIARY
DEMON ORORON, THE
DEUS VITAE
DIABOLO
DIGIMON
DIGIMON TAMERS
DIGIMON ZERO TWO
DOLL
DRAGON HUNTER
DRAGON KNIGHTS
DRAGON VOICE
DREAM SAGA
DUKLYON: CLAMP SCHOOL DEFENDERS
EERIE QUEERIE!
ERICA SAKURAZAWA: COLLECTED WORKS
ET CETERA
ETERNITY
EVIL'S RETURN
FAERIES' LANDING
FAKE
FLCL
FLOWER OF THE DEEP SLEEP
FORBIDDEN DANCE
FRUITS BASKET

G GUNDAM
GATEKEEPERS
GETBACKERS
GIRL GOT GAME
GRAVITATION
GTO
GUNDAM SEED ASTRAY
GUNDAM WING
GUNDAM WING: BATTLEFIELD OF PACIFISTS
GUNDAM WING: ENDLESS WALTZ
GUNDAM WING: THE LAST OUTPOST (G-UNIT)
HANDS OFF!
HAPPY MANIA
HARLEM BEAT
HYPER RUNE
I.N.V.U.
IMMORTAL RAIN
INITIAL D
INSTANT TEEN: JUST ADD NUTS
ISLAND
JING: KING OF BANDITS
JING: KING OF BANDITS - TWILIGHT TALES
JULINE
KARE KANO
KILL ME, KISS ME
KINDAICHI CASE FILES, THE
KING OF HELL
KODOCHA: SANA'S STAGE
LAMENT OF THE LAMB
LEGAL DRUG
LEGEND OF CHUN HYANG, THE
LES BIJOUX
LOVE HINA
LOVE OR MONEY
LUPIN III
LUPIN III: WORLD'S MOST WANTED
MAGIC KNIGHT RAYEARTH I
MAGIC KNIGHT RAYEARTH II
MAHOROMATIC: AUTOMATIC MAIDEN
MAN OF MANY FACES
MARMALADE BOY
MARS
MARS: HORSE WITH NO NAME
MINK
MIRACLE GIRLS
MIYUKI-CHAN IN WONDERLAND
MODEL
MOURYOU KIDEN: LEGEND OF THE NYMPH
NECK AND NECK
ONE
ONE I LOVE, THE
PARADISE KISS
PARASYTE
PASSION FRUIT
PEACH FUZZ
PEACH GIRL
PEACH GIRL: CHANGE OF HEART
PET SHOP OF HORRORS
PITA-TEN
PLANET LADDER

# STOP!

## This is the back of the book.
## You wouldn't want to spoil a great ending!

This book is printed "manga-style," in the authentic Japanese right-to-left format. Since none of the artwork has been flipped or altered, readers get to experience the story just as the creator intended. You've been asking for it, so TOKYOPOP® delivered: authentic, hot-off-the-press, and far more fun!

# DIRECTIONS

If this is your first time reading manga-style, here's a quick guide to help you understand how it works.

It's easy… just start in the top right panel and follow the numbers. Have fun, and look for more 100% authentic manga from TOKYOPOP®!